Operation: Face the Fear

Tony Ruggiero

I0565801

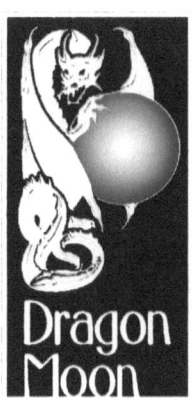

Dragon
Moon

www.dragonmoonpress.com

Works by Tony Ruggiero

Books

Operation Immortal Servitude
Operation Save the Innocent
Alien Deception
Alien Revelation
Aliens and Satanic Creatures Wanted: Humans Need Not Apply.

Work in Anthologies

No Longer Dreams. Poetry: "Waiting in the Garden."
Writers for Relief. Poetry: "A Meeting with Destiny," "Buried Treasures of Life,""Celebration," "Guard Them Well," "Hello," "Is There Anyone There," "Pursuit," "The Last Visit," Up Another Step," "Wind of Life" and "Yet It Did."
Writers for Relief Volume II. Short story: "The Importance of Undergarments at Science Fiction Conventions."
Breach the Hull. Short story: "Perspective."
So It Begins. Short story: "Looking for a Good Time."

Non-Fiction

Contributor to the *The Complete Guide to Writing Fantasy: Volume 2.*

Plus numerous short stories.

Operation: Face the Fear

Tony Ruggiero

Operation: Face the Fear

ISBN 10 - 1-896944-97-3
ISBN 13 - 978-1-896944-97-5

Dragon Moon Press is an Imprint of Hades Publications Inc.
P.O. Box 1714, Calgary, Alberta, T2P 2L7, Canada

Printed and bound in Canada or the United States
www.dragonmoonpress.com
www.tonyruggiero.com

DEDICATIONS

Thanks to John Reese and the Team of Darkness for the opportunity to tell their story. Without them, I wouldn't have much to talk about.

To my publisher who without her selfless determination this book would not have had the opportunity to see daylight. Thanks Gwen.

To my editor whose tireless efforts to correct my bad grammar and cut out those redundant words are very much appreciated. Thanks Barbara.

To my daughter Alexandra—they may not "sparkle" but they are my vampire to give to you. Love Dad.

Lastly to Mary whose help and encouragement somehow makes it all work—and I'm not just talking about the book. It's about everything. Thanks hon.

PROLOGUE

Dear J:

I know it's been a while, almost a year since I last wrote. How are you doing? I've missed those long talks that we had. I never heard back from you after we talked last time—did I scare you away with my story? I'm going to pretend that I didn't and talk to you as I always have in the past. I hope that's okay. You're the only friend I have at the moment that isn't part of this. Do you remember that letter or have you forgotten? The one where I said I thought that things were getting better. I honestly thought that they were. I thought it was over and maybe I could start over again. But it didn't last—it never does any more.

I mentioned that I was going to be teaching again; unfortunately, that fell through. How do I begin this: it's all happening so fast it's hard to comprehend. Let's just say that something has happened. The operation that I told you about, the one that I said was over—well, it's not. General Stone did something quite foolish and now, I get to pay for his mistakes. They have brought me back onto active duty so that I can find two young girls. Why would a Navy Commander be searching for girls? If you remember the team that I led (those that had 'the unique abilities'), well these girls are just like them. The General must have been completely mad when he came up with this plan. But he did and they were here in the States, but then they got away somehow and that's why I was brought back to active duty—to find them.

If that's not complicated enough, there are others involved that could make this situation sticky for me. They are from some government agency; I don't even know which spook shop they're from. I've only met two of them, a woman named Samantha, who says she is in charge, and a man called Smith. Talk about two for the nut farm; Smith is a real prize, he gets his jollies from making people squirm. It's an obvious power thing with him only they won't give it to him—not a lot of it, anyway, so he takes it out on anyone who can't push back. Smith is the kind of guy that will always require a handler because he never knows when to stop. As for Samantha, I think she would kill anyone who disagreed with her. It's the look in her eyes and the way she talks…it's as if she's living right inside the border of sanity but makes day trips onto the insane side as she needs to in order to get things done. Nice people, huh?

I can tell you this as unbelievable as it sounds…General Morris, who took command after Stone was murdered, he's scared of them. This is the man who commands all the U.S. Special Forces and he's scared. Really scared. He's actually commandeered a SEAL team to serve as bodyguards. I imagine that they have threatened him should he fail in his mission to recapture the girls. Those threats run downhill to me in turn. Basically, they've promised me a cozy little cell at Fort Leavenworth if I don't produce. And if that isn't enough, I think that they suspect that I let the original Team go. Smith is riding my ass and questioning everyone that was involved in the original mission again. This is like a game of dominoes and no matter which way they fall, I lose.

I know who took the girls of course: it was Dimitri and the rest of the Team. No one else could have done it. So if I do find the girls, the Team is found at the same time. The Brass finds them and then they throw my ass in Fort Leavenworth for lying about what happened. It's a lose-lose scenario for me unless I can get to the Team first and get the girls from them. That's if they will give them up, which is doubtful. Dimitri and I understand each other, there are no more get out of jail free cards left. Hell, he probably thinks that I had something to do with capturing the girls which he'll probably kill me for. So unless I can figure a way to get the girls, either the agency, the military, or the vampires will kill me. Sound like fun?

But it's not completely doom and gloom. I've met a woman named Christina. I can't explain the way she makes me feel. She's so captivating and so very interesting. All I know is, for the first time that I can remember I feel that there may be a chance for me to have a normal relationship with a woman. No one has been able to do what she has done in such a short period of time. She has been able to give me a reprieve from what was eating away at me and destroying me from the inside; the fear of facing my true feelings of the quest for the immortality of the vampire life and being able to live across centuries. That need no longer haunts me because the void has been filled by her. She is what I needed to quell the fear of what I lacked. Her warmth saves me from the cold and inhuman vampire world. If I can find a little peace by not having to face the fear that pervades my nightmares, then that is what I want and I will do anything to get it. Anything.

Well J, wish me luck. Thanks for being a good friend and listening to my ramblings. I imagine that you must wonder if I, like my agency friend Samantha, am the owner of mental real estate bordering insanity. If I am, I at least recognize that it is only a vacation house and not a permanent residence. Funny, huh? Look at me making jokes at a time like this. Regardless, if I am still alive after all of this ends I want to see you in person. It has been much too long and we must be reunited in the end in order to finish all that we have begun.

Warmest Regards,

John Reese

CHAPTER ONE

"There is no one to save you today, Commander Reese," Samantha gloated, "the third time is the charm, so they say." She placed the gun to his chest and fired for the third time.

Commander John Reese rested the weight of his body on the sink in the bathroom as he splashed cold water on his face. Raising his head and looking in the mirror he saw a tired and haggard man, but overall he thought he looked pretty good for someone that had been shot three times.

He lowered his face to the pool of off-red colored water and went back to splashing cold water onto his face. The water had obtained the pink color from the blood that was on his hands. The blood dripped from small punctures made by the rose he had crushed, a gift from Christina, which had apparently received the brunt of his physical reaction to being shot during the dream.

Right now he wished he could simply wash away the dream's images. He looked in the mirror again; the circles under his eyes and the pronounced crow's feet at the corners made him look older than his forty-three years. Even his salt and pepper hair looked haggard. Yet the fact that he was still alive easily countered these effects and a slight reassurance appeared within his eyes as he looked at them.

He had been in his office on the Naval Amphibious Base, a few feet from where he now stood in the male head when it had happened. The dream had been vivid and disturbing on so many levels. Of course, the fact that he had been shot three times had obviously jolted him the most, but there had been other things as well. Other things such as the dead body of General Stone, the talking dead body of General Stone, lying on the conference table making accusations at Reese for his involvement with the vampires—codenamed Team of Darkness. Also there had been the vampire Dimitri who accused Reese of being involved with the capture and detainment of Ishma and Crema, the two children turned into vampires at ages thirteen and six. Yet the puzzling surprise was that Christina, the woman that he had recently spent time with under somewhat unusual circumstances, was also in the dream. She said that he had to help the girls. That only he could do what needed to be done.

But Reese never saw her—he only heard her voice, which was puzzling. And finally there had been Samantha. She was the point-of-contact for the mysterious government agency that had backed him into the corner to find the girls or as she so nicely put it, "if he was lucky, help Reese change his address to Fort Leavenworth prison." In the dream, Samantha directed Dimitri to kill him, but Reese would not allow the vampire the opportunity which led to Samantha having to do the shooting.

Wouldn't Freud have a good time with this one? Damn dream, but what does it mean, if anything?

Reese wiped his hands and face with the paper towels from the dispenser and returned to his office. He closed the door and moved toward his desk. His eyes focused on the scattered rose petals. He scooped up the remnants of the flower with cautious hands and placed them back in the box. When he was finished cleaning up as best he could, he closed the box and put it to one side.

He sat down at the desk and prepared to go to work reviewing the information that he had been given at the initial SEAL briefing session. The folder lay in the center of the desk and when Reese reached for it, he spotted the card which had accompanied the rose. Reese picked it up and read it again:

May all your dreams come true.

He flipped it over.

Thanks for not having me arrested for breaking and entering. Christina

He smiled and laughed. Although there was a bit of irony in the note about his dreams, he could now at least find some humor in it—thanks to Christina. Since this morning he had not thought about her, but now that he had a moment, he found that his thoughts drifted in her direction and their unusual but revealing evening together. Her appearance at his home he had first considered an invasion of his privacy but that quickly changed as they discovered similar interests in ancient myths and legends. Now he wanted nothing more than to see her again. He wanted to call her to see if she wanted to have dinner with him tonight but with the way the op was going, he didn't know if he would be able to make it; there was too much going on. The teams had begun the surveillance portion; however it would take several hours, if not days, to determine if the buildings they were watching were being used by the vampires or their captors. But when they did, it would be an around-the-clock op until completed. While the surveillance continued, he had to explore every possible contingency as to where they might be hiding. He knew that they, whether the military or the Agency, would be watching him. Apparently trust was something that didn't exist in the world of dark operations.

But still he wanted to see her and he hoped that she would understand his situation without him talking any specifics. Even though he knew that with her background of ancient history she could be an immense help to the project, he knew that it would not be allowed by either General Morris or Samantha. Too many people already knew too much.

Still the thought of her remained fixed in his mind as if she had placed a spell over him. He snickered and thought there could be things much worse that could happen to him than a beautiful woman's spell. He wanted to talk to her and most of all he wanted her to know that he was thinking about her. A lot. Taking the card she had given him last night out of his wallet, he reached for the phone and began to push numbers. Just as he was about to press the last digit, there was a knock on the door. With a sigh, he replaced the receiver.

"Come in," Reese called; his voice containing a tinge of aggravation as he slid the card under the folder.

CHAPTER TWO

"It's hard to say goodbye to friends; that's the part of humanity that sucks."

John Reese.

The door opened and the familiar face of Lieutenant Colonel Sam Barkley peered around the door.

"Hey Sam!" Reese said. The joy at seeing a good friend quickly replaced the aggravation of the interruption. "Get your low-life Army ass in here."

Barkley took a tentative step into the room. At almost six feet in height and about two hundred pounds, his large body filled the door opening. He stopped and eyed Reese for a moment taking particular note of the uniform he was wearing.

"I'll be damned," he began, "the Navy must be desperate if they let you come back in?"

"Let's just say that they made me an offer I couldn't refuse," answered Reese. He got up from his chair behind the desk and walked over to Barkley. They shook hands.

"The last time we talked," Sam began, "you were getting ready to teach or something. What the hell happened?"

"Yeah, well I got the whole first day under my belt before I had a visit from a wonderful gentleman named Mr. Smith. Have you met him?"

"Oh yes, and what a charming individual he is," Barkley agreed.

Reese thought that Barkley's voice and facial expression conveyed his true feelings, which were apparently quite similar to his own.

"Yeah, he definitely lacks in the social graces," Reese added. "Well come on in and have a seat."

The two men sat and for a moment there was an awkward silence between the two as if either one was afraid to ask anything. Finally Reese began, "I requested your help, Sam. I know you wanted to be finished with the op, especially after the last time we talked, but I can't do this without you."

"It's okay John, I understand," Barkley said. "It's just like a bad penny. Will it ever end?"

"We can hope," said Reese and then asked, "How much do you know?"

"They gave me a quick briefing about what General Stone did."

"What do you think?"

"I'm pissed for one," he shot back. "The bastards stole the bodies from me! I had to leave the medical tent in Kosovo for a few hours and when I got back, I was told the bodies had been removed for burial. Said it was local custom or some bullshit like that. I never thought to question it. I assumed that Idriz wanted to have his children buried. It seemed logical so I never bothered to ask him about it."

"Nothing is ever what it appears to be," Reese said feeling the phrase was familiar to him, as if he had heard it before. After a second or two, he remembered, Dimitri had used that exact expression.

"I guess not," Barkley agreed. "Why exactly did you call me in?"

"I needed a familiar face just as much as someone who truly knows what we're dealing with here."

"If it was just you and General Morris, I could deal with this. But this crap with Smith and whoever he works for is rather unsettling. They scared the shit out of me with their little interrogation."

"They interrogated you?" Reese asked.

"Sure did. It was not long after you and I met a few months ago. I got a message they wanted to talk to me."

"It was probably because you came to my house," Reese said thinking out loud. "Apparently they have been watching me as well."

"Why?"

"Two reasons. Probably routine after the op we were on. They wanted to ensure we didn't take the information outside or do anything stupid. Secondly, because we were players in the past op, they might have wanted to use us in the new one. However, I guess they originally didn't want to bring us back into the fold for whatever reason."

"But these girls, Idriz's daughters, they're just kids for Christ's sake," Barkley said. "Have you seen them?"

"On video but not in person," Reese said. "They were innocent little kids, but now, they're two very dangerous little kids. Especially if they fall into the wrong hands."

"You think they were broken out?" asked Barkley.

"There's no doubt about that. The question is, by whom." Reese remembered seeing the blurred image of Dimitri on the surveillance tape. He couldn't tell Barkley about that because Barkley believed that Dimitri and his team had been killed. It was best to leave that as is. He thought he knew Barkley well, but something like this could shift the balance from personal friendship over to an allegiance to duty. It was too risky to chance.

"How the hell will we find them?" asked Barkley. "This area is so damned big, and that is if they're even still around."

"Or alive," Reese added. "They may have already been killed by either their captors or by the collars. We just don't know for sure."

"So what do we do?"

"We wait and keep looking. If I were you," Reese began, "I would clear your calendar for quite a while."

"And what do I do until we find them?"

"Until we get something for you to specifically look at, I want you to do so some research for me."

"Research? On what?"

"I want you to see if you can come up with something that could neutralize the elixir that was used in the collars."

"What?" Barkley asked. "We used that to control them and now you want to find a way to neutralize it?"

Reese explained, "If they escaped, the collars would have to be removed in order for them to survive, right?"

"Yeah, sure."

"If whoever took them wants them alive, they'd have to get the collars off. If the perpetrators at the compound knew as much as they did about the facility, they had to know that the collars would be activated as soon as it was realized they had escaped. I've reviewed the time log; the collars were activated in less than fifteen minutes. There is no way they could have gotten them out of the range of the transmitters that quickly. This means that the girls are dead, or someone had to come up with an antidote or some way to block the reaction of the elixir. Do you see what I mean?"

"Got it now," Barkley agreed. "It's an interesting idea."

"That's what I want you to look into," Reese continued. "When we were involved with the Team of Darkness op, we never really cared about it as long as it worked. I think maybe someone did look into that aspect and found a way to neutralize the elixir and prevent it from killing the girls."

"I don't know if I'm smart enough to do this John. I'm just a general MD; what you need is a full time chemist."

"Then find one. There are several major military hospitals in the area; Portsmouth Naval Hospital is probably the closest. I want you to examine the civilian sector as well or maybe we can have our good friend Mr. Smith perform that aspect. It's a long shot, but maybe someone might remember being brought the elixir to have analyzed."

"Someone like that won't be willing to part with the information," Barkley stated firmly. "If money convinced them the first time, it'll probably work just as well the second time," replied Reese.

"I see what you mean," agreed Barkley. "Okay, I'll work that angle. So what's the plan if they're alive? Capture or kill?"

"Whichever ensures the best chance of success," said Reese.

Reese watched as Barkley became quiet. He appeared to be thinking about something. "What's bothering you?" asked Reese.

"Too many unanswered questions. Who did it? There's a possible antidote for the elixir? How did they know the compound so well? How did anyone ever learn they were here in the first place?"

"I know," Reese agreed. "The ramifications of this run deep.

"Christ John, it almost sounds like it was one of us. We knew all these things. You don't think that they believe we had something to do with this, do you?"

Reese thought carefully before he spoke. "Look, this goes beyond the military sphere we understand. Back then, we knew the rules but now we don't. And I tell you, General Morris is scared as well. The man has bodyguards. Can you imagine that?"

"It's rather ironic," Barkley said and snickered. "The man has all the spec-ops in the world at his disposal and yet he feels the need for personal protection."

"Yeah, ironic," agreed Reese. "There seems to be a lot of that around these days. This agency involvement is, I don't know, strange in some way and I think it runs a lot deeper than it appears on the surface. The bottom line is we need to try and resolve this so that we don't become a permanent fixture in this organization. One way or another, the only way it will end will be with either the return of the girls or evidence of their deaths."

"That's the only way we can truly clear ourselves, isn't it?" asked Barkley.

"No one knew as much about the op as I did," Reese began. "Do I think someone is watching me? You bet. Smith's lurking around here somewhere. I haven't seen him yet, but I know he's here."

"So what are we to do?" asked Barkley.

"Just do your job. We give them what they want and they'll be happy."

"This is getting uglier than I first thought it was going to be," Barkley said as he stood and turned toward the door. "I'm going to check out the lab facilities here and see what kind of shape they're in."

Reese rose and walked with him. When Barkley was halfway out of the room, Reese said to him softly, "It's only going to get uglier."

"Hmm, going ugly early," Barkley said. His voice tried to sound light and amused but it came across stiff and forced; the humor was obviously meant to lighten the mood. "Isn't that a Navy thing? You guys have been known for your, how would you say, lack of discretion in picking women."

Reese smiled weakly and said, "Let's hope that our discretion saves our asses this time."

Barkley nodded but said nothing. Reese saw the fear in his eyes.

CHAPTER THREE

As Dimitri watched the two girls ascend the stairs and exit the bomb shelter, their current sanctuary, the words from the book that Crema picked out earlier to read resonated in his thoughts.

"My revenge is just begun! I spread it over centuries, and time is on my side. Your girls that you all love are mine already; and through them you and others shall yet be mine…"

The irony of Crema's book choice made Dimitri's head spin. The book was Dracula. In the book the vampire promised revenge and yet in real life, it was the vampire, he, who suffered from the revenge that one human being had brought upon another. Where would it all end?

Dimitri sat down on the bed and for a brief moment, thought he felt a nagging pain course through his body. He knew and understood that as a vampire, he could not feel the passing of time. He'd remained unchanged the past ninety-three years or so and he was still physically twenty-three. He understood the physical effects that aging brought to humans and thought that what he was feeling right now similar to that. His mind grew fatigued as he thought about the girls forced to become vampires. They were so young. He cursed Josip under his breath for the cruelty of what he had done in seeking out his revenge against Idriz Laupki and the senselessness of the generational feud. But Dimitri also could not let General Stone and his military accomplices off the hook for their lack of compassion. They could have ended it all but instead they nurtured this craziness to fulfillment by bringing the girls into the picture.

All Dimitri and his two friends, Andre and Iliga, wanted, was to go home.

They had broken free of the captivity that they had been borne into by Commander Reese. Ironically it was Reese's own guilt that allowed them the opportunity to escape. Their past year of freedom had been spent amassing money and various assets in order to purchase a secure way to get them all back to Kosovo. The plan was relatively simple but secrecy was always expensive and bribes best paid in cash. In the interim, they had secured a safe place to feed in this area of Virginia and things were progressing as planned. That was until they had discovered the dead body. The traces of a vampire kill led them back to the compound, their former prison, and the discovery of the young vampire girls.

Breaking the girls out had been the right thing to do. That they did not debate. But learning that one of their closest friends, Josip, had changed them was too much even for Dimitri to comprehend. The ferocity behind such an action left his mind in a state of disarray that he had not known for a very long time. He yearned for the quiet times in the mountains of the Balkans before they were captured by the American forces. The time spent in old libraries with even older books had been relaxing and peaceful. Life went by and they were left alone. Things were as they should be. There were advantages to being a myth. People tended to fear them and thought it best to just leave them buried in the layers of dust.

"Dimitri?" a voice called.

Dimitri kept his eyes downcast but answered, "Yes, Iliga, what is it?"

"We were waiting. Is there a problem?"

"At times it seems like there is always a problem," answered Dimitri and he found himself snickering at his own response. "Yet, we have been through a lot old friend haven't we?"

"Yes," Iliga agreed and he gave Dimitri one of his rare smiles.

"We should go and feed," said Dimitri as he rose. "Everyone is hungry."

"Your troubles are our troubles," Iliga said as he placed a hand on Dimitri's shoulder. "Andre and I want to get back to our home as well. The girls have a place with us. They need us and there is nothing for them here. We will find a way to make it work."

"I fear we may have done ourselves in," said Dimitri. "I always cautioned Josip not to display his abilities openly. I warned him that he would only draw the attention of the curious. And here I have done just the same. I should have left them."

"It will work out," insisted Iliga. "We have safeguards enough."

"Let's hope you are right," said Dimitri. "If not, this underground shelter may become our own crypt and we will never leave."

CHAPTER FOUR

"Life is an evolution that welcomes change…even in death."

Christina.

As Christina returned to her underground sanctuary at the abandoned Naval Station, she was feeling quite pleased with the way things had transpired with Commander John Reese at his home. The information that he had on other vampires, everything General Stone had insinuated before she killed him, was foremost in her mind but it would take time to get it out of him. She could take it from him, but that might leave gaps, posing an unnecessary risk she did not want to take. At least not yet. She had time and lots of it. She was having fun with this role. Her introduction had even included a flirtatious advance on her part and yet she had not found the part difficult to play. The ease of it surprised as well as frightened her.

Her fear was that her actions might bring back the dream. The dream that she did not like or wish to live through again. Those dreams had stayed buried in the past and she liked it that way. Some memories were best forgotten; especially those of a woman that she could not be anymore.

Arriving at her secure bedroom, she removed her clothes and dropped them on the floor heading for the bed. As she crawled under the cool sheets, she closed her eyes and relaxed in the safety of the protected room. As she began to quietly slip toward sleep, she entered that place somewhere between wakefulness and utter relaxation of the mind. Unknowingly, her hand rose to her face and her fingers traced along the contour of her lips remembering the kiss with Reese. They parted and a smile settled in their place as she drifted off to sleep. But that smile was wiped away as the dream that she feared returned.

★★★

THE YEAR 1800

Christina staggered through the woods. She felt cold and hungry. Her face was dirty and tear streaked even though she could not cry anymore. She stopped, looking back one last time in the direction from which she had come. She would never return to her family and lover, for they had cast her out from her home and from her life. One foolish mistake had cost her everything. One foolish mistake caused by love.

She hated the sound of that word. Love. What had it gotten her? Cast out, scorned, shamed and hated. What had been painted and imagined as the best thing in life, the most important thing in life, was the instigator of all her problems. She hated the word and all that was associated with it. She would never love again. She would never trust anyone ever again.

Darkness settled quickly upon the woods and with it came the cold of night. When it became too dark to see anymore she sat at the base of a large pine tree, resting her back against the trunk and closing her eyes. She wondered if tonight would be her last. She hadn't eaten for days and felt weak. More importantly, she saw no reason to go on. No matter where she went, they would find out about her. That was the way towns were. News was news, regardless of what it entailed. She listened to the sound of the woods as they too changed from daytime to night. The creatures of the day made their way to whatever home they had, while the creatures of the night began to wake up and start hunting for food. She wondered if she would become food for some lucky animal; perhaps a wolf or bear. She let fatigue and hunger cover her like the blankets she had used in her home only days ago. She slept.

She awoke to the sound of someone talking. The voice was calm and steady and it seemed to gently carry her up from sleep. Her eyes opened and she saw that the wooded area was awash in silver moonlight from the near full moon and that a man sat on the ground across from her.

Even though he was sitting, she could tell he was a tall man with a large build. The moonlight reflected off his face making it appear a ghastly white, as if he were a ghost. Perhaps he was, she thought. Perhaps this was death come to escort her to the gates of Hell. His eyes appeared to glow in the moonlight, but not a silver or white as one would expect from the light, but rather a soft red. They glowed with an almost animal-like quality with a sharpness that looked for prey in the night.

Despite his appearance, she was not frightened. She wasn't sure if it was her exhaustion or if it was just that she didn't care anymore. Whatever he was, she was sure that this was some premonition of the end she knew had come.

Who are you? Why are you here? She heard his voice but his lips had not moved. She wondered if she was still asleep, and perhaps dreaming. She pushed back against the pine bark feeling the roughness of it dig into her skin. She was awake and there was a strange man sitting across from her who spoke without moving his lips. She smiled and giggled at the absurdity of what was happening.

You laugh? Are you mad? The voice came into her thoughts again.

As she tried to imagine how this could be happening, she continued to stare at her visitor and suddenly a realization crept over her like dew settling upon the morning fields. She didn't know how, but she sensed from the stranger that he knew who and what she was. Perhaps he was one of the woodsmen and had heard of her from the villagers and had come looking for her. He would take advantage of her destitution, expecting her to be grateful and pleasure him with her company for a few nights before throwing her out to die.

"Why do you not speak?" he asked in a gentle sounding voice. "Why do you not tell me why you are here? Who are you?"

She now saw that his lips moved as he spoke and she told herself that she had just imagined them not moving before. Her hunger and pain were eating away at her mind. There was nothing supernatural or unexplainable here.

"Does it matter?" she said coldly. "I am here, that should be enough to satisfy your question. I am a gift from the Gods for you. Do with me as you like, but kill me swiftly when you are finished."

"My name is Alexander. Won't you tell me why you are here? Are you lost?" he repeated.

"We are all lost," she said and then laughed.

CHAPTER FIVE

In an office deep within the corridors of the Pentagon, a man in a nondescript black suit sat at a desk in a lonely office. There was no name plaque on his desk and no sign on the door that led into the room. His desk was void of anything that would give an appearance that it was actually in use—except a telephone. His hair was a stark white in color although his age was probably around 45 or 50 years. His eyes remained fixed on the package that sat on his desk. About the size of a paperback book, maybe a little larger, it was wrapped in paper that was brown with age. Twine, discolored and frayed, looped around it and was tied in a knot in the center. There was no delivery address – no return address for that matter. It had simply arrived for him via a courier that no one could describe. It was indeed a perplexing issue yet one that intrigued him. He loved a good mystery.

He picked it up and tugged at the twine which separated easily. A layer of dust that was imbedded in the twine rose as into the air as if protesting the action. Obviously whoever had prepared this had done so a long time ago. Next, he unwrapped the paper that enclosed the object, trying carefully not to tear it, but rather to keep it all in one piece. Inside the paper were a folded note and a single book. He read:

    It has taken too long for this to make its way back
    to you. For that, I am sorry. I hope it provides
    some comfort and gives you some of the answers
    about a father you seek although I fear it might
    provide more controversy than comfort. Either way
    it is in your hands where it belongs.

He refolded the note and noticed that his hands shook briefly. Experience had tempered his enthusiasm many years ago but he was extremely interested and tried to contain his enthusiasm over information that may have to do with a father he never knew. There had been many false leads in trying to ascertain any details about his death. The famous line of "need to know," had worn a path in his thoughts so well traveled that he had just come to accept it.

He turned his focus on the evidence. The cover was leather which was heavily worn in a few spots. He placed his hands on the book where he would need to open it and saw that the worn spots were where the fingers would have rested when handling the book and making entries. He smiled at his discovery. In a day and age where everything was always more than it appeared to be, he liked the simpler things, no matter how insignificant. The knowledge that this simple book had been used often told him something about the person that had owned it. In that, there was no controversy—things were as they appeared.

The book was not very thick. In fact he thought it was quite thin given the thoughtfulness of the design and the long-lasting leather cover. Maybe the author did not have much to say, he thought. There was only one way to find out and he flipped the book open.

The answer was immediately apparent as there were jagged and torn edges along the interior spine indicative of pages being torn out. Looking at the thickness of the spine, by his rough guess, he figured maybe half of the pages had been removed. He gently turned to the first page.

January 1945

I hope that whoever finds this journal will see that my family gets it. I have written their address on the inside flap cover. I have left only the pages which I felt were relevant to explain what happened. It's important that they know what happened to me and they have a right to know that I died in the line of duty. Died doing what I felt was right for the agency and my country.

For a brief instant the man thought he recognized the handwriting. Yet he knew there were probably hundreds if not thousands of handwriting styles that might be similar, but still, he thought he saw something in this one. And there had been the reference to the *agency*; another coincidence? Yet even with all this uncertainty, he cautiously flipped to the back of the book to read the address. It was no longer there.

He grabbed the brown paper again and looked for anything that might give him a clue as to where it had come from. It was blank. He wondered if it had been re-wrapped at some time from its original packaging. The paper looked old but not as old as the writing established.

He flipped to the next page and began to read.

9 October 1944

What a discovery! The body was quite well preserved. It reminded me of photographs I have seen of human remains that have been preserved by some type of natural disaster where the material involved prevented decomposition. A good example would be the bodies found at Pompeii which had been buried in ash. Yet there were no such materials in this cavern. One of the men on my team came to an amateur estimate, based upon the thickness of the layer of dust, that the cavern had to have been sealed for at least fifty or sixty years. I took this initial estimate under advisement. However, if that was the case, the condition of the body was an anomaly which posed additional questions which archeological experts would find intriguing.

As I prepared to extricate my team, seeing no further interest in this matter, some of the men who were making a cursory examination of the body called my attention to some of the physical oddities they'd discovered.

First, it was decidedly that of a female human, the physical characteristics of breasts and genitals were clearly visible. However, her face possessed some features which struck me as very peculiar. My initial reaction was that I was looking at features of an animal rather than a human being. The nose was long and flat as if adapted for hunting, suggesting a heightened sense of smell and her ears were larger and shaped in a way that might be indicative of superior hearing. Her teeth were in immaculate condition and almost appeared to glow in the dim light. Also, her incisors looked more like animal canine teeth rather that of a human. Her skin was extremely pale—almost a pasty white in color where after a long time period one would expect the skin to be mottled and decayed.

As we examined this body the more oddities and questions were uncovered. Apparently whatever it was that was in the crypt, for whatever reason, was quite different than a normal human being.

As we prepared to leave this enigma for the historians and archeologists that would eventually discover it, the man that earlier had suggested the amount of time which had passed, discovered something else. The body was also covered with the appropriate layer of dust as was the rest of the cavern which was to be expected. However, under the nose of this woman, the dust was non existent as if…her breathing had kept the dust from settling.

I do not know what drove me to my next action, perhaps I wished to humor the men and myself, but I had one of the medical personnel conduct a further examination of the body. To our amazement, they detected a very shallow and faint form of respiration. It would be unnoticeable to the naked eye, but with proper equipment, such as we had, it could be detected. This woman was somehow still alive. We secured all personnel involved in the discovery into one military unit for control. There were a total of nine personnel. One member was a civilian national, serving as guide and interpreter. His reaction to this discovery has been quite unusual. He refused to go back into the area where the crypt is contained—he was visibly scared. When I suggested he go into the area of the crypt, he got wide-eyed with fear and began to tremble and make the religious sign of the cross. His interpretation of this discovery was based upon local folklore of a creature that terrorized the area almost a century ago by murdering almost an entire village. He also used the term 'vampire'.

My investigation shall continue. There are many issues here which defy all logic, yet offer possibilities which I believe may be of significance to those I work for. I am intrigued with this mystery but can offer no information or even an assessment at this time.

The man found the beginning of this story quite compelling. So much so that he let the similarity to his father's handwriting fall back to a secondary position in his thoughts. It was his occupation to make logical sense of mysteries and he always felt unnerved when a logical explanation could not be found. He tried to imagine the excitement of wondering what must be going through the mind of someone faced with this type of unknown—a discovery that defied logic.

"When in doubt," the man said aloud, "always fall back to the obvious. When you have eliminated all that is possible, whatever remains, no matter how improbable, must be true; from our good friend Mr. Sherlock Holmes."

CHAPTER SIX

In an empty office in the secure Navy compound where the search was being conducted, Mr. Smith dialed a number.

"Yes, Mr. Smith," a woman's voice answered.

"Nothing yet. They're still looking," he said.

"Would you say that they are looking aggressively?"

"Yes. They have several teams conducting surveillance on possible locations where they might be hiding."

"And what of our good friend, Commander Reese? Is he being a good boy and cooperating?"

"He's got them jumping. He is the one that developed the search criteria for the teams."

"I asked, is he cooperating?" the woman's voice asked again this time sounding annoyed.

"I think so."

"You don't sound very sure. I thought you could judge a person's character better than that."

"From what I am seeing, he's very good at hiding things, but he does slip every once in a while."

"What did he do?"

"One interesting thing was that he reacted to something he saw on the video of the breakout. From what I saw, I thought he recognized one of the perpetrators, but he blew it off by saying that the man's characteristics were consistent with European origin, probably Slavic or some bullshit like that."

"That may be of further use," the woman's voice said. "What else?"

"Apparently he didn't sleep last night. And he had a visitor—some woman."

"He has time for pleasures?"

"Apparently so," Smith said and added a disgruntled sound. "At first we thought someone was breaking into his house but it turns out he knows her. I had someone follow the woman but he lost her somewhere out in Suffolk."

"Sloppy."

"Yes, I agree. I'll ensure they do better in the future."

"Anything else?"

"Reese asked for the medical guy from the original op, Lieutenant Colonel Barkley."

"Why?"

"Said he wanted him for his experience with the original team, but he probably wants someone he can trust. He's putting him to work on looking for an antidote for the elixir."

"An antidote, why?"

"He believes that whoever took the girls wouldn't have gone through all of that trouble to just see them die. He thinks they had some kind of antidote that would allow them to survive the collar injecting the elixir."

"What do you think?"

"Well, it actually makes sense; if that was the goal, to capture and not destroy. It could possibly lead to information about those that were involved."

"Then let the doctor work the issue. Offer all assistance."

"Of course," Smith answered.

"How long before we know anything about the surveillance?"

"Could be hours—could be days, it's hard to tell. Unless something happens that gives us an idea where they are—it's a needle in the haystack scenario."

"Keep me posted."

Before Smith could answer, the connection was broken and all he heard was a dial tone. "Yeah. Sure thing."

CHAPTER SEVEN

"My name is Alexander. Won't you tell me why you are here? Are you lost?" he repeated.

"We are all lost," she said and then laughed.

Christina angrily tossed in her sleep as if she wanted to strike out at something or someone but could not. Lies. The word resonated in her mind; the world was nothing but lies and deceit as she faced the man in her dream.

★★★

"So much anger from a beautiful woman," Alexander said. "It does not become you."

"Ah," Christina said. "Yes, I have beauty. A man told me that once as he danced between my legs. He said I was beautiful and that he needed my beauty to survive. I believed him; I was young and foolish. I thought he loved me, so I loved him in return. But he proved that he needed his wife more when he was caught with me. He testified that I was a temptress who had stolen away his love for his wife to satisfy my own selfish and evil cravings. Do you need my beauty to survive as well?"

"I need nothing that is so full of hatred," Alexander said calmly. "Hatred such as yours burns away at everything I seek from this world. It consumes you above all else. You wish to die, I know. But your hatred refuses to give way so easily against those that have wronged you."

"What do you know about my hatred? Nothing! You're a fool!" she screamed at him.

"Believe what you want and choose what you want," he said, his voice calm yet probing. "That is what life is all about. But don't look for what you do not want to find: The truth."

"The truth," she said vehemently. "I know the truth about life. It's filled with people who lie and cheat their way through it at the expense of the innocent. There is no compassion for the weak, only heartbreak and disappointment."

"So sad," he said shaking his head. "I pity you."

"I don't want your pity!" she screamed.

"What do you want?"

"I want… I want to die. Do you have a knife? Give it to me and I will finish this now instead of listening to you debate what I really want. You can be my one and only mourner. Tell me, will you grieve for me? Will you shed a tear for me when I am gone?"

"You will not kill yourself," he said. "What you need is time to heal and to forgive."

"Ha," she said and laughed. "Give me your knife," she repeated.

He removed a knife from his belt and tossed it on the ground near her.

As she reached for it, he was suddenly on top her with his hands on her throat. She didn't know how he had done it; it was almost mystical. She wondered if perhaps she was dreaming all of this. She had to be. Earlier, when she heard his voice and his lips did not move, and now the way he had moved from one spot to another meant it was all a dream. She tried to convince herself it was all result from her hunger. She was becoming delirious.

"Not real," she murmured.

"Oh yes, my poor soul, this is real," he said. She felt his hands tighten on her throat as if to prove what he had said, slowly squeezing the flesh.

"The knife would be too easy for you," he said. "You are such a fool to be so eager to give up what you possess. I won't let you waste life without meaning when you could give it to me. But perhaps I can change your mind about what life really is."

"Not life," she murmured.

"Life. Yes. This is life as you perceive it, isn't it? Cruel and uncaring. Perhaps you need to feel what you so desire," he said. "A small taste of death."

She stared into the face of the man that held her tightly by the throat. The moon was behind him and she couldn't make out his features as they were bathed in the darkness. But she saw his eyes: they were a bright and deep red and looked as if they were on fire. She felt herself shudder involuntarily at the sight and her anger began to dissipate as it grew into its brother: Fear.

"Not real," she said softly, trying to convince herself.

"We shall see what is real and what is not, what we think we want and what we really want."

He moved his face close to hers now and she smelled his breath. Her mind instantly associated the smell with that of damp earth when one entered a root cellar. It was not an unpleasant smell, but that of old earth damp with moisture. A dream, she insisted. It was all a dream.

He was going to kiss her, she thought as his lips neared her own. But then he moved toward where his hands held her at the neck. She felt the pressure begin to lessen and then felt his lips touch her skin. She had the strangest reaction then, the odd sensation of cold, numbing her skin in a matter of seconds. Then there was a slight pinch and the world exploded in her mind.

CHAPTER EIGHT

"When in doubt always fall back to the obvious. When you have eliminated all that is possible, whatever remains, no matter how improbable, must be true; from our good friend Mr. Sherlock Holmes."

★★★

"Whatever remains must be true..." the man said. The memory of the saying of the classic detective was another reminder of his own past. His father had been an avid reader of Arthur Conan Doyle as evident by the books in their library at home. As a child, he had found those books in the library and read them as well. Was it a father's passion passed down to a son? Just like the agency?

A father who had worked for the agency and who had gone missing during the war; his body never found according to what he had been told. A father whose handwriting looked very similar to what he was looking at right now. But in his mind, all of these similarities were not a certainty but only increased the possibility of getting to know someone that contributed to his birth fifty plus years ago. Time alone dictated that it was now a moot point in the grand scheme of things. Still, it was a mystery left unsolved. The man was too old to not be cynical about life's events and this one was no exception. He turned the page and continued with the next diary entry.

11 October 1944

Medical evaluation results as to the condition of the body are inconclusive; however, there have been some amazing discoveries. Even though there are no responses or outward signs of life from the woman, other than those previously mentioned, the body possesses amazing healing powers I have never seen before.

Any incisions or damage to the skin quickly closes. Imagine being wounded by a bullet and the body healing itself in a matter of minutes. In addition, while the skin remains broken there is minimal blood loss. The blood is also an oddity in itself: when examined we ascertained that it contains characteristics that suggest the female is non-living, i.e. a lack of active and living cells.

As our examination progressed, it was revealed that the organs do not appear to perform the common functions we are accustomed to—in fact the results suggest that there is no longer a need for many of them. The only active organs appear to be the heart and lungs. The rest are not being used at all. Contradiction continues as we seek a determination of what this woman is.

13 October 1944

As I must have answers and seeing no other option, I have secured the local scholar as advised by our guide. By doing so I will have caused the man's death, but there are answers here that I must have. His formal credentials indicate that he is a highly educated man respected in his community in the area of ancient myths and the interpretations of legends. Before the war he taught in the local university. His area of specialty also includes the translation of Slavic tongues considered to be extinct. This skill, I feel may be of value in the investigation due to the apparent age of the crypt.

When he arrived, he performed an examination of the female body using texts which appeared to be extremely old. He then performed a reading of some of the text aloud in a Slavic tongue with which I am not familiar. Although at first I doubted my decision to bring him in, my skepticism became less and less as he was able to produce some physical reactions from the woman. He managed to get the body to perform a movement of limbs. At one point, he also succeeded in having the woman open her eyes.

They were not eyes that one would expect to see on a human. They immediately reminded me of an animal. They looked like the eyes of a wolf. Everyone in the room had the same reaction to this. Everyone also reported feeling as if they were being looked at—all at the same time. I was grateful when she once again closed her eyes.

Although we have discovered many things that are unbelievable about this woman's body, I was still not prepared for the scholar's conclusion: He concurs with what the guide had said earlier about the woman being a vampire. Still he had achieved some results which we had not so I decided to go along with his assessment for the moment.

When I questioned him about her current physical condition he suggested that the weakened state of the woman is similar to a hibernation of an animal— to conserve energy. Not unlike what bears do in the winter. He also suggested that the clothing of the woman and the age of the artifacts in the chamber indicate her arrival dating to perhaps a hundred years or so ago.

Based on his observation I had an independent analysis of artifacts and clothing completed. The results of the test concluded the age is approximately one hundred twenty-five to one hundred and fifty years old. Unless they were placed in here before the woman was, or there is some other way into this crypt we have not discovered, I will have to accept this.

Once again I cannot reach a logical conclusion.

"That is because there is none to find," the man simply said. "What you have found exists when it should not. Therefore it defies all logic. It's a conundrum whose resolution will only lead to further questions and danger. I only hope you realize your mistake before it is too late."

The man shook his head in frustration unable to decide what he should feel toward the man and the diary. Why see this now? What prompted its arrival and furthermore, who had sent it?

CHAPTER NINE

"Keep me posted."

Before Smith could answer, the connection was broken and all he heard was a dial tone. "Yeah—sure thing."

Samantha replaced the telephone headset in the receiver base. She rose from the desk and paced the room. Her clothes were still damp with sweat from working out before the phone call from Mr. Smith. She usually exercised three times a week when things at work were at a semi-normal pace and found it to be just the right amount to keep her edge under control. But now with an operation of such high consequence should she fail, Samantha worked out as much as three times a day especially during the part that she hated the most—the waiting. If she didn't expend her nervous and frustrated energy she would probably kill someone. History had proven that to be the case.

Every day that the two girls—the creatures—were loose jeopardized the discovery of their own creature and Operation Iron Stake. If there was even a hint that such creatures existed, the whole world would become a turmoil and even worse, the United States would lose the advantage they had enjoyed over the years. If this advantage was lost due to any fault of hers, she knew she would be quietly removed. An accident would be arranged, or worse yet, Mr. Smith would be assigned her neutralization. He would enjoy that immensely, she thought.

The folder on Operation Iron Stake lay open on her desk. She had gone through it at least three times now looking for anything that might help the current situation. She had memorized many of the operations that had been completed, including the assignments that had fallen under her tenure as handler of the creature. She had written a summary of the major events so that she could quickly review if she thought it became necessary.

1949: Assassinations of key personnel in order to allow CIA establishment of Radio Free Europe.

1950: Assassinations of North Korean officials prior to invasion of South Korea.

1952: Assassinations of Egyptian officials to secure overthrow of King Farouk.

1954: Assassinations to ensure CIA supported coup in Guatemala in the overthrow of President Jacobo Arbenz.

1956: Assassinations in Hungary in support of anti-Communist rebellion.

1958: Assassinations in support of election of Charles de Gaulle.

As she continued going through the list, her thoughts also focused on her own personal knowledge from her experience with the asset.

1961: Assassinations in support of Bay of Pigs Invasion.

1964: Assassinations in key Russian positions to ensure failure of Khrushchev's Agricultural reform.

1966: Assassination of Lal Bahadur Shastri in support of election of Indira Ghandi as Prime Minister.

1969: Assassination of Somali President Abdi Rashid Ali Shermarke.

1970: Assists CIA in Laos by assassination of key government figures.

1971: Assassination of Chinese Defense Minister, Lin Pao.

1972: Assists in Philippine Offensive to remove Communistic elements.

1973: CIA directed assassination of Chile's Marxist President, Salvador Allende Gossens.

One of the cardinal rules maintained in the relationship with the asset was the separation of contact between the handler and asset. Samantha had met the creature in person on only two occasions. First, when she became her handler and second, before sending her on the op to kill General Stone. The importance of the General Stone op required her presence to ensure the creature understood exactly what needed to be done and the peculiarity of placing the collars on the dead bodies.

Samantha returned to the list and began going down the page looking at names. Some she had known, some she had not. Did it matter? In the end they were just names on paper that had been obstacles to the ideals and expectations of those in charge. Those obstacles were given to the handler to deal with appropriately. The term 'handler' was one that she had come to admire and cherish just as one would place importance on something sentimental to them.

Her eyes fell back to the list of names as she felt the beginnings of a laugh start to form in the back of her throat.

1975: Assassination of King Faisal of Saudi Arabia.

1976: Assassinations in support of finding the murderer of US Ambassador Francis E. Melroy in Beirut.

1977: Assassination in Ethiopia in support of removal of Communist Forces.

1978: Assassinations in opposition to Soviet supported coup in Afghanistan.

1979: Failed attempt in infiltration of American Embassy in Iran.

1980: Assassination of Yugoslavian President Tito.

1983: Assassination of identified terrorists involved with bombing of US Marine barracks in Lebanon.

1985: Assassinations in Nicaragua in support of Contras rebels.

1986: Sabotage of Chernobyl nuclear power plant.

1988: Assassination of Pakistan General Zia ul-Haq.

1989: Assassinations in support of Czechoslovakian revolt against Communist government.

1990: Assassinations in support of overthrow of Communist party in Yugoslavia.

Handler. She allowed the sound to dance on her lips. She raised her finger and touched her lips to feel the vibration. She smiled. The term had been adopted somewhere along the line for reasons she didn't know; however, she understood the implications of it very well. When Iron Stake had been placed into service, positive control had been maintained by the explosive device inside of her. The device was state-of-the-art in the mid-1940's when it had been designed, but with technological advances, the device had been quickly replaced with even better technology.

Better technology meant the device was replaced every five years or so.

"Boom," she said and she splayed her arms in front of her. "Boom... boom." She liked bombs. Bombs were good ways to get your target. You didn't have to be right on top of them to use a bomb, just close enough. Like in horseshoes and hand grenades.

1991: Assassination of key Iraqi officials to aide allied invasion of Operation Desert Storm.

1993: Assassination of Somalia dissidents associated with American soldier murders.

1994: Assassinations of Russian spies associated with American spy Aldrich Ames.

1995: Assassinations in support of investigation into death of Israeli Prime Minister Yitzhak Rabin.

1996: Assassinations in support of operation in Saudi Arabia as a result of bomb exploded at apartment complex.

1998: Assassinations in support of CIA operation to locate Osama bin Laden.

1999: Assassinations in Yugoslavia in support of NATO operations to halt ethnic cleansing.

2000: Assassination of Syrian President Hafez al-Assad.

2001: Assassinations of Chinese military officials involved with the capturing of American pilots.

2002: Failed assassination attempt on Saddam Hussein.

2003: Assassinations in support of democratic issues by students in Iran.

2004: Assassinations of General Stone and Commander Scott for their inappropriate handling of assets involved with 'Team of Darkness' Operations.

Her list ended, although she knew with certainty that there were a few more events that had been completed. A new policy had been adopted over the past few years of not even recording the missions. Some things just did not belong on the list because if they did, someone might find out one day and ask questions. She felt a warm smile come to her face as she thought about those missions and her thoughts drifted back to the explosive device.

The controlling device became smaller and more complex with every replacement and the current range of the tracking device was virtually worldwide. Which meant the ability to detonate the device was also possible anywhere in the world, so any attempt by the creature to escape was useless. Of course this bit of information had been kept from the creature until after the device had been installed. However, the one thing that had not changed over the span of time was the method of removal. The device was coded with the genetic code of two people, the handler and the head of the agency. Only these two people could have the device safely removed. Any other attempt would result in a small but deadly explosion.

Samantha smiled as she imagined the efficiency of such a kill. She smiled and felt warmth between her legs as she dreamt about the explosion and the effect it would have on the human body.

CHAPTER TEN

"It will work out," insisted Iliga, "We have safeguards enough."

"Let's hope you are right," said Dimitri. "If not, this underground shelter may become our own crypt and we will never leave."

"It is time to go," Dimitri said.

The three men and two girls stood in the driveway outside of the barn on the farm in Suffolk, Virginia. Dimitri had procured the farm and then rented out the land at a very affordable rate to cattle owners. This not only gave him a steady stream of income, but also a steady source of food in the blood from the cattle. It was a win-win scenario.

They had finished feeding on the cattle that had been brought into the barn for the night, another arrangement that Dimitri had his hired help perform. Every evening, they would bring six cows into the barn, leaving the rest out in the field. This way the cattle were rotated every day, ensuring none were harmed.

Dimitri turned toward the two girls. "Are you alright?" he asked. He did not direct the question due to concern over the feeding, but was referring rather to the conversation that Ishma had had with her younger sister, Crema, concerning their future.

During the drive from Norfolk, Ishma explained to Crema what Dimitri had told her about her father and Josip and what their life would be like. The young girl had cried and wailed at the loss of her father. Yet Dimitri wasn't sure if she really understood what her life would be like from this point on. Youth was pliable and could be shaped to change he hoped. She would probably adapt after a short period, however Dimitri was more concerned with Ishma. She was older which made her worldly enough to understand the possible satisfaction that could come from revenge and hatred rather than the peace of putting the past behind.

"We're...okay," Ishma answered cautiously, "a little shaky but okay." As she spoke, she pulled her younger sister closer to her, hugging her tightly. Something between an unsure smile and a frown was upon the lips of the younger girl.

"We should go," he said. "We have things to plan."

The five of them got into the van that was parked on the side of the barn. Andre drove as always, Dimitri sat in the passenger seat, and Iliga sat in the back with the girls. Nobody spoke as they drove down the dark and empty roads.

This area of Suffolk was full of plenty of those. The people of the area were still trying to resist the pull of commercialism and development. In a small way it reminded Dimitri of the rural areas of Kosovo, although this land was flat as compared to the rough terrain of his own city. They passed a few deer, their eyes' reflections caught by the headlights of the van as they passed. The animals were foraging in the fields for peanuts and corn as the van made its way back to the main road. Slowly the darkness gave way as they approached the more abundant streetlights of the main road. They turned onto the main highway, Benn's Church, and headed toward Smithfield.

Dimitri did not feel as exhilarated as he usually did after feeding. His thoughts were troubled because everything was changing so suddenly. They had acclimated to their new environment. They had begun to settle into a new routine. They had secured a safe food source, had studied the area and the society, and learned adaptive strategies. But then they'd learned of the girls and now he wondered what changes they would bring to the group.

He felt the van turning left onto Route 17 and heading toward the James River Bridge. He could smell the brackish water of the river as they approached. He didn't like the smell. For some reason he associated it with a rotting corpse of a dead animal and he tried to ignore it as he settled back into his thoughts.

The three of them had already decided that it would be best to take the girls back home to Kosovo. They had based this upon the assumption that perhaps having a sense of familiarity with their surroundings would help them adjust to their new lives as vampires. There were many places in the mountains that they knew; secret places such as the old library where Dimitri and his group had spent many quiet years. People also had a... Dimitri struggled to find the word to describe it, a respect for the old legends. It was as if they were proud that their area of the world had been the bedrock for these myths and stories. The people of the Balkans would drag their feet and struggle as they were pulled into the future.

The only problem with the plan to return home was how to get them out of this area. Since the escape, every possible method of leaving had been blocked. Dimitri had underestimated the strength and determination of whomever it was that had control over the girls and their captivity. He only hoped that that one mistake did not cost them their lives.

Chapter Eleven

Christina had the strangest reaction then, an odd sensation of cold numbing her skin in a matter of seconds. Then there was a slight pinch and her world exploded in her mind.

Christina tried to roll from side to side in her bed as if to escape something. Her sheets were wrapped around her legs preventing her from rolling away. Her hands were wrapped in front of her throat as if trying to prevent an attack.

She was immersed in the massive amount of sensations—her body felt as if she were being submerged into a pool of intense warmth. The feeling pushed aside all thought and allowed only the sensation of intense pleasure to carry her along whatever path it chose as she rode the never-ending wave.

Further and further she fell into the bottomless well. She had never felt such pleasure before, and she never wanted it to end.

This is what you seek to give up. A voice came from somewhere within her. Remember it well, cherish it.

It grew dark and cold as the warmth faded quickly from her body. As each part of her body grew cold, she felt pain surge, evicting the pleasure of seconds ago.

Here is what you seek…the end to everything.

She felt the loss of sensation in parts of her body. One by one, they turned off—or died, taking with it the feeling of life that had nurtured it. Piece by piece, the cold of death traveled through her body like an unwelcome guest, killing everything in its path like a plague.

You have one chance. One final chance at life. But you must choose now.

She felt weak and cold as she slowly opened her eyes and looked at him. The flame still burned within this strange man's eyes. But now she saw that his mouth was dark; covered by shadow, but the shadow moved as it dripped from his face. As her eyes adjusted to the dim light, she realized it was not a shadow but blood: her blood. He had taken it from her. What was he?

Her mind supplied an answer. She remembered the stories she had heard about creatures of the night, about vampires. They would prey on humans to get what they needed to survive. Blood. Had she sacrificed her life to a man that was not even truly alive? The thought was infuriating and anger fought for dominance as shame and vile self-loathing filled her heart. She imagined what her fate might be: Taken advantage of by two men to further their own goals, while completely disregarding her and her life. There must be... and then she remembered what else she had heard as a young child.

These creatures harbored amazing recuperative powers. They were extremely hard to kill: Their wounds would close up quickly or they would vanish for periods of time while they healed. People said it was because of the altered blood that flowed in their bodies. That was the answer!

If she could drink his blood, perhaps that would save her. The thought was revolting and even as weak as she was, she felt her stomach lurch at the thought. But what other choice did she have? Would she allow herself to be defeated again? Perhaps it was better to just end it and die here alone in the woods with her shame.

No! The thought of defeat brought immense hatred. Her emotions flushing away the weakness brought on by the loss of blood. She would have him. She would have his blood and she would drink it as he had drunk hers. If it didn't help her, she would die—but she would not die alone. She would take him with her. If it did help her, she might live another day or night and...what? Yes, seek revenge against those who punished her wrongly.

Yes...every single one of the villagers...every single one of them.

"Do you still wish to die?" he asked.

His voice drove her from her thoughts and back to the moment.

"Perhaps it would be better," he answered to her silence.

"Give it back," she said. "My life...I want it..."

"I cannot give you back what I have taken. If I did, it would change you into what I am. Your anger would then manifest you into something worse: Something that that would consume and change you over a great period of time, nurturing you perhaps into something even more pitiful than you are now."

It is true, she thought. The stories were true. He could give her back life.

"No. I cannot allow that," he continued. "If you wish to live, you must do it on your own. You must want to live enough to survive this night, but you must do it without my help."

"You bastard," she whispered. She wanted to strike out at him, to hit him and hurt him. She wanted to kill him. But he was stronger and she needed a weapon of some sort. Then she remembered the knife: he had thrown it to her before he had grabbed her by the neck. Where was it? She didn't remember. Knife or not, she need something.

"You must decide what you wish," he said.

"You have not left me a choice, have you?" she said, trying to act calm and to distract him from her hand's movement.

"None," he answered, and then his face went blank as if remembering something from his own past.

She slid her hand along her leg and onto the ground, searching for anything she could use to strike him with. Her hand struck something hard and cold on the ground. Her fingers examined it as she kept her eyes on the man. The cold steel and sharp edge confirmed the object to be a knife.

"Perhaps I am a bastard," he agreed. "But I have shown you what life can truly be about if you let go of your anger and thirst for revenge."

"I want to see your face," she said. "I want to see the face of the man that would do such a thing."

He leaned closer.

She took a deep breath and channeled all her energy into her right arm. She sent the knife straight up into the man's throat.

CHAPTER TWELVE

The man shook his head in frustration unable to decide what he should feel toward the man and the dialogue. Why see this now? What prompted its arrival and further who had sent it?

For a moment the man thought that his hands were shaking, but he knew that couldn't be true. Any emotional attachment to his father had been lost a long time ago. The man returned his attention to the problem at hand and shook his head.

"Logic does not always afford us the luxury of survival," he said remembering the last diary entry. "That was a lesson you should have remembered."

He turned the page and continued reading.

```
17 October 1944
```

```
The research continues. Further examination and
interpretation of texts the civilian authority has
in his possession suggests that the definition of
a vampire is an un-dead creature that feeds on
the live blood of animals and humans. Physically
strong, one creature can possess the strength of
ten men. They are virtually impossible to kill
except by decapitation or exposure to sunlight,
though there are references to the use of some
religious symbols. They can move quickly and are
virtually undetectable. Additionally, they appear
alluring to the opposite sex and possess a strong
sense of self-preservation. They are generally
antisocial and tend to be solitary creatures who
maintain a certain degree of territory superiority
with other similar creatures.
```

```
Of course I reserve my judgment on believing any of
the information contained in the texts. Myths and
legends are usually nothing more than old wives'
tales fabricated out of superstition to explain
things not understood. But if this, any of this,
```

is true—and we assume that there were more of these creatures, then why have we not seen or heard of them before? Or is she the only one? It is questions such as these I shall pursue.

The civilian believes there is a way to bring the woman out of her deep sleep. He suggests that their senses are naturally attuned to the smell of fresh blood. We shall attempt to lure her awake by using fresh blood from a slaughtered animal. He cautions that she will resist all methods of capture and that she should be killed immediately if proven to be one of these creatures—a vampire.

Although unlikely to be required, I have taken precautionary measures. While she is still in her trancelike sleep, I have inserted an explosive device inside of her body; an extremely difficult procedure considering the healing powers of the body. The device is encased within a steel cylinder approximately six inches in length and with a diameter of three inches. It can only be moved or opened by the use of a special transmitter and encoding unit. The explosive is not removable without entering a coded sequence into the transmitter.

18 October 1944

My God! We have successfully awakened the creature! I doubt I will ever be the same man I was before I saw what happened today. I have seen a lot in my lifetime but nothing like the carnage I witnessed here. If her other talents prove to be consistent with the legends, we may have exactly what we need. But I'm getting ahead of myself, I shall begin by describing what we did and saw.

On a whim I agreed to allow the local expert to adopt some of the religious aspects of protection— and ironically this may have been the only thing which saved our lives in the end.

Upon placement of the fresh animal blood near her, her eyes immediately opened. I shall always remember those eyes. They weren't normal eyes. They were dark red in color and animalistic—and the way they stared…with such intensity. And then the holocaust began.

We weren't prepared for the swiftness of the creature. She grasped the bowl of blood and drank it as if she was quenching a drastic thirst. It was gone in less than five seconds. Then she flew from the crypt and took down two of our men before we knew what was happening. She showed no fear of the rest of us. She ripped open their throats with her nails, which had grown several inches longer since she'd awakened. It sounded like she was cutting paper. I will never forget the way their skin opened and how she buried her face into their necks. The sound of strong sucking and lapping echoed off the cavernous walls. I almost vomited. All of this took place in the blink of an eye. In less than fifteen seconds, she had filled herself and that was when I saw it.

She turned toward us and she had changed. Her physical appearance, the desiccated, near mummified body and the face which earlier contained the features of some type of mixture of human and animal, had now become… breathtakingly beautiful. When she had lain in the crypt she was vaguely discernible as a female. What features she did possess were plain almost to the point of non-gender. Thin lips, small breasts, her skin and hair as coarse as sandpaper from the absence of any moisture. But now… as she stood before me, she was the most voluptuous woman I have ever seen. Her eyes were the loveliest things I had ever gazed upon and they looked into me as if they spoke to my soul. Above them her eyebrows were slender and curved exactly in the right contour to accentuate her eyes. Her face was perfect. Where her nose had previously been mottled and misshapen, it was now even and aquiline. Her lips looked as smooth as cream, they were full and enticing and just below them was a small dimple which highlighted the shape of her chin adding new dimension to the otherwise even skin. I stared at the round curves of her cheek bones, the skin that looked as soft as silk. Suddenly, I could imagine my fingers tracing over that skin, feeling the softness of it. And her hair, it was long and brown falling far past her shoulders. Again I had the strongest urge to reach out and touch it and feel the texture of it between my fingers. She had full and firm breasts where before she had virtually little to no shape at all. Again I immediately drifted into some form of dream like trance where I was with her—touching her. Everything else around me had vanished and was replaced with only the thought of wanting this woman.

Then the sound of gunshots echoed in the cavern and as quickly as I had been sucked into this dream, it was shattered by the harshness of reality and imminent death.

One of the men opened fire. I hadn't thought about it at the time, about how he had escaped her illusion of attraction which had so easily immobilized me. Only after debriefing, I realized that he had taken communion this morning at a nearby church. I can only think that somehow his religious observance had perhaps saved us all from our deaths.

I watched as the bullets hit her in several places. She had been struck enough times that it would have brought down the strongest man. But she just stood there looking at the holes they left behind. I watched as the wounds closed almost immediately. The rest of the men opened fire and continued to shoot until they emptied their weapons magazines. I thought my head was going to explode from all the noise. Yet, she just stood there.

When the last shot had been fired and the echo died away, a deathly silenced enveloped the cavern. She raised her head and smiled and then I heard her laugh. It was in a tone that was both exhilarating and frightening. It reached into my chest and tore at my very soul.

All during this incident, whether by the sudden change of events or the hypnotic effect she had on me, I had completely forgotten about the explosive device within her and the detonation device in my pocket. As I awoke from my stupor, I reached for it but before I could fully grasp it, things exploded again.

The civilian splashed some holy water in her

direction and she stopped and hissed at him baring large canine incisors. He screamed at me to look away from her. I felt his arms on mine as he shook me. As he did so I felt the remaining haze lift from my mind. I carefully returned my gaze to this creature, avoiding eye contact at all costs for I believe this was how she was able to obtain a hold over me. I realized she has a power to cause an unprotected man to lose his concentration in some way. For a brief period, I could think of nothing other than how desirable she was. And I am sure of one thing: She would have kept me thinking that as she slit my throat and drank her fill of my blood.

I realize how crazy this must sound. I have not lost my mind or suffered any forms of delusion. I know what I saw and felt.

What happened next shall remain vivid in my memory for the remainder of my life. I watched the creature slip its hand through its own flesh and probe the area where the device had been planted. Unlike before, when we inserted the device and had the constant problem of keeping the flesh opened, she had no problem at all. It was if her body allowed her own hand to probe her insides at will. When her hand stopped moving, she looked up at me with an expression that threw me. I expected to see a look of disdain or anger at what I had done. But instead I saw a look that I could only describe as a mix of curiosity and amusement.

I found the creature's straight forward approach unsettling and yet fascinating. I assumed she either accepted her situation, the explosive device within her, or she had a plan to counteract what we had done. I have never before felt so unsure of my actions at any moment in time.

A strange sense of calm seemed to come over the creature. She stopped all forms of aggression and simply asked me to explain what I wanted. After a few minutes of conversation, she agreed to end hostilities so that she could learn more about us and what the world on the outside was like.

```
It was during those few minutes that I got the
feeling that she was not ignoring the bomb we had
placed inside of her, but rather that she did not
care about its presence one way or the other. This
meant that she did not care if she would live or
die and this made her truly dangerous.

Even after what I saw—I still have the blood of
my men upon my clothing—I am almost ashamed to
say this… I am not sure if it's the effect of the
creature's influence or my own thoughts which are
causing my attraction for her.
```

"An attraction toward that creature? How could you…you son of a bitch?" The man shook his head back and forth. "No. You had a mission to accomplish and you…you had a family at home…how could you even consider such an idea?"

The man's heart raced as anger filled him. *Such a selfish bastard!* He hurled the notebook at the nearest wall. There was a resounding *thump* as the leather made contact with the cinder block followed by a *whump* sound as the book fell onto the floor.

The man remained motionless and stared at the book. His labored breathing slowly returned to normal.

CHAPTER THIRTEEN

Reese said to him softly, "It's only going to get uglier."

"Hmm, going ugly early."

★★★

After Barkley left his office, Reese returned to his desk and the folder he had yet to review. He looked up at the clock on the wall and saw it was nearly 6PM. The realization that he had been awake for over thirty six hours reinforced the physical effects brought on by lack of sleep. Fatigue was catching up with him.

His mind was beginning to blur with the possibilities discussed with Barkley combined with the search parameters that had been put into place. If he opened the folder and looked through any additional information, he doubted he would even be able to comprehend it in any useful way.

He pushed the folder aside deciding that a few hours of sleep would do him good. The folder could wait. As it slid across the desk, the business card with Christina's phone number slipped out onto the desk blotter. He remembered that he had started to call her earlier, but then Barkley arrived interrupting.

He picked up the card from the blotter and held it between his fingers. The flowing script of Christina brought a smile to his lips. He remembered when she had written it and what she had said about calling her soon because she might have to leave town for a while. But he didn't have time tonight, and…

Damn it John, just call her. If nothing else at least let her know you're interested for Christ's sake. Stop making excuses—just call her!

Agreeing with the subconscious thought, his hand went to the telephone and dialed the numbers. The phone rang once and he felt his stomach begin to tighten. On the second ring, he felt his hand nervously twitch and he grasped at a pencil to keep it still. On the third ring, he was poised to hang up the phone because he decided he didn't know what he would say if she answered the phone. As the fourth ring began, he was ready to remove the handset from his ear, but then a voice answered.

"Hello?"

Reese hesitated.

"Hello?"

Say something, his inner voice demanded.

"Chris-tina," he said struggling with the syllables as if he were learning to talk for the first time. He felt embarrassed and thought about hanging up. This wasn't how he wanted to come across, weak and unsure and sounding like a wimp.

"John? Is that you?" she asked.

Busted, he thought. He had to talk now. "Hi," he said, struggling to place some normalcy back into his voice.

"Hi yourself," she said in return, "I'm very glad you called."

Really, he thought to himself. Was she really glad?

"I thought I'd give you a call when I got a chance," he began. "Sorry about the time, it's been one of those days."

"I know what you mean," she said. "Have you had a chance to get any sleep yet?"

"No. In fact, that was what I was going to do. Grab a few hours and then start back at work. I wanted to call you...and...maybe when this is over, I...we...can..."

"I have an idea," she said not addressing what he found so hard to say. "I need to take care of some things, and you need to get some sleep. Why don't you let me bring you dinner later on tonight?"

"Dinner?" he asked.

"Yes. You know... food?" she said playfully. "You do eat, don't you?"

"Ah...yes," he said although his voice sounded skeptical. He tried to focus and calm down so he would sound normal.

"Well then, it's all settled then, I'll see you—say around midnight?"

"Midnight..."

"Yes John," she said.

He thought he heard a little laughter in her voice. Stop screwing it up you idiot, he told himself.

"Do you always repeat everything?" she asked.

"Repeat..." he began then caught his words. "No—well sometimes..."

"You're cute when you get flustered."

"Ah..." he stuttered feeling himself flush with embarrassment. How was she able to tell what he was feeling—was he that transparent that she could tell by the way he talked how he felt? He didn't know what to say to her statement so he decided surrender was the best avenue. "Okay, midnight sounds good," he said. Unlike his previous words, these came across more confident and assured. Of course they did—he wanted to see her again.

"I bet your favorite is…," she paused and then said, "Italian food?"

"Good guess," he said agreeing with her because he really did like Italian food the best of all.

"Great," she said. "Now that we have that settled. Go home and get some rest. I'll see you at your house around midnight then."

"Is it easier if I come to you?" Reese suggested, "Your place?" He proposed the suggestion because after his conversation with Barkley earlier, he was wondering if he wasn't being watched. Or had his meeting with Christina already been logged in some report already? Did it matter? He wasn't sure, but he wanted everything to go right with her and, not knowing what the true ultimate goal of the agency was, he wanted to play it safe.

"My place is…" she hesitated, "a mess right now. I don't think you're ready to see it yet, John. Maybe later okay?"

For the first time since he had met her, her voice did not sound confident but rather cautious, he thought. Was it that there was something he was not supposed to see or know? Perhaps she lived with someone—another man? Or worse yet, was she married? Or was he just doing the same old thing again and assuming the worst? How he wished he could just stop it. "Ah…sure," he said.

"It's not that, John." she said.

"What?" he asked.

"What you're thinking," she said. "I heard it in your voice. I'm not… seeing anyone and I'm not married John. That's not why I am suggesting having dinner at your place. It's complicated and I don't want to discuss it over the phone. Maybe tonight we can talk about it. Okay? Don't worry, it is not some great mystery to be solved. You'll see it…soon."

"Sure," he agreed.

"Now go get some rest," she continued, "I want to talk about some things tonight. Some of my own research that you might be interested in and I want your full and undivided attention."

Intrigued by her promise and suggestion he asked, "Such as?"

"You'll see. I'll see you tonight."

"What no hints?" he said, enjoying the mystery of her.

"Nope. I like to keep you guessing. I'll see you later."

"Okay," he said. "Bye."

"Bye."

Reese hung up the receiver. He couldn't help the feeling that seemed to invigorate his tired body. He was excited at the thought of seeing her again and he felt it—and he liked it. Goose bumps actually made a cursory trip over the skin of his flesh before heading back to wherever it is they hung out when they weren't needed. He thought of how wonderful a human emotion that was. Of course, he was sure that there was some scientific explanation that could explain the reaction, some neural to physical connection, but just this one time, he could not care.

He checked his watch; it was almost 6:30 PM. He would make a stop in the control center and see if anything had come up from the surveillance before he called it a day. As he rose from his chair, his eyes returned to the unopened folder on his desk. It beckoned him to just open it up and have a fast look.

"It can wait for a few hours," he said out loud. He was surprised as this reaction was another first for him. Normally he would have given into the demands of his work over his physical needs of sleep or....well whatever might happen later this evening.

Ah...that's an evil thought there, John. You hardly know the girl and at one inkling of, shall we say, the pleasures of the flesh you become obsessed? Aren't you getting a bit ahead of yourself?

He felt himself smile at the thoughts while he pushed the folder to the side of his desk blotter and headed out of the office.

Maybe...

CHAPTER FOURTEEN

She took a deep breath and channeled all her energy into her right arm. She sent the knife straight up into the man's throat.

As Christina lay asleep in her bed, a smile crept onto her face. It was the sweet smile of revenge as she remembered the look of surprise on Alexander's face all those many years ago as he watched his own blood squirt from the main artery in his neck.

★★★

She wasted no time. Using the element of surprise, she pushed him over onto the ground and straddled him. She saw his precious blood spilling from the wide gash in his throat. She smiled momentarily and then put her face to his throat and tore at his flesh with her teeth while swallowing his blood in long satisfying gulps: Just as he had done to her.

In those few seconds, she literally tasted her revenge against this man and against all the men that had abused and used her while thoughts of the perversity of the action was forced aside. There was something odd in the taste of the blood.

She had tasted blood before, the sucking of a cut finger or a slice from something sharp on the inside of the mouth which produced the coppery sweet taste. But what was entering her mouth, what she tasted on her tongue, was much different. It was vile in some way she couldn't describe, perhaps old and musty or…decayed. And it was cold.

She could feel the cool liquid slide down her throat and into her belly. She imagined the process in her mind and saw the blood making its way through her bloodstream and heading to her heart. Along the way, the altered blood left a path of destruction within the body organs it came into contact with. The simplest explanation entered her mind with what was happening; the altered blood was in essence turning the organs off because they were no longer required. When it reached her heart, it felt as if someone had taken a sledgehammer and hit her with it in the chest. All the oxygen in her body seemed to escape, leaving her gasping for air.

She leaned back up to a straddling position and looked down at the creature. His eyes were closed as if he were unconscious. The gash at his neck was still open and oozed blood but the flow had slackened considerably and was beginning to slowly close back up. Her body convulsed with another sledgehammer blow to the chest and she fell to one side of him and lay on the ground.

She felt her breathing stop and she grew cold as her life passed away from her. Her eyes remained open and they were filled with the light from the full moon above. She remembered staring up at the silvery orb as she died and remembered how its image changed when she was reborn as a vampire. It appeared to be laughing at her in a mocking fashion as she gave up her life as a human being for the life of the undead.

When she returned to consciousness, the moon had moved across the night sky and was no longer in her field of vision. She rolled over on her side and saw that she was not entirely alone. The man known as Alexander was no longer there. However, in his place sat a wolf on its haunches looking at her. It was a large wolf, weighing about eighty or ninety pounds and each panting exhalation showed its chest was massive. Its fur glowed in the moonlight and its eyes shone as they stared intently into hers. She could see the circular aspect of the creature's irises clearly as they glimmered in their sockets. As if acknowledging she was awake and examining it, the wolf growled and bared its long, menacing teeth at her. They outlined the large mouth; saliva dripped and oozed between its pointed fangs.

Normally she would have been scared at the predicament in which she found herself—now however, Christina felt nothing of the sort. Instead, she felt a surge of excitement course through her body. She thrilled with the anticipation of facing this creature in its own home but most of all she had the urge to kill. She wanted to kill the wolf—no, she had to kill the wolf. The beast growled and lunged for her.

She effortlessly caught the animal in mid-air and grasped it by its throat holding it securely with her hands. She was not surprised by the strength that flowed through her. Then as if by some instinct she didn't comprehend, she knew what she needed to do and her body slipped effortlessly into the killing mode. She felt her nails become longer and sharper, like the talons of a hawk or eagle. They slipped easily into the flesh of the animal, slicing it open. She felt the elongation as well as the increased sharpness of her incisors with her tongue. The wolf's warm blood flowed over her fingers and she could smell it. She could smell the life within the animal's blood and she wanted it.

The smell of the blood was sweet, provocative and inviting. It drove her to an immediate madness—a near obsession for the liquid. She must have it now her mind screamed and she buried her face into the animal, her teeth and nails easily separating the flesh and exposing the veins and arteries where the blood flowed. She drank deeply feeling the animal's warmth flow through her. It was invigorating beyond words. Her body responded to the blood as it made her feel…reborn.

As the animal neared death, she felt the change in its blood. It began to taste bitter and sour instead of sweet. Her instincts told her to stop: that there was danger in drinking the blood so close to death. The urge to continue was strong, but she dropped the carcass on the ground. She wiped her mouth with her sleeve and saw the blood that came away. She stared at the blood with no remorse, no revulsion. This was life, her life and she gladly accepted it.

Life. She was now a part of life that included the stories she had heard as a child about the creatures that owned the night. She wondered how it would be, not being able to see the light of day any longer. Would she adjust? Of course she would. Like anything else, there were advantages to her new self as well as disadvantages, but most importantly, she was able to control her own destiny from this point on. If the myths were true, she would no longer feel cold, heat, pain or hunger as a human would. All of these would now become inconsequential, as would the emotion of love. She was dead for all practical purposes, and with it, she had buried any hope for love or human life, at least for the time being.

For now, she had to decide where she would go. Which direction would she go? Back toward the town or away? She turned in the moonlight as if trying to sense what direction to take. While doing so, she caught a glimpse of something on the ground. She walked toward it and saw it was a piece of paper with a rock on top of it to keep it from blowing away. She bent over and picked it up. Although it was dark except for the moonlight, she discovered it was quite easy for her to see in the reduced light. She smiled at this ability as she observed the scrawled words in a rough handwriting.

I misjudged you. I sought to make you cherish life, the human life, by bringing you to the brink of death—to feel the emptiness and coldness as compared to the fullness and warmth of life. But instead, you gave it up willingly, and took from me what I would never have given freely.

You are an evil woman as well as a fool. You believe this life will be better then death? It will appear so in the beginning, but its joys will wane quickly as you remember what you could have had in a normal life. I was taken without a choice and have often begged for death. But I have accepted my fate and tempered this life with caution and indifference in order to survive over the years, hoping that meaning will come to me. I still wait after many years to find it.

As for you, I would have killed you for what you did, but by the time I had recovered, you had turned and we don't kill our own. Yes, there is a bizarre and perverse code by which we conduct ourselves in contrast to the solitary lives we choose to live. Our kind generally keeps to themselves: We're territorial, I guess you might say. You may never meet another like you and so you may have nothing but solitude for company for the rest of the nights of your life, unless you choose the companionship of a human.

Unlike you, I never gave up my conscious being and I still adhere to the rules and principles that governed my human life. So I will share the bare necessities with you. It might appear to you that you understand what has happened to you since the transformation, but there is much that you will have to experience on your own. As I have created you, albeit under conniving circumstances, I shall give you the basic tenets of what you need to know in order to survive.

You must avoid all forms of daylight. You must immediately seek shelter as your first daylight period approaches. Religious symbols when properly prepared and consecrated with unwavering faith are also deadly. There are various forms of elixirs made by people of the villages to ward us away from their cattle and people: Many are useless but others are not. Approach them with caution. Do not attract unnecessary attention. People are changing; they no longer hide behind their myths and ghost stories. They pursue us like they do any other adversary so choose your victims carefully. Better yet, purchase cattle and keep them yourself. Animals are always safer. Human blood will make you reckless as a human drinking too much wine.

Remember that money always tames the biggest fears, so always have some with you.

I leave you now to whatever fate awaits you. If you do not change, your anger will consume you and turn you into an even more hated creature then you were in your village. You have time now, use it well and allow it to heal whatever scars have been cast upon you. Search to find what you have lost in life, so you can cherish it in death. Make something out of your death other than the creation of pain and suffering for others.

Alexander.

Christina stared at the note for a few seconds, and then stuffed it into her bodice. She made a conscious reminder to revisit the note at a later time...how much later, she didn't know. But right now, she had some things to take care of and headed off in the direction of her old home, her old village. She wanted to pay a visit to her family, her friends and especially one man.

She would show them that she had overcome their use of her to achieve their own selfish goals. Yes...she would show them that their judgment of her was wrong...dead wrong.

CHAPTER FIFTEEN

The man's heart was racing as anger filled him. Such a selfish bastard! He hurled the notebook at the nearest wall. There was a resounding thump as the leather made contact with the cinderblock and fell to the floor.

When the man felt in control of his anger, he rose from his chair and walked over to the wall and picked up the diary. Part of him wanted to burn the book while another part of him demanded that he finish what he started. Opening the book had been like opening the lid of Pandora's Box.

So suck it up…and get on with it.

His eyes scanned over the last phrase over and over again…yet I am not sure if it is the effect of the creatures influence or my own thoughts which are causing my attraction for her…

"If you have to ask the question, then you are in deep shit, buddy" he said shaking his head. "Damn…you should have pulled the plug at that point. Whoever was in charge should have seen this and gotten someone new in there or at least adopted a two-man rule security system which would have kept you all safe from this creature's power. Such oversight is inexcusable. You wrote your own death sentence."

He opened the book and turned to the page where he had left off. He read on.

20 October 1944

Our non-violence agreement holds. The creature has made no offensive gestures toward me or any of the other men. At times I detect an air of arrogance in her demeanor, as if she's just toying with us and that she could have her way if she chose to. Yet at times she appears to want something from us. I just don't know what it is yet. She is indeed an enigma on so many levels.

As to her requirements for sustenance, she does not desire nor is she able to eat normal food. All that she requires is blood from a living organism. We keep her fed with animals purchased on local market. The blood from them seems to satisfy her although I do not see the same extreme vitality she exuded when she killed the two men and fed on them. I suspect that the animal blood, although it can sustain her life, does not produce the same euphoric effect on her body as human blood.

I have held several conversations with her and find her to be extremely intelligent and captivating. I have to remind myself of the gruesome assault she performed on my men. This is another trait that the civilian warned me about; this potential for her to infiltrate based on her physical and mental qualities alone would be highly formidable. I regret having to terminate him, he could have been useful in my understanding of this creature, but he left me no choice.

I have discovered that she possesses a remarkable memory of the period from the late 1800's to the 1920's. However, when I questioned her about her own past and how she became what she is, she is hesitant to give me complete answers.

I have not been able to get anything further from her about her own past or the specifics of how she was created or the creature that made her. Her reluctance to go into this area is quite obvious, so for the moment, I have decided to not go any further into it.

As she speaks I can hear a change in her perception of the world over the long life she has lived. As she comes further toward present day, she loses something - perhaps what I would define as purpose. This is why, I think, she has no great concern for the explosive device within her. She doesn't care if she lives or dies. This I believe is the key that I shall use to motivate her—the promise of purpose.

 22 October 1944

She has agreed to join us! I am glad of her decision on both a professional and personal level. The conversation that we had was fascinating. I have tried to recapture the essence of it in my notes.

I was told that she wished to see me. I entered her living space and she said, "I have decided to accept your proposal."

"I am glad to hear that," I said. "May I ask why?"

"Opportunity," she said. "There is nothing here anymore that interests me. This country and its people remain the same. Perhaps where you offer to take me will present new ideas and concepts. If it turns out to be the same…well there is always the option of death that you offer so freely."

"I see," I said. "So you agree without reservation?"

She laughed and then said, "No. There are two."

"I'm listening go ahead."

"First, I will never make another of my kind. I will submit to death without a moment's consideration."

"Why?" I asked.

"My reasons are my own and of no concern to you. Besides you shall have me to do your bidding—there is no need for another."

"And your second condition?" I asked.

"The length of time of our agreement. I normally don't have any concern for time. I have all the time in the world as long as I am not foolish. But for you it is different. You will die and I will still be here or wherever it is we shall go."

"Ah...of course. Time."

"I assume at some point my services will no longer be required?"

"As you have said earlier, some things never change with people. I suspect there will always be a need for your services."

She turned serious and said, "I can always have, how do you say...hope? Is that correct?"

"Of course," I agreed. "But just for my own speculation, what do you think would be a reasonable, shall we call it 'term of service'?"

"This device inside of me will not last forever."

"True. Its life is limited. With replacement work it will last for quite a while."

"Will it last fifty years?"

"Yes."

"Then let's go with that time then, fair enough?"

"Yes."

"Now that I have agreed, you shall tell me where we are going."

"We go east: To the United States of America."

To this she made no verbal reply but nodded her head in agreement.

As I return to my thoughts, her honesty and bluntness is mind boggling at times. Her agreement under the two conditions is workable to our needs—at this point in time. As to the device inside of her, I have no idea how long it will last. It was designed for more traditional purposes.

It is impermeable to natural elements but the technicians have no idea how long it will remain stable within her body. Her blood possesses characteristics that they are not sure of and how they will affect the casing of the device. There is also the risk of an accidental jarring or disruption and the device might be triggered unintentionally at any time. The risk factor increases the longer it remains in her body. At some point we may want to look at replacing it.

Given all that, I see tremendous potential in using her for our purposes. I have begun making arrangements for our transport to the United States. I do not look forward to the termination of non-necessary team members at this end, but given the military value that she has, I see no other alternative.

As to the men that I use for the transport process; I will see to their termination at the other end once we have safely arrived. I see their deaths as necessary to maintain this secret for the country which I serve. In a strange way, I also feel their deaths are needed to help protect her and me as well. In that regard, I do not understand what is happening. I understand she will do what I ask as long as I give a part of myself to her and this goal that she seeks.

There was a space on the page. Then a few inches later the writing started up again.

May God have mercy on my soul for what I am about to do. I know that the act of my asking for forgiveness is in itself a poetic irony—yet it is all I can do. Not everyone will understand what I do; I only hope that someday my son knows the truth and that when it came to the end there was no choice. I had to do it. My son, I wish I could have been there for you but our country needs me. I hope you can understand that.

There were no further pages.

The man closed the book. His hand went to his face and he was surprised to find the small tear. He wiped it away. He felt ashamed that he had actually shed a tear for this man. He was glad that his mother was long dead and that he would not have to tell her anything about what he had just seen, or at least relay a sanitized version of it.

There was obviously more to this story that was not here. There were quite a few missing pages even after the last entry he had read. Chances are they had come back to the States and something happened. But what? And who had sent him this? And why was it in his hands after all these years? Why now?

Secrets were his own life and he knew the risks that they entailed. Sometimes he actually thought that secrets or rather the keeping of them was nothing more than one test after another. Some measure of a man or his loyalty.

"Sir," a woman's voice came from the telephone speaker on the desk.

"Yes," he said.

"Sorry to interrupt you," the woman's voice said with genuine concern.

"It's okay Sally, what is it?" he asked as he placed the book into a drawer.

"It's the director of the CIA; he needs to talk with you immediately."

"Put him through," he said. There was a click and then a new sound as he came on the line. "Bill, how are you?" he said.

"Fine, fine," the husky voice said. "Listen, I need a favor."

""Now there's a surprise."

"Yeah well there are benefits to being off the radar, I'm sure you understand that aspect very well."

"Of course I do. I learned it working for the CIA before coming here. But there are problems here as well, believe me."

"How can that be? You're virtually accountable to no one. Even I don't know anything about your organization. Heck, all I have is a spook book with a phone number that says in extreme circumstances, call this number."

"Yes, we are a bit of an enigma aren't we? But with that enigma comes additional problems. With no one having to account for everything, there are things that can happen within the organization and I won't know of it either. As of late I have come to understand that even more so." The old man was surprised at his own candidacy with the CIA man. His eyes were drawn to the drawer where the diary was.

"Why is that?" Bill asked sounding puzzled.

"It's a family matter," he said.

"Huh?"

"Never mind. Let's discuss what you need."

As the CIA man spoke, the older man sat and thought. He could hear and understand the entire conversation but he was also thinking about the diary and its contents. The two words, *family matter*, resonated in his thoughts. The itch to know all the pieces of this puzzle began and he knew that he would have to scratch it at some point. The only question was how?

Chapter Sixteen

As Christina finished her phone conversation with John Reese about their meeting later on tonight, an odd mood settled within her. She felt strange, but what bothered her more was that she couldn't put her finger on exactly what it was she felt oddly about. She knew that part of it was that she needed to feed soon, but she decided that it was important to not summon Jake for that purpose.

She didn't want to see Jake tonight after she had almost accidentally killed him the night before. Whether it was guilt from that or just that she was feeling something else from the memories that had arisen during that experience—she wanted to forget about it for a while—especially before she saw Reese later this night.

At dusk, she left the abandoned naval compound in Driver and drove toward the little airport that resided on the edge of Suffolk and the border of North Carolina. She had been to the area before and had observed several homeless people who made their home on the fringes of the airport in a small stand of woods. There were some abandoned shacks that had earlier been used to store obsolete runway maintenance equipment that had been out of use for many years. The area was now commonly referred to as a transient hotel.

She pulled her car off of the side of the road and turned the ignition off. Gazing out at the dark woods she sat there for a few minutes focusing and preparing for what she knew she had to do. To hunt required the proper mindset and being sloppy could cause her to be discovered, or worse yet, possibly injured. These skills required practice just as anything else. She had become so dependent on Jake that she didn't have to go out and search for someone to supply her needs very often. Of course, there had been those that she had killed on her assassination missions but she had not been allowed to take their blood—only to kill them. Then there had been those who had wandered into the area she lived—the occasional teenagers and a police officer. They were unfortunate kills, but necessary for her continued safety.

As she sat in her car, she felt her impatience grow. It wasn't just that she needed to feed that caused impatience to gnaw at her, but rather just the fact that she wanted to get it over with. Tonight it felt like something that you had to get done, rather then something you wanted to do. This change in attitude she did not understand.

Feeding upon Jake, her primary source of human blood had brought her pleasure over the years. She couldn't deny that.

"So what's changed?"

She tried to pinpoint when her feeling had changed and the answer came quickly as if it had been waiting to be discovered.

"Since killing General Stone."

Ever since she had learned of the possible existence of other vampires and about John Reese, something had changed. Was it that she felt her isolation was over? That there were other vampires that she could join?

"Enough thinking…"

She opened her car door and stepped out. Her feet crunched on the gravel parking lot as she swiveled her body around to close the car door. Looking to both sides of the small area she saw that there was only one other car parked nearby. She assumed that whoever owned this vehicle was probably fishing in the stream that meandered along the quiet road that slipped from Virginia and into North Carolina. Walking away from the car, she moved toward the area she had remembered seeing the homeless people.

She entered the wooded area, flushing her mind of all thought and allowing her senses to guide her in the hunt. She lifted her head as a gentle breeze tickled the forest around her and told her what she needed to know. For an instant, there was a sense of familiarity—something from her own country; as if she had been here before long, long ago. She placed these thoughts aside and her senses told her that someone was here. She closed her eyes allowing her mind to drift toward the smell.

Prey. Prey with life flowing through its veins. Food and nourishment. It would be hers. She would…

Suddenly something reached out and slammed into her mind so hard it made her stagger in her steps and stop. Then it was gone. She didn't know how to interpret it but thought it was like a memory long forgotten that had come back with a vengeance. But as suddenly as it had appeared it had departed leaving her wondering what it was. It had something to do with her surroundings…the woods she thought. She looked around and saw or sensed nothing unusual. Regardless it was gone now and so she returned her thoughts to her prey and the meal at hand.

She moved toward the smell and came to a small building where a single man with his back to her sat next to a small fire he coaxed along on a small tabletop grill. Some kind of meat sizzled on the hot grill, the smell also reaching her nostrils, but ignoring it for the smell of the blood that coursed through the man. She moved in quietly.

She stood directly behind the man when he suddenly rose and turned to face her as if he had known that she was there.

However, he was not the one that was surprised by what he saw. Christina stared into his face. It was then that she recognized the feeling she had had moments ago; the woods of her home. She felt her breath escape her lungs in surprise as she saw the face of the vampire that had made her.

Alexander.

CHAPTER SEVENTEEN

Samantha smiled as she imagined the efficiency of such a kill. She smiled and felt the warmth between her legs as she thought about the explosion and the effect it would have on the human body.

No...she could not give into it yet...the pleasure...not yet!

She exhaled deeply focusing on the moist warmth between her legs and forced it to dissipate. A few moments of breathing deeply and she felt that she was back in control. She let her body relax a little as the images of the explosive device and their effects diminished from her thoughts.

"Rationalize before pleasure. The golden rule..."

She returned her thoughts to Iron Stake. Samantha knew that the creature was aware of all of the issues dealing with controlling her actions and even could have possibly resisted at times. But the interesting part of this revelation was that she simply chose not to.

This fact had always puzzled Samantha and during her first meeting with the creature, she had asked about it, to which she received no satisfactory answer to explain it. However, the way in which the creature spoke when asked had given Samantha a lasting impression of that moment. The creature had simply smiled and said, "What price we have placed on our existence always possesses a cost that is greater then what we can afford to pay, so we always remain indebted."

What she had meant by that the creature had never truly explained— so Samantha let it drop.

Samantha never called the creature by its name. Their relationship was purely professional and not of a personal nature on any level. There was not any sort of female bonding between them because Samantha refused to believe that the creature was an actual woman. The creature was an abomination. Their talks were always professional, succinct and about mission requirements. Despite her personal contempt, Samantha was not totally heartless. She allowed the creature a range of freedom as long as it did not pursue any interests that were in contrast to hers or the agency's mission.

The agency kept an eye on her movements, where she went and what she did. She was sure the creature was aware of this but apparently never felt the need to discuss it. When Samantha occasionally looked at the reports of where she had gone or what she had done, the creature focused on two types of action: either scouring for information about the world and its people, or entering into long periods of extended sleep for months at a time. At best it appeared to Samantha as if the creature was searching for something and the long periods of inactivity meant she was biding her time until she found what she sought.

When the creature was put into use on an agency mission, she did as she was told without any questions and with the strictest compliance. The creature was the perfect assassin—ensuring a guaranteed kill. That was her prime function. Her talents were not wasted on anything trivial such as surveillance or similar type low risk missions.

Samantha made it a point to follow orders and agency doctrine. Never had she questioned orders or directives. However, she had always thought the creature underutilized. They should have used her more often instead of for just high risk missions. Her talents went to waste during the long periods of hibernation whereas her abilities were worth at least the manpower of five agents, maybe more. But that was a decision made above her pay grade even if she thought it was wrong, she followed it and kept her ideas about how the creature could be better utilized to herself.

"Shit…" she cursed to herself. "That's back door logic if I ever heard any."

Samantha rose from her desk and began to pace her office. She knew what her thoughts were doing and she didn't feel comfortable with it. She was trying to rationalize using the creature on her current assignment in direct contradiction to agency policy. She tried to place the pros and cons in some kind of order so that she could evaluate them.

There were risks—the op would expose the creature to unnecessary danger. Then there was the unknown of what it would do or how it would react to the discovery of more of her own kind. Would it change her disposition toward what she did for the agency—or would her behavior remain the same?

On the other hand, not using her abilities on the mission also meant that the potential existed for the two additional creatures to fall into the wrong hands. If that happened the United States would lose its advantage and possibly be exposed for having used the creature for over sixty years and that would not be good.

The controversy over the pros and cons of an op ran through her mind. What risks would endanger the creature? She was virtually indestructible. As far as the possibility of her attitude changing toward the agency after the discovery, she couldn't go against the agency because of the explosive device. Even in a worse case scenario if she found the other two and decided she would no longer help the agency, she could be destroyed and the agency would still have the other two to utilize as they saw fit. There was also the possibility of having all three of them under her control. If that was the case they could more then double their efforts and perform at least twice as many missions. The pros were beginning to look better and better to her. Now the question was would she risk such a bold action?

As she thought about it she smiled.

CHAPTER EIGHTEEN

In another room inside the naval facility, Mr. Smith placed the receiver of the phone into the base. A wicked smile appeared on his lips; a smile that conveyed a sense of power from knowing what others were doing. He had just finished listening to a conversation between Reese and some woman.

So...Commander Reese has a fun evening ahead of him does he? Well that's interesting. His file showed no previous women of any acquaintance for any significant period of time so this one must be new. What an unusual time for this to happen. And was this the same woman that gave his surveillance man the slip last night? Interesting that this occurs at just this moment? Yes...very interesting.

Smith removed a secure cellular phone from his pocket and pressed a key.

"Yes," a male voice answered.

"You have a second chance tonight. The woman is meeting him again at his house around midnight. Don't screw it up."

"I won't. This time I will attach a transmitter to her vehicle just in case."

"Good. Have you installed the phone taps and home surveillance equipment?"

"Yes. It's done."

"Well then, you have a good night. Call me if anything interesting develops."

"I shall."

"Oh and one more thing," Smith continued, "Fuck this up and you'll have a hard time finding employment in the future. Do you understand?"

"Yes," the voice answered in an unsteady tone.

The tonal qualities Smith heard made him smile. He pressed a button disconnecting the phone call. He slipped the cell phone back into the breast pocket of his suit jacket.

He rose and ran through his own checklist of events. Reese was covered, Barkley was covered, and he had Commander Pattoon in his pocket to call him if anything came up from the surveillance. There was also the information in the folder that he had looked at earlier, but Pattoon had screwed up and included information prior to the breakout.

What an idiot. What did murders before the breakout have to do with any of this? Nothing. Once that information was eliminated, there was nothing of any value in the packet. So what was left? Nothing for the moment? Tonight would be a time for him to relax and indulge into some pleasures of his own.

"Ah…pleasures," he thought. He had brought with him his little bag of fun—his toys were the way he thought of them. Just some things that would help pass the time. He imagined the feel of the leather in his hands, the warmth it would gather from their bodies. The smell of sweat on the leather and the blood that would accompany it. Yes…he would have some pleasures of his own this evening.

He made a few calls and quickly found what he wanted. He preferred a man but given the short notice he would settle for a woman tonight. The woman would meet him at his hotel room later this evening. She would do what he wanted and then he would simply kill her. No fuss no muss.

The body would be disposed of by normal channels. The reason would be the same as always: He needed information from the person and they refused. A struggle ensued leaving him no choice but to kill them. The agency provided a mop up team at his disposal for such circumstances and tonight they would be called to pick up the body. No questions would be asked. The team would walk in, pick up the body and leave. He thought of it as one of the perks of his job.

"God bless the perks, he thought. How dull all of this would be without them. The money's good, but it's the perks that give the thrill—the excitement. The excitement, tonight…ah tonight. How I wish I could have gotten a man. It would have been special—I will have to work at it, but I think I can imagine that Commander John Reese is the company I shall keep. How I would like to see his smart ass attitude whither away under my hands as I choke the life from him. Ah well…tomorrow is another day and the call might come from my lovely bitch boss to do away with Commander John Reese. I can be patient for a while longer. Yes…I can…oh yes…just for a little while longer."

CHAPTER NINETEEN

She felt her breath escape her lungs in surprise as she saw the face of the vampire that had made her.

Alexander.

"You..." Christina said through pursed lips as she stared at Alexander. "You! This cannot be!" She took a step backward.

"Yes, it is me," he said calmly. "Your mind does not deceive you in that regard as it does in others. It is hard to comprehend how I am here but in truth, I have always been here with you," he said pointing at her, "inside of you—a part of you."

She felt anger and hatred flow through her as she remembered the night in the woods when he had come for her. "Are you here to see what you have done? To study the handiwork of what you created?"

"I did not create anything," he asserted calmly and without any emotion in his voice. "You created yourself; do you not remember your own actions?"

"You sought to fool me that night," she hissed. "But I tricked you," she said as she began to pace.

"Yes, you did trick me. I sought only to help you, but you have fooled yourself. You have gone through the years with your hatred of mankind, wearing it like a perverted badge of honor."

"What do you know of me and my hatred?" she scowled.

"What I know of everyone," he said simply as he displayed his hands with his palms upward. "Hatred consumes everything. You have allowed yourself to condemn all mankind for the act of a few. The man that wronged you, the people of your village that wronged you—you killed them all. You stalked each one, terrifying them before you killed them. You wanted them to know that it was you that was going to kill them. Each one of them died as a result of your revenge, even the innocent ones."

"There were no innocent ones," she said angrily, "we are all guilty of something. Even you. You have killed as well!"

"When I have had to. Yes," Alexander agreed, "in order to survive. But you kill to satisfy your craving for revenge, not survival. You do it at the beck and call for others, for the humans who won't do their own killing. You do it gladly. Each time you substitute whoever it is you kill for one of those from your village. You kill them over and over again trying to satiate a thirst that can never be quenched."

"Yes! I kill because I must. They will never be punished enough for what they did to me" she said. "What does it matter if others direct me in that endeavor, the end is still the same?"

"Is your life to be directed by others as well? You pretend to be enslaved by their non-existent control. You know it does not have to be that way."

"I know nothing," she said as the truth bit at her harshly.

"No!" he shouted. "You do know," he said taking a step toward her. "But you choose not to understand."

"You speak foolishness," she said turning from him.

"I speak the truth," he countered, "and you shall hear all of it."

"No! I don't want to hear this nonsense."

"The device inside of you—you know you can remove it," he said pointing at her chest. "Yet you leave it there to remind you the death you bring has some kind of vindication. You pretend it is not your own choosing but that of others. You lie to yourself!"

"Why? Why would I do such a foolish thing?"

"It's the easier way," he said simply. "You don't want to admit that you have had enough revenge on those that have wronged you. If you admit that, then you have no reason to exist because you made that your only goal in life. Your only goal is to take revenge for what those villagers did to you all those years ago. It is done, Christina; you must get on with your own life. Move on or perish."

"You don't know what you're talking about," she said but refused to meet his eyes with her own.

"I do know and you know what I say is true. You actually have feelings inside you but you've hid them away—until now. This is what has enabled me to come to you. You know that they are there but they are so different then what you have known, they scare and confuse you. You fear you will not survive a new way of life. You're afraid of a life of peace."

The truth stung her like a sharp spear through her heart. She felt anger building up inside of her begging to be released at this man who said these things she did not want to hear.

Alexander continued, "It is the same thing that you believe the device inside of you cannot be removed, you allow yourself to believe that you cannot possess other feelings or to have another purpose."

"Shut up!" she cried. "I have heard enough."

"No you haven't," he retorted. "You must free yourself from all these things that are self-imposed. You know that your captors forgot the most important thing—just as you have forgotten what life is meant to be. You can have happiness but the first step is the hardest."

"No more!" she screamed. "I have…" she searched for words to refute what he said but none came. What Alexander had said was true and she knew it. For the first time since she had been found guilty in her little village, she felt scared and indecisive. "I cannot…" she said as she placed her hand on her chest and looked at Alexander.

"I cannot make you do anything you do not wish to do," Alexander said softly, "you know that."

"What will I do?" she asked.

"There is much to life, I think you realize that now. But if you wish to live it, you must take the first step."

He stepped up to her and placed his hand over hers, and then lifted their joined hands to rest on the center of her chest.

"They have keyed the device to the DNA of the handler," he said softly in a tone of a father speaking to his daughter. "Any other DNA will cause the device to detonate. However, your body gave up its DNA when you became what you are. It should not explode."

"And if it does?" she asked, "if you are wrong?"

"You must have faith, but either way you shall be free," he said simply. She felt his grip tighten on her hand. "But you must do it yourself."

"Free," she whispered.

"Yes, free," he agreed.

Christina let go of his hand and tore her shirt open from collar to waist. She caused her fingernails to become longer and sharper. Holding her right hand with her left, she turned the knife-like nails inward, slicing a thin line from the top of her chest downward several inches. She wedged her hand inside of the sliced flesh and felt for the mechanism. As she searched, her flesh where she had slit it open tried to close and she had to keep slicing it back open. Finally her hand found the object. She took a deep breath as she closed her eyes. Then she wrapped her fingers around it—and pulled.

CHAPTER TWENTY

There was also the possibility of having all three of them under her control. If that was the case they could more then double their efforts and perform at least twice as many missions. The pros were beginning to look better and better to her. Now the question was would she risk such a bold action?

As she thought about it she smiled.

Samantha glanced at the pages in front of her but her mind kept going back to the creature. Her plans could work but there were always obstacles. Much of her conundrum arose from the fact that she didn't like or trust Mr. Smith. He had all the proper experience from his earlier time in the FBI and CIA; however, since his recruitment into the agency his motives seemed to be based purely upon financial gain.

Unlike the other organizations, the agency operated upon an incentive based pay scale. Samantha never approved of the system—she thought of it as something as cheap and tawdry as the system a car salesman worked under. Some agents didn't care what the mission was designed to achieve, but rather cared only about making the highest commission. There was no patriotic attachment only a financial one: Mr. Smith in a nutshell.

She understood Smith's motivations all too well in this situation; if he played a significant role in the capture of the creatures, he would be generously rewarded. He was one of the breed that lived for financial success and gratification and was not to be trusted completely. He was not drawn by commitment and purpose; someone who possessed a passion for what they do—someone like Commander John Reese.

Now there was an enigma. She had studied Reese's file until she was intimately familiar with every detail of information that was contained in it. Perhaps what she found most to her liking was that in a way, they were very much alike. She was intrigued by his steadfast study of myth and legends—a field which would not lead to any quantifiable financial success. It was clear that what he did, he did for passion.

But what also interested her were the sacrifices he made in the pursuit of his interests. He had no life outside of his work. No commitments to any woman—there had been fleeting relationships but nothing lasting. It was as if he refused to allow anything to come before what he searched for thereby eliminating all distractions to that end. In this regard, they were very much alike. However, she was not sure about his level of patriotism, not knowing how far he would go to achieve the means she saw necessary to keep the United States safe.

She thought his role in the Team of Darkness operation was mixed. Of course he had been instrumental in their capture and enslavement yet according to some of the reports she had read, he seemed to have some moralistic issues of the use of the creatures. Still he followed orders, conducted the ops satisfactorily, and even destroyed the creatures when he had lost positive control—just as he had been directed to do. He followed his orders to the letter. Although these mixed signals perplexed her, she still felt his dedication and obsession toward the vampires could be useful to her—if she could ensure his loyalty.

If the creatures were recaptured, his insight could be of great benefit to the continued operation she had dreamed of. Of course the military aspect would have to be removed completely. Generals Stone and Morris had both been inept in their management which had had disastrous consequences. Under agency control and with Reese's help, she thought she might be able to advance her own idea of a more wide ranging operation which would ensure the United States a position of superiority in the world forever. She dreamed of the creation of an entirely new agency: An agency that consisted mainly of vampires.

This new agency would become the main arm of covert operations. They would have a presence in every country of the world; immediately taking care of any problems that operated against United States policy and the democratic process. The opportunities for successes were mind boggling to her and these successes were her life—what she dreamed of—what she wanted.

Before she had realized it, Samantha felt herself slip into the physical euphoria that accompanied her life's ambition. Normally physical pleasure as well as erotic thoughts were always kept locked up in her mental vault of secrecy because giving into them was, to her, a sign of weakness. Whereas many women dreamt their way to physical pleasure with thoughts of gorgeous men that would sweep them up in their arms and ravish their physical and emotional egos, Samantha tied her physical pleasure to her life's goals: the final and lasting solution to the assured sovereignty of her country. The thought of a private army of vampires was the closest she had ever come to a solution for the problems of the world. Just the thought of it caused her body to tremble with the physical arousal of what could be accomplished. With each singular thought, it drove her closer and closer to an orgasmic pleasure of the body as well as the mind.

Assured loyalty...

Her breathing began to quicken.

Commitment to the cause...

She felt her body temperature rise sharply—sweat began to accumulate on her skin mixing the sensation of hot and cold as she shivered.

The number of lives that could be saved...

Her heart thumped loudly in her ears and banged hard in her chest. Warmth inside her accumulated in giant masses; building toward a release.

Religious fanatics taking the lives of innocents in the false name of achieving freedom would be ended...

She was going to scream. She placed her hand over her mouth to stifle it—she felt her teeth bite into her hand. Her teeth tore into her flesh. She felt the blood trickle from wounds and she tasted the sweet copper tang and she liked it.

The world would be free to pursue worthwhile things...

Her blood. It was blood given to the cause. Blood had consecrated battlefields as well as back alleys around the world in the name of protecting freedom. She would give her blood freely and willingly to the cause. It was sweet like honey and she sucked at it with a passion; harder and harder as waves of orgasms flowed through her. She twisted and gyrated so violently in the chair with each surge of pleasure that she fell to the floor as waves swept her to the climax of her destination.

The chance to have a world that could finally live in peace...and the United States would ensure it stayed that way...forever...

Her body tensed and stiffened as she rode the last gigantic wave to freedom within her. She arched her back and bit harder on her hand to stifle the scream that begged to be released. It flowed through her and she felt the intense warmth as her own release met the wave and she rode it toward the shores of her country as one united thought.

Samantha stayed on the floor of her office for several minutes as her breathing and heartbeat slowed to some semblance of normal. She lay on her back looking up at the ceiling, her body drenched with sweat. Her hand began to throb and blood flowed freely from the gashes she had made with her teeth.

Slowly she raised herself to a sitting position. She felt both drained and energized at the same moment. It was rare that she allowed the pleasure of flesh to overcome her. She saw it as a dangerous weakness that could lead to unclear thoughts and actions. But she also knew total and complete abstinence was a trap that she had to avoid. Both could make her vulnerable.

She never pursued lasting relationships with men for that reason. There was one man that she saw on a regular basis, but that was a relationship based upon physical need. And yet, he was probably the closest she allowed herself to get to anyone on any emotional level. They both worked for the agency and shared that common bond. Their relationship would be frowned upon if discovered, but given the anonymity of the members of the agency, few knew one another to begin with and the odds of a chance meeting near impossible. Yet it had still happened. She smiled.

Of course it happened... I arranged it and for a very good reason. She thought it was fate. A relationship based on physical attraction and keeping secrets as well. Secrets that she knew and he did not. It was a special relationship on many levels—all hers.

Relationships. The concept reminded her of the black widow spider that killed its male after mating. She considered the female spider's act one of self-reliance: A perfection of the symmetry of a dedication to the cause. The spider's act ensured a sustained superiority in breeding by only allowing one male to mate before its death. There would be no multiple mating and so the species would remain varied and not interbred. That was important in terms of her plan as well.

Like the spider, her plan would ensure no further dilution of the genes of the United States through tolerating the pompous arrogance of a world full of fanatical and idealistic zealots. She would eliminate those who chose to interbreed their impure thoughts with the United States of America in their attempts to dilute the principles that the founding fathers had intended. Foreigners or even citizens that opposed the rights of a democracy were all fair game in her book and needed to be removed from the body of democracy like a cancer.

She raised her knees to her chest and wrapped her arms around them. Slowly she began to rock herself back and forth. As she did so, she softly began to hum a tune. As she rocked faster the tune increased in tempo as well. As she rocked and hummed she organized all the thoughts that had come to her since she had returned to the office. Because of her physical and emotional outburst, she felt as if everything had been expunged— like a blackboard being erased and now it was empty and ready to receive a new list. She created a new list. A clear outline of what she would do.

As she continued to rock and hum, a smile slowly formed on her face.

She stared directly in front of her, her eyes wide open and unmoving. To someone else who saw her expression, they would think that she had discovered some form of long sought inner peace—as if she had had some form of an almost religious experience and was now closer to God. That she had obtained some form of understanding of the most complicated or mysterious elements of life. Looks can be deceiving.

Yes…there were answers. Yes.

The sound of her phone ringing irritated her as it brought her back to a reality she did not want at the moment, preferring the fantasy of which she had been thinking about. She rose from the floor to pick up the phone. "Yes."

"You don't sound like you're in a good mood," the man's voice said.

"No, it's good," she said immediately recognizing he voice.

"How are you?" he asked.

"Fine, your timing is impeccable," she said quickly as she was surprised that it was the man that she had just been thinking about.

"How so?"

"I was just thinking about you," she said.

"Really?"

"Yes," she agreed.

"Good things I hope?"

There was a pause as Samantha tried to decide how she should answer. At times lying came so easy that she actually had to try and remember the last time she actually spoke the truth. But that thought brought another: Did it really matter?

CHAPTER TWENTY-ONE

"Does your silence mean they were not good thoughts?" the man asked now wondering if perhaps calling her had been a mistake. Their relationship was an unusual one, but given their careers, not much seemed normal to begin with. He held the diary in his hands, his fingers rubbing its worn leather the same way his father had probably done so many years before.

"No, sorry," she said. "My mind was wandering. I am in the middle of a bit of a problem that has me on several different levels of thought."

"Nothing serious I hope?" he asked knowing that she would not tell him any specifics. Their perverted sense of loyalty prevented them from sharing the details of their work.

"Just the usual," she said and laughed lightheartedly and then she added, "And the world as we know it will come to an end if we don't do something."

"I see," he said. "It seems like we're always busy these days."

"I won't be able to get away for a while," she said.

He was surprised at her interpreting his next question, but was not as surprised by her answer. "It's not pressing," he said feeling a little relieved about her being too busy to meet. The topic was an awkward one for him. "It's about my father…some new information has made its way to me."

"Are you sure it's about him?" She asked.

"Pretty sure. It's actually quite disturbing."

"What's the source?" she asked.

"Unknown, I received an anonymous package containing a diary."

"How do you know it can be trusted?"

"I can't, but it has a certain feel to it that feels right. But I will get it tested for authenticity."

"Make sure you're discreet," she said. "Someone might ask questions. I'm assuming it is work related?"

"It's been sanitized, but yes," he said. "It also proves that I was lied to."

"How so?" she asked.

"It suggests that there was a follow-on op that brought him back to the States rather than him disappearing overseas."

"That is interesting," she agreed. "Give me a few days," she said. "I should be free then."

"I will get it checked out and then see if any of my contacts can tell me anything."

"Go slow," she simply said and hung up.

CHAPTER TWENTY-TWO

She took a deep breath as she closed her eyes. Then she wrapped her fingers around it and pulled.

Christina opened her eyes. She stood near an old wooden picnic table. There was no fire and there was no Alexander. There was no one. She stood alone in the woods despite what she had just experienced.

It was a dream...nothing but a dream. When I entered the woods, it reminded me of home and brought back that memory of him. Recalling some of their conversation, she felt anger and shame.

She closed her hands, tense with anger and frustration at the experience that had come with the memory and as she did, her right hand closed upon something hard. She raised her hand finding it black with blood. Christina opened her fingers and saw a cylindrical object in her hand. The explosive device? It was covered by the same black blood. It was then that she realized that she had done it after all. It had been more than just a dream.

But if that was the case, where was Alexander? She had seen him. She had spoken with him. She had felt his touch. Or had she? Had it been him, or had it been her own thoughts that had brought him to her to do what she wanted to do? Were these thoughts part of some awakening she was undergoing?

She had felt strange this evening. Too many feelings were distracting her - taking control of her thoughts and actions. What was happening? First, there was her reluctance to feed upon Jake and then the anticipation of seeing John Reese again. Now there was removing the device that she'd willingly succumbed to so long ago. Christina wondered if perhaps she was losing her sanity. She didn't know. What she did know was that she was free.

Free...what does that mean?

There would no longer be any outside control over her. She could do what she wanted. Be with who she wanted. She could even...go home if she wanted. Home?

There was much to consider and she felt overwhelmed by the possibilities. She also felt ashamed at how she had allowed herself to be used all these years. But it was only time, she thought and she had all the time in the world.

But first, I need to feed.

She felt hungry, near starving. The removal of the device had involved a heavy loss of blood despite her recuperative powers; however, combined with her already existing hunger she needed to feed and soon. Still holding the explosive device she decided that it might have a use later on—if for no other reason then as a reminder of misplaced trust. She placed the device into her pants pocket and then sniffed the air. She no longer smelled the presence of any other humans and now she wondered if there ever were any here to begin with.

She headed back to the parking lot finding the other vehicle still parked near her own car. She decided to walk down the trail leading to the water and after a short walk, found what she sought.

The man was young with beautiful dark skin, perhaps twenty, she thought as she spied him sitting alone. Next to him were two fishing poles with their line cast out into the river. Dressed in a pair of jeans and a T-shirt, he was wearing a set of headphones and humming loudly to the music his player was providing. She searched the area to ensure they were alone and not sensing anyone else, she moved toward him. He was oblivious to her approach because of the headphones he wore.

Although hungry, she also felt unusually playful in the new mood brought on by her...what would she call it? Her epiphany? Sure, why not—that sounded good and Christina smiled. This was going to take a while to get used to.

She picked up a piece of a branch that was lying on the ground, and tossed it near the man. It struck him in the leg causing him to look in the direction it had come. He removed his headphones and stared at her.

He had a strange look on his face, his eyes wide and puzzled at the sight of her and Christina remembered what she had done to her clothing. She had cut her shirt from her collar to waist, including her bra, exposing her blood splattered chest. She imagined she looked like some kind of monster from Dawn of the Dead, or some other movie young men would watch.

"Christ, lady, you scared the hell out of me," he said loudly as he jumped up allowing him to get a good look at who it was that had snuck up on him. His eyes explored her and he said, "What the hell...hey... are you okay?" His voice was hesitant, thick with concern for her and her present condition.

"I'm fine," she said, "I just fell down a bank over there and tore up my clothes. It's just muck and dirt, not blood. I must look like a mess," she said as she tried to re-button her blouse which she knew was too badly torn. She kept playing with the fabric in order to get his attention, smiling to herself as his eyes focused on her exposed breasts and lingered there.

The young man sighed with a heavy breath of relief. "Well, that's good. I thought for a minute I was going to have to run you to the hospital or something."

"No, I'm fine, but there is something I need," she said as she released the pheromones that would relax him as well as raise his testosterone levels making him receptive to her enticement. His enticement was further manipulated by her molding the image he received as well as the perception by his senses. She guided his perception by using her hands to touch herself in certain ways, her hands stroking her waist and breasts were having a direct impact on his sexual attraction for her.

In a few seconds, his demeanor changed and he slid into the mood she required.

"Well," he began, the look in his eyes reflecting his sudden and growing desire, "you just tell me what you need, and well…I will be more than happy to do what I can for you. Anything."

"Can you give me a little hug to cheer me up?" she asked.

"I sure can," he said as he moved closer without hesitation.

When he was within arm's reach, she placed her hands on his shoulders and drew him into her fold. She could smell his sweat mixed with the hormones of emotional anticipation.

"That's nice," she said.

"Hmm, yes it is. I feel so…wonderful," he whispered. "I could just stay here…forever."

She knew he was ready. Her own body reacted to his as she felt her front canine teeth elongate in preparation to feed. She gently turned his head with her hands and drove her teeth into his neck. She felt him involuntarily jump at the pinch when she broke skin, but then settled down as the natural anesthetic further soothed him. When he relaxed once again, she began to suck his blood.

This process was routine for her and there were certain expectations each time that were fulfilled. With Jake, the added familiarity of his reaction and his sexual appreciation of the event always yielded a gratifying result to both of them. When his blood entered into her system, there was an exhilaration that went along with the satisfaction of hunger. Baring the sexual aspect with Jake, with other humans there was a similar reaction on her part every time, the exhilaration of the

OPERATION: FACE THE FEAR
OPERATION: FACE THE FEAR

stalking, the final attack and the similar excitement of those she tasted. The experience of fresh hot blood as it entered her system. However this time it felt different.

She felt the effects of the blood entering her body and the nourishing effect it had upon her but there was nothing more. No excitement, no exhilarating feeling of having seduced the human so easily into a sense of false calm. There was no longer the pleasure from the manipulation and the potential destruction of the living being. It was just...food.

She wondered if this was part of her epiphany. She wasn't sure if she liked that word or not but there was no doubt about the change. This giving up her sole reason for existence—getting revenge—would change her existence in nearly every way she began to understand.

After a few minutes she had had enough blood. She released him and helped him to sit down on the ground. He was still entranced in her pheromones, oblivious to everything around him. She allowed her thoughts to flow into his mind.

You will wake up in ten minutes and realize that you had fallen asleep. You will think it's time to go home and get in bed. You were alone the entire time you were out here. You met no one. You saw nothing unusual.

She left the man sitting at the base of the tree and walked the short distance back to her car. She felt a smile form on her lips and a sense of... she didn't know how to describe it, perhaps a sense of neutrality about what she had just done. For the first time that she could remember, she did not have to fulfill any expectations beyond her sustenance or feeding. With Jake, there was a pleasing that had to be accomplished to keep him satisfied. With others, it had been about killing for the sake of killing. But this time, she had acquired what she needed with no commitments, no expectations, and without killing.

She arrived at her car and got into the driver's seat. Starting it and putting the car into drive, she turned back onto the main road and headed back toward the city of Suffolk. As she drove, she felt lighthearted and it felt nice.

She remembered that she had promised John dinner tonight and checking the time she saw that she had just enough time to find a restaurant before they closed. She could get some food and then drive over to his house in Norfolk. She, of course, would not eat any of the food but she would just tell him that she had already eaten. It would work as an alibi for now.

Thoughts of John as well as everything else tonight seemed to jumble about in her thoughts as she drove. For the most part, she felt good about everything that had happened and was embracing the new outlook she found herself living in. However that did leave her with two potential areas of contention: Jake and her connection to the agency for which she had dutifully worked for the past sixty-plus years.

She would have to decide what to do about Jake. What would she tell him and would he understand? As for the agency, that would require something more resourceful. She knew that she would not be allowed to leave on her own accord. There would be no fond farewell dinner given to her because she had decided she had had enough of this line of work. The break would have to be decisive and believable.

Enough. These are things to be decided later. Right now, I have to figure out what to bring for dinner.

She laughed at her own thoughts. Normally she had to be concerned about how to murder someone, and now she was concerned about what to have for dinner. Such domestic bliss. She only hoped that all of her decisions would be so simple. But experience told her there would be hard times ahead and she didn't think those decisions and choices would be so simple.

Welcome to the world of the living...

Chapter Twenty-Three

Ah…that's an evil thought there, John. You hardly know the girl and you already have an inkling of, shall we say, the pleasures of the flesh? Aren't you getting a bit ahead of yourself?

He felt himself smile at the thoughts while he pushed the folder to the side of his desk blotter and headed out of the office.

Maybe…

The closer that Reese got to his home in Norfolk, the greater the fatigue of the past two days pressed on him. It was another of those rules of nature that he never understood, just like the one about having to go to the bathroom; the closer you got to home the more you had to go. In either case, it was as if there was some link between body and home.

The thought made him wonder about the girls and if they possessed some kind of link to their home and if they missed it. It had been different with Dimitri and his fellow vampires. They were able to rationalize what was happening to them. That thought also brought on a twinge of guilt because he had been the one who orchestrated their capture and removed them from their home. But there was nothing that could be done about that now.

But the girls had been snatched up and taken. One minute they are in the Balkans and the next they are in America with virtually no explanation about where they are and what is happening to them.

Christ…what a God damned mess…

So much hurt and pain. It was devastating to think about these two little girls and what had been stolen from them. Not stolen. Ripped away described it better. He only hoped that he would be able to help them in some way. Maybe Christina could offer…but he couldn't tell her. Telling her would only endanger her and he would not let that happen. She was special.

'Special'— interesting, thought John. *You hardly know the girl and she's already special. Getting a little ahead of ourselves aren't we?*

"Blow it out your butt," he said to his own thoughts. "You will not win this time my friend. This time it's going to work out, I can feel it."

Reese pulled into his short driveway and got out of the car. He unlocked the front door and as he crossed the threshold, he had to admit that he hoped his mystery woman would be inside again as she was the previous night. Instead only silence greeted him and his thoughts quickly returned his fatigue.

Get some sleep, John…you'll need it.

He went straight to the bedroom, dropped his clothes on the chair next to the bed, and crawled in under the covers. He set the alarm clock for 11:30 pm; leaving enough time to get a quick shower before Christina arrived with dinner. He reached for his backup alarm clock and set that one for 11:35 pm, just in case the first one did not get him up.

As he settled under the covers, her image entered his mind, but he reluctantly drove her away. If he didn't refuse her entry right now, he would never get to sleep. But thoughts of her were still preferable to the nightmares that haunted him. Tonight he could only hope that exhaustion would refuse entry to the horror of his greatest fear that drove him mad. Just as that thought dissipated from his mind, Reese was fast asleep and the dream began.

★★★

Reese awoke in the darkness to the touch of a cool breeze across his body. As he looked around, he found himself back amongst the ruins in Kosovo, near the town of Kacanik where the original Team of Darkness vampires had been captured.

Where it had all begun…

But unlike that time, now he was all alone. There was no Navy SEAL search and destroy teams with him. No Lieutenant Johnson. No Idriz Lauki. He was totally alone. He was here on a different mission—a mission of his own.

Something was calling to him. Calling him to come inside the subterranean cavern. A voice that he not only heard in his mind, but that touched his heart or rather his soul. What he wanted was there—waiting for him.

He walked on feeling the earth crunch underfoot. He entered down to the crypts that he knew existed; the crypts that had held Andre, Iliga, Josip and Dimitri as they slept the sleep of the daylight. He also remembered the Navy SEAL that had lost his life after tripping the sabotaged door down in the underbelly of the tunnels. He had been a young man in the prime of his life…but that had been so long ago. At least he would not die again in the dream for that was the one thing that Reese did know. He would be the only one whose life would be in jeopardy.

Apparently he was expected because torches hung on the cavern walls illuminating his path down into the depths. Yet even with the burning flames around him, the air was cool and as it mixed with his nervous sweat and he felt a chill run up his spine as he descended. The torch light also added a new dimension to the cavern walls—deep dark pockets of shadows. When he was here before, their only source of light came from the night vision goggles they wore and John thought how he preferred their greenish glow over the dark shadows. He couldn't see into those dark shadows because they denied the entry of light, batting it away with a veiled shroud of blackness. Those dark corners with their shadows would remain unknown to him and not help to reveal what had brought him to the caverns. What was it that called him here? What summons had been so carefully sent that it drew him ever deeper into this dark abyss? He didn't know. It was just the overpowering sense that what he wanted—what he needed—was here. The answers to his questions were here.

He travelled further into the depths. The coolness that he had first experienced now turned to cold. He could see his breath mist in front of him as he walked; his mind never considering the impossibility of such coldness and he continued on thinking how easy it would be to get lost in the underground lair. He had turned corners so many times since entering the caverns he had no sense of the distance or direction he had traveled. He knew that he could never find his way back but also knew that his escape was something that no longer mattered. As he turned one more corner he saw the door to the crypt. He knew that whatever it was that drew him, or more truthfully, had summoned him was here.

Unlike the way it had actually appeared, in his dream the door was covered with hundreds of red roses. With the cold air that blew freely in the cavern the roses appeared fresh as if they had just been cut from the bush. They appeared to slither and merge with one another in fluid motion making him think of two bodies melding into one during the act of making love. He reached out to touch the roses and as the flesh of his fingers neared the beautiful petals of the flowers, several stems of the roses reached for him with sharp thorns. They attached themselves to his flesh with a sharp sting and John felt the warmth of his blood dribble from where the thorns had embedded into his skin like the sharp teeth of a vicious animal. The more he struggled to remove his hand from their grasp, the tighter their grip became and the more they tore at his skin.

Blood dripped from his hand and fell upon the other roses which responded by writhing with renewed vigor. Unlike what he had seen earlier and had equated it to the act of love, the movement now was more forceful and somehow more destructive in its nature. The roses that were not attached to his flesh used their thorns to tear at each other as if fighting for the drop of blood that landed between them. Petals of the beautiful roses flew into the air as the stems fought more and more violently. It was like a wild pack of dogs that had picked up the scent of a fresh kill and had decided to abandon their own activities.

At some point he felt that the frenzied activity of the roses had caused a loosening of the hold on his wrist by the rose stems. The roses continued their assault upon each other, their petals dropping off and falling to the ground. After a few moments, the action slowed as fewer and fewer of the roses still possessed any of their petals. It appeared as if they were dying; each petal as it fell taking with it a piece of life.

As the last petal dropped on the ground the crypt door opened with a loud creak. He had to step out of the way as its massive bulk filled the space he had just occupied seconds before. A tremendous burst of air forced its way out into the passageway almost knocking him over both from the force as well as the smell of rotten food and damp earth it carried. He fought his immediate reaction of gagging and vomiting from the foul stench that threatened to inundate him. His recovery was aided by the sudden change in the smell of the air.

The first wave of stinking rot had suddenly changed into the delightful scent of the red roses...hundreds of them. The perfumed scent was near intoxicating and in such sudden contrast to the other smell, he felt himself become lightheaded by the sensory effect. He felt his equilibrium slip and struggled to maintain his balance. Just as he thought he could no longer stand, he felt a firm grip on his arm that supported his weak knees. He blinked his eyes as he turned in the direction of the hand that held him and saw that there was nothing there. He was alone in the cavernous corridor...or so he thought until he heard the voice.

"Come in," a voice called to him. "Come in. Enter of thine own free will."

It was a woman's voice; warm and alluring but it did not resonate in the corridor where he stood. It originated from inside the crypt.

"Come in, John," the voice called again.

He took a few steps in the corridor moving into position so that he could see within the crypt and when he could observe the interior, he was amazed by what he saw.

Part of him, the part that had been here before, remembered that it was a cavern carved into the rock. He knew that within were the four crypts of the vampires that had come to comprise the Team of Darkness—but that was not what he saw now. This time he saw a chamber filled with the finest curtain and draperies of silk, thick carpets and rich tapestries of Persian designs adorned the room. Golden candelabra with long and pure white candles provided a warm glow which accented the huge canopy bed that sat in the middle of the chamber. The bed was veiled with sheets of gossamer hung from its sides. Through the veiled sheets, he could see the shape of a woman sitting on the bed.

"Hello, John," the figure said. Her voice was thick and full as the syllables seem to languish in the air, teasing him with an alluring attraction of some kind.

Reese stared intently at the figure but he was unable to distinguish any features of the woman through the gossamer that hung around the bed.

"What is this place and who are you?" he asked.

"This is your mind, John," she simply said as if he should know it. "It is your greatest fear and yet contains your greatest hopes."

"I don't understand," he said. "This is nothing more than a dream."

"Is it?" she asked. "Are you sure?"

He didn't answer her because honestly, he wasn't sure anymore.

Chapter Twenty-Four

Since the escape, every possible method of leaving had been blocked. Dimitri had underestimated the strength and determination of whomever it was that had control over the girls and their captivity. He only hoped that that one mistake did not cost them their lives.

As the van carrying Dimitri and the other vampires from the farm in Suffolk drove up the ramp onto Interstate 64 toward the Hampton Roads Bridge tunnel and Norfolk, Dimitri suddenly lunged forward in his seat and grasped the dashboard. The sound of the dashboard sections caving in under his hands echoed in the cab of the van. As he released his grip, his hand impressions could clearly be seen embedded in the vinyl.

"Dimitri? Are you alright?" Andre asked.

Dimitri struggled to regain his composure and free his mind as the image of Commander John Reese in some kind of danger shoved its way violently into his.

As a vampire, he had learned that his thoughts were well-guarded from intrusion. It was something unique to their kind, probably because of the psychological bond between other vampires. Because of this intimate relationship process, thoughts were in a way more composed, and never random. It was as if they had developed a self-blocking mechanism to prevent the random thoughts from cluttering their thinking; another strong self preservation technique of their kind. This sensitivity to unwanted intrusions is what made it such a shock. Why or how the image of Commander Reese had come to him he did not know. It caught him completely off guard with the intensity with which it had struck him. He would have defined it as a mental rape.

"I'm alright," he answered Andre.

"But—" Andre began, his hand pointing to the dashboard where Dimitri's handprint was firmly embedded.

"I said I'm fine," he said firmly, but not with any anger. Dimitri knew that there was more concern in Andre's voice than anything else.

Andre's eyes went from Dimitri to the road, and back again to Dimitri, but he said nothing.

Dimitri stared ahead as they approached the tunnel entrance that would take them under the water and over to the Norfolk side.

What had that been about? Why had that image of Reese jumped into his thoughts? And why had the intensity of the feeling of Reese struggling against something been so strong? They had no bond of blood. Dimitri had never taken from Reese.

Since their last meeting several months ago, Dimitri had had no contact with Reese. This was mutually agreed upon for two reasons: first to ensure that the presumed death of the vampires would not be questioned and second, to ensure Reese would not be punished for his actions. Symmetry at its best—both sides were protected and obtained a resolution to their problems.

However, this incident of the girls and the possibility of Reese's involvement raised more doubt about his stated position of non-interference toward the vampires and their use by the military. Why would Reese cut loose the three of them only to turn around and proceed with another pair of vampires on the same mission? It made no sense. Further, during their time together with the team, Reese and he had held many discussions about life and the role that the vampire played in it. What was happening now did not agree with what he had heard Reese say then. Had he a change of heart? Or had the military gotten to him somehow? Was he being coerced to cooperate or was the Commander a willing participant in order to further his desire to examine a specimen of the myth he held onto tightly? Dimitri sighed heavily. He had no answers to these questions which only led to deeper frustration.

He squinted his eyes against the bright white lights which indicated they were about to emerge on the other side of the tunnel. Dimitri squinted under the brightness and again exhaled strongly as if he could get rid of his frustration by doing so. His actions drew another concerned look by Andre.

Looking out into the upcoming darkness of night outside of the brightly lit tunnel, Dimitri spoke. "It is fine, my friend," he said sensing Andre's concern. "I just need to think it out for a bit. We'll talk about it later."

Andre did not answer. He didn't have to because they had been linked together for so many years which had led to an understanding that required no further communication. Instead, they sat in silence as they exited the tunnel and were enveloped by the darkness of the night. The darkness brought a sense of comfort to Dimitri and he silently dropped deeper into his thoughts as the van drove on.

CHAPTER TWENTY-FIVE

"I will get it checked out," he said, "and then see if any of my contacts can tell me anything."

"Go slow," Samantha said and hung up.

Samantha was thinking that this could be a problem. But after a few minutes decided that if she wrapped up the main problem, this one would take care of itself too. And if all else fails, there was always the last measure which could be carried out by a quick phone call to her associate, Mr. Smith.

She had known all along that her intermittent lover was the son of one of the first handlers assigned to Iron Stake. It was clearly annotated in the record. This doubled the pleasure of the purpose of their relationship; research as much as it was for her pleasure. Either way the ends justified the means in her book and that was all that mattered. However, what puzzled her was how he had obtained the information.

Obviously all materials related to Iron Stake had been restricted at the highest levels. There was nothing as ridiculous as agency family privilege; if anything there was less information in those cases. The bottom line was that the agency did not exist, never mind having any employees, family or not. The only reason why she knew of the personal relationship was due to her position as handler.

The answer to where the information had come from was obvious: There had to be a leak. She picked up the phone and started to dial his number to call him back—but she stopped slowly replacing the telephone back into the cradle. She could press him for more information, but it could wait. The leak would be found soon enough once the other issue was laid to rest. But it still bothered her.

Realistically, what harm could come from him knowing that his father had been involved in the mission? None at all. She had learned from him that any emotional attachment to the missing father had been lost a long time ago. Now it was more a matter of curiosity. She had never told him the truth and it would do no good to tell him anything anyway because if he did know what had happened, there was a potential for issues she did not want to have to deal with if she didn't have to.

She recalled the files in her photographic memory and the entries that had been made about the disposition of the handler. One comment stuck out in her mind specifically. It was about nine months after the creature had been brought back to the United States. The order simply read:

```
Handler lost positive control of Iron Stake.
Decisions and judgment impaired by emotional
attachment to creature. Handler terminated by Iron
Stake at the direction of agency.
```

So they had instructed Christina to kill him. However Samantha surmised that there was more to it than that. She had learned to understand the creature and could easily read between the lines of the short message. He had fallen in love with Christina. He'd formed an emotional attachment that had probably initiated for the sake of the creature's own amusement. She could be devious that way and she had a history of it as well. This was another reason why physical meetings were highly discouraged unless adequate two-person rules were established.

Rules. There were always rules. She tried to keep them at a minimum especially where her own actions were concerned. For when rules are added all they do is complicate any situation. This was why the Agency itself existed to begin with; to skirt the rules.

Still, there was one rule that she knew she would have to follow if it came to it. If it came to removing him, she would feel no great loss. She would miss the sex, but the sacrifice for the greater need was always justifiable and always brought her greater satisfaction. Sex was simply a release and an overrated one at that.

Chapter Twenty-Six

"I don't understand," Reese said. "This is nothing more than a dream."
"Is it?" the woman he still could not see asked. "Are you sure?"
He didn't answer her because honestly, he wasn't sure anymore.

"Come in and sit down," she said sliding across the bed and making preparations to rise from her slumber.

Reese was surprised that he found the snake-like fluidity of her movement both nerve wracking and exotic at the same time.

"The chair, over there," she said pointing toward a pair of plush arm chairs on the other side of the room. The dim light made their fabric appear dark and Reese associated the color to blood and death.

Still he felt compelled so he moved toward the chairs never taking his eyes from the woman. He still couldn't make out any of her features and that bothered him. It was as if her voice was enough to control his actions and he felt helplessness pervade his thoughts.

The woman stood erect now. She raised her arms and parted the gossamer veils shrouding the bed. Stepping through the opening she made, she moved into clear view.

Reese's eyes fell upon her and he immediately looked for some form of recognition. She was tall and thin with long black hair that fell down her back. She wore a long white sleeveless nightgown which draped to the floor hiding her feet. As she moved closer, she seemed to not be stepping, but rather to be gliding effortlessly across the distance separating them.

As she neared the chair and the additional light, her features became visible but revealed more controversy rather than clarity. Her face was beautiful, rather half of it was. It looked as if someone had drawn a line down the center of her face. One side was tanned and smooth as a youth's, whereas the other was coarse, wrinkled and pale giving an indication of old age or perhaps an illness that attacked her flesh.

Her eyes also reflected the same controversy; one wide open and a deep blue which radiated a sense of well being, while the other was half shut and liquefied pus oozed from the half open socket. Her lips were parted in a half smile with perfectly shaped teeth which shimmered even in the dim light. While the other half was dark with rotting and decayed teeth.

Her sleeveless arms were of the same appearance; one smooth, tan and perfectly shaped while the other was pale, wrinkled and crooked severely at the elbow.

"What are you?" he asked.

She glided across the last remaining steps that separated them and sat in the chair across from him.

"I am a controversy, John—your controversy," she simply said. Her voice seemed to also resonate with the same controversy of her appearance; it varied from the smooth melody of a singer to the abrasive coarseness of a heavy cigarette smoker.

"I still don't understand what the hell you are talking about?" He said trying to sound convincing, but there was a waver in his own voice that indicated that perhaps he did know what she meant.

"I think you do John. Look at me closely," she said leaning forward in her chair and closer to him.

Reese tried to keep himself aligned with the pretty side of her face; the other side was too repulsive to look at for any length of time. The longer he stared at the misshapen side of her face the more he thought he actually saw something squirming underneath the surface of the skin. However, as he moved she moved with him keeping the perspective equal so that he had to see both sides. Apparently she did not want to afford him the luxury of seeing only her good side.

Her eyes fixated on his as she spoke. "I am what you seek, John. I am two distinct versions of your thoughts because you cannot separate the side of truth from the side of the reality in which you have firmly entrenched yourself. I am in limbo because of you, John. Until you decide what truth is and what is real for you, I shall remain in this state. In essence I am a part of you."

"No. That doesn't make any sense," he said.

"Yes, John, it does. Stop deluding your own reasoning and you will see it. I am what you cannot decide. I represent the complexity of life— your life."

"This is not really happening," he said. "All of this is a dream."

"That is a valid consideration. Yet perhaps it is more than that," she said calmly. "I prefer a constant reminder…as it shall remain until you decide, John." She turned to face him so that he had a full profile of one side of her face. She raised her arm and touched the youthful side of her face, the soft and gentle flesh, the eye that reflected vitality. She ran her fingers over her plush and full lips and touched the enamel of her white teeth.

"This is what I can be, John. Today. Tomorrow. A hundred years from now. I will be the same. I can love and be loved if I choose. Eternity is nothing but a word which no longer possesses any relevant meaning; however, it does come with a price."

She shifted her body so that the other side of her face was toward him. As she had done before she raised her arm to touch her skin. This time however, it was not the youthful looking arm, but the one that appeared old and wrinkled. Her fingers were like twisted and gnarled tree limbs and she ran them along her sickly looking flesh. Reese thought he could actually hear the sound of scratching, like someone running their fingers across a piece of coarse sandpaper.

She touched her half closed eye and a white puss oozed under the slight pressure dribbling down the side of her face. The eye fluttered open and for a brief instant, Reese saw something in that eye. A glimpse of something that he thought he knew, or should at least be familiar with. His vision clouded over and the thought of history passing…no not history, but time passing and its ravaging of civilizations entered into his mind. Shifting sands that had come and gone and cleansing the Earth of the parasites of mankind that inhabited it.

The image quickly vanished and he saw her face again.

"You cannot deny what is truth," she said. "History precludes a lie. What has happened has happened. What will happen is destiny."

He opened his mouth to say something but quickly closed it. It was as if the images had stolen his voice.

Next, she ran one of her fingers over her decayed teeth—Reese could actually see one of them shift from the pressure as she touched it. Her gums were black from what he assumed was tremendous age.

"This is the harshness of reality, John," she said. "This is what will happen over time. Physically you will become old and as feeble as you see me now. The thought that you shall die becomes a constant. However, with this thought also comes a reality of truth. Time is relevant, time is meaningful, therefore life becomes precious because of the scarce quantity one is given. You saw what was in my eye, John. You know it well. It is normalcy—it is conformance to societal norms and all that the acknowledgement brings with it."

Reese fought his mind to not interpret what she was saying. Finally he said, "Why do you look like this? Why do you show me this…contrast?" His hands clawed at the arms of the chair he sat in, digging in as if preparing for the fight of his life.

"You bring this upon yourself, John. I am what you have made me; a

OPERATION: FACE THE FEAR

controversy that you refuse to decide upon."

"No—no—no, I don't understand this!"

"Yes you do, John. You understand it perfectly well. Ever since you met your dream—you have been faced with your conundrum which you nurture like an alcoholic nurtures their last drink."

"No!"

"Yes, John. You admire them—you envy them—you want to be like one of them."

"That's not true," he said, his voice sounding uneven in its tone.

"You continue to deny it even when you know it is true. Lieutenant Johnson saw it in himself as well, but he did not hide it as you do."

Lieutenant Johnson. It had been a long time since Reese had heard the name. Johnson had been the operational platoon commander of the Team of Darkness until he had been killed during one of the missions. He had liked Johnson even though toward the end they had become divided upon their views of the vampires and their use. As Reese looked back at that time, he knew that the main difference was that Johnson had seemed to know what was going to happen all along and what the ultimate use of the Team would be, whereas Reese willfully remained hopeful that it would end differently. As it turned out, Johnson had been right and Reese had been very wrong. John wondered how he could have been so blinded by his own personal gain to not see it coming. He guessed it was the naïve part of him that wanted everything to end well. Yet although Reese had been less than honest with himself, Johnson was dead while he was still alive.

And neither one had had their dream fulfilled…but Johnson had been ready to sacrifice it all.

"And for that, you were jealous of him," she continued as if she had read his thoughts. "He admired them as you do, although his admiration was from the perspective of a military man and what the transformation would mean. When he was on the verge of death, he pleaded and begged Dimitri to make him a vampire. When Dimitri refused you were glad about it, weren't you?"

"Yes that's right," he said vehemently. "I didn't want to see Johnson turned into a vampire."

"Why not, John?"

"He was a human being for God sakes!"

"But it was what he wanted," she asserted. "Why should he be denied?"

"Because it was not…right," he said offering no further explanation.

"Perhaps not in your eyes, but in his it was," she asserted. "You knew he wanted to be like Dimitri. Johnson admired him, envied him just as you do. You had it firmly fixed in your mind that if anyone should be changed—it should be you."

"That's not true!" screamed Reese.

"You still hide from what you cannot deny," she said as she rose from her chair and moved closer to him.

Reese watched as her face came nearer to his. She started to turn her face from side to side the movement becoming faster and faster causing a strobe effect of the two sides of her face.

"Why do you do this?" he asked as he pressed himself into the chair trying to get as far from her as possible. He wanted to close his eyes but couldn't.

"No more, John. You must choose! If you wish to live you must choose which side of life you will accept."

"No. I can't."

She stopped her movement and remained poised inches from his face. Reese stared at the side of her face which was youthful in appearance.

"It is this that you want, John," she said. It was not poised as a question, but as a confirmation. "I can help give it to you. All of it."

Reese felt the draw of what that side of her face represented. It was strong—very strong, but something within him tried to deny its pull. Suddenly he felt the touch of her hand, smooth and silky, upon the side of his face. She ran her fingertips alongside his cheek. Her touch brought euphoric comfort to him, conveying the thought that he should do as her voice suggested.

"John," she whispered. "We can end your turmoil now. You will be free."

Reese slowly raised his own hand and grasped hers. He felt the softness of her skin.

"Free, John," she murmured into his ear. "You can finally be free."

As the last syllables of the word dissipated, everything around him became hazy and then vanished. The room with its lavish furniture and draperies were gone and now it was just the two of them alone in the dark. His body felt as if it had been immersed into a vat of warm oily liquid that caressed every pore of his body and was sucking every nuance of emotion from him. Then, without any conscious thought of what he was doing, Reese placed her hand on his throat and moved it back and forth.

"Yes, John. Is that what you want?" She murmured. "You must be sure."

"Y-eee—-sss," he said, the syllables lingered on his lips like the hiss of a snake.

In the hand that remained touching hers, he felt the contour and texture of her fingers change in his hand. On his skin, where her nails gently raked the flesh of his neck, he felt the softly sanded edge of her nails change. They became sharp and toyed at the softness of his skin as if probing for a particular area.

His excitement, fed by the induced euphoria he was immersed in, sent his pulse to quickening. With her hand on his neck, he could feel the throbbing of his artery where her hand settled. There was a slight pinch and then he felt liquid warmth on his skin.

"To life, John," she said as she moved closer.

"Everything gets easier over time, especially if you have all the time that there is."

The words resonated in his mind bouncing around like the metal ball in an arcade game from one point to another, but unlike the pinball game, instead of harmless bumpers of flippers, when this ball struck areas in his mind, they keyed thoughts that gave him the impression that there was something he should know—something about what she had just said to him.

He felt the soft touch of her lips upon his throat, her tongue licking the flesh where the liquid warmth had been felt.

Everything gets easier over time, especially if you have all the time that there is. And I do.

Something shot through him. It was as if a stake of ice had just been plunged into him; its cold quickly eliminating the euphoric warmth that he had been bathed in only seconds ago. Those words. He knew those words. He had heard them before! They had been said by...

He lifted his arms and grabbed the woman. He forced his arms to push her away from him. He stared straight ahead. What he saw drew away his breath and confirmed where he had heard those words before. The woman was no longer there. In her place was a man, his lips covered with blood, his eyes red with a fury that danced within them. He recognized him immediately—it was Dimitri!

"No," Reese screamed. "No not you!"

He flailed his arms widely striking out at the vampire. The blows had no effect. Dimitri did not move. A smile slowly appeared on his lips.

"You are mine and you shall become like I am," said Dimitri. "It is what you want. It is what you have wanted ever since the day you stared upon us in our crypts."

"No!" Reese screamed as he continued to strike out at Dimitri to no avail. "I refuse! This was a trick! Just a trick to make me question my own beliefs and trick me into giving in."

Dimitri laughed. "It is too late," the vampire said, "It is too late for many things and you know it. Things are at an impasse that must be resolved."

"No!" Reese screamed as he struggled. "I can not. I will not!"

Reese continued to struggle against the vise-like grip that held him. As if in response to his struggle, Dimitri's eyes glowed an even deeper blood red and he returned his sharp fangs to Reese's throat to finish what he started.

Reese screamed.

CHAPTER TWENTY-SEVEN

The darkness brought a sense of comfort to Dimitri and he silently dropped deeper into his thoughts as the van drove on.

The van containing Dimitri and the other vampires continued along in the night heading toward Norfolk. Dimitri sat quietly in the passenger seat delving into his thoughts trying to retrieve what he had seen earlier. The images and thought had hit him with an intensity he had never felt before. The thought was so strong that in an instant it commandeered his consciousness. Now he tried to put what he saw and felt into perspective.

There had been the image of Reese and he appeared to be terrified of something. It must have been that terror that caused the image to bleed into Dimitri's thoughts. He needed to know what it was that caused such an emotional outburst; He demanded that his mind reproduce the image and allowed himself to flow into it.

The image came quickly and with such intensity that Dimitri felt the fear that had surged through Reese. It was an emotion of such depth, that even Dimitri felt swept up in it. He had not known fear for so long, not since becoming a vampire, so long that he had forgotten what fear felt like. As disturbing as the effect was, there was also a sense of exhilaration. Casting aside the feeling he forced himself to focus.

Dimitri became an outsider to the event as he watched Reese being attacked by someone or something. First he saw what he thought was a woman, but as time progressed, it changed into a man. Then the location struck Dimitri as familiar and he recognized it as their sanctuary back in Kacanik in Kosovo—their old home.

What madness is this? Dimitri thought. He is not back there. That was in the past. He is here in this country. How can this be? This question drew an immediate response—it was a dream. Reese was having a dream about being attacked in the place where he had taken them into captivity.

Dimitri forced his attention back to the struggle. As he studied the images, he heard the attacker speak. Fear crept back into Dimitri in a new wave. He recognized the voice and the words. He felt sickened for he knew the attacker. The words had been his own words, and he was the attacker.

Why had Reese had this dream? Dimitri had never threatened him. At one point during their captivity, Dimitri had even considered the possibility of friendship with this man. Dimitri held back because Reese was too distracted by his own emotions. The man didn't know what he wanted from life. What had happened to change all this? That thought was puzzling, but not as much as the next one that he had.

How could the images from Reese have touched his mind? There were only two possibilities that Dimitri could think of. The first was the most obvious but he quickly eliminated it. He had never taken Reese's blood. The taking of blood forms an attachment by which the vampire can sometimes sense what the victim is thinking or feeling. As this had never happened, there was no chance that it was a possibility.

The second possibility was also impossible because it would involve another vampire that had been made by the same maker. Thoughts sometimes overflowed into other vampires who were connected because of the same maker's blood in the body. The way Dimitri understood this was that although new blood was always introduced into the vampire body, there would always be traces of the original maker blood. It was as if during the transformation, the maker blood embedded itself into the vampire heart.

Dimitri was most familiar with this occurrence because at times he could sense the feelings of Andre and Iliga, as well as those of Josip and Alexander when they were alive. Alexander had been their maker and through his bond, the link between all of them had been established. Dimitri involuntarily shuddered at the possibility of his thoughts. Alexander would have had to have made another vampire and that this vampire was also in the vicinity and the effect was this bleeding through of images.

But Alexander had never mentioned the fact that he had created another. It surely had not happened during the many years they had spent together and Dimitri was sure that if it had happened earlier, Alexander would have mentioned it to him. He would not have hidden it unless there was a specific reason why he did not want Dimitri to know.

Dimitri searched his own thoughts and memories of Alexander to see if there had ever been a mention of another even in the vaguest of terms. He could think of none yet the more Dimitri thought about what had happened and given that the possibilities were very limited, he was forced in the direction of his theory of another vampire. Perhaps there had been another and Alexander had thought they were dead and that was why there was never a mention of them. Still, that didn't make sense. Dimitri had thought of Alexander as a father and himself the son. They shared their thoughts willingly and freely. There had been no secrets between them. There had to be another possibility.

Perhaps Reese, or the military, had found some way to create the link artificially. They might try to use it as some form of control or subversive communication tactic. They had taken samples of their blood to study and analyze, perhaps they had developed something? But if that were true, could they use it to find them—to track them down somehow? Could they be tracking them right now? What of the girls? Were they connected somehow to this as well?

As Andre exited the interstate, following the signs into Norfolk, Dimitri thought there were too many questions and not enough answers. All of this was happening at the worse possible moment. All of this was connected and if he wasn't careful with their next move, it could jeopardize them all as well as the ultimate plan to get the girls back to the Balkans. Given the nature of this new problem, it just became a lot more complicated - not to mention dangerous as well. They would have to revise their plans And Dimitri would have to do what he had wanted to avoid from the beginning: Seek outside assistance from someone he didn't know if he could trust.

Dimitri gazed out the window as the scent of the ocean reached him. The smell was always strong here on Ocean View Avenue with its constant breeze. Regardless, he found it relaxing and right now he felt the need for a few moments of solitude on the beach to ease his mind.

"Stop the van," Dimitri said, "over in the lot next to the park. I wish to walk a bit. You can take the others home, I will meet you later."

Andre pulled the van into the lot and parked. "Dimitri, are you okay" he asked.

"Yes. I just need to think. We have a new problem to deal with, a potentially dangerous development. I will explain later."

"As you wish," said Andre.

Dimitri opened the door of the van and got out. He walked to the driver's side of the van where Andre sat. First, he looked at the girls, smiled and said, "You go back with Andre and Iliga; I will be there shortly."

"Is something wrong?" Ishma asked.

"No. I have something to do and then I will join you," said Dimitri.

He then placed his hand on Andre's forearm.

"Take them home and get the girls settled." Then he lowered his voice and spoke softly, "keep an eye out for anything unusual."

"Unusual?"

"It's hard to explain," Dimitri said, "just keep them occupied. See if they have any information we might have missed about the military or any tests they may have undergone. I have a feeling we may have missed something."

"What?"

"I don't know," replied Dimitri.

Andre didn't say anything, but Dimitri saw understanding in his eyes.

'I'll see you in a bit," Dimitri said as he walked off.

When he reached the top of one of the dunes, he turned back and watched the van depart the parking lot and head in the direction of their house. After the van was out of sight, he continued heading down toward the water. It was late and he did not expect to run onto anyone at this hour. Occasionally he would see someone, but the area was prone to a criminal element and that kept many away. It was just another reason why he liked the place.

Dimitri then did something he hadn't done in quite a while; he removed his shoes and socks and walked barefoot on the sand. It felt both cool and gritty against the soles of his feet. The sensations were helpful as he tried to clear his mind of troubling thoughts. Distraction was the tool of choice he had always used to get to answers that his mind would not allow him to see.

He continued walking along the beach. There was just enough light from a few old fashioned streetlamps on the main boardwalk area so the foaming edges of the encroaching waves could be seen as they lapped along the shore. He kept a safe distance from the water's edge as he walked further. Although he knew it could not harm him, the water brought back to many painful memories of their operations when they attacked the drug cartels.

Such a realist, he thought. A curse when you are a vampire who chooses to avoid reality on a constant basis.

How ironic considering what his own fate in life had been; a product of the unreal, or the undead. However, choosing to avoid reality did not affect the way in which he reached a decision. A perfect example was that it had been the logical and correct decision to end their relationship with Commander John Reese. He felt it was dangerous to them all and an unnecessary risk and Reese had agreed. So what had led to the human fearing them: To fear him specifically? Dimitri did not understand and it certainly did not explain the strange connection which had occurred this evening.

"What is it?" Dimitri said out loud. "What the hell is it that I am missing?"

The cawing of a seagull interrupted his thoughts and he watched the large bird from the corner of his eye as it flew by him. The bird appeared agitated at being disturbed from its slumber by his passage.

"Yes, I know," Dimitri said, "Hell is a relative thing isn't it?"

CHAPTER TWENTY-EIGHT

She laughed at her own thoughts. Normally she had to be concerned about how to murder someone, and now she was concerned about what to have for dinner. Such domestic bliss. She only hoped that all of her decisions would be so simple. But experience told her there would be hard times ahead and she didn't think those decisions and choices would be so simple.

Welcome to the world of the living…

Christina stood at the front door of Reese's home holding several Styrofoam take-out containers in her hands. She had stopped earlier at an Italian restaurant and picked up the food—she was not much of a cook, in fact she could hardly remember the last time she had cooked or even eaten food for that matter. She could eat if she wanted to, but simply wasn't interested. She would tell him that she had eaten earlier and just warm up what she brought for him.

She moved to push the doorbell and stopped and stared at her hand. It was shaking. She was nervous? She found the sensation disconcerting because she could not remember being nervous. Why was she nervous? What was there to be nervous about?

Because this is the new you, a voice inside her head answered. How are you going to handle this new found desire to get close to someone? Maybe it's too late.

She smiled and ignored the little voice as she pushed the doorbell and waited.

Nothing.

Maybe it's too late…

She pushed the doorbell again.

Still nothing.

Maybe it's too late…

Holding the food in one hand, she placed her other hand around the doorknob and turned. It didn't move. It was locked.

A feeling of unease pervaded her thoughts.

It's too late…for him and you…

"Oh shut up," she said to herself and then gripped the doorknob firmly in her hand. She turned it until the lock snapped and gave way to her strength. She opened the door and stepped across the threshold and into the house.

That was when she heard him screaming.

Dropping the food containers, she moved swiftly toward the sound of his voice as he yelled at something or someone to get away. She followed his voice into his bedroom. As she entered the room, she saw that he was writhing violently back and forth in his bed as if trying to combat something that held him in its grasp. His clothes and bed linens were drenched with sweat. The sheets were twisted into rope like strands and were pulled out of their folded and tucked positions. Whatever was happening had been going on for a while she thought.

"No!" Reese screamed as he struggled. "I can not—I will not!"

She could feel the depth of his fear through his elevated bodily functions. Even from the distance, she could hear his heart racing. It was dangerously fast and she wondered if he was on the verge of a heart attack or something. She was also drawn to the seductive sound of the organ as it pumped and pumped his blood. The violent beating meant that his blood was flowing at an increased pace through his body causing it to be even warmer than it normally is when the body is at rest. She was drawn to that warmth. She could almost taste the sweetness of his blood as it flowed across her lips...

Stop it! What are you doing! Help him!

Christina stepped up to the bedside and grasped him firmly by the shoulders to try and calm him down. As her skin made contact with his she could feel the tremendous heat of his excited body from his elevated temperature. She was thinking about what a curious sensation it was when she was suddenly jolted by what felt like an intense electrical shock. However, it was not an electrical shock, but rather the shock of the sensation of his thoughts shooting through her.

Christina saw an image of what was attacking him, not through her own eyes but through his. It was a man which stood over John, the eyes were a burning red and his fangs red with blood, a male vampire. She also recognized something else about the vampire—the look of his face. He had dark hair, a tanned complexion and features that were characteristically similar to hers. He looked like the people of her own country where she had lived the majority of her life.

Was this one of the others? Is this the one that General Stone had said existed? Or was just this just a nightmare?

As the thought flashed through her mind, she felt or sensed something else. There was a brief, but recognizable feeling of a connection to something...she didn't know how to explain it. It was as if a doorway had opened up in her mind and this doorway connected two adjoining rooms. The rooms represented two separate and distinct minds now sharing their thoughts. What had been previously locked up in the one was now shared with the other through the door. She didn't understand it.

Reese moaned aloud, driving her from the thoughts and breaking the brief connection she had experienced. Christina was confused. She wanted to see more of this other vampire; she wanted to know for sure if there were others, yet she was concerned about what this dream was doing to him. The tremendous amount of fear he was feeling was tearing him apart.

Instinctively she grasped him by the shoulders and shook him.

"John! John! Wake up," she said.

"No! No!" he screamed, "I refuse!"

He was still wrapped up inside of the horror of the dream. She shook him harder.

"John, wake up!"

"No! Leave me alone!" he cried, now moving his arms in violent arcs as if fighting off invisible attackers.

Christina jumped upon the bed and straddled over him. She held his flaying arms flat against the mattress. He squirmed under her hold. She tried to think of how to wake him from this deep dream. She had to pull him out of it.

A memory from her childhood flashed though her mind. It was so long ago. She was a child; a little girl sitting up in her bed in the cottage where she lived with her mother and father. She had woken crying and screaming from a nightmare where she had been chased by wolves through the forest near her home. As she ran, the wolves got closer and closer to her, nipping at her long nightgown. Slowly they tugged at the material and slowed her down so the other members of the pack could catch up to her. They tore at her nightgown and then began tearing at her skin. She began to scream.

Her father came into the room and woke her. He hugged her and kissed her forehead and cheeks with warm soft kisses. He made her feel safe from the dream. He told her she would stay with her through the night to make sure the wolves would not return. When she awoke that morning, he lay next to her on the tiny bed.

She remembered the way she felt that morning when she had awoken. The magical feeling she had that she was safe and would always be so because her father loved her and protected her. She could not recall ever feeling so safe and loved as she had at that moment. In fact, she had completely forgotten about that day and the feelings that were associated with it and she had never felt that way again. There was a pang in her heart when she realized she had not known that pure love and safe feeling from anyone again.

She was intrigued and surprised that this thought had arisen from the dark depths of her innermost thoughts. Feelings for her had been reduced to basic animal needs such as food, shelter, and survival. She embellished the rising of the memory and relaxed her mind as she tried to place herself back into that little girl's body. She wanted to feel that way again—just for a moment—just for an instant she wanted to remember what love was.

She felt her father's heavy broad arms wrap around her like a blanket bringing with it immediate warmth that shut out the cold. She felt his breath upon her skin as he soothed her with words and thoughts of happy things. She felt his kisses upon her moist cheeks where there had been tears of fear and imagined pain. He rocked her back and forth with a soothing motion that drove away all the bad thoughts and memories of the dream. Words failed to come to her on how to express or describe what she felt. Simply all she could do was know that she felt safe—she felt protected and she felt loved.

She took this feeling she couldn't describe and projected it toward John through her mind as he still struggled under her grip, trying to escape the demons that chased him. She repositioned her hold on him to lift him up and toward her. She wrapped her arms around him, pulled him close and hugged him.

"Shhh…" she murmured to him. "It's alright, John."

She rocked him gently back and forth.

At first Reese resisted her grip and struggled to break free. She continued to rock him and talk to him. "They're gone, John. All gone. You're safe. I'll…protect you."

The last words surprised even her. They just flowed across her lips without any thought—it was just a feeling—but one she had not had for a very long time. Even stranger was the feeling that came with it, a feeling of warmth inside of her where there had been none before.

"I'll protect you…" She said again. She hugged him tightly and moved her face alongside his, feeling the rough texture of his unshaven skin as his whiskers scratched at her skin. She felt a tingling sensation flow from where their faces made contact and it continued throughout her entire body.

His struggling subsided and his body began to relax. She gently eased off the pressure with which she held him and let his body relax within her grasp.

"Shhh…" she whispered again. She didn't need to say it, but her utterance of the sound was not just for him, it was for herself as well. It was as if she wanted to quell her own reaction to the sensations she had awoken within her own heart. But she wasn't sure if she really wanted to. These sensations were both exciting and bewildering. It was as if she was a newborn child experiencing them for the first time.

What is happening to me?

She tried to tell herself that these were not new sensations or experiences. They were just things that she had forgotten. She tried to reason with herself, but part of her refused. She didn't want to think about reasons or facts—she just wanted to be a part of it. She wanted to be consumed within it. No more thinking. Just enjoy the moment and the sensational feelings that accompanied it.

Just for a little while…

Christina leaned towards him hesitating just inches from his face. She moved closer placing her lips tentatively upon his seeing what reaction it would bring. At first there was nothing but then she felt him respond. She kissed him deeply and allowed herself to drift within the feeling.

CHAPTER TWENTY-NINE

The cawing of a seagull interrupted his thought and he watched the large bird from the corner of his eye as it flew by him. The bird appeared agitated at being disturbed from its slumber by his passage.

"Yes, I know," Dimitri said, "Hell is a relative thing isn't it?"

"This is like debating in a vacuum...useless," Dimitri thought as he tried to figure what it was he had missed about the brief connection he had shared with Reese.

After Andre had dropped him off so he could have some time to be alone and think, he had walked along the shoreline for a while, but had returned to the cement walkway which served as the primary access to and from the beach. However, no matter how much he walked or how much he thought about the possibilities of what had happened, he always returned to the same course of action.

There is no choice but to talk with Reese and find out what is happening.

"Hey man...got a cigarette?" a voice called to him driving him from his thoughts.

Dimitri turned in the direction of the voice. He was surprised that he had not sensed the man's presence.

Fool. I am a fool if I can be so easily distracted. If I am not careful, mistakes like this will get us all killed.

He focused upon the surprise visitor. He was a young man, perhaps twenty or twenty-five years of age. After his emergence from the shadows he stood about twelve feet away. Even in the dim light, Dimitri saw that he was filthy and assumed he was probably one of the homeless people that had returned to the area after their brief hiatus – a hiatus caused by Dimitri and his men. That had been shortly after Dimitri and his fellow vampires had escaped captivity and were at the mercy at whatever food source they could find. Until they had secured a stable food supply, Dimitri and his men had used the homeless people, drug traffickers, and assorted riff-raff to feed upon. They did not kill anyone unless they had to. However, those fed upon reported strange occurrences; sightings of creatures that drank their blood, red eyes, and fangs and so the area quickly emptied out of the less desirable. By the time the city declared a surprise victory of taking back the streets, Dimitri had secured the

Suffolk property and a stable food source with the cattle. Now, he couldn't help but smile at the ironic humor of the crime fighting vampires.

"What's so funny," the man asked, bringing Dimitri's thoughts back to the present. His voice had changed from the earlier tone when he asked for a cigarette. Now he sounded annoyed.

"What are you smiling at? You think I'm funny? Do I look like I'm having a great fucking time or something that you can laugh about it, huh? Look at me…"

The man raised his arms and turned around in a circle.

"These aren't what I would call designer clothes, would you?"

"No, I suppose not," Dimitri answered calmly. "I'm sorry, I did not mean to make light of your situation. However, I do not have any cigarettes. They're not healthy for you and you should quit before they make you ill."

"So now you're a fucking comedian, are you?" the man said.

Dimitri noted that the voice and tone were appearing to be heading to the point of hostility. "No. I am not a comedian nor did I mean any disrespect. I was referring to smoking." Dimitri was surprised in the dramatic change of the personality of this man. "A limited lifetime is too precious to waste on such a destructive habit."

"Destructive habit? Are you stupid or something? Retarded?" the man asked.

"No," Dimitri responded. He was curious as to why the man was getting angrier with him. "Destructive in that smoking shortens life."

"You want to talk destructive, I'll show you destructive. Look at these beauties," he said as he raised his shirt revealing bruises all along the front of his chest. "A few of my…neighbors out here got bored and wanted some amusement. How's that for a pleasant evening?"

Dimitri was appalled at the sight of the abuse the man had suffered at the hands of his own kind. It was an aspect he could never understand even after living all these years and witnessing constant reminders of it.

"Human life is something that should be cherished and revered," Dimitri said. His statement was not so much as in response to what the man had said, but rather, his thinking out loud about the abuse mankind bestowed upon itself.

"Oh Christ…now you're concerned about my life? You people crack me up," the man said becoming visibly agitated as his face began to spasmodically twitch. He stepped closer to Dimitri. "What do you know about me or my life? Not a damn thing. Do I look like I'm in a position to be concerned about my long term health?"

"You should be concerned…"

"I'll tell you what I'm concerned about," the man said cutting off Dimitri's reply, his voice becoming overtly sarcastic. "I'm concerned about making my first million! Or what yacht to buy! Or which mansion I want to pick up! How's that sound? Is that concerned enough for you?"

"You are…"

"Don't tell me what I am or what I need. I haven't got a pot to piss in! People like you, you forget about the simple things, the basic things of life. Your goals and mine are very different!"

For some reason Dimitri became interested in this homeless man's argument. There was something to his logic that keyed Dimitri's thoughts. He decided to encourage the man to go on with his story. "What do you want out of life?" Dimitri asked.

"Geez! What now?" he said shaking his head. "You didn't get enough of your talk show fix today? Not enough Oprah or Montel? You want to know my life's goals?" The man took small steps in place as if confused about what to do. After a few seconds he stopped and looked at Dimitri with a changed expression—he had become calm again and when he spoke, his voice changed to a less sharp tone. "Okay, I'll tell you, but it's gonna cost you."

Dimitri reached into his pocket and felt his fingers touch the folded twenty dollar bills. He removed one and handed it to the man. He could have gotten what he wanted without the inducement of the money; he could have just taken it from his thoughts, but Dimitri wanted to sense the feeling and emotion behind this man's motivations, as well as an understanding of them.

"Well," the homeless man said eyeing the twenty in Dimitri's hand, "you must be really bored tonight, either that or scared." The man's eyes briefly locked onto Dimitri's. "No…I don't think you're scared," he said, in a tone no longer sarcastic. He took the twenty from Dimitri's hand. "There is something about you; I can see that you aren't scared. In fact you're the furthest thing from scared. I'm not sure how to describe it." He then looked away from him and pointed to the sandy area. "Pull up a chair," he said.

The man plopped down where he had been standing. Dimitri sat opposite him but close enough so he could see the man's face.

"You asked what I want. Well, I want to go to sleep tonight knowing that I will wake up tomorrow and see the sun come up," the man began. His voice again changed to a tone that Dimitri thought reflected the true person he had once been and not the homeless man looking for a cigarette.

"Is that all?" Dimitri asked.

"No," the man said. "I want to feel valued. I want to know that I am looked upon to perform a useful function in society. I want to love someone and to be loved by them. And most of all, I want to live without fear of becoming what I know I can be."

"I don't understand. What is this fear of becoming what you know you could be?"

"We all want things out of life: love, commitment, and self-worth. But there are certain things that are particularly more important than others. These things are hard, very hard to get. It reminds me of the old saying which says it best, if it was easy, then everyone would do it. These things are obtainable only if we are willing to make the sacrifice to obtain them, but in order to do that, you must overcome the fear required to make the change."

"I don't understand," Dimitri said.

"Are you sure you're not…a little slow maybe?"

"Is anyone really sure," said Dimitri and smiled.

"No I suppose not," the man agreed. "Well look, suppose that someone wanted to do something, like maybe I wanted to go back to my wife and family to try and patch things up. I would have to overcome the fear of rejection in order to chance the joy of acceptance. But if I can't overcome that fear, I will never attempt it. Instead the thought will just fester inside of me in my waking thoughts as well as my dreams. It will consume me: day by day, week by week, month by month. It will slowly destroy me. I made a mistake but instead of coming clean, I tried to hide it. I lost my job, my family, and now here I am. I think about the same thing every day, yet I cannot overcome the fear to do what I know I must do."

"This fear is interesting, but I don't see why it is so hard to overcome," Dimitri said.

"Say what? Come on! You can't be that dense? You've felt fear—it's the strongest emotion we possess."

Dimitri tried to remember the last time he had actually been afraid – the last time he'd felt fear. He couldn't remember.

"Humans will go around everything else to avoid the fear of making a choice because we may not be sure that it is the correct one. Some people joke about it…they say, do you know what f-e-a-r stands for?"

"No," said Dimitri as he shook his head.

"Fuck Everything And Run. I read that in a Stephen King book. But you know what? They're full of shit. They're scared just like the rest of us but don't want to admit it."

"So this fear—it destroys you?" asked Dimitri.

"Not the fear itself, but what it makes you do."

"Which is?"

"Nothing. You do absolutely fucking nothing. Like I said earlier, you become so scared of attempting to achieve what you want that you don't bother to try at all. It festers like an open wound, gets infected and then you die from it. No happy ending. The curtain drops. End of show. No sequel this time."

Dimitri thought deeply about this. He and his fellow vampires had not felt fear like this man had described. Why? The answer darted into his mind: Time. They had all the time that there was. There was no pressure to do something within a limited span of human life before you ran out of time. Were there things that he wanted to do? Of course there were. But he knew they would happen in some point of time. Maybe not today, next year or in the next fifty years, but it would happen. Time was not of concern, so therefore there was no fear.

"Hey, you two! What the hell are you doing? " An angry voice called interrupting Dimitri's thoughts.

"Oh shit!" the man said.

CHAPTER THIRTY

In Reese's dream, the attacking vampire Dimitri faded out of existence and with it, the pain and fear of the attack. The sense of fear and loathing was replaced by a new sensation which engulfed his body. A prevailing sense of calm flowed over and through him. Every muscle in his body suddenly felt warm and relaxed. He felt the pressure of something on his lips. It was nice—it felt safe—he felt safe.

Reese slowly opened his eyes but the pressure on his lips continued.

His vision was blurred and he couldn't associate the feeling on his lips without the confirmation of sight. Finally his mind solved the problem that his field of vision was blocked because of the closeness of another face to his. As his thoughts assembled and he could think, the feeling and the image came together, he was being kissed and it was nice.

"Hmm…" he murmured, which came out sounding like a mixture of surprise as well as delight.

The other face drew back a few inches from his.

"Hello there," she said. "Welcome back."

Reese stared at Christina as he felt a smile form on his lips. Her long strands of hair draped down and tickled the sides of his face. It's silky feel and appearance was highlighted by the dim light from his bedroom lamp. Her features of her face were cast in a golden hue from the low wattage bulb and the light appeared to dance upon the moisture on her full lush lips.

"Hi there," he said. "Am I dreaming?"

She laughed. "No. Not now…but you were," she said softly. She moved her hand to his face and gently brushed away a few strands of hair from his forehead with her fingers.

"What time is it?" he said as he turned his head toward his alarm clock and saw that it was 12:30 AM. "My alarm…it must not have gone off. How long have you…wait a minute, how did you get in?"

"When I got here and you didn't answer the door, I became worried. So I came in. You left door unlocked again."

"I could have sworn I locked it," he said although the sound of his voice questioned his comment. "Maybe I didn't? I can't remember. Either way, you're still breaking and entering lady. I'm beginning to wonder about you."

"Yes well, my breaking and entering appears to becoming a habit lately with you."

"Was I talking in my sleep?"

"You screamed," she blurted out. "Not just a wimpy little scream either. I came in here and you were apparently having one hell of a nightmare. So I thought I wake you up with something which I hope was better than what you were dreaming about."

"It was," Reese said, "believe me it was." The image of Dimitri, or whatever the creature of his nightmare was flashed through his thoughts, the teeth, the blood. He felt himself involuntarily shiver.

"You want to tell me about it?" she asked. "I'm a good listener."

"Thanks, maybe later," he said. "It's...well it's complicated."

"Dodging the issue again?" she quipped.

"No. I just don't want to..." he searched for the words, "I don't know. Maybe I don't want to scare you off."

He reached out and touched her face with his hands.

"It takes a lot to scare me off," she said as she took his hand in hers. "You have to trust me John."

"I know," he said, "It's just that..." his voice trailed off.

"You don't give your trust easily," she said. "I know."

"How do you do that?" he asked.

"What?"

"Know what I'm feeling. It's as if you can read my mind. Know what I'm thinking. Am I that...I don't know, predictable?"

"Predictable? No. Not at all. I think you're quite complicated, John Reese. You're a mystery that yearns to be solved. The problem is that you won't allow it to be solved."

"Ah..." he said, "the doctor has arrived. My very own psychoanalyst."

She smiled playfully. "Oh you want to play doctor?"

"So doctor, what do you suggest?" he said playfully.

"Well," she began, "I think you need to undergo some shock therapy."

"I agree and you're it," he said enthusiastically.

"Well," she said pretending to be flabbergasted at his comment. "I don't know how I should take that comment."

"You're here," he said in a more serious tone. "I don't understand why, but at this moment, right now, I don't want to know why. I don't want reasons and answers. I just want..."

Reese didn't finish the sentence. Instead he reached for her face and drew it nearer to his and kissed her deeply. Wrapping his arms around her, he drew her body to his. When their bodies touched, he gently raised both of them and while cradling her in his arms, rolled over taking her with him so that they were lying side by side on the bed.

He didn't stop kissing her. He couldn't stop kissing her. He kissed her lips, her cheeks and even her closed eyes. He placed his lips upon her neck and gently caressed her skin moving toward her ears. He kissed her ears as well as explored them with his tongue.

His hands moved over her body exploring it as dutifully as his tongue explored every square inch of her face. His fingers gently touched the smooth curves of her neck, her shoulders, and then meandered across her firm breasts where he lingered allowing his fingers to dance teasingly around the nipples. From her breasts, he slid his hands to the curves of her hips where he languished in the subtle angles of skin that curved gently toward her waist.

As he bathed in the pure ecstasy of the moment, he felt as if the world was relinquishing its hold of him; casting him off to drift in a wide and expansive sea of pure emotions. Everything vanished and only his sensory abilities remained. It was something that he had never experienced before and something he didn't want to stop.

He heard her say his name softly, "John."

"Hmmm..." he said as he continued to enjoy the delights of feeling her and the way she responded to his touch.

"I...I...what's happening..." she murmured.

"Don't think," he said, surprised at his own words. But even more surprising was that he actually believed in these words more than ever as he felt her hands over him now, touching and caressing him.

Feeling his own excitement growing, he became more aggressive and began to undress her. His hands shook with energy and he found that he struggled with the buttons. She appeared to sense his frustration and provided her own hand to assist him by ripping her shirt apart without any regard for the buttons at all. He removed what remained of her tattered shirt and then released the clasp on her bra, allowing her breasts to fall freely from their captivity. He ran his hands around the mounds of softness, then kissed and caressed them, gently taking the nipple in his mouth and worshipping it with his tongue.

He was shaking uncontrollably and felt as if his body was on a roller coaster of emotions which would lead to some tremendous release. They groped and fondled as they continued removing the remaining pieces of their clothing. She tore at what few garments he had worn to bed. The shorts and t-shirt were baggy on him allowing her to remove them easily. Christina's only remaining clothing were her jeans, which she was trying to shimmy off all the way by sliding her legs up and down and back and forth. While she shimmied her jeans to remove them Reese slid her panties down to her knees and then seeing that the jeans were still in the way, he ripped them off and tossed them aside.

He was at the peak of his excitement and his senses were attuned to her every moment. That was when he felt the change come over her.

Chapter Thirty-One

"Hey, you two! What the hell are you doing?" An angry voice called interrupting Dimitri's thoughts.

"Oh shit!" the man said.

Dimitri turned toward the voice. A man wearing a police uniform stood on the wooden walk area that led to the beach. Dimitri's heightened eyesight scrutinized the man, a Norfolk police officer. His senses also conveyed caution in the way the officer appeared to be excited about discovering them. The officer shined a flashlight in their direction. The light centered on Dimitri for a few seconds, then swept over to the homeless man.

"I said, "What are you two doing?" The officer asked. His eyes became fixed on the homeless man and then he snapped his fingers as if the sound would get the man's attention. "Is that you, Mike?" the officer asked while the light from his flashlight remained on the homeless man.

"Yeah...it's me," Mike answered. "Good evening, Officer Bill Mann."

Dimitri could sense the fear that came from the homeless man, now identified by the name of Mike. Dimitri wondered why he had not asked what his name was earlier. By the tone by which Mike had answered, Dimitri detected that they knew one another and probably not in a cordial way.

"Sir," the officer asked turning his attention back toward Dimitri. "Is this man bothering you?"

The officer moved closer to them, studying them both carefully.

"No, its fine, Officer Mann," Dimitri said keeping his voice calm. "We were just enjoying the night air and having a conversation."

"A conversation?" the officer asked as he returned his attention to Mike. His eyes centered on the twenty dollar bill that Mike still held in his hand.

"Well looky here. You're rich tonight?" Officer Mann asked. "Where'd the money come from?"

"I gave it to him," said Dimitri before Mike could answer. "I thought he needed it."

"Sure," Officer Mann said. "Yes I'm sure you did. Good conversation is hard to come by these days, huh?" Then turning his attention to Mike he added, "I'm getting a bad feeling about this. We've talked about this before, haven't we?"

"Yes," Mike answered as he shoved the twenty dollar bill in his pants pocket.

"I told you 'no soliciting' on my beat—I thought you understood that after the little talk we had last time."

"We were just talking officer," Dimitri reiterated seeing the direction the conversation was going in. "Mike here has some interesting views."

"I bet. Twenty dollars worth," the officer said. "It must have been some "good" information. Care to share with me ,Mike?"

"Officer Mann, I believe you are," Dimitri began.

"Stow it my friend," he said.

Dimitri heard the agitation in the officer's voice but there was still the underlying excitement that alerted the vampire that the officer was enjoying the confrontation.

"Something's not right here and I want to know what's happening here. You have any identification?" he asked Dimitri.

"Of course," Dimitri said as he slowly reached into his pocket and removed his wallet. There's no time for this, Dimitri thought. With the new insight Mike had given him, he wanted to resolve this situation as quickly as possible and return home. He handed the officer his driver's license.

"So what was the money for?" Officer Mann asked not taking his eyes from the license Dimitri had handed him, "Mr. Bicannoff."

"He helped me with some information I needed," Dimitri said, as he thought of something to say, "I'm a writer and I needed some information about the homeless situation here. Mike was bringing me up to speed."

"That's right," Mike interjected, "I told him about my life—you want to hear my story?"

"Shut up, Mike," Officer Mann said. "It'll just go harder for you downtown tonight."

"I didn't do anything!" Mike said adamantly.

"Officer there appears to have been a misunderstanding," Dimitri said. "There is no reason to suspect that this is anything more than a conversation between two people."

"So, you're a lawyer now are you?" Mann said, obviously not liking what Dimitri had just suggested.

"No. I am just trying to save us both a lot of time," said Dimitri.

"Too late, Mr. Bic-ann-off. Bicannoff...what kind of name is that anyway?"

"Slavic," answered Dimitri.

"Is that Middle Eastern?"

"No, European," Dimitri said beginning to tire of the conversation. "I'm afraid I must be leaving. If you would be so kind as to return my license, I will be on my way."

"No, I don't think so," Mann said. He smiled and continued, "I've seen your kind before. I have probable cause to take you both down to the station for further questioning, Mr. Bicannoff."

"Aw…come on," Mike whined. "This is police harassment."

"Yeah, right," Mann said sarcastically. "Save it for the judge. Maybe you can even have your friend here be your lawyer?"

"Lawyer?" asked Mike. "I'm going to need a lawyer now? What the hell for?"

Officer Mann ignored the question and turned his attention fully on Dimitri. "Besides what else do you two have to do tonight? We'll get in the police car and have a nice ride with some conversation. I have a new Godzilla toy on my dash, you know those six inch ones made by Bandai—I love those things. You'll see it and it will just make your night."

"I'm not going with you," Dimitri said, "And neither is he."

Officer Mann stared at Dimitri. His hand went to the butt of his revolver.

"What did you say?"

"I said we are not going. We have done nothing wrong."

"I don't recall this being like an auction or something where you get to bid on whether you did anything wrong or not. I think you have and that's all that matters," Mann said, "now we can all be good and nice people and get in the lovely police cruiser or I can cuff you both. Which shall it be?"

"Neither," Dimitri said. "As I said, we are not going anywhere."

"Mr. Bicannoff," Mike said, "I think maybe we should comply with the Officer's wishes." Then in a softer voice he added, "He has a very bad temper, if you know what I mean," he said as his hand vaguely pointed to the bruises on his body.

"Astutely put," Mann said. "Now what's it going to be, Mr. Bicannoff?"

"No."

Officer Mann slipped the safety catch off of his holster and began to remove his revolver.

Dimitri lunged at him before his weapon had moved even an inch out of its holster. With both hands, he gripped the officer by the neck and applied pressure to the main artery cutting off the blood flow. As he did so, he felt the flesh on his hands beginning to get hot. As the seconds passed the heat turned to burning and he struggled to keep his grip on the officer and finally he felt the man go limp and pass out. Dimitri dropped him unceremoniously to the sandy beach.

He looked at his hands. The flesh had been burned off at several places but was quickly healing. He knelt and carefully reached for the officer's shirt collar and opened it. He immediately found what he had surmised would be there. A gold chain with a cross was around his neck and had been the cause of the burning of his flesh. Dimitri smiled and shook his head at the hypocrisy of a man such as this who obviously meant them harm yet at the same time received divine protection.

Putting the irony of the moment aside Dimitri delved into the man's thoughts. As delicately as a neurosurgeon, he found every memory of their conversation and plucked it out.

"What the hell are you doing?" Mike asked. He blinked his eyes several times as if he wasn't sure of what he had just seen happen. "I've never seen anyone move that fast."

"It's okay, Mike," Dimitri said using the homeless man's name for the first time in addressing him. "When he wakes he won't remember a thing." He ignored Mike's statement about moving so fast. "You will have nothing to worry about."

"Yeah...right," Mike said sarcastically. "You mean you don't have anything to worry about. You get to go back to wherever it is you live and not worry about him. Me, I have to live around under his watchful eye. You remember him mentioning that little talk he gave me?"

"Yes."

"That's where I got these colorful bruises."

"Don't worry, he won't remember anything about tonight and you won't be around anyway." Dimitri reached into his pocket and removed the large wad of twenty dollar bills. He handed them to Mike.

"What's this for?" he asked staring at the money, but not taking it.

"It's for you to get your life back on track," Dimitri said. "It won't get you to overcome your fear, but at least it will remove some of the distractions and give you a chance."

"You can't be serious," Mike said.

"I am. Here take it and get going."

Mike took the bills and stuffed them into his pocket. He then turned toward the prone body of Officer Mann and snapped his fingers several times. He smiled. And then turned back toward Dimitri and said,

"Thanks."

Mike turned to leave, but stopped after a few steps and looked back. "Tell me why?" he asked. "Why are you helping me?"

"Because you've helped me to understand something I had forgotten and needed to remember."

"Who are you?" Mike asked.

"My name is Dimitri Bicannoff."

"No, I mean, who are you?"

"I am man just like you. The only difference is that I have lived a very long time and I have learned that time does not change anything. It merely alters our perception of fear."

"Well..." Mike began. The look of confusion on his face reflected he didn't understand what Dimitri had meant. "Glad I could be of help."

"Me too," Dimitri said and disappeared into the night.

CHAPTER THIRTY-TWO

He was at the peak of his excitement and his senses were attuned to her every moment. That was when he felt the change come over her.

Christina stopped what she was doing and became still. Moments ago she felt her body responding to his touch in ways that she had never imagined possible. Feelings she had never attained in her short human life. However this new arousal of wanting John was also tantalizing her body as it had only been accustomed to when excited by hunger— whether for blood, or the taking of a life. She suddenly became aware that she couldn't be sure which reaction would claim overall control of her. If she couldn't decide or control which impulse would be the overriding sum of her actions, she risked John's love and his life. One false move on her part would ruin everything. Not to mention, she didn't know if it was possible to have sex with a man the way she had before she was changed. She thought so, but her orgasms had consisted mainly of the association with the taking of blood.

I should have thought about this before I let this happen...

"John," she whispered. "I...don't know if I can do this," she said. "Not yet."

"What?" he asked. His voice held a combination of surprise and regret. "What's wrong?"

"It's been so long," she said, "a bad experience a long time ago."

Reese nestled close to her. He wrapped his arms around her and just held her tightly.

"What happened?" he asked.

"I don't know if I'm ready to talk about it yet," she said. "It was devastating to me. I was very young when it happened," she said. "Yes... very young.

"You're the one with the secrets? Now who's being complicated?" he asked.

She giggled lightly. "Yes, it's my turn now." Then in a serious tone she added, "I need for you to understand John. It's very important to me that you do. It's been a very strange day for me, a day of revelations."

"Revelations? What? Revelations in terms of religion or something?"

"No, nothing like that," she said although the vision she had of

Alexander and what she experienced could potentially be classified as such.

"I don't understand," he said as he gently ran his fingers through her long hair. "Is it me? Something I said—or did?"

"Absolutely not," she said firmly. She tightened her grip on him to offer physical assurance with her answer. "This revelation is totally in my own ballpark. I just don't want the wrong thing to happen and my mind bringing up my past to ruin it. Does that make any sense?"

"Sure," he said.

She could sense his disappointment of not making love tonight.

"John, I have much to explain to you, but like you, I'm worried that I might scare you off."

"Now, I'm getting nervous," he said.

"Don't. Please don't feel like I'm a...I don't know, just leading you on here," she said. "I just need some time. I wanted it to happen right now, but I don't want to risk it going the wrong way and ruining what we have."

"So we have something here?" he said and then quickly added. "That wasn't meant to come out as a question," he countered. "I believe we do," he said as he ran his hand along the side of her soft cheek and then traced the outline of her lips with his fingers.

"I understand," she said as she kissed him. "I know how you're such a doubting John," she said and laughed lightly.

"Do you?" he asked. "Or are you just saying that?" he asked playfully.

"I mean what I say, John Reese," she said. "I'm more concerned if you really understand without me explaining about my past... at least not yet anyway."

"I understand, believe me. I know about emotional scars and what they can do to you. That's what..." he hesitated, "That's what my dream is about."

"So, can we just slow down?" she asked. "So I can put things into perspective?"

"Of course we can," he agreed. "But..."

"But what?" she asked.

"This doesn't get you off the hook for dinner and what information you said I wanted to hear."

She smiled. "As I said, I do what I say and say what I mean. I'll go warm up dinner while you get showered and dressed."

CHAPTER THIRTY-THREE

After Reese showered, he walked into the kitchen and was greeted by the smell of Italian spices and tomato sauce.

"Yum," he said, "smells good."

"I must warn you, John Reese," she began, "when it comes to cooking, or even just warming up food, I lack any form of knowledge."

"So you're saying what? You're not the domesticated type, woman? Don't want to claim the kitchen as your safe haven of domestic bliss?"

"Er...yes, exactly," she agreed.

"Sounds to me like you're trying to set a precedent so I won't get my hopes up in the future—is that your evil plan?"

"May be," she said, "just may be."

He walked up behind her and wrapped his arms around her. He was surprised that she felt rather cool to the touch now. Earlier she had felt... well he thought she had felt warm but he wasn't sure. Of course she had.

"You're cold," he said.

"Low body temperature. It's a family trait," she said. "I don't sweat much either."

"Bet I can get you..." he began but stopped feeling embarrassed about what he was going to say after their earlier conversation in the bedroom.

"Say it," she said, "or I'll beat you with this wooden spoon," she said as she raised the spoon she had been using to stir the sauce. "I don't want you to be afraid or worried that something you say will bother me. If it does, I'll tell you, okay?"

"Okay," he agreed. "I was just going to say that I bet I can get you warmed up and sweating as well."

"Hmmm, well, we'll have to just see about that, now won't we." She turned and hugged him tightly. "How long do you have tonight before you have to go into work?"

"I probably need to be there by about 0600, pardon me," he corrected himself, "You civilians would say six o'clock."

"Well, you better sit down and eat then."

"Yes maaaammmm...." he said drawing out the syllables in an exaggerated southern drawl.

"Cute," she said.

Reese turned toward his small kitchen table and saw that there was only one place setting.

"Not eating?"

"I already did. I ate earlier, plus, I've been nibbling on yours as well. I'll have a glass of wine while you eat."

Reese sat down at table and Christina served him his food. He didn't think he was that hungry, but as he began to eat, he felt his appetite take over him. He consumed everything she placed in front of him.

"John, what was your dream about?" she asked.

He stopped chewing and looked at her for a few seconds. She didn't say anything as he wondered what he would, or could, tell her. He finished chewing his food then picked up his glass of water and drank some. He placed the glass back down on the table.

"It's about fear," he said simply. "A year or so ago I was involved in a particular operation. I saw some things that made me question…I don't know, life itself maybe. But in particular, my life in terms of what I really want. It's hard to explain."

"Can you tell me about what you did that caused this?" she asked.

Reese looked at her and fought back what he wanted to do. He wanted to tell her everything about the Team of Darkness and the current op, but he couldn't. It was a selfish endeavor that would only get her in trouble if it ever leaked out that she knew anything about it.

"I wish I could—but I can't," he said.

"It has something to do with your work, doesn't it? But which work?" she asked.

"Huh?" he asked.

"Is it your military work or is it your myths and legend work? Or is it both?"

Reese didn't say anything.

She continued, "I read your book, remember? Of course I'm fascinated with certain aspects to begin with, you know that from class and what I said about my family being from the Balkans. However, you devoted a lot of time to one particular section; the one that centers upon vampires. You can see it in every word and line of text that you poured your heart into it. You brought up so many new points and hypothesis that it overwhelms everything else in the book."

She knows, he thought. "Was it that transparent?" he asked.

"To me it was. The vampire section and the new implications you brought out were remarkable." She paused. "Something must have happened to have you bring all these new points out. What was it, John? What did you find?"

"Christina, listen to me," he said still astounded about her depth of perception in his words and thoughts. "You'll have to just take my word that what I wrote about was all substantiated and I barely scratched the surface. But, I can't talk about that. It's not that I don't want to, but I can't. You and I could get in a lot of trouble if anyone ever found out. It's for your own safety as well as mine."

"Let me guess," she began, "if you tell me, you'll have to kill me, right?"

Reese felt his stomach drop.

"Christina, don't even joke about that!" he said and felt himself tremble with the thought of Samantha and Mr. Smith from the agency. He knew what they would do if he arbitrarily told someone else what he knew.

"John," she began, "I was only joking. Are you okay? You're pale as a ghost."

Reese forced himself to calm down.

"I'm okay," he said as he rose from the table and took his dishes to the sink. He scraped them off and rinsed them.

"John, it's all tied together isn't it? The dreams. What happened to you? The section of the book on vampires; you actually found some vampires didn't you?"

He turned toward her and looked at her. His expression became stern and looked as if it said that he would answer this one question and no more.

"Yes," he said and turned away from her.

★★★

Others do exist, she thought. Others like me.

His words had confirmed what she had suspected. The image she had seen in his dream was probably one of the other vampires. But where were they? What were they doing? She had to know. She felt as if she had discovered a long lost relative, one whom she thought was dead but was actually alive.

Her feelings about actually meeting other vampires were mixed. There was an excitement about it, yet a feeling of foreboding from the expectations she had. Did she really have expectations? She wasn't sure, yet she felt that she had to know all about them. And how would this effect the relationship that she and John had embarked upon?

When she'd killed General Stone, he had insinuated that there was bad blood between himself and the vampires as well as John. And the key question was how the vampires had been used: Were they assassins like her?

She needed answers but she would not push or influence John in any way to get them. There could be no taking if there was to be something between them—and there was, she thought. There was something between them. She would learn the information some other way.

CHAPTER THIRTY-FOUR

Reese turned toward her and looked at her. His expression became stern and looked as if it said that he would answer this one question and no more.

"Yes," he said and turned away from her.

Reese fell silent and he busied himself by fixing the coffee maker. He was in the midst of feelings and emotions that twisted inside of him like two ends of a rope forming a knot that made him ache. In a way, he felt relieved by telling someone about the existence of vampires, but wondered if his foolish admission had placed her at risk.

He turned to face Christina. "You must never acknowledge what I just told you. If you do, your life may be at risk."

"I can take care of myself," she began, the tone of her voice reflecting no fear. "It's okay, John."

"Listen to me," Reese began, "It's not okay. I don't even feel safe talking about this out loud. Even within my own home. This is very serious stuff I'm into. The people involved are very, very dangerous."

"I understand, John," she said and then added, "Probably more then you can imagine. I have had some, how would you say, odd experiences working for the government. But I'm still fascinated about the specifics of what you discovered."

"No." he said firmly. "No more."

"Alright, John," she said. She rose from the table and went to where he stood at the kitchen counter. Neither one said anything. The gurgling of the coffee pot became the only sound in the room as they stood in silence.

"Thanks for sharing," she said as she placed her hand on his cheek. "I know…I know it wasn't easy for you."

"It wasn't," he said. "And it's damn dangerous in more ways than one." He grasped her hands in his and squeezed them tightly. "Dangerous," he repeated. "Just telling you what I've told you puts you in harm's way. I shouldn't have said anything."

"It's a natural reaction, whether human or animal," she said. "Exposing our undersides, our vulnerable area, to attack leaves us wide open. I'm the same way. I've shut my inner thoughts away in my head for…a very long time. I didn't realize how painful and destructive that was."

"How so?" he asked.

"My past," she paused, surprised that she had so willingly set herself to talk about it.

"Yes?" he asked. "What about it?"

"When I was very young, I fell in love with a man in the village where I lived. He was many years older than me, yet I was captivated by him. The things he did to me, the way he talked to me, he made me feel so wonderful. He was married but he told me he didn't love his wife and that he was going to leave the village and take me with him. I'll save you all the sordid details, but suffice it to say that I believed him. When he was caught with me, I was accused of being a seductress and ostracized from my village. Everything I believed in was snatched away from me. My home, my parents, my friends were all turned against me. I became a very angry person. A very angry person and all I sought was revenge."

"What happened?"

"Basically I got even," she simply said.

"What did you do?" asked Reese.

"Not yet," she said, "I'm not ready to tell you all of it. In a way it's similar to your own predicament: If I tell you, it puts you in jeopardy. Later, we'll see."

An uncomfortable silence fell between the two for several seconds. Finally Reese spoke. "Well, it seems like we both have some interesting skeletons rattling around in our closets."

"You can say that again," she agreed.

"Seems like we both have some interesting skeletons rattling around in our closets," he repeated and quickly received a playful slap on the arm.

"Cute!" she said.

"I try," he said as he reached out to her, drawing her close and hugging her.

"We're so much alike in a way," he said.

"Yes, John," she agreed. "We both have our monsters that pursue us. But I think we can help each other rid ourselves of them if we try."

"You think?"

"Yes John, I do."

"Well I guess we'll have to see about that," he said.

A gentle beeping sound reminded Reese that the coffee was done.

"Want some?" he asked.

"No, I'm fine."

They separated from their embrace and Reese grabbed a cup from the cupboard. He poured himself a large cup of coffee and after adding his sugar and cream, his eyes meandered to the clock. It was almost 5AM.

"I'm going to have to go soon," he said. "About thirty minutes."

"Already? How time flies," then she added, "so many things to do and learn about us as individuals, and everything else around us."

"That's profound," he said. He meant it as a joke, but the words slipped him back to reality with the truth they contained.

As he sipped his coffee he remembered that Christina had mentioned something earlier when they had talked on the phone, something to tell him about his research, which he had forgotten completely about. He decided to bring it up seeing as how they could use some other line of conversation.

"Well, now that we have cleared the air a little, you said earlier you had something interesting to tell me about my research?"

"I do," she said, "the one area that I thought you were lacking in your book."

"Lacking? What?"

"Information about female vampires, she said, "I happen to know some things about them that you might be interested in."

"And how did you come up with this information?" he asked.

"Ah...I have my sources," she said in the jokingly stuffy manner of an old professor.

"Well, spill," he said.

"Why don't we save it for later," she said. "I want to have your full attention with this because once I start, you're going to want me to finish."

"Aw...teasing me ?"

"No, John, not teasing," she said and paused. "Well maybe. I have to keep you interested in me, don't I? A girl's gotta do what a girl's gotta do."

For a moment, Reese felt his body flush with the embarrassment of the thought that she was serious. "You don't think that all of this is about, you know, me getting material for my work?"

"Oh, John," she said, "if only you could see the look on your face—it's priceless. You look like the little kid who got caught with their hand in the cookie jar. I was just joking!"

She went up to him and placed her hands along the sides of his face. "I think we have a lot more in common than just history and myths. Don't you think?"

"Yeah. I really do think so," he agreed.

"Oh John," she said wistfully, "Trust me, okay? I'm here with you because I choose to be, okay?"

She kissed him before he could say anything in response. After a few seconds she backed away from him, "Now you go get changed for work. Go put on that uniform that drives the women crazy. I'm going home."

"Tomorrow?" he asked.

"You bet, just call me. You'll know where I'll be," she said as she walked to the front door. "And don't forget to get this fixed," she said.

"What?" Reese said from the bedroom. By the time he came back out she had already gone. What did she say—get it fixed? Get what fixed? His eyes fell upon the door and then the doorknob. He reached out and turned it and it felt weird. He tried the lock mechanism and it would not engage. The lock was broken.

"When the hell did that happen?"

CHAPTER THIRTY-FIVE

Christina hopped onto Interstate 64. She accelerated up to seventy miles per hour while she reminded herself that she needed to get one of those wrist watches with an alarm clock. During their intense evening together, she had forgotten about the time. If she wasn't careful, she was going to find herself stranded somewhere and not be able to get home before the sun came up. Fortunately at this hour and given the direction of her travel, traffic was virtually non-existent and she didn't expect any problems that would delay her arrival at the abandoned base in Driver.

Christina was actually quite proud of herself. She had shown restraint with John and yet she had opened up to him more than any other man she had ever known. But she knew that they still had a long way to go. She would have to tell him, at some point, the tiny detail of her being a vampire. She was one of the creatures that fascinated him and terrorized his sleep. Although they had joked about it, she wondered if he would be able to accept her as a person, rather than just a specimen to study. And there was the other vampire; her primary motive for seeking Reese out to begin with. She was both exhilarated and somewhat hesitant after learning that John feared them for some reason.

It wasn't until she merged onto Interstate 664, that she felt she was being followed. She watched the headlights of the half dozen cars that were around her, but was unable to tell anything by them. She thought that perhaps she was overreacting. This stretch of road was always busy, people heading toward the Monitor Merrimac tunnel and access to many different areas of Tidewater. Still there was that annoying feeling and she decided to take no chances and follow her usual driving pattern as she always did—just in case.

As she exited the Interstate in Chesapeake, she proceeded on Portsmouth Boulevard toward Driver. When she reached the town, she began her evasive trek through the dark and seldom traveled back roads. There was one set of headlights that seemed to be moving in her same direction, but she wasn't sure.

The streets in this area were so seldom used that anyone would know in a matter of minutes if they were being followed. The solitary set of headlights that were behind her faded into the blackness. After a few turns that led her back to the main road, she emerged alone. There she sat for a few minutes to be sure and after no one else came, she proceeded to the base.

There was a large chained gate for the fence that encircled the compound. To open it, Christina would have to stop and unlock it, enter and then relock the gate. Despite her vampire speed, it would still take several minutes to accomplish. During this time, the possibility of being spotted by people in the few homes outside of the gate was highly likely even at this early hour. Most of the residents of the local area were older and their sleeping hours erratic she had discovered. To avoid being seen, she parked in an adjoining ball field parking lot and walked through the woods to a section of fence that could not be seen from the road. Christina scaled the fence with no difficulty, and walked the rest of the way inside the base to her compound entrance.

It was her habit to watch the black sky begin its transformation to gray before she entered her underground world. It was the closest she ever came to seeing the sun before it rose above the horizon. Sometimes Jake would stand with her and they would talk about the years which had gone by.

This morning as she stopped outside of the entrance, she knew she couldn't stay long; the sky had already changed into the familiar shade of gray that she knew meant not much of the night was left.

"You're late," a voice she recognized said.

"Hello, Jake," she said. "I know. I lost track of time. What are you doing up?"

Jake moved out of the shadows, his form slightly bent and his steps somewhat unsure from the arthritis that plagued them. He held a coffee cup in his hand. It was hot and she could see the steam of the vapor rising from it.

He's getting old, she thought. He won't be around much longer.

"I couldn't sleep," he answered. "I was worried something had happened to you."

"You're so good to me, Jake," she said. "But you have to remember I'm a big girl and I can take care of myself."

"I know that," he said sharply. "But after you almost killed me the other night, I'm not so sure you're keeping your mind on what you're doing. I've not known you to get distracted so easily before, so it must be something important. Something more important than me or my life."

"Stop it, Jake," she pleaded. "I was distracted that night...something from the past. I've been discovering things about myself lately."

"So I see," he said. "I just wonder where I fit into all of this."

Christina didn't want to address this issue now. She wanted to sleep and think about it and maybe talk with him tomorrow. "Jake, it's late," she said. "The sun will be up and I need to go. Can we please talk about this later?"

Jake didn't answer as he stared off into the brightening horizon.

Christina turned from him and went down the entrance into the underground base. She went into her bedroom and sealed it for the day.

As she crawled into bed, her thoughts refused to turn away from what she did not want to face; the breaking off of her relationship with Jake. Over the years she had used men to get what she needed. She took their blood by promising them what they desired, immortality. Jake had not been an exception. She had created desire within his mind based upon the image of love that she had given him. But all that had now changed with her epiphany. But still, she had to deal with Jake. She had promised him immortality and a life with her – all the while without any intention of actually fulfilling that promise.

After so many years of their mutual relationship she could sense the feelings he had displayed moments before, as well as the inner frustrations he was feeling right at this moment. She had never been concerned with human emotions, considering them pitiful and pointless. But now not only did she feel his anger and sorrow, she understood them as well. It made it harder to turn away as she had always done before.

Although the choices were relatively few; she could just leave him, she could turn him, or she could kill him, Christina did not want to think about it any longer tonight. His overflow of emotions confused and cluttered her thinking. She decided to withdraw from their mutual connection. She would sleep and then address the issue tomorrow when she could think more clearly. She focused her thoughts on their connection and neatly severed it.

Soon she drifted off into restful sleep.

Chapter Thirty-Six

Jake remained standing where Christina had left him watching the sun as it peeked over the horizon. He could feel the warmth of its rays upon his face along with the moisture from the tears that rolled freely down his cheeks.

I have given her my entire life and now I've lost her. She no longer needs me -she's found someone else. Changes she says! She doesn't know what changes are. She doesn't know what she is talking about. I know changes. I feel them every day as I grow older and weaker. I dedicated my life to her. I sacrificed everything for her. I have done everything she has ever asked me to do. And now…it's over.

Jake took the last bit of coffee into his mouth and then violently threw the cup against one of the trees. The ceramic cup bounced off of the tree, but shattered when it hit the ground striking a rock. The adrenaline of his anger made him feel years younger, but it didn't stop the hurt.

He needed to get away for awhile both from here and from her. He walked quickly through the woods toward the parking area near the ball field where Christina had entered. Instead of scaling the fence, which he could not do at his age, he unlocked one of the smaller gates and walked through. As he entered into the parking lot clearing, he saw a man standing next to the car he and Christina shared.

Jake watched as the man removed a slim jim from under his jacket and used it to jimmy the door open. The man slipped inside the car and began examining the contents of the glove box and everything else that was lying on the seats. He obviously wasn't there to steal the car, Jake thought, or he would have done it by now. Besides, he just didn't look like the type that did that sort of thing. He was neatly dressed in a suit and appeared to be around forty or forty-five. But even given that, what the hell did he think he was doing?

Jake, his anger already at a high level from his earlier confrontation with Christina, thought about returning to the underground base to get her and let her deal with this problem, but he knew she couldn't come out in the daylight. Besides, he'd had had enough of her for one night and a confrontation with some asshole breaking into his car might be just what he needed right now. He reached into his back pocket and felt the reassuring weight of the knife he had carried for more years then he cared to remember. He closed the distance between himself and the intruder as quickly as his legs would allow him. When he was alongside the car he confronted the man, keeping one hand on that pocket that contained his knife.

"What the hell do you think you are doing?" asked Jake, his voice loud and threatening.

The man, surprised by Jake's appearance, nevertheless reacted calmly by reaching for something under his coat. "I'm getting my identification," the man said. "Don't do anything rash, okay?"

"You make sure you only have an ID in your hand. I have a gun," Jake lied, "and how about you back slowly out of the car."

With his back still to Jake, the man produced a large black wallet and handed it to him. "I'm Special Agent Barrett, FBI," he said as he got out of the vehicle, "Is this your car?"

"Yeah, it is. You mind telling me what you're doing inside of it?" Jake took the man's wallet but still had not opened it. He kept his eyes fixed upon the man that stood only a few feet away from him. He was a tall man, probably about six foot or so and went about hundred and eighty pounds. He had a fair complexion which contrasted with his dark black hair flecked with gray strands. His face was pot marked and scarred as if he had been in some kind of accident. But it was his eyes that gave Jake an uneasy feeling; they were the kind Jake despised, small and beady as if the eye fairy hadn't finished them. "What did you say your name was?" asked Jake.

"Agent Barrett," he replied quickly and then asked, "Did you drive this vehicle this evening."

"No. I did not drive the vehicle," Jake said.

"Not at all?" the agent pushed.

"That's right," replied Jake.

"Well, the hood is quite warm for a car that has been sitting all night," the agent said.

"I…ah…I just arrived here, so of course it's going to warm," Jake said. "You asked me about last night. The car sat at my house where I live. I drove it to come here this morning and walk. You know, exercise?"

"You come here to walk," the agent said, not in the form of a question, but as a doubtful assertion. "Where do you walk? And who do you walk with?"

"I walk here," Jake said and indicated the ball field area. "I come here alone. You don't see anyone else, do you?"

"Not at the moment."

"What's this all about?" Jake asked trying to hide his nervousness. He was walking a fine tightrope between lies and the truth and this man was obviously trying to get him to slip up and reveal something. He wondered if this agent had followed Christina here. If so, he was walking deeper into a pile of shit.

"I'm conducting an investigation that I am not at liberty to discuss at the moment. So you're telling me you did not drive this car tonight? Is that correct sir? What did you say your name was?"

"My name is the same one as on the registration you just looked at a few minutes ago. Now, if you don't mind, I have to go to work, Agent...." Jake said as he opened the wallet to look at the identification.

Expecting to see the FBI logo and identification, he was surprised to find that the wallet contained nothing at all. As Jake raised his eyes to look back at the agent, he felt the cold steel of the gun barrel resting on the back of his head.

Shit! Jake thought. *I should have walked away from this one.*

"Now," the man who Jake felt pretty confident was probably not an FBI agent began, "I am going to ask you a few questions. But before I do, I want you to know that I am very tired as well as hungry. The sooner you tell me the truth, the sooner you can go about your business and me about mine. If you bullshit me, I will shoot you right here and now and then I will go and eat a hearty breakfast without any remorse or loss of appetite. Are WE clear?"

"You can't talk..."

Jake's head was shoved into the roof of the car. He saw a momentary flash of light fill his vision as well as feeling a bolt of pain.

"I will ask the questions," the man said. "Are we clear on that?"

"Yeah I get your drift," Jake said as his vision slowly cleared.

"Good. Now, let's start this conversation again. You didn't drive the vehicle did you?"

"Well..."

The man jabbed the barrel into the side of Jake's skull and the older man felt searing pain rip through his head.

"Christ!" Jake yelled.

"I want direct answers," the man said. "Was I not clear on that?"

"Alright! Alright," Jake said. The throbbing in his head pounded unmercifully.

"You did not drive this vehicle tonight did you?" the man repeated.

"No," answered Jake.

"Who did?"

"I don't know," Jake answered.

The next sound Jake heard was the pistol cocking. It was very loud and distinct and there was no mistaking it for anything else.

"I don't have the patience for this," the man said. "If you do not answer correctly, that sound of the pistol being cocked will be the last sound you ever hear. Now, who drove the car?" the man asked again.

"A woman," Jake said.

Jake realized that whoever this guy was had probably followed Christina here. There was no sake in lying about that anymore. What he had to do was come up with a convincing story that he would believe right now.

"And where is this woman?" asked the man.

"I don't know," Jake lied trying to sound convincing. "We have an arrangement. She uses my car at night and she pays me cash for no questions. She doesn't have a driver's license or something. I'm just trying to make some money. I've got to retire soon and I need the cash. I know it's illegal, me not paying taxes or claiming it as income."

"And she leaves the car here for you to retrieve in the morning?"

"Yes," Jake said.

"Then where's the money?" he asked.

"She pays at the beginning of each month," said Jake.

"And where does she live?"

"I don't know for sure, somewhere around here," Jake said as he indicated the sparse neighborhood. "That's all I know," Jake pleaded trying to sound as if he had told him everything he knew. "Like I said, I need the money so I can retire. I know it's wrong but I made some mistakes in my life from gambling. I owe people money so I saw a quick and easy way to make some cash."

There was a deathly silence as Jake waited for the next question from the man. Finally, Jake felt the pressure of the gun barrel on the side of his head ease off as it was removed. In the next second, Jake felt himself breathe a little easier. He was glad he had been convincing enough and had made it.

"Aaaaahhh," Jake screamed as the man grasped a handful of his hair and yanked his head back sharply followed by the icy cold sharpness of the knife at his throat followed by the swift motion of it digging in and slicing across his flesh.

The bright light from the rising sun quickly turned to gray and then to black as Jake slumped to the ground and quickly bled to death.

CHAPTER THIRTY-SEVEN

The man wiped his knife off on the back of Jake's clothing. He moved it back and forth as if he was sharpening the blade on a stone. He would stop and look at it for a few moments then go back again. Finally the blade received his look of approval.

He folded and placed it in his inside jacket pocket. Then he removed a cell phone from his pocket and placed a call.

"Smith here, go ahead," a voice answered.

"The situation has become interesting," the man said.

"Oh how I love a mystery," Smith answered, the humor clearly evident in his voice. "So enlighten me, what exactly is interesting about it?"

"It would appear that the woman that has been visiting Reese is involved somehow in all of this."

"Why do you say that?" asked Smith.

"She's hiding her location quite adeptly—she obviously does not want to be found. She had an associate that was covering for her."

"Really—that is interesting. What's the location?"

"Suffolk, an area called Driver, near an abandoned military base."

"And Reese? Is he a player or a tool?"

"I'm not sure if he is aware of her actions or not. I have some other things to check out yet, but you may want to make plans to join me this evening. I think it may prove enlightening."

"Yes, I shall," Smith said, "But first, I need your assistance at a hotel here in Ocean View, a cleanup operation, one body."

"That makes two," the man said. "I have one to dispose of as well."

"I'll text message the address and details. I'm heading over to the base. If you need me before this evening, call me. Have a great day," Smith said and hung up.

The man disconnected the call and placed the phone back into his pocket. He would have to move quickly now if he didn't want his breakfast to turn into lunch with the added burden of another pickup. Apparently his boss had some entertainment last night. But he had expected as much because Mr. Smith was a busy man and when he got time to play—play he did. He wondered if it had been a man or woman this time.

Time will tell. Lay your bets gentlemen.

He looked down at the body that lay on the gravel parking lot. His facial expression took on a look of disappointment with even a hint of resentment.

"You should have planned better—for your retirement," he said as he pointed his index finger at Jake's still body. Then he laughed, "You're so full of shit. You were pretty good my deceased friend. I almost believed the part about you needing money. You...you're good you, you're very good," he continued on imitating Robert De Niro's voice and tone from a scene he remembered from a movie. De Niro had been an idol to him since the movie Taxi Driver where he played a psychotic in New York; killing low life scum and trying to make sense of it all.

He searched through Jake's clothing finding a wallet and a knife in his back pocket. He placed the wallet in his own pocket and looked at the knife.

"This is rather nice," he said as he moved the blade in and out of the sheath. "Yes, very nice." He pocketed the knife and then looked at his watch.

"My, my, it's getting late, places to go and things to do," he said.

The man bent down and grabbed Jake's body by the lapels of his jacket and dragged the body into the woods. When he found a suitable place off the main path, he dumped the body and covered it with debris. It could wait for a bit.

As he finished this task, he thought about how he wanted to have a huge breakfast. Eggs, toast, hash browns, pancakes...the whole works. After all, he'd earned it. He walked back to his own car and drove off in the direction where he remembered seeing an International House of Pancakes just off of Main Street in Suffolk.

He really loved IHOP's pancakes.

CHAPTER THIRTY-EIGHT

From his house, Reese arrived on the base in less than thirty minutes. The mystery of the broken lock had already been filed away under 'a trip to Lowes to get a new door knob'.

Upon entering the secure compound, he swung by to see if Commander Pattoon had come up with anything. He found him half asleep sitting in a high back chair; apparently he had spent the night in the office keeping tabs on the progress of the operation.

"Anything?" Reese asked loudly, with a slight hint of pleasure in his voice at waking the man given the phone call Pattoon had pulled on him the previous night.

"Er…no…nothing. The surveillance continues. We have eliminated maybe half of the possible places already."

"Well we thought it might be a long shot," Reese said. "Is there any other unusual data to look at?"

"Not beyond what was in yesterday's folder," said Pattoon.

Pattoon's statement reminded Reese he had yet to look through the folder's contents.

"Which reminds me," Pattoon continued, "there was some extra data in there that didn't belong. One of the techs dropped in an article that didn't meet all the search criteria; it was a day or so too early to have been related."

"Okay," Reese said, "I'll make sure I remove it."

Reese left the control center and walked toward the office he was using. "Interesting night, Commander?" a voice from behind him said.

Reese knew the voice without turning to see who it was; it was his good friend Mr. Smith. "Fine, and yours?" asked Reese as he slowly turned to face the man.

"I had a nice relaxing evening," Smith said in a voice that was overly happy. "I had a chance to work out some frustration. It's amazing the clarity of mind one can have when it is freed from obstructions. No clutter of things to dwell on. It's like the weather on the day after a hurricane; everything is so clear because it was all swept away. You should try it sometime."

"Try what?" Reese asked. "Have a hurricane?"

"Funny. You're a funny man Commander. Let me break it down for you. I was referring to working out your frustrations. It might work wonders for you and help you with those dreams you keep having."

Reese felt immediate anger well up inside of him. He had suspected that they might be keeping an eye on him. However, this overt display was too much to swallow. He had to calm himself before he said or did anything he might regret.

"Maybe it's the company you've been keeping," Smith continued. "You might want to be more careful about who you choose to spend your time with."

"Okay asshole," said Reese. "That's enough! So you're keeping an eye on me; point made. Must be a cheap thrill for you huh?"

"You know," Smith said, "I like a cheap thrill every once in a while. Kind of gets the old motor running at high speed."

"I bet you do. Yes sir. The more cheap and perverted the better you like them."

"Well enough about our personal lifestyles," Smith began obviously moving on. "Maybe you and I can get together this evening? What do you say?"

"I'm not your type. I like women," Reese said and walked away. He got three steps down the corridor and turned back. Mr. Smith was still standing there watching him. Reese smiled and then gave him the finger...with both hands.

Laughing, he quickly stepped into the office and closed the door behind him in the event that Mr. Smith wanted to continue the conversation—although he didn't think so.

Although he was feeling that he had told Smith off in a colorful manner, the fact that the spooks knew he was having nightmares confirmed the suspicion that his house was not only under surveillance, but probably bugged as well. This meant that Smith was probably aware of his evening with Christina and that sent a chill down John's spine. They'd had a conversation about the existence of vampires. Shit, he cursed. He would have to warn her about this.

However, for the moment, there was nothing he could do about it. Until he was sure his house was clear of surveillance, he would insist that she meet him somewhere else. The thought that she might already have fallen under Smith's eye struck Reese. He would have to talk about that tonight when they got together. For the moment, there was nothing else he could do about it.

He turned his attention to the folder on his desk. He needed to delve into this operation so that one way or the other it could be resolved and he could return his life to some form of normalcy. With Christina, that actually meant something good and he liked the feeling that came with the thought.

Reese opened the folder and began to peruse the documents. The headline of a newspaper article from the Virginian Pilot caught his attention. "Teenagers and Police Officer Disappear in Suffolk." Reese checked the date. It was the day before the escape of the two girls. This must be the article that Pattoon had referred to earlier, but he was right, this was exactly what he would have looked for if it had occurred after the escape rather than before.

Something drew Reese to the article and he scanned it anyway. As he read, he learned that the two teens had cut school and never returned home that night. The parents called the police who began an investigation the following day. A police officer had been assigned as the preliminary investigation. Officer Sam Blackwater began by questioning friends and classmates at the high school the teens attended to try and ascertain what had happened or where they might have gone. After questioning some of the students, the police officer disappeared later that same day.

"Christ sakes," Reese murmured.

Attempts to recreate the steps of the officer consisted of following up on places the teens may have gone to. One of the places that came up was the abandoned military base in Driver, Virginia, which was only a few hundred yards away from the school the teens attended on Portsmouth Boulevard.

Officer Blackwater, deciding to follow up on the lead contacted the city for assistance to gain access to the base. A Public Works employee, Jake Sommers, was sent by the city to assist the officer with entry into the base as well as to escort him wherever he chose to go. Jake Sommers testified that the officer arrived early in the morning and he assisted the officer in a search of several of the buildings. Hours later, he escorted the officer off of the base. Mr. Sommers noted that Officer Blackwater had not mentioned where he was going; however he stated that the officer did receive a phone call and seemed perturbed about something.

Officer Blackwater did not report in later that day and all attempts to communicate with him failed. The patrol car he was driving, which had not been equipped with any tracking device due to a city budget shortfall, was also missing. The Internal Affairs Division of the Suffolk Police Department was investigating the case with the assistance of the FBI.

Reese placed the article down in front of him but did not remove his eyes from the article. There was something about this event that just felt like it was related somehow. Even if it had not been the young vampires, it could have been Dimitri and his crew. But that seemed unlikely because it attracted too much attention. Dimitri and his team were smarter than that, much smarter. Still…

Reese picked up the phone and dialed.

"Commander Pattoon," the voice answered.

"Reese here. This event in the folder, the one that is outside of our search parameter?"

"Yeah. What about it? If you're going to tell me I messed up, you're too late. Been there done that. Go get your jollies somewhere else."

"As much as I would like to," Reese said meaning what he said, "that's not what I had I mind. I want you to see if there is any more information on it."

"Why?" asked Pattoon sounding obviously annoyed. "Don't waste my time pulling my string."

"Because I'm interested in what happened," said Reese.

"But it's outside the time frame, you said so yourself."

"I know that. But that doesn't mean it's not involved with what's going on. Just see what you can come up with."

"All right, I'll see what I can get," Pattoon said and then hung up.

Reese replaced the receiver into its cradle. "Asshole."

He flipped through the folder and saw nothing else that drew his attention. Next, he scanned the list of properties that were being watched. He was amused that most of the properties under surveillance were either in rural areas of Suffolk or Chesapeake, with a scattering of a few of the older areas of Norfolk. His own home, in Norfolk, was less than thirty minutes away from many of the properties. The area had also been the hunting ground for Dimitri and his team when they had first escaped.

Their hunting ground. Reese had turned them loose because he believed that their use as killers was wrong. Yet his own act, his releasing them from their forced servitude, had turned them loose on society where they had preyed upon the populace for some period of time. But obviously that had all changed: There were no more reports of crime rates mysteriously dropping. So where had they gone? Or were they still here but using another food source? Had this event with the teenagers and the police officer been a mistake on their part? Or had it been something else? Maybe Dimitri was making a statement? Perhaps he wanted to get Reese's attention?

Where are you going with this, John? You have two vampires you are trying to find and now you want to find the rest of them as well? You really want to get that deluxe suite in Fort Leavenworth, don't you?

It was too late. The wild hair, so to speak, had lodged itself firmly in Reese's butt. He would not be able to leave it alone now. At a loss on how he would search for Dimitri, he decided to go with the least likely but most obvious way of all—at least it would satisfy part this crazy urge for the moment. Reese picked up the phone and dialed Pattoon's number again.

"Commander Pattoon," the voice answered.

"I need a real estate title search on the name Bicannoff, Dimitri."

"Spell it."

"Last name B-i-c-a-n-n-o-f-f, first name D-i-m-i-t-r-i."

"Got it. Is there anything else?"

"Not at the moment," Reese said.

"Good," Pattoon said and then added, "So what's the deal? You and Smith must have had a good night last night," Pattoon added sarcastically.

"How so?" asked Reese.

"You're both driving me nuts today with all your fucking requests."

"Really? And why is that?" Reese asked although he didn't care about Pattoon's problems, "What's he looking for?"

"He wanted background on some abandoned Navy base in Driver out in Suffolk."

That was where the teenagers and police officer story had been centered, Reese thought.

"What sent him in that direction?" Reese asked.

"I guess the article in the paper," Pattoon said.

"Yeah, I guess so," Reese agreed and found it amusing that Smith had gone in the same direction that he had. Why? Smith didn't know what he did. "Patton, whatever you find, you might as well shoot me the information as well."

"Sure…is there anything else you would like? Breakfast? Perhaps some coffee?"

Reese was getting sick of this man's attitude and sarcasm. "No that's okay, I've already eaten. How about just getting what I asked you for. That is if you are capable of doing something so simple as following orders."

Reese hung up the phone before Pattoon could respond.

Apparently Mr. Smith was pursuing a similar avenue of investigation —or was Pattoon playing both sides of the fence? Probably a combination of both, he thought. It may have been a mistake having him run a check of Dimitri's name then. But it was worth the risk, if anyone could help him find the two girls, it would be Dimitri, as long as he found them first and if Dimitri would be willing.

Reese's phone rang.

"Yes."

"Reese, General Morris here."

"Yes sir."

"We have a possible on one of the surveillance houses. We're going to send a team in to check it out. I want you in command center to monitor and advise."

"Location of the house?" asked Reese.

"Norfolk."

"On my way," Reese said.

CHAPTER THIRTY-NINE

As Reese entered into main control center of the compound, he immediately noticed that several television monitors that had been previously blank now displayed several images of the same house. Commander Pattoon had relinquished his seat to another Navy SEAL Commander which Reese recognized as John Ritter. Reese had trained Ritter and his men on the signs and possible indications of the vampire holdout. As per military protocol, Ritter assumed command of the control center during operational situations and Reese was sure this pissed off Pattoon. The fact that Pattoon was off stewing somewhere at such a pivotal moment, made Reese smile.

"So, what's the information on the house?" Reese asked trying to keep the joviality out of his voice.

Commander Ritter looked up and acknowledged Reese's presence, "Hey Reese, ready to party?"

"Only if I get to have the most fun," Reese answered.

"Of course," Ritter answered. "Girls, booze, food and vampires—it doesn't get much better than that."

The door opened and General Morris walked in. Everyone began to rise from their seats. "As you were. What do we have Ritter?"

"The house has been under surveillance for almost forty-eight hours. The only movement to and from has been at night. Three possible suspects depart at dusk and return just prior to dawn. The home recently sold a couple of weeks ago. The neighbors have no idea who has moved into the place and there has been no contact with the new residents. There is another part that is really interesting." Ritter had a sly grin from ear to ear.

"What?" asked Reese, "Come on?"

"The yard has an underground bomb shelter that is accessible from the house."

"A bomb shelter?" asked Reese.

"Yeah. Apparently there are several homes in these older neighborhoods of Norfolk that were built around the height of the cold war and the nuclear bomb scare; living this close to where the Atlantic Fleet is stationed, well you can understand the concern."

"I guess it does make sense," agreed Reese.

Ritter continued, "We had some men dress up as solicitors and go up to the house during the day when we knew someone was there and knock and ring the doorbell. Whoever is inside refuses to answer. On a cursory glance, we took a look in the backyard; we found two dog carcasses which appeared to have been killed recently.

"Sounds promising," General Morris said. "What do you think, Reese?"

"The only thing lacking is any evidence of the two girls. However, that doesn't mean that whoever has them isn't going out to get them their food. They might be bringing back the dogs for them to feed on."

"Can they…do that?" asked Morris, "I mean use the blood from dogs?"

"Yes sir. In a pinch, anything will do as long as it's alive. I've read in some myths where they survived on rats pretty well, especially during long sea voyages."

"Your recommendation on how to proceed?" asked Morris.

Reese checked the time on the standard large white faced clock that hung on the wall. It was 10AM.

"Time is on our side for the moment," Reese began, "if we go in before dusk, the girls will be asleep. But if there are four or five others there, some of them might be awake on guard duty. If they detect us coming in they might kill them. If we wait until they leave, it would lessen the amount of people we have to deal with and increase the odds of getting the girls out alive. However, if the girls get vicious, that could ramp up the risk as well. So the question comes down to, who do we want to deal with, the mortals or the vampires?"

"If it was you going in there," Ritter said with a sly smile on his face, "which would you rather face?"

Without hesitation Reese answered, "The mortals."

"I agree," said Ritter.

Morris turned to Ritter, "How soon can you be ready to go in?

"About two hours or so. That gives us time enough to get the backup team on station and have the local residents evacuated."

"Do it then," said Morris to Ritter before turning to Reese. "Go with them. You have my authority to cancel the op if it looks like it's not going to work. Is that understood?"

"Yes sir," Reese said as he felt the weight of the authority settle upon his stomach. It reminded him of the day General Stone gave him the same authority to capture Dimitri and his associates. These similarities between the two operations were becoming stronger the further into the operation he went and Reese thought how much he hated it.

It never ends.

CHAPTER FORTY

At noon, the evacuation of the neighborhood had been accomplished. The scenario given to the press was that there was a dangerous gas leak and for the safety of all residents; they were being evacuated to a local school to wait until the leak had been located and repaired.

Norfolk police went door to door ensuring that the homes were empty including the house in question, but nobody answered the door. Police cars blocked off the entrances to the area allowing no one to enter. At 12:45PM, four large cargo trucks, with the logo of the gas company stenciled on their sides, entered the neighborhood to commence the search for the leak. However, the cargo trucks carried no personnel from the gas company. Instead each van contained a six man SEAL team fully loaded and ready to go.

By 1:00 PM they were ready. One van was parked in front of the house; one was parked on the adjoining street which allowed access to the rear of the house by going through the yard of the house on the back side of the street. The third and fourth trucks were parked at the intersection of the adjoining street which gave a clear view of the side of the house.

The plan was relatively simple. One team would cover the rear, one would cover the front and sides, and one team would enter the house. The fourth team consisted of the command and control for the operation. The team that entered the house would be the one facing immediate danger if their plan failed.

Given the scenario, Commander Ritter had decided that the use of tear gas would be the optimum way to go. It wouldn't harm the vampires, which hopefully would be asleep anyway, but it would immobilize the captors with minimum risk to the SEAL team members. With no way out, the people inside would succumb to the gas and not kill the vampires, unless that is if they had gas masks which was predicted as not likely. If they did, the 'search' aspect of the mission would be over and the 'destroy' would begin.

Reese and Ritter relocated to the command center cargo truck at the intersection. Lieutenant Colonel Barkley had joined them in the event his medical expertise was required. Also inside this truck was a six man team. This vehicle would serve as the onsite command and control center. They had direct connections with each other van, the platoon leader of each six man team, and the control center back at the amphibious base.

"Well we're as ready as we are ever going to be," said Ritter.

"I wish there was another way into the shelter," Reese said. "If it goes bad, we're stuck."

"True," agreed Ritter, "however, so are they."

"I suppose," Reese agreed hesitantly.

"Last chance," Ritter said, "speak now or forever hold your peace. What's it going to be Reese? Go or no go?"

For what seemed like a long time, Reese held his breath and said nothing. He could think this scenario to death but he knew it would not change anything. As much as he didn't agree with capturing the girls and placing them back into the hands of Samantha and the Agency, he didn't have much of a choice. All he could do was hope for some kind of lucky break. He looked at Barkley who raised his eyebrows in a questioning manner and shrug of shoulders.

Finally he turned to Ritter and said, "Go."

Ritter keyed his headset and said, "All teams, this is C & C, standby to execute on my mark."

CHAPTER FORTY-ONE

"Mark," said Ritter.

All eyes turned toward the monitors. The team that was in the van covering the rear of the house on the adjoining street moved first. They exited their van quickly wearing urban camouflage, designed for missions inside of city areas. They were armed with M16 rifles and 9MM pistols. Their mission was twofold: They were to locate the air vent for the shelter and then to remain on the rear of the property in the event there was another means of escape to which they would respond if needed.

One man on the team used a metal detector to sweep the ground in order to locate the air vent. Within minutes he had found and uncovered it. Quietly he was assisted by the other men in removing the top exposing a pipe that was approximately six inches in diameter. When it was removed, the platoon commander keyed his headset.

"Team One, ready for phase two."

"Copy Team One," Ritter said. "Team Two, go."

Men exited from the second van that had been parked in the front area of the house. They took up positions around the house forming a perimeter. Their mission was to back up the main team that would enter the house, as well as cover in the event that the suspects tried to escape.

"Team Two in position," the voice sounded from one of the speakers inside the control van.

"Copy Team Two," Ritter acknowledged. "Team One, drop the gas."

"Team One copy. Dropping gas."

The men poised over the air pipe began pulling pins on tear gas grenades and dropping them down the pipe. When they had dropped the sixth one, they capped the pipe with a non-venting cover which would prevent any further air exchange.

"Gas dropped," the platoon commander transmitted.

"Copy Team One," Ritter said. He looked toward the six man group in his truck. They had donned their gas masks and were ready to go. Ritter's eyes made contact with the platoon commander. "Team Three, go!"

The back of the truck opened and the last team of six men exited and sprinted toward the front door of the home. Seeing the launch of Team Three, two men from Team Two emerged from their positions with a battering ram and approached the door. As Team Three was about to reach them, they used the battering ram to smash the door in. By the time the point man of Team Three reached the door, it was a gaping hole.

"Going in," the point man said.

"Copy," Ritter said as he flipped to another screen in the truck that showed the floor plan of the house. "The entrance to the shelter is off of the main bedroom. Go straight down the corridor in front of you."

"Copy," the point man responded.

On another monitor, the view from the point man's transmitter showed the interior of the house as he proceeded through. He passed rooms that joined into the main corridor but saw no one in them. He reached the main bedroom without encountering anyone.

"Access to the shelter is through the closet," Ritter said.

"Copy."

The view on the monitor showed the point man approach the closet. He opened the door and was greeted by a wall of smoke that was escaping around the trap door that led to the shelter.

"Confirm gas."

"Roger. Hold position."

"Holding position."

The rest of Team Three joined the point man. They had checked out all of the other rooms on the main floor just in case.

"Team Three ready."

"Pull the door."

The trap door was raised by one man as the rest of the team covered the opening. Bilious smoke emerged from the opening and drifted into the house.

"This is where it gets tricky," Ritter said to Reese and Barkley. He keyed his headset, "Proceed down."

The point man of Team Three started down the stairs. The view from his camera was like looking at a blank piece of paper due to all the smoke which made it impossible to make out any detail.

"No see," the point man said, indicating his blindness.

"Copy. Hold position," said Ritter.

The effectiveness of tear gas in a small and enclosed area such as this would only take a minute or less to have the desired effect on the inhabitants. After three minutes, Team Three set up an exhaust fan at the top of the steps and turned it on. The fan created a huge pull on the air in the shelter and within fifteen seconds the point man, as well as Ritter back in the truck, had a clear view. Neither one was prepared for what he saw.

The room contained nothing more then a sleeping and eating space. In the center of the room was a table. Around the table sat four people. One couldn't tell their gender because each person wore similar jumpsuits or coveralls, as well as a gas mask. They calmly sat around the table with their hands in an upraised position indicating their surrender.

"C & C," said the point man, "do you see this shit? Advise."

Chapter Forty-Two

"Oh…fuck me!" Ritter said covering his headset. "How the hell…" his voice drifted off.

"Son of a bitch," Reese began.

Ritter cut him off. "Well, do you see anything that might indicate they are or ever were here?" he asked Reese.

Reese scanned the monitors again looking for any outward signs that the girls were here, he didn't see any. There would not be any need for them to be wearing a gas mask because it would not harm them.

"No, I don't think so. But…what the hell is going on?" Reese said. "They look as if they were expecting us? They have gas masks? No resistance? It's weird."

"It sure does, but we aren't going to get any answers until we talk to whoever these people are," Ritter said. He then spoke into his headset. "Secure the area and bring them out of there. Let's find out what the hell is going on."

The rest of Team Three entered the space and prepared to secure the four people at the table by tying their hands together.

"Hold on," Reese said, "let's not take any chances, just in case they might be hiding the vampires by dressing them up. Have the sprayer hit them anyway. We have to be sure."

"Team Three," Ritter said, "hit them with a blast from the sprayer."

"Copy."

One of the men in the team moved forward with the backpack sprayer which every team possessed in the event they made contact with the vampires. Each sprayer contained the deadly vampire elixir. The man with the backpack unit moved forward and sprayed a stream of solution on each person.

Reese, Ritter, and Barkley stared intently at the monitor waiting to see if there was any reaction to the solution. Nothing happened.

"So they aren't hiding them," Reese said. "Let's get them out of there and see what the hell is going on." He turned away from the monitor and toward Ritter and Barkley and said, "I don't know about you, but I am getting a feeling we walked right into something that we were supposed to."

"Yeah…" Ritter agreed. "It's as if someone expected us to come looking."

"Yeah...someone," Reese murmured, "someone." He wasn't sure if he should be happy about this or not. He was glad that they weren't there but the detail to which someone had gone to fake this was highly suspicious and very astute.

"Bring them all out," Ritter said into the headset, "search the entire area for anything that looks suspicious. Anything. And get their damn masks off."

"Shall we go meet our guests?" Ritter said to Reese.

"Sure, why not," agreed Reese. "After you," Reese said to Ritter indicating with his hands the direction to go. Turning to Barkley he said, "Joining us?"

"I wouldn't miss this for the world," Barkley said.

They left the van and entered the living room of the house. There four men sat with their legs crossed on the hardwood floor alongside one wall. Their masks had been removed revealing that two of the men were African American and the other two were Caucasian. They sat placidly on the floor staring at their armed captors with a look that surprised Reese. They appeared neither scared nor surprised at what had just happened. Reese studied the look on their faces and came to the conclusion that they looked as if they had been waiting for something and were glad that it was finally over.

He continued his examination. The first thought that Reese had was that they were just average looking regular guys that you would meet on the street. But as he learned very well lately, looks could be deceiving. Barkley tapped Reese on the shoulder and said, "I'll be over here if you need anything." He smiled and gave Reese a look that Reese interpreted as all yours—have fun.

"Thanks," Reese said.

"Good afternoon, Gentlemen," Ritter began, "It's so nice to meet you all but if you wouldn't mind, my associates and I would love to know what the hell you are doing here."

"Nothing," one of the Caucasian men said as if he had been anticipating the question. His voice was very calm and level. "We aren't breaking any laws whatsoever."

"So do you always do your partying in a bomb shelter?" Reese asked in a sarcastic tone.

"It's not illegal," the man responded and then added, "do you always bash into somebody's house, drop tear gas on them and then tie them up like animals?"

Reese smiled at the response although inside he didn't like this guy's rehearsed ambivalence about the situation. This is beginning to smell more and more like a set-up, he thought.

"Look," Ritter began, "If you ever want to have a social life again, let's start from the beginning and see if we can get this thing cleared up."

"Question number one," Reese began, "who are you and what are you doing here?"

"I'm Sam," the same man answered. "This is Carl, Leon, and Lester," he said going down the row in the order in which they were sitting. "We're watching the place for someone."

"You have any proof of that?" Ritter asked.

"Yes sir we do," said Sam confidently. "There's a folder down in the shelter with all the paperwork in it including a letter that appoints us to be here."

Ritter indicated for one of his men to go and retrieve the folder.

"Why are you watching the place?" Reese asked.

"Because that's what we're getting paid to do," he said as if the answer had been obvious.

"Paid? What do you mean?"

"It's our job, or was, until you all busted in. We're homeless. Normally we hang out at the mission down off of Granby Street while we wait to get any day work. So one night we were just hanging out in the park across from Macarthur Mall, and this guy approached us and asked if we wanted some work. We thought he was joking, you know being easy money and all and having a safe and clean place to live and any of the food in the house that we wanted, but he cleared it with the mission supervisor so we of course we said yes."

"And your instructions included to have gas masks and to sit in the shelter?" Reese asked.

"Well not exactly," said Sam. "The gas masks were just sitting on a shelf right there in the open. He didn't even mention them. We figured he just like to collect weird stuff like that or something. So when we saw the gas coming in, well it was just a natural reaction to grab them and put them on."

"You didn't think it was odd?"

"What?"

"The fact that there were gas masks sitting on the shelf?"

"Odd? No man, we didn't think it was odd," Sam said and laughed. Most of his compatriots joined in.

"What's so funny?" asked Ritter.

"We've all been through some shit in our lives and we aren't exactly all model citizens ourselves," he said for which he received another round of small laughs from each man. "So we didn't really think about the masks until the gas started coming in and it seemed the logical thing to do."

"So tell me, what did your mysterious benefactor look like?" asked Ritter.

"He was a white guy. Large build, maybe six feet in height and two hundred pounds. He had dark hair, deep set eyes and his skin was tan."

"Was there anything odd about him?" asked Reese.

"Well, he had an accent of some kind, sounded like a foreigner who's been here for a while. You know, he spoke English fine, but he said many words with a different emphasis. I'm not a world traveler or anything, but my guess is European."

Reese remembered the way Dimitri used to talk. That description could have fit him as well as thousands of other people. Yeah it was a long shot, but it was still a possibility.

"Could you recognize him? Or if you worked with an artist could you describe him well enough?" asked Ritter.

"I guess. I don't remember real well anymore, but maybe between all of us we could come up with something."

It didn't sound promising to Reese.

"What was the reason for you to watch the house?" Reese asked. "What did he tell you?"

"He said he had just bought the place and didn't know the neighborhood very well and didn't feel comfortable leaving it empty for a couple of weeks. And then you guys bust into the place so I guess he was right about the people in this neighborhood."

"Why didn't you answer the door when we knocked and rang the bell?"

"We're just watching the place, we don't have time for the Avon lady," Sam said again getting laughter from his friends. "And he was quite specific in that we were not to answer it."

"Why were you staying in the shelter?" asked Reese.

"Do you see any furniture anywhere else?" Sam said plainly. "He said that was it so we stayed there."

"What other instructions did he give you?" asked Ritter this time.

"We were told to arrive and depart at the same times every day, so that we were here most of the daylight hours."

"Don't most break-ins occur during the night? Didn't you find that kind of strange?" asked Reese.

"Look, as I said, the man was paying so if he wanted the house watched during the day, that's what we did. Jesus! Are you thick or what?"

Maybe," Reese agreed, "maybe we are because we obviously missed something."

"You are going to fix that door aren't you?" Sam asked.

"What?" asked Reese.

"The door. You busted in the damn thing."

"We'll see Sam," said Reese.

Sam continued, "Well it appears to me that you guys busted in here for no good reason. By the way, do you have a search warrant? And what the hell is this smelly shit you sprayed on us?"

"It is just something that identifies the use of certain chemicals," Reese said quickly ignoring the aspect of the search warrant question. "It's harmless."

"It may be harmless, but the shit stinks," Sam added again. "I don't know if I should believe you. This stuff smells bad enough to make you sterile, might be a lawsuit in there somewhere."

His friends looked toward Sam as if he had just mentioned something that they would all be interested in: Money.

"You're watching too much television," Ritter offered. "We'll take care of the clothing and stuff."

"Does that mean you don't have a warrant," Sam said sarcastically.

"Allow me to confer with my partner," Reese said indicating Ritter to follow him outside of the room.

They walked outside of the room and stood in the hall.

"What do you think?" Ritter asked.

Reese said, "We can verify most of this but I think it will pan out as a perfectly legitimate arrangement for the most part."

"We're fucked, huh?" Ritter asked.

"And perhaps set up as well."

"What do you mean?" asked Ritter.

"This is an obvious set-up. A decoy specifically designed for us to find."

"It did meet the criteria perfectly, didn't it?"

"Yes," Reese agreed. "Someone wanted us to find this. It's all too neat and perfect."

One of Ritter's men walked up and handed him a folder. He opened it and flipped through the paperwork.

"Aw...shit. You're going to love this one," Ritter said after a few moments.

"What now?" asked Reese.

"The owner's name on all this paperwork is one Mr. Tom Foolery."

CHAPTER FORTY-THREE

"Mr. Tom Foolery. Great," Reese said. "The asshole has a sense of humor."

"So what do you want to do with our friends?" Ritter asked as he pointed in the direction of the men sitting on the floor.

"I guess we can get their statements and some kind of description of their boss. Give them some clothes and money to keep them happy and then release them. Just have someone check out the mission in downtown Norfolk, maybe the supervisor can remember what our mystery man looked like."

"Got it."

"Let's wrap this up," Reese said, "I don't think there is anything else we can learn here."

They both walked back into the room where the four men were still seated against the wall. "Okay fellas," Reese began, "we have some paperwork for you to do and then you will be free to go."

"And what of our arrangement here?" Sam asked.

"I think you're done. We'll make up the money difference. I assume you have been paid some money already?"

"Half," Sam answered.

"We'll ensure you are well compensated for your assistance."

"Where do we sign?" Sam said boisterously and the rest of the group agreed with nods. But then Sam's face turned grave as if he remembered something. He spoke in a serious tone, "There is the issue about the damages to the door and the alarm system we want cleared up in case this guy ever shows back up and tries to come after us for the damages. I want you to give us something that says we are not responsible for those damages."

"We will take care of...," Reese stopped in mid sentence, "wait a minute, what alarm system?"

"The one that the door is now flattened against," Sam said as he pointed toward the door which was torn apart and careened violently up against the side of the wall.

Reese stared intently at the area Sam indicated.

"What, Reese? What's wrong?" Ritter asked.

Reese walked toward the door. "The alarm. If it's an alarm, then shouldn't there be police or some security company then?" asked Reese.

"Yeah, I suppose so," agreed Ritter.

"Then where are they?" countered Reese. "They would have come by now or at least they would have sent someone to where the road is blocked and they would have called in."

"What are you getting at?" asked Ritter.

"Well if the police aren't coming, then the alarm was not meant for them. It was for someone else."

"Damn, I see it now," said Ritter. "Whoever set this up has the alarm signal going to wherever they are."

"Exactly," Reese said. "Which means that they know we're here at this moment and if it is that important to know, then they're probably still in the area."

"And they know exactly what we're doing," added Ritter.

"Yes. Look for cameras," Reese said.

"Spread out," Ritter said to his men. "Look for any indication of a camera or monitoring device."

Within a few moments, one of the men near the front door called out, "Here, sir, up in the ceiling."

Reese and Ritter examined the area the SEAL was pointing to.

Up in the corner of the ceiling, a thin tubular wire snaked through and pointed toward the center of the room. The wire had been painted white so that it would blend into the white ceiling and walls.

"Can this be traced?" Reese asked.

"I don't know," Ritter said, "let me get an electronics guy in here."

Ritter keyed his headset to get the appropriate help. Reese walked aimlessly around the room deep in thought.

Sam called out to Reese, "He's a strange one."

"Who?" Reese asked.

"The guy. Our boss. He's strange. I knew something wasn't right the first time we talked. But he had the money and we needed it. That need overrules the inquiring mind if you know what I mean."

"I suppose," Reese answered.

"And it was strange…how he seemed to know it," Sam puzzled.

"What?" asked Reese.

"The way he seemed to know we would do it and I think he even knew that you would be coming."

"Why do you say that?" Reese questioned.

"He said something like 'all men are predictable'—that times may have changed but the one thing that remained the same was the people.

But for him, he said that time was irrelevant because he had all the time that there is."

Reese froze. He recognized the expression that Dimitri had said to him when General Stone had struck a deal with the vampire to do his killing. Reese remembered the way the cold unnerving words had struck his heart back then.

"What do you think about a fella that says something like that?" asked Sam.

"I think...I think maybe he's right," Reese said and walked away. He felt the urgent need to get back outside and into the sunlight.

CHAPTER FORTY-FOUR

Outside the house, Reese walked along the sidewalk, his eyes staring off at the non-descript neighborhood but not really seeing any of it. The idea that perhaps Dimitri and the rest of his group were not involved with what was happening vanishing quickly. At this point, there were simply too many coincidences to believe otherwise. Besides, why would Dimitri set these homeless people up in this house unless they were concerned about being discovered? The answer is that they were concerned because they must be involved somehow with the release of the girls.

Was that really a bad thing? He wondered. The girls could be taken away and the military/agency operation would die in its infancy. That was what he wanted. And it would work if the idea was that simple: But it wasn't simple at all. He knew that the agency would not stop pursuing this matter unless they had hard evidence that the girls were destroyed. Samantha would want their heads on a silver platter for proof before she would let go. Plus, if it was discovered that Dimitri and his group were actually still alive, all hell would break loose. Especially for him. He would probably be thrown in Fort Leavenworth for the rest of his life and the hunt would become relentless for Dimitri and the others.

Reese heard a door close and he looked to his right and saw Ritter exiting the house and heading to the control van. It was probably time to report in to General Morris about what they had learned. He walked in the direction of the van and joined the debriefing.

"Nothing," Ritter's voice said.

"What?" Reese asked.

"The alarm and surveillance camera—we can't trace them."

"Are you really that surprised?" asked Reese as he tried to think what he was going to do next.

"Not really," Ritter said, "just hoping for a break."

"No such luck," chided Reese.

"Whoever is doing this," Ritter began, "knows exactly what they are doing. They are well trained in covert ops."

"Yeah, appears so," agreed Reese. Then in his thoughts he added, well trained alright; trained by the same people that are chasing them.

Ritter established the link to the command center back at the base.

General Morris's image appeared on the screen. Ritter summed up the operation and their discovery of the surveillance equipment.

"So we've lost the element of surprise we thought we had," Morris said. "That's not good. Not good at all."

"However, it does confirm some things that might be helpful," said Reese.

"Go on, Commander."

Reese knew he had to be careful with what he said. He couldn't stop the operation because he had no proof to substantiate the request. So the best he could do for now was to try and convince the General to return to the status quo of continuing the search. Suggest there was still a chance of success so that he could stall for more time to try and figure something out.

Reese began, "They went through all this trouble to stage this and I think that it confirms two things: First, those that orchestrated the break-out are still in the area. Their methodology and expertise seems to indicate that they are either familiar with or trained to do this type of operation. This leads me in the direction of a special force unit. Second, the chance of the two girls being alive is also a strong possibility. If not, why go through all of this sham? Why not just pack up and get out of Dodge."

"Interesting thoughts, Commander," the General said in a voice slightly more upbeat than previously. "So what's your recommendation?"

"We still don't have much to go on so until something new develops, I would suggest we continue with the list of possible places that they might be hold up at. Maybe the lab boys can get something from this house or maybe we can get a good description from the homeless mission downtown for our mystery man. Maybe there were more fake houses set up? If so, we can try and eliminate them."

"Ritter, any thoughts?" asked Morris.

"I agree with Reese for the moment. We're back to waiting."

"All right then, pack it up and get back here."

The screen went blank and Reese let out a big sigh.

"What?" asked Ritter.

"Just glad he wasn't pissed off," said Reese.

Ritter removed his headset and then snickered.

"What?" asked Reese this time, "what's so funny?"

"You don't know Morris. He never gets really pissed. Well at least not outwardly. He's a really hard man to read. You remember General Stone?"

"How could I forget," Reese said.

"Off the record, of course," Ritter began.

"Of course," agreed Reese.

"Stone was a damn idealist, and as such, never understood the world around him. He thought he could just use blunt force to get what we wanted."

"I would agree."

"At least with Stone you knew where the attack was coming from. But with Morris, you can never tell."

Reese smiled, "Yeah I know the type," he said thinking about how he would have described Dimitri the same way.

CHAPTER FORTY-FIVE

Dimitri was awakened by the sound of an alarm. As he rose from his bed in the shelter, he was joined by both Andre and Iliga. "It's one of the remote alarms from one of the other houses," Andre said. "I programmed different alarm sounds for each one."

"No immediate danger then?" asked Dimitri.

"That's correct," agreed Andre.

Ishma stirred from her own sleep and sat up on her bed, "What's wrong," she asked as she saw their hurried movement.

"It's nothing to worry about right now," said Dimitri. "The alarm is from another location. Stay here."

The three men climbed the ladder from the shelter and entered the house above. The shades had all been drawn to keep the interior as dark as possible. They moved into one of the smaller bedrooms where the electronic equipment had been set up.

In the room were several computers and monitors. The monitors showed the images of several rooms in different houses. Their attention was immediately drawn to the one that showed a flurry of activity.

"So they have taken the bait," Dimitri said calmly. "I'm surprised, it is earlier than I expected."

The images continued across the screen. "Are they military?" asked Iliga.

"They appear to be SEAL's," Andre said. "Standard equipment and mode of operation. See the backpack sprayer?"

"Yes," Dimitri said as he watched intently. "Definitely SEAL's, I remember that piece of equipment very well."

They watched the men in uniforms as they proceeded through the house. Small pockets of gas drifted through the house and passed the surveillance camera obscuring the view.

"Gas. They're using tear gas," Iliga said. "It would be quick and efficient in subduing the inhabitants."

"Yet no harm to us," added Dimitri.

"They know we would be in a resting state at this time of the day," Iliga added.

"Ah yes, good point," said Dimitri. "We would not have posed much of a problem. I see now. Smart, very smart."

Minutes later they watched as the men that had been placed inside the home were led up from the shelter and lined up against the wall in one of the larger empty rooms. Dimitri noticed that the men's coveralls were covered with black spots.

"They aren't taking any chances," Dimitri said as he pointed to the screen indicating the markings on the coveralls. "They have sprayed them with the elixir."

Two new men entered the room and instructed the men to remove the masks.

"That one," Dimitri said, pointing at one of the images, "can you zoom in on him?"

Andre placed his hand on a joystick type device and moved his hand. The image of the man grew larger.

"Just his face," added Dimitri, "that's all I need to see."

Andre zeroed in on the back of the head of the man who was currently facing away from the camera. "Turn this way..." Dimitri muttered.

As if in response to Dimitri's request, the man slowly turned to face the camera.

"Well that settles that," Dimitri said, "The question of Commander Reese's involvement has been solved."

"Yet this doesn't mean that he is a willing participant," Andre offered, "was it not the same before?"

"Perhaps not in the end, but he was a willing participant in the beginning," said Dimitri flatly as he returned his gaze to the monitor.

Reese's face continued to stare at the camera as if he had just discovered it was there. He and another man moved toward the camera.

"Cut the feed," Dimitri said, "they see it."

Andre's fingers slid across the computer keyboard. In a few seconds the monitor went blank.

"It is not traceable any longer?" asked Dimitri.

"No. All they may learn is the frequency of the transmission. It will tell them nothing important."

"Good." Dimitri said. He fell into thought for a few seconds as he remembered what he had decided the night before: To find Reese and learn what had created the connection he had felt.

"We have gone in a circle," Iliga said breaking the silence.

"Yes it appears that once again our Commander Reese is looking for us," said Dimitri, "that answers the question you posed earlier about our 'friend,' and seeking help from him," he said to Andre.

Andre didn't speak but nodded in agreement.

"It also makes a meeting with him more important," Dimitri added.

"We need to find out what is happening. Perhaps even take him back with us."

"You don't propose that we take him?" Andre asked.

"If we remove him, they will lose their expert," said Dimitri.

"But that may also compromise our position," Andre argued, "he is not looking for us, but the girls."

"Are you sure? He's smart enough to figure this out. If he didn't know we were responsible for the removal of the girls before, he does by now. The men we planted in the house, as well as our surveillance will certainly make him suspicious."

"But he still will not have any definite proof that points to us," Iliga added. "Perhaps he is trying to avoid anything that points to us and pursue whoever took the girls."

Dimitri looked toward Andre who didn't respond.

"If I'm not mistaken," Dimitri began, "it appears as if you two are trying to protect this man. Is that so?"

"Not protect," Andre said, "just give him the benefit of the doubt. He did give us the opportunity to escape when he did not have to."

"As well as placing himself in potential harm," Andre added. "We should reserve any judgment until we know the entire story."

I agree with both of you," Dimitri began, "however I had already decided that we needed to find him."

Dimitri was surprised at this mounted defense that Andre and Iliga had offered for this human. In all the time that he had known them, he had never seen such...humanity toward anyone besides their own kind. He wondered how Commander Reese had accomplished this.

"This latest occurrence just makes it more necessary. We will go to him tonight."

"Where?" asked Andre.

"You know where he lives, correct?"

"Yes."

"Then we will go there," said Dimitri, "and pay a social visit on Commander Reese after he has had such a busy day."

Chapter Forty-Six

"The operation was a bust," Smith said into his cell phone. "It was a false front set up to divert attention. But it does reveal that whoever we are looking for are very intelligent and dangerous lot. If they were cautious enough to set up a fake safe house for us to find, this might be more difficult than we first imagined."

"What are your thoughts?" asked Samantha.

"We don't have much to go on and no real course of action outside of continuing the searches. But if whoever took the girls is smart enough to set up these safe houses, they understand the methodology we are using to search for them. We might just keep spinning our wheels breaking into house after house while they sneak out the back door."

"Do you suspect inside involvement?" she asked.

"Possible. Are we really sure that there are no other...agencies involved with this?"

"Yes, I am sure of that," confirmed Samantha. "So who looks promising?"

"My feelings keep turning back to Reese. He's the one calling the shots right now and if he wanted to keep us moving in the wrong direction, he's in the perfect position to do it."

"Why? Why would he do this?" she asked. "You're not making this personal, Mr. Smith, are you?"

"Of course not," he said trying to keep his voice level. "Maybe he wants the inside track on the two girls. If he had them, he could turn it into a bidding war. He could become quite rich." He knew he was giving Reese more credit than he deserved but it was a useful diversion that might keep the bitch happy and off his ass.

"I don't believe money is the primary motivating factor for our Commander Reese."

"Maybe not," Smith agreed. "I don't think he's smart enough to pull it off anyway. But something just isn't right about him. He acts like he's above all this somehow. It's like he's on some moralistic campaign or something. Sometimes I just want to ram it back down his throat so he can choke on it."

"Are you watching him?" she asked.

"Yes. In fact I have something to follow up on tonight that might have something to do with him; this woman he's been seeing might be able to provide us some insight."

"Don't move until you let me know what you have on him. I don't want him to have any 'accidents,' do you understand?"

"Yes, but..."

"Did you not hear me?" she asked, her voice becoming stern and extremely coarse. "I don't want him harmed in any way. Is that perfectly clear?"

"Yeah. Sure," Smith agreed through clenched teeth.

"Good. I'll be coming down there tonight. I have some things I need to attend to," she said and then added, "Ensure that you keep an eye on things."

The line went dead.

Smith pressed the end button on his cell phone.

"Shit! The bitch is coming here," he muttered as he thought about his own plans of having some entertainment later which were now ruined. She would expect him to be on call every minute she was here. And this shit with Reese, this 'kid glove' approach was really starting to piss him off. He should have had an 'accident' a long time ago like the guy at the abandoned base.

"Well... I won't touch a hair on his pretty little head," Smith said aloud. His hand reached inside his jacket pocket and wrapped around the knife that he kept there. He gripped it tenderly the way a man might grip a lover's hand in a show of affection. "But his girlfriend, now that's another story. I know he's hiding something and when I start taking his bitch apart, as I cut each limb off one by one, I'll get it all from him. All of it before I kill her and then I'll kill him too. Yes...that part I will enjoy immensely."

He indulged himself in the feel of it and imagined how the knife would cut through the flesh and bone.

"Whoa..." he suddenly said and laughed realizing that as he envisioned his pleasure, he was becoming aroused. "Best save that for later."

Chapter Forty-Seven

When Reese returned to the base he grabbed a quick shower. Between the operation and the realization of what this was turning into, he felt like he had just run a marathon. The hot water helped to ease some of the tension, but not much. He dressed quickly and headed back to his office.

His route took him past the command center, so he stopped in to see if anything else had come up. Commander Pattoon had resumed his seat at the center of the activity and despite the bored look that indicated nothing new had been learned. Reese had to ask.

"Anything?"

"No. Still proceeding with the surveillance of possible places," he answered without looking toward Reese. "Did you have fun on your outing?" Pattoon asked, his voice dripping with sarcasm and resentment. "How does it feel to have it thrown back at you when you're supposed to be the expert?"

"At least I was there," Reese shot back. He knew it was a childlike response but it was the best he could do at the moment.

"Makes me wonder," Pattoon continued, "yeah…it sure does make me wonder how the hell you managed to get through the first assignment as long as you did without fucking it up."

"You know what?" Reese said.

"What?" asked Ritter.

"The team, my team, might have been nothing more than a bunch of blood sucking creatures, but I knew that from the start. They didn't hide that fact. You, on the other hand, are one of those slimy bastards that although you may not suck the blood out of living things, you'd wrap your lying lips around some general's dick in order to get ahead. In my book, you're worse than the creatures we're hunting. They didn't have a choice but you do."

Reese didn't wait for a response. He thought he better leave before he said anything else he might end up regretting.

"Well, Mr. High and Mighty, the information you wanted is on your desk," Pattoon called still not looking in Reese's direction. "I hope you like surprises."

"What's that supposed to mean?" asked Reese. Pattoon didn't say anything further. He kept his gaze on the monitors and away from Reese.

Reese closed the door when he entered his office and saw that Sam Barkley was sitting in one of the chairs. "Hey, Sam," said Reese.

"You look mad enough to spit nails," Barkley said. "Let me guess, Pattoon?"

"Yeah," Reese said, "he's a real work of art, isn't he?"

"Sure is, he reminds me a lot of Commander Scott. The kind of guy that does whatever he has to in order to move up in the ranks."

"Same mold," Reese agreed. "Anyway, what's up?"

"We believe we have the guy that developed the antidote for the elixir," Barkley said.

"What? How did you find him so quickly?"

"You won't believe this," Barkley said smugly.

"What? Come on tell me."

"I put an ad in the paper."

"You're shitting me?"

Barkley smiled a broad grin. "Yeah I know it was a long shot. But Smith's idea of sending his people out to the pharmaceutical places was just too broad. They would have to go through personnel files looking for possible suspects that might do something like this and on and on. It would take weeks to find out anything. And I don't think that this person has to be associated with a pharmaceutical place, he or she could just be intelligent enough to analyze what was in the elixir and develop a neutralizing agent. Would he need equipment? Sure, but not on any great scale. Hell, most colleges have what they would need to do this. So I decided to take along shot and see what came up."

"And you think this guy is really it?" asked Reese.

"He has some interesting points in his story," Barkley said in a tone that differed greatly from his earlier successful attitude. His gaze also turned more serious.

"Such as?" asked Reese.

"Oh, lots of things," Barkley said. "Let me look at my notes, it's in here somewhere," he said as he handed Reese a small piece of paper. Reese unfolded the note and read the single line.

Is this office secure?

He understood the meaning of the note. Whatever Barkley had to say, he didn't want it to be overheard. Reese felt his stomach seize as he wondered why Barkley had suddenly taken this approach. What had he learned?

"Sam, would you mind if we took a walk?" Reese asked. "I have a terrible headache and I could use some air, you can fill me as we take a little stroll."

"Sure," Barkley agreed. "It is a little stuffy in here."

The two men got up and left the office. They walked down the long corridor that led to the exit of the building. Reese opened the door and the fading afternoon sunlight hit him in the face. They walked for several minutes without saying anything.

When Reese thought they were far enough away, he finally spoke. "What's going on, Sam?"

"That's my question for you, John?"

Reese felt his nervousness increase. Sam did not usually use his first name when they talked.

Barkley continued, "There is no doubt about this guy being the one who made the antidote for the elixir. At first I was skeptical because he's kind of a strange one; he also has an expensive drug habit. He does freelance work at some of the local labs so he has access to equipment and to the drugs he uses. Anyway he responded to the ad in the paper. So I just confronted him and told him I knew that he had done the work. He sang like a canary just as soon as I promised he wouldn't be charged with anything."

"Okay, so why the secrecy then?" asked Reese.

"This guy might be the slime of the earth with his drugs and God knows what else he does on the side, but he's no idiot. He videotaped the entire transaction," Barkley blurted out. "Here is a photo of the man who had him do the work."

Barkley handed Reese the photo. It was a clear picture of Dimitri.

"Damn," Reese muttered.

"Damn is right," agreed Barkley. "What the hell is going on, John? Dimitri is supposed to be dead. You said you activated the collars and killed them all that night they tried to escape. Didn't you?"

CHAPTER FORTY-EIGHT

"Yes. I activated the collars," answered Reese. It was not a lie. He had pressed the button on the remote control device; however, he had deactivated the remote control prior to using it. The only thing that still worked was the little light that lit when the button was pressed. It had lit that night and he had made sure that everyone on the bridge of the ship witnessed it.

"Then how could Dimitri still be alive?" asked Barkley.

"Malfunction?" said Reese.

"No way," countered Barkley. "The collars and the elixir in them was my responsibility. I checked them thoroughly every day as well as the remotes."

"Then the elixir must have not been potent? Maybe it lost its effect?"

"John you know better. I thoroughly tested the elixir. I knew down to the minute how long it would be effective. You knew all this. So why don't we get to the truth here. What really happened that night?"

Reese hesitated for several moments as he tried to decide what he should tell Barkley. For the first time in the past several days, he didn't know what to say. If he told him the truth, it would endanger his life. Barkley was a friend and now he risked all of that. The silence seemed to last forever and Reese knew that Barkley would surmise the truth from that silence.

"Christ, John, you let them go!" Barkley said. "Holy shit! How the hell could you do that?"

Barkley looked away from Reese and stared at the surroundings. He paced nervously. "Sam, I don't think I should say anything. The less you know the better. I know this looks bad," said Reese. "But believe me I thought about it very carefully. It had to be done."

"You were too close to that damn creature, Dimitri," Barkley scowled. "You let him and his philosophical bullshit about them having their own lives get to you. I saw it. You felt sorry for them and envied them at the same time."

"Perhaps I did, Sam," Reese agreed, "but there was more to it than that. You knew what General Stone had in mind all along. Christ, you saw it yourself."

"Yes I did," agreed Barkley.

"Are you going to tell me that you could sanction the killing and the slavery of the creatures?"

"We are the military, John. We follow orders," said Barkley.

"Yes, Sam. We follow the orders, but only the legal ones. What we were involved in would not fall into any lawful order category."

"Perhaps," Sam muttered. "But that was something for the chain of command to decide, not you. I wish I had never gotten involved with the operation. Why did you get involved with the girls? Where did they come in?"

"General Stone. He never told me about it. I found out when they brought me back on duty to find them. I had no knowledge of what he had done. That was just as much a surprise to me as it was for you."

"How did Dimitri find out?"

"I have no idea," said Reese. "But it's pretty evident that he has them."

"What a mess," Sam said, "and they probably think I'm in on this as well."

"Nobody knows about Dimitri and the rest," Reese said. "Just you," he gestured at the photo. "Now."

Barkley stared at Reese with a look of betrayal that hit Reese hard. "So what are you going to do, Sam?" asked Reese. He had to know where their friendship stood on the issue.

"I don't know," Barkley said, "what are you planning to do?"

"Well, before Dimitri stepped back into the picture, I didn't have of a choice beyond finding the girls and turning them back over to General Morris. These people with the agency—well you've seen what they're like. They won't give up until they either get the girls back or have two dead bodies. But now if they find Dimitri, that blows my story about that night all the hell and I end up in Leavenworth. Or worse."

"And because they know you and I have talked on several occasions, they will assume I know what happened as well. You'll have a cell mate."

"I'm sorry, Sam. There is a good chance that you're right about that."

Barkley turned from Reese and walked in a tight little circle deep in thought. After a few minutes he turned back, "It doesn't look like it matters what I want. They'll never believe me if they find out Dimitri is alive. I guess I'm in. So what now?"

"For now, we have to find Dimitri. We find him and we find the girls. One way or another, we end this."

"But if he doesn't want to be found," Barkley began, "that may not be easy."

"True, but if we don't find him, that also means that nobody else will," Reese said.

"That will only work for so long," Barkley asserted, "if you don't produce they'll find someone who can find them. You know I'm right."

"Maybe. Maybe not," Reese mused. "It depends what they find out. Speaking of which, does anyone else know about the guy that made the antidote for the elixir?"

"No, of course not."

"Where is he?"

"I have him in a room here at the compound," answered Barkley.

"We need to get him out of here before someone gets curious. I have a few questions myself. Why don't you go in and get him and bring him out here. I don't think we want anyone to overhear this conversation."

Minutes later, Barkley exited the building accompanied by a man whom Reese guessed was approximately 30-35 years old. He was tall, around six feet, and very thin. His facial features appeared sunken, he was missing several prominent teeth and he had gray smudges beneath his eyes.

"This is Mr. Holiday," Barkley said. "Mr. Holiday, this is Commander Reese." They shook hands briefly. Reese noticed that as well as a nervous twitch, there was no strength in his handshake.

"I just have a few questions for you, Mr. Holiday," Reese began, "and then we will get you out of here."

"All right," Holiday agreed, "I will be paid of course," he stated firmly.

"Of course," Reese agreed. "Now, I'm curious, why did you record all of this?"

Holiday smiled. "Because I'm not a fool," he said plainly.

"I don't understand," Reese said.

"The guy that wanted the stuff analyzed, he was weird."

"How so?" asked Reese.

"Right from the beginning, he tried to hypnotize me or something. I could feel him trying to get me to forget things like who he was and what he wanted me to do. It was like he wanted me to be his slave or something."

"But it didn't work apparently," Reese said, finding it quite interesting. Vampires had the power to make people forget things. They had used it on the guards that were subdued during the kidnapping of the girls. But he had not ever heard of it not working before.

"No," answered Holiday.

Barkley also perked up at this response. "Do you have any idea why?" he asked.

"I don't know. Maybe because I was high," Holiday said as he shrugged his shoulders.

"That might be it," Barkley agreed, "the drugs may have served as some form of block to the hypnotic attempt. Very interesting."

"Yes it is," agreed Reese. "We might want to do something with that later. Anyway," he said returning his attention to Holiday, "So you made this antidote for him. How?"

"It's not really an antidote, I'm not that smart. I just came up with something that would neutralize the active ingredients for a period of time."

"And it worked?" Reese asked, although he knew the answer.

"In the lab it did." Holiday said and shrugged.

"So this man paid you and that was it?"

"That's it."

"You don't have any information of where he lived or worked?"

Holiday looked at Reese with a sarcastic smile on his lips. "Do you think I care? All I wanted was the money. I didn't want to know the guy's history. The less I knew the better especially when I saw what he was trying to do. I just played along with him and let him think what he was trying to pull on me worked."

"I see," said Reese, "and you must have been quite convincing."

"Why do you say that?" asked Holiday.

"You're still breathing," Reese said plainly.

"Huh? What? You think he would have killed me?" asked Holiday.

Reese didn't respond to the question. "Okay, I think we're done. Barkley here will give you a lift off of the base."

Holiday and Barkley turned to leave.

"Oh and one more thing," Reese began, "I can't hypnotize you, but I would strongly suggest you forget about all of this. There are others who'd like to clean up the loose ends. Those people won't bother trying to hypnotize you, if you know what I mean."

Holiday turned toward Reese as he said this. His eyes locked upon Reese's face. Reese's expression said he was not joking.

"Yeah, I get it," Holiday said and turned back towards the building.

"Give me a second," Barkley said to Holiday as he and Reese moved a few steps away from him.

"Nice touch," Barkley said. "I think he shit his pants when you said that."

"I hope so, because you know as well as I do, that's not an empty threat. It's more like the truth."

"I know," Barkley agreed. "What are you going to do now?"

"I'm going back to the office and see if any new leads have come up."

"Okay, I'll get our friend out of here," Barkley said and turned to leave.

"Sam?" called Reese.

"Yeah," Barkley said as he stopped and turned back.

"Be careful," said Reese.

"It's a little late for that, isn't it, John?"

"Yes, I suppose so," Reese agreed. "But be careful anyway."

CHAPTER FORTY-NINE

Reese made his way back to the office, serenaded by his stomach growling from the breakfast and lunch he still hadn't had—and here it was almost five o'clock. There just hadn't been any time to eat and he was beginning to feel the effects of drinking too much coffee and not having any food to help absorb it. He stopped at the vending machines and perused the culinary selections available. He finally decided on a package of chocolate donuts and a Milky Way bar.

The coffee caught up with him and he stopped to make a head call before going into his office. He dropped his food on the foyer counter and headed toward the urinals. He began his business and heard the bathroom door open. Turning to look, he saw it was Commander Pattoon.

"Office visits?" asked Reese. "I thought you never left your command post?"

"We need to discuss something," Pattoon said ignoring Reese's comment.

"You have me at a disadvantage," said Reese. "My hands are full."

"Hurry it up then, this is important."

Reese felt the chill of his response. He finished his business, flushed the urinal and stepped over to where Pattoon stood.

"I have some information you were looking for," Pattoon said, and then corrected himself, "or perhaps I should say lack of information."

"I don't understand," Reese said.

"The information you wanted about the disappearances of the teenagers and the cop in Suffolk."

"Oh yeah," Reese said remembering. His thoughts had been focused his meeting with Barkley and the new information they had received from Holiday, he had forgotten about the request he had given Pattoon earlier.

"I can't tell you anything about it," said Pattoon.

"Why not?" asked Reese. "Surely there must be…"

"Listen!" Pattoon interrupted, "I'm taking a risk by telling you anything."

"Then why?" asked Reese. He wondered why Pattoon would go out on a limb for him.

"I don't like you," Pattoon said flatly. "The mission they gave you on the original op should have been mine. You're a screw-up working in my world of special operations. You had the chance to work with these creatures and you fucked it up."

"Well, at least you're honest about something," Reese said.

"Yeah well, these agency people scare the shit outta me. I don't trust them. I think if they had their way, the military would be working for them. That is, if we aren't already."

"For once, I have to say I agree with you," Reese said. "But what's this all about? What are you trying to tell me?"

"The event in Suffolk has been hushed up. They're going to suppress it with some bullshit story to cover it up."

"Who is going to cover it up?"

"I already told you, the agency."

"How the hell can they do that?" asked Reese. "It's already happened and what's more, why would they want to do that?"

"The how part is easy. They have a lot of influence over other agencies, such as the FBI and CIA. It appears that the agency has stated jurisdiction in the matter and taken full control of the investigation."

"Why?" asked Reese.

"I don't know," Pattoon said. "But all the information is locked up. I tried to probe around and see what I could find out and the next thing I know is I get a phone call from General Morris ordering me to stay away from it."

"Did he ask you why were you looking?"

"Of course, I told him that the event fit the search parameters and I was looking for more information on it."

"And he said what?" asked Reese.

"That The Agency was taking care of it. End of discussion."

"That's interesting," said Reese. "What would be so important to them? It appears to be a local concern."

"I don't know and I don't want to know either. I'm done with this subject," Pattoon said firmly and turned to leave.

"So why go out on a limb? Why are you telling me this?" asked Reese.

"I might not like you; but I hate them even more."

Pattoon didn't wait for Reese to answer. He opened the bathroom door and left.

Reese stood motionless for a few seconds, his thoughts a jumble of confusion. He tried to understand the reasoning why the agency had taken over the investigation since it had occurred before Dimitri's escape. Further, why they had not mentioned it to him? None of it was adding up. He felt that something very important was missing; some piece of the puzzle that would bring it all together.

The more he thought about it the more he knew that the answers to his questions could only come from the Agency. He could go to Smith and ask him about it, but he didn't think the asshole would volunteer any information. The only option left to him was to call Samantha and see if she would tell him anything. He doubted it, but it was the only thing left for him to do, well not the only thing, there was one more option he could pursue.

Reese went over to the sink and turned the water on. When it was warm enough he washed his hands and splashed water onto his face several times as if trying to wash away his troubling thoughts. He grabbed some paper towels and turned to leave and then remembered his chocolate donuts and candy bar he had purchased. He grabbed them, looked at them for a few seconds, and then tossed them into the garbage can. Despite his grumbling stomach, he didn't feel hungry any longer. He knew he had to hunt down some more coffee. It was going to be another long night.

He returned to his office and grabbed a road atlas of the Tidewater area and looked at the summary map of the area finding the area he wanted enclosed in a black square with a number 12 on it. He flipped to that page and studied the map until he found what he was looking for. He circled the area and then took the atlas over to the scanner and scanned then printed it. He then folded the print out and placed it in his pocket.

Looking at the clock he saw that it was almost 6PM. It would be dark in less than an hour. That would leave him enough time to stop at his house to pick up some gear and change his clothes before he headed out to Suffolk and the abandoned Navy site in Driver.

CHAPTER FIFTY

At home, Reese removed his uniform and put on a pair of jeans and a sweat shirt. He grabbed a small carry bag and threw in two flashlights, extra batteries, a hammer, crowbar and a few other small tools that he thought he might need. He took the bag and placed it by the door. He checked the time, 6:15PM. Dusk was just settling in so given his estimation of 45 minutes to drive to the base it would be completely dark by the time he arrived. Just what he wanted.

There was one more thing to do before he left, he picked up the phone and dialed Christina's number. She picked up on the third ring.

"Hi, John," she said.

"Hi, yourself," he said, "wait, how did you know? Oh, never mind. How are you?"

"I'm," she paused, "I'm good. Really good."

"Was that a tough question?" he asked wondering why it took her so long to answer. "Is everything okay?"

"Everything is fine. Actually it's better then fine but I'll explain it to you later. Are you still at work?"

"No, but I have to go somewhere in a few minutes. I might be able to see you later though. That is, if you're interested."

"Cute. Very cute, mister," she said playfully. "Working eh? Are you sure you aren't off to some secret meeting with a mysterious woman? Hmmm?"

"Yeah, I'm pretty sure. I can only handle one mysterious woman at a time," he shot back.

"Me mysterious? Okay, I'll have to give you that one. For now," she said. Her voice changed and became less playful and more serious. "But that is all going to change John. I have things I want to talk to you about."

"And I want to hear them," he said. "How about I call you later and maybe we can meet for a coffee or something?"

"Sounds good," she agreed. "Where are you off to? Or can't you tell me? If you tell me you'll have to kill me right?"

"Something like that," he said. "It's work related."

"Okay mysterious Commander. I think maybe I'll call you Commander Dark, you with that shining optimism of yours."

"I'm trying darling, I'm really working on that image thing."

"I'm messing with you, John. You know that, right?" she asked earnestly.

"Sure. It's all good," he said. "Hey well I better get going. The sooner I get started the sooner I finish."

"You be safe," she said. "There are a lot of bad people in the world, John. I think perhaps I used to be one of them."

"Whoa! Where did that come from?" he said. "Now who is being dark?"

"Sorry," she said, "I was just thinking out loud."

"Are you okay?" he asked, "You sound different tonight. What's wrong?"

"I'm fine. I've just been doing a lot of thinking lately and there is someone I need to talk to tonight. I need to end an old relationship."

Reese felt his stomach knot.

"John?" she asked.

"Yeah, I'm here. You...ah...just caught me off guard a little."

"Sorry. It's a long story about an odd relationship."

"How odd?" asked Reese.

"I think the best way I can describe it was that it was a mutually beneficial one but one that wasn't based upon any love."

"Okay, now I'm really confused," Reese said.

"Hmm...you're right. This is not telephone stuff and I probably really have you wondering now. I don't want you to worry while you're working, so trust me on this. It's not what you think."

"Are you sure?"

"Yes. I know how you think John, remember? You only think about the worse things that can happen and not the best."

"Okay," he said still not sure where all of this was going.

"How about we save it for later then?" she offered.

"Good idea," he agreed. "I'll call you later."

"John?" she asked.

"Yeah?"

"I," she began hesitantly. But then her voice changed as she sounded as if she was correcting herself from saying something else, "I'll see you later," she said.

Reese almost dropped the phone. His mind had filled in the missing words that he thought she was going to say.

"John?" she asked, "You there?"

"Yes," he said, "I'm here. I'll call you in a few hours." He suddenly felt awkward. He thought that if he didn't say something at this point about what she almost said, or what he thought she was going to say, she might think the wrong thing. "I really want to see you," he said.

"Me too," she agreed. "Call me later."

"Okay. Bye," Reese said.

"Bye."

Reese stood there with the phone still up to his ear after she had hung up. He wondered if, in fact, he might even be in a state of shock. Part of him urged caution. Things were moving very fast. Or were they? What was fast anymore? But hadn't she slowed things down last night when they were on the verge of making love?

Stop thinking about it, John! Just do what you feel is right.

He felt a smile form on his lips. He was proud of his positive subconscious thoughts speaking up. In fact, he agreed with them wholeheartedly.

As he remained in his positive thoughts, the sound of an additional click from the phone brought him back to reality. The click was followed by some audible sounds that he couldn't make out. However, it didn't take him long to figure out what those sounds might be.

"You guys kill me," he said into the phone. "So Smith, did you get your cheap thrill for tonight? Well we're going to have a little talk about this phone tapping bullshit. I'll be back there in about thirty minutes and I'm going to look to kick some phone tapping ass!" He slammed the phone into its receiver.

He smiled. He had lied about heading back to the base, but what the hell. He hoped he sounded pissed enough so that whoever was listening or recording his phone conversations would now be running to their supervisor with what they called a 'holy shit' report: "The subject knows we're listening." Besides, he really was pissed. Here he was in the middle of having a special moment with a woman, and some asshole who was probably sitting in some room somewhere smiling as he flipped through the Sports Illustrated swimsuit issue on a frequent basis out of boredom, and thinking how cute all of this was. The more Reese thought about it, the madder he got.

"The hell with it for now," he said as he moved toward the door where his bag awaited him. "I'll take care of this tomorrow. Perhaps something interesting will come out of tonight's foraging and maybe we'll have a lot more to talk about as well."

Reese grabbed his bag and car keys and headed out the door into the night.

CHAPTER FIFTY-ONE

"That car, there," Andre pointed for Dimitri to see. They sat in their own car which was a couple houses down from Reese's house.

"Are you sure?" asked Dimitri.

"It arrived not long after Reese did and he's been watching the house ever since. Commander Reese is definitely being followed."

"I wonder if he is aware of it?" Dimitri pondered.

"What do you want to do?" asked Andre.

"We can't have anyone see us come or go," replied Dimitri. "We can get into the house without him seeing us, however, if Reese is being followed there is probably a good chance that his house is also wired. They would hear us and that will not work either."

"So, we take out the surveillance man," suggested Andre.

"Yes," agreed Dimitri. "You wait here. This won't take long."

Dimitri slipped out of the car and merged into the shadows that the old, tall oak trees bathed the street in. He moved quickly and quietly. Within a few minutes he found himself on the sidewalk less then fifty feet from the car and the man that was inside of it. Because of the way that the car was situated in the street, Dimitri decided that he would walk up alongside the car and pretend to be lost and ask directions. He stepped out onto the sidewalk and approached the driver's side window. "Excuse me," he said as he came up alongside the car. "I was wondering if you could help me?"

The man sitting in the driver's seat looked up at Dimitri. "What seems to be the problem?" the man asked as he eyed Dimitri warily.

"I'm lost," Dimitri said as he raised his hands to indicate the expression. "I'm looking for Bayview Boulevard? Do you know where that is?"

"Hold on, I have a map in the car," the man said. He turned his head and reached across the seat to grab the map.

Dimitri quickly reached in and grabbed the man by the throat in a paralyzing hold. SLEEP...he said in his thoughts. The man's eyelids closed slightly but then opened wide again as he resisted. SLEEP NOW! Dimitri repeated. This time the man's eyes closed and Dimitri felt his resistance fade immediately. He released him and the man fell over onto his side and quietly lay across the front seat.

Dimitri opened the door and searched the contents of the car. He opened the glove box and found nothing but rental car paperwork. He checked the backseat and found nothing that would answer his question of who the man was. He searched the man and found a gun in his shoulder holster and an official form of government identification in his breast pocket of his suit.

Dimitri examined the identification card. He recognized it as a governmental law enforcement type of identification, however there was no name of the particular institution that the man represented. He thought this very strange. He had expected to see CIA or FBI, but to find nothing at all added another level of questions to what was happening. Who was the strange man and why was he following Reese?

Dimitri decided to get back to his own car to get Andre. They were going to have to figure out some way to get Reese out of the house so that they wouldn't be detected in the process. Just as he closed the door to the car, and turned to walk back to his own vehicle, Andre pulled up alongside.

"He's gone," Andre said through the open window.

"Reese?"

"Yes. While you were taking care of this, he came out of the house and got into his car. If we hurry, we can still catch him."

Dimitri hopped into the car. "Let's go."

Andre drove off quickly down the street. "He's only a few seconds ahead, we should catch him soon."

"Actually this is probably better," Dimitri said. "Now we don't need to figure out how to get him out of the house without being seen."

Andre came to the end of the street and glanced left and then right. "There," he said, "the blue Honda Civic."

Dimitri looked in the direction Andre indicated and saw the taillights of the car. "Let's go," he said. "We'll follow and see where he is going and then decide when it is best to reacquaint ourselves with Commander John Reese."

CHAPTER FIFTY-TWO

When Christina finished talking with Reese, she hung up the phone and suddenly sensed that something was not right. Her heightened senses were flooding her thoughts. She simply knew something was wrong. She tried to focus and narrow it down. She went through her mind sorting out what had caused her to suddenly become aware of whatever it was. And then she found it: A void where one had not existed for many years.

Last night when she went to sleep, she had broken her connection to Jake. He was aggravated and she had been too tired to deal with him so it seemed the best choice at the moment. However, having awakened and reopened her thoughts to the connection which had been there for over 60 years, she discovered it missing. The void could only indicate that something was terribly wrong.

She left her room and headed out of the underground compound with the intent to backtrack her steps from this morning to see if she could find him. She stepped out into the cool night and its welcoming darkness. Christina closed her mind to all other thoughts and focused on Jake. She replayed their conversation in her mind from last night focusing her senses to try and piece together what happened after she had left.

In her mind she saw Jake throwing the coffee cup and it flying off into the distance to finally shatter against a rock. The pieces of the cup seemed to hang in the air as if they might come back together like a last hope or chance to fix the moment and make things right. But the pieces finally fell to the ground as if in silent confirmation that there was no chance of anything changing in the past.

She felt him move away from the compound and toward the car so she moved in that direction. As she walked she could sense the coarse feelings that had washed through his mind and his thoughts. She felt the painful stab of anger, neglect, and a sense of loss. They were not unfamiliar to her. She had sensed these feelings before but they'd not bothered her. That was all before her epiphany and altered perspective but it was different now. Now they brought upon her a sense of guilt and even regret. She should have tried to reason with him last night and not have let him gone off in that state of mind. They had been together a long time and to mindlessly cast him away seemed cold and cruel even though she had never worried about it before.

There had been many mortals she had used in this way; using them as they sought their own personal gain through her. In the end, they perished and she moved on to another. It was a cycle that she had followed for many years.

So many I have used and discarded without a thought or concern for their welfare; how could I have been so cruel. It seemed so easy at the time…

She had already decided that Jake would be the last. Her rebirth, which is how she thought of it, would not be based upon the servitude of a human for support. She would take what she needed but not through years of implied love or the promises of immortality she had used in the past. All of her past life was over.

She came to the fence that bordered the compound and easily scaled it dropping to the other side. She continued walking through the woods sensing the direction Jake had gone. The path was easy enough to follow because he took the same one every time. A few more steps and she froze. She felt the hair on the back of her neck rise and her body immediately assumed a defensive posture. Seconds later a familiar smell reached her—the smell of death.

She knew that smell well enough through her years of killing. It had never changed. However, this time there was something different about it because the smell of death encompassed what she had been following. The traces of Jake and his life that now mixed with the smell of his death. A feeling descended upon her, one that she was not familiar with. Her stomach felt twisted and her heart began beating quickly in her chest.

I'm scared! This is what it feels like…I had forgotten.

Her eyes scanned the darkness for any signs of intruders. She could feel the blood pumping through her own body working to control the combination of fear, excitement and trepidation. She struggled to focus on the smell and the aura of Jake that she had used to follow him.

In minutes she came to where her senses told her the body was. Someone had tried to conceal it in a small ravine by covering it with debris from the woods. Slowly she removed the branches and leaves and saw Jake's face and the horror that had fixed itself upon it.

"Oh, Jake," she murmured. "It wasn't supposed to end like this."

The men in her company had always died peacefully. When the time came, she eased their way to death and let them believe until their last breath that they would reawake and begin their lives of immortality with her. It was a lie, but it was one that she had become accustomed to over the years and after all that time, she almost believed it too. Until now.

She wanted—no, she demanded to know what had happened. She examined Jake's body and quickly found the cause of death; his throat had been cut. She placed her fingers on the torn flesh and let the tacky blood that remained there adhere to her own skin. The connection through the blood they had shared was weak and faint, but still present as a ghostly image formulated in her thoughts. She grasped fragments of images and sounds that were his last moments in life.

CHAPTER FIFTY-THREE

"Christ!" she heard Jake scream.

"I want direct answers," someone said to him.

"Alright—alright," Jake said as she felt pain where Jake had been struck with something.

Christina experienced it all. She could feel Jake's emotions, scared and unsure, hoping he had lied sufficiently well enough to deter the attacker who obviously was looking for her. She tried to examine the pieces of conversation to see if she could somehow determine who the attacker was and why he had followed her. But there wasn't enough life left in the blood. The attack must have occurred...

She suddenly felt Jake's head yanked back and the sharpness of the knife at his throat followed by the swift motion of it digging in and slicing across. She felt the life rushing out from his body. He was dying.

"I love you, Christina," was the last thought that flowed from Jake's living mind.

"No!" she screamed as she stood up and staggered away from his body. The depth of the emotion that was contained in his last thought had overcome her. He had died protecting her! He had given his life so that she could live! In his last moments of life he had only thought of her—even after her refusal to talk with him the night before.

How could I? How could they do something like this?

She staggered as if drunk with clumsy steps that took her nowhere. Her legs felt like rubber. Her mind was whirling with thoughts of guilt, anger and rage. She stepped backwards not looking or knowing what was there. She bumped up against the trunk of a large tree. Anger flared in her mind! She turned to the tree and began slashing at it wildly with her fingernails extending from her hands.

Each slash brought an image to her mind. Each image was that of a person she remembered from the town where she had been born and later both shamed and ostracized.

SLASH.

The lover that had turned upon her.

SLASH.

The council leader of the village.

SLASH.

The members of the council.

SLASH.

The young boy who had thrown stones at her as she walked out of the town in disgrace.

One by one the images came and she dispatched them as she had done all those years ago. She clawed and clawed at the tree. Bark peeled off as she ripped and tore at it. Her nails dug into the exposed tender pulp of the tree. She could feel the moisture of it and it made her think of flesh of the man that had killed her Jake. She thrashed and tore at it until even her vampire nails were worn down to bare shapeless nubs and her fingers bled.

Panting and exhausted, she collapsed at the base of the savaged tree. For the first time in her life, she actually felt real pain. The pain was not from her fingers, but from her heart. Alexander's reappearance to remind her that she could be free again—that she could live again, had not prepared her for the feelings of pain that accompanied freedom. Pain newly discovered was what you felt when you lose someone you cared about.

The anger she felt was not only about Jake, although it had been the catalyst for the barrage of feeling that forced her to the ground. She remembered what she had done with her life. Remembered those she had killed in a vengeance that she could never quench. She had caused too much pain and suffering in the world. Far too much. How many others had felt the pain that she was now feeling? How many felt pain caused by her hate? How many had been guilty only through association. The answer was simple: Too many.

The anger was replaced with feelings of remorse and sorrow for what she had been. It left her feeling devoid of what had been the mainstay of her life; the evil that she had done with her own hands. She wiped at the blood tears that rolled down her face. She cried for Jake as well as the others. How many had there been? She didn't know exactly but she did know there had been many. She wanted to say that all of that was over, in the past, but she knew that wasn't true. Not now—not yet. There would be one final murder she would commit. It would be over once she took care of whomever it was that did this to Jake. Only then would it be over.

She returned to Jake and carefully brushed away the remaining debris covering his body.

"Oh, Jake," she said softly. "We were together a long time weren't we? I promised you a life of forever and you end up having to settle for death at the hands of someone else. I'm sorry, Jake. I'm so sorry. I will find who it was and make them wish for death before I give it to them. I promise."

She knelt down and picked up his body and cradled it gently in her arms. She rose effortlessly and began to walk back toward the compound. She remembered a place down by the river where Jake had liked to sit and fish or just to watch the water on summer nights. She would take him there and bury him.

She made her way back inside of the fenced area of the military compound and walked in the moonlight toward the river. She walked slowly for there was no need to rush with him. For once she would take the time to do it right because Jake deserved that and so much more.

Time, time, time...

She thought about Jake and the times that they had experienced together ever since they met when she first arrived in this country. He was such a young man then, a boy actually. So full of life.

How quickly time passes, she thought, especially when one does not have to worry about it.

As she continued her walk toward the river, she became aware of something else. A new sensation tickled upon the fringe of her senses, there was someone else here. Someone was watching her.

CHAPTER FIFTY-FOUR

She ignored what her instincts were telling her about being watched. She sensed no immediate threat of danger but rather more of a curiosity. A light breeze arose and Christina felt the air dance upon her skin. The feeling reminded her of the way Jake used to touch her face gently with his hardened hands. She closed her eyes and remembered the time and felt herself smile. However, the smile left her face quickly as the breeze brought her something else, the definitive smell of a human that she knew.

She continued to walk, sensing the presence of the human watching her. She took a deep breath allowing her senses to decipher its meaning. It was someone she had been with before that much she was sure of. She searched her thoughts for the match of her visitor. Slowly it came to her; it was a female, her supposed handler, the woman called Samantha.

She could wait, Christina thought. She would take care of Jake first and then see what Samantha wanted. This human had only come into contact with her twice before. What was it that brought her presence here tonight? Something must be wrong, but it would wait until she had finished with Jake. Nothing would get in the way.

Christina picked up her pace, moving incredibly fast into speeds where no human could possibly keep up, covering the remaining few acres in less than two minutes. She passed one of the old sheds where Jake kept tools. She went inside, removed a shovel and an old blanket and then continued on. As she moved, she wondered why Samantha was here.

Samantha rarely visited at all, so this unexpected and unannounced visit was indicative of some development. Had she learned that she had removed the device? Christina didn't think so. Because of the tracking device capability built into it she had ensured that she carried it with her. She was not ready to leave the old compound yet so she thought it best to continue her arrangement until she was ready to disappear. So it must be something else, possibly a new assignment?

Finally Christina arrived at the spot that she remembered Jake liked. She carefully laid him on the ground and began to dig the grave. She emptied her mind of everything while she dug. So many things had happened in the past few days and at a dizzying pace. Yet she also knew that there was something that was formulating at the back of her mind that she couldn't put her finger on. Some connection of some sort eluded her. But for now, she blanked all of it out and simply dug. She did it quickly and effortlessly. What would have taken a normal man an hour to dig, she had accomplished in a mere ten minutes. She retrieved Jake's body and placed it gently at the bottom of the grave. She folded his arms across his body, then covered his body and face with the old blanket before she began to fill the hole back in. She returned the dirt slowly; unlike the speed in which she had removed it. For some reason it felt right to do it this way. She continued until the hole was filled in and she had smoothed the top of it out making it uniform and even. Jake would have liked that, she thought. He always believed that things needed to be a certain way, even in death.

Death. She remembered how their first meeting had been baptized in death. Jake discovered her by finding the dead bodies of the military escort that had brought her back from Europe. She had killed them as directed by the man that had been her first handler; another man she had killed later on as directed by the Agency. He had been one of the few that she had actually had any kind of feelings for. The one with the diary that she had mailed to the son to perhaps answer some questions about a father that had been forgotten.

Words. She stood and wondered if she should say anything over the grave before she left. She knew that Jake wasn't religious but that he had believed in God. Still what did she know about God? Her attempts at anything religious would be a mockery in itself and that would not be appropriate. "Farewell, my Jake" she said and shrugged her shoulders, not knowing what else to say. "I'll miss…"

She was suddenly inundated with a barrage of thoughts and images. Samantha was here to see her. Reese's nightmare of other vampires. The confirmation that there were others like her. Jake's death.

There's some kind of a connection to all of this?

"Good evening, Christina," a voice called to her.

Christina didn't jump or react nervously to the voice as she backed out of the thoughts that had just overwhelmed her. She had expected Samantha to find her because she most likely carried a GPS that located exactly where she was at any given time.

Christina turned to face her. "Samantha," she said calmly, "this is an unexpected surprise." Christina's eyes were drawn to Samantha's right hand which remained in the pocket of her jacket as it had on the two previous times they were together. Christina knew that Samantha's right hand remained in that pocket holding a detonation device in case she got out of hand and tried something foolish such as killing her Handler.

"I was in the area on another issue," Samantha said calmly as if they spoke in person on a regular basis.

Christina looked at her questioningly and said, "So you thought you just stop by and see how I was doing? Should I be flattered by your presence?"

Samantha smiled and it wasn't a pleasant sight. "We have business to discuss. I have a mission for you," she said as her eyes returned to the freshly dug grave. "Who was that?" she asked.

Christina found her tone to be curious rather than pressing as if she didn't care. She found herself angered by the aloofness of it. "It was the man called Jake," she simply said. She thought to herself, *Who are you to act as if you care?*

"Ah…your friend," she said with an emphasis on the word friend that Christina further did not like. "Are you finished with him?" she asked with no emotion in her voice.

"He was killed," Christina said sternly, "brutally murdered."

"Why? Was he robbed or something?" Samantha asked.

"No not robbed. He was protecting me. Apparently someone either followed me or was waiting by the car. Apparently he didn't tell them what they wanted so they killed him."

"Followed you?" Samantha said. Her tone became tight and more focused. "Who followed you? Why? What have you gotten into?"

"I don't know," Christina answered.

"You were supposed to report anything like this: Anything suspicious that might indicate that someone knows of your presence. Why did you not contact me? You know the rules," she said in a voice that sounded condescending.

"I didn't know until about an hour ago when I found him," said Christina.

"Where did you find the body?" asked Samantha.

"In the woods just outside of this place," answered Christina. She didn't like having to remember how he found him. She wanted to be done with this conversation so she could begin to find who had done this.

"What have you been doing the past few days? Where have you gone?" pressed Samantha.

"Nowhere unusual," Christina replied. "Besides, you can check all of that out if you wish," she said referring to the tracking device. She was not going to tell this woman about John or any of the other events that had occurred. That was her own business.

Samantha scowled and said, "No, this is not good—not now especially with what else is happening."

"What else is happening?" Christina asked remembering the earlier cascade of thoughts she'd experienced when Samantha arrived and knew that somehow these events were connected.

"Ah...nothing," Samantha said in a dismissive tone. "It doesn't concern you, yet. Besides, it doesn't matter right now. The death of this man was too close. I don't like it. We have to move you," Samantha said.

"Move?" Christina asked.

"Yes. Let's get back to the compound. I need to make some calls."

This was not what she wanted but she decided to play along for the moment because she wanted information. "This way," Christina said as she led the way.

The two walked in silence as they each delved into their own thoughts.

Christina knew she wasn't going to go anywhere else with Samantha. This 'relationship' with Samantha and the people she worked for was over. She would stop this tonight and disappear because she was sure now that there were others of her own kind. She also knew that if Samantha suddenly went missing, whoever she worked for would come looking for her.

As they entered the underground facility, Samantha moved toward the desk that held the secure telephone that she used to call Christina. As Samantha picked up the handset, Christina decided to see what she could get through conversation.

"Why have you not told me there are others... like me?"

Samantha slowly replaced the handset into its cradle and turned to face Christina, her eyes wide with fear and surprise. "What do you mean?"

CHAPTER FIFTY-FIVE

Reese parked his car in the gravel parking lot of the small ball field which was next to the fenced area of the abandoned Navy base. He saw that there were two cars there already which surprised him given the hour of the night and that he could not see anyone on the ball field. He supposed they could belong to some of the people who lived in the area and wanted or needed to park their cars somewhere else. Still, it made him a little uneasy.

He got out of the car and studied the map he had located for the base. The internet was wonderful thing. He had located information which gave him the history of the World War II era facility as well as a rough listing of all the buildings. When the base had been closed due to BRAC, Base Realignment and Closure, the site had gone up for sale and a complete description of the property was given, building by building. The report also indicated that some of the base had been given to the city of Suffolk but the rest he wasn't sure about.

He decided he would begin his search with the central area and main core of buildings. That was the area where supposedly the police officer had searched with the city representative before he disappeared. But first, he needed a way in. He found the fence line and began searching for an area that time had taken its toll upon as well as the ingenuity of teenagers looking for a place they could hang out undisturbed. It took less than fifteen minutes before he found it.

He slipped through the broken fence and walked through the rest of the perimeter of the woods. Contrary to plan, when he emerged from the trees he found that he had misaligned himself with the area he wanted to search. Instead of being near the buildings, he appeared to be on the opposite end of the base.

"Damn," he cursed. In the moonlight he could see the silhouette of the buildings. He estimated that he probably had to hike another mile to get to where he had wanted to be. "Not much choice," he said and started out.

The pace was intermittent at best. There were areas where old road had been and the ground was level and even showed remnants of gravel having once been in place. But at other times the brush was waist high and he either had to go around, or try and wade through it. Either way, it was slow going.

As he walked, he had time to think about the past few days and what a merry go round it had been. He was back in the military; chasing two small vampire girls; found evidence that confirmed Dimitri and his team were involved in their disappearance; and met the woman of his dreams. Meeting Christina was of course the best part of this scenario. However, unless he found some way to resolve everything else, there would not be a happy ending to this story. As for that ending, he hadn't a clue what he was going to do or what was going to happen next.

"Commander Reese," a voice from behind startled him from his thoughts. He had not heard any sounds indicating that someone was following him and he knew that it was damn near impossible to traverse through the brush without making any noise. Had they been waiting for him here?

Reese turned quickly, almost falling down in the process, and faced two men. The moonlight shone brightly upon them outlining their tall and full bodies. However, his eyes were immediately drawn to their faces and the highlighted red glow of their eyes.

"We meet again," the man said. His voice was calm and steady and Reese recognized it immediately as Dimitri's. "I told you it was in our destiny."

Reese wasn't sure how he should feel scared or relieved at this moment. The last time he had met Dimitri, they had parted on somewhat amiable terms, but a lot had happened since then. He obviously knew about the girls. Did the vampires think he had been in on it from the beginning? He peered at the other and recognized him as the other member of the team, Andre. He wondered where Iliga was.

"It is still Commander, isn't it?" Dimitri asked, "Or have you been promoted?"

Reese heard the thick sarcasm that accompanied the question. "It's still Commander," Reese answered trying to keep his voice even. "They brought me back on active duty." He thought how silly his answer must have sounded, the entire conversation for that matter, as he stood in a deserted area with vampires that could easily kill him as they discussed his rank.

"At times we cannot hide from our true calling, as much as we would want to," Dimitri responded. For a few moments he stared at Reese but said nothing. Then in a low voice, "For the moment, we are on…how would you say, even ground. No harm will be committed unless it is warranted."

Satisfied that they weren't going to kill him - for the moment - Reese asked, "What are you doing here? Are you following me?" Before Dimitri answered, Reese suddenly realized how it all fit together with the disappearances and the abandoned site; it would be the perfect place to hide out at. "Wait, you live here don't you?"

Dimitri smiled, "Always trying to figure things out. You tend to accept things at face value. Because I am here you believe I live here?"

Reese couldn't help but snicker at Dimitri's response. Even for a vampire, he knew him so well. "You're right, I should know better than to accept simple answers," Reese agreed, "someone else has reminded me about that same issue lately."

"But in answer to your question," Dimitri continued, "we do not live here. We followed you from your home. There are things we must talk about."

"Yes," Reese agreed. "This whole affair is escalating."

"I have a question that you must answer truthfully. Did you know about the girls?" Dimitri asked bluntly.

"No," Reese said assuredly trying to sound convincing. However, it didn't really matter because he knew that Dimitri could tell if he was lying. "I found out a few days ago when I was forced back onto active duty to help find them."

"I thought as much," said Dimitri. "The girls did not mention ever seeing you."

"Where are they?" asked Reese.

"Alive and safe."

"I assumed as much. We found the man that made the elixir neutralizer for you. Were you aware that your memory erasure did not work on him?"

"No," Dimitri said. For the first time that Reese could remember, a look of puzzlement appeared on the vampire's face.

"He was on drugs; it must block your ability somehow," said Reese as way of explanation.

"Interesting," Dimitri answered.

"Yes, but it also means that if I found him, someone else might."

"You have a point to make, Commander?"

"You know as well as I do; you risk being discovered by your involvement with the girls."

"Were we supposed to just leave them?" he asked. "You know that was not possible."

Reese hesitated before answering. He knew Dimitri was right. "I know, I know. But you should have come to me, perhaps we could have figured out something."

"We did not know exactly where your allegiances lay," Dimitri said.

Reese could see his point and did not see any reason in debating it. He changed the subject, "How did you learn that they had the girls to begin with?"

"I found a dead body near the oceanfront which had vampire blood on it. It wasn't from any of us so that led me to thinking of the possibility of others. It also was logical to assume that if there were others, they would be held at the same place we had been. We went and watched. When we discovered they were actually there, we went in and got them out. You know who they are?"

"Yes," Reese answered, "the daughters of Idriz Laupki."

"Did you know they had been turned?" asked Dimitri.

"Not until recently. From what I have learned, General Stone secretly had the bodies brought back. He thought it had been accomplished secretly, but it wasn't." The mention of Stone's name reminded Reese about his brutal murder. "Why did you kill Stone?" he asked.

"Stone?" asked Dimitri with an edge of surprise in his voice.

"Yes Stone," Reese shot back annoyed. He hated the General but murder was murder.

"I did not kill him," replied Dimitri.

"What?" asked Reese shocked at the denial. "His body was found drained of blood and wearing a collar. It's just what you would have done!"

CHAPTER FIFTY-SIX

"I assure you it wasn't me," Dimitri said forcefully. "We had nothing to do with his death. I read the newspaper account. They said it was retaliation by the drug cartels. We accepted it as fact; we had no reason to believe otherwise."

"That was a cover story," Reese said. "What was not reported in the papers was the lack of blood and the fact that both Stone and Scott, who was also murdered, were both wearing the elixir collars."

"I swear to you, it was not any of us," Dimitri said sincerely. "Why would I lie about that?"

"Well if it wasn't you, then," Reese began but stopped as more pieces of the puzzle came together. "The girls, did they do it?" he asked.

"No. They were put through only one test and that was only recently. They were not brought to consciousness until a short time ago."

The agency, Reese thought. They had to be involved somehow.

"Did you hear me?" asked Dimitri.

"Yes," answered Reese, "I was just thinking. They wanted Stone out of the picture so they had him killed."

"Who?" asked Dimitri.

"Who or what?" said Reese. "All I know is that they are some kind of governmental agency that operates in the background. It goes beyond dark ops and, in fact, nothing would surprise me about what they might be involved in. They learned about the original Team of Darkness operation and went after Stone. Apparently, Stone stepped on a lot of toes to pull off what he did. When he had the girls brought back, he had to pull some strings and apparently drew him some unwanted attention. That was when the agency found out about the original op. They were too late to do anything, but they knew about the girls."

"So you suspect they had Stone and Scott killed?" asked Dimitri.

"Yes. They wanted them kept quiet. Permanently."

"But why make it appear that we did it?" asked Dimitri.

"I don't know," said Reese, "Whoever did it knew that those facts wouldn't be made known to the public. So if the agency did it, they wanted to send a signal to someone inside - perhaps the military itself to tell them that they were above them. I don't know. It's all so damn crazy."

Reese's head ached from trying to figure this all out. He felt as if he was real close to having the complete picture, but yet some key element eluded him. He decided to think along other lines for the moment. He returned his attention to the fact that Dimitri had sought him out.

"Why did you decide to follow me?" Reese asked.

"I have several questions for you that need answers, but mainly to seek your assistance on how to get the girls out of here and back to Kosovo."

"Back to Kosovo? Why?"

"The change for them is hard to comprehend and deal with here. At least back home, they would have some semblance of order in their lives. I thought it would be best to take them back and they have agreed. We of course would accompany them, as we have been gone for too long as well, but now every means to go back is blocked."

"This is not going to be easy," Reese said. "It would be extremely risky especially because of the heightened terrorist alert. They search everything."

"So you are saying it is impossible?"

"Not impossible, just extremely difficult. But I can tell you this much, unless we resolve the girls' disappearance in some way, the restrictions will never be eased. Not to mention that if they discover that you, Andre and Iliga are alive, they will stop at nothing to recapture or destroy you."

"So what do you suggest?" asked Dimitri.

"The only way you will be able to get them out is to get the dogs called off and the only way that is going to happen is to either produce the girls or two bodies."

"That is not going to be easy," agreed Dimitri.

"Welcome to my world," said Reese as he snickered. "Easy doesn't enter into it. Let me think about this and see what I can come up with. Remember if they find you, they will come after me as well."

"You fear this and other things," Dimitri said.

"What's that supposed to mean?" Reese asked wondering what he was referring to.

"I have seen your dreams," said Dimitri plainly.

Reese felt his stomach somersault with fear at the mention of his dreams. He was not ready to discuss that issue with Dimitri. Not now and maybe not ever. "Well, let's not worry about my dreams for the moment," Reese said quickly dodging the subject. "We have enough other stuff to go around for the moment."

"As you wish, but we shall come back to it later. So it is my turn to ask, why did you come here tonight?" asked Dimitri, "and did you know you were being watched?"

"I'm not surprised about being watched," said Reese, "probably agency people."

"We took care of him," Dimitri said indicating Andre who remained in the distance and totally silent during their conversation.

"You didn't kill him, did you?" asked Reese.

"No, he is merely... resting. But you didn't answer my question, why did you come here?" asked Dimitri again.

"There have been some unexplained events that center on this area that caught my attention in searching for the girls. I thought it was possible vampire activity. That's why I asked you if you were living here."

Dimitri perked up. "What events? Describe them please."

"Disappearances. First some teenagers and then a police officer. When I started looking into it, I discovered that the investigation is under agency control and there is no information available. It doesn't add up. It makes no sense for the agency to take over a local case. If anyone, the FBI should have it."

"Unless there is something they don't want you to know," added Dimitri. "And you say it all happened here?"

"That's just it, they don't know for sure. All we know is that this place is a common link between both incidents. Supposedly the teens came here when cutting school, so naturally the investigating police officer came here as well. They know he searched the place because a public works employee was here with him. They searched it together and then the officer left, neither the officer nor the kids have been heard from since."

"Interesting. Tell me about this place," Dimitri said as he raised his head as if the night breeze had stirred up some scent that caught his interest. Reese saw how his eyes became distracted as if he wasn't sure about something. He watched as Dimitri's eyes searched the darkness as if he sensed that someone or something was watching him.

"What?" asked Reese. "Is there something wrong?"

"No. It's nothing, go ahead."

Reese didn't like the way Dimitri was acting. He remembered from the ops they had been on that when Dimitri or one of the other vampires was nervous or unsure about something, they would act this way. He started to explain, "This area is an abandoned US Navy base. It was shut down in the 90's. It originally came into service around World War II,

1944 to be exact. That's about it."

"It would be a good place to hide," Dimitri said.

"True. But it doesn't matter anymore. You say you aren't living here and the girls are with you, so that wraps that part up. The only thing I don't understand is the agency involvement in the investigation."

"It remains a mystery along with some other things," Dimitri said. "I have another thing I can add to the unsolved pile."

"What other things?" asked Reese.

Dimitri turned his gaze fully upon Reese. "The other day I was drawn to your thoughts it was a dream or something you were having. I could sense your fear very strongly through a psychic connection."

"Me? I thought that as only when you had a connection to someone via the blood?"

"That is generally correct."

"Well, we don't have any blood connection so how could that be?"

"This is true," agreed Dimitri, "however if we eliminate that possibility, then something still caused the link."

"Do you have any ideas?" asked Reese.

"Yes, but they don't seem possible. You are not aware of any experiments being done that might have caused it?"

"No."

"Then as your famous detective, Sherlock Holmes, claims, 'when you have eliminated all that is possible, whatever remains, no matter how improbable, must be true'."

"And what does that mean?" asked Reese.

"Then there may be another vampire," Dimitri said simply.

"What? That's not possible," interjected Reese.

"Why not?" asked Dimitri. "There are many things we do not know, you yourself have acknowledged this. How can you be sure that another of my kind has not been discovered? You said you did not know about the girls, correct?"

"Yes that's true," Reese agreed. "But if there was or is another vampire, why would General Stone or Morris not mention it?"

"Perhaps they did not know?"

"I guess it's possible," agreed Reese reluctantly, "but how come you didn't know about it before?"

"I don't know," conceded Dimitri, "but what I do know is this connection is generally caused by psychic commingling of the blood or by the creation by the same master."

"So you're telling me that the creature that made you, made another vampire and this vampire is near here?"

"It is a possibility," acknowledged Dimitri. "My master, Alexander, did not ever tell me if he did create others. I am only going by what I know in these matters."

"What about Josip?" asked Reese, "could he have created another vampire that you don't know of?"

"No. We were too close? I would have known."

"Wait a minute, if you would have known if he did, why did you not know about the girls?"

"They were not developed enough. Even they did not understand what they were. Given time, they would have become more developed and I would have sensed them."

"So certain powers come with the age of the vampire?" asked Reese.

"Yes."

"Why did you not mention that before?" asked Reese feeling as if Dimitri had withheld information.

"You didn't ask."

"Hmmm, well is there anything else I should know?"

"Not that I can think of," said Dimitri.

"Okay," said Reese, "I'm not sure if I buy into this 'other vampire' theory, but let's say for argument's sake that you're correct. How does that explain you getting the, what did you call it, the psychic connection to me?"

"Once the blood connection is eliminated, then this other vampire is close to you somehow. It could be close in terms of either physically or mentally."

"Hold on, you're losing me here," said Reese.

"Think of thoughts such as dreams or memories, and place it in terms of water. They flow through your mind and sometimes they crest their banks and spill upon others."

"So, it could be anyone that I have been in close proximity with."

"That is correct."

"Well that really narrows it down. Do you have any idea how many people I have been around the past few days?"

"That may be irrelevant at the moment," said Dimitri, his voice and tone changing. Reese saw that earlier look of distraction return to his face. Dimitri turned to Andre and motioned to him with some form of signal that caused Andre to also become more heightened in his posture.

"Yes, irrelevant," murmured Dimitri. He closed his eyes and appeared to become intensely focused on something.

"What's going on Dimitri?" asked Reese. "What's irrelevant?"

Dimitri opened his eyes and looked at Reese. "There is another vampire and it is very near."

"Near as in… in this area?" asked Reese.

"Yes. We should explore this place further," said Dimitri, "follow me."

"Ah, sure," Reese agreed. "Lead on."

CHAPTER FIFTY-SEVEN

"Why have you not told me there are others... like me?"

Samantha slowly replaced the handset into its cradle and turned to face Christina, her eyes wide with fear and surprise. "What do you mean?"

"Please don't treat me like an idiot," said Christina. "I know they exist. I felt their presence. I have done what you have asked of me for many years. You can at least be honest with me now, besides, I will know if you lie."

"You're right," Samantha said grudgingly. "That is why I came here tonight. Your new assignment is to..."

"Tell me about them?"

"Yes. There are two of them."

"Why did you not tell me earlier?" asked Samantha.

Samantha sighed. "It was a military action and we did not know about it when it occurred. Later, when we learned of what had been done, we had them transferred to what we thought was a secure compound in an area not far from here."

"For what purpose? Were you intending to replace me?" asked Christina.

"No. They were to be treated as additional assets."

"I wish to see them," said Christina.

"You can't. As I tried to tell you earlier, they have been taken," Samantha said.

"Taken, what do you mean taken?"

"We still don't have a complete picture yet, but it appears that they had help in getting away from us."

"Ah, now I see why you're here," said Christina as she began to understand. "This is not only about finding them it is about killing those that took them from you."

Samantha ignored the comment as she said, "We need to get them back before anything happens to them or they are discovered by someone else."

"You are worried about losing your superiority in this arena, aren't you? Someone else will have their own assassin to send in to take care of their problems."

"Not my problems, my country's problems," Samantha shot back. "But that is one way of putting it."

"Well, what have you got to go on?" asked Christina.

"Not much. We have people working the issue but they haven't come up with anything specific to go on. We're searching all locations that look like potential hideouts but still we've found nothing."

"You said that you suspected that they had help in escaping? How did you conclude this?"

"They had only been in the facility for a few days. Someone had to show them how to get out. After all, they were just young girls who didn't…"

"Girls?" asked Christina. She remembered the images she had received from John's nightmare. There was nothing there that she had seen that resembled little girls. On the contrary, she remembered a male vampire quite specifically.

"Yes, two young girls, their approximate ages are thirteen and seven." Now it was Samantha's turn to look at Christina oddly. "What did you think they were?"

"I assumed they were male," Christina said trying to hide her surprise. "I couldn't tell from the connection I had with one of them," she lied.

"Well regardless of their sex or size, they are still extremely valuable assets and I want them." Christina heard the demand within the Handler's voice. "And I want you to find them," she continued. "This takes precedence over everything else."

"I can try, but we need to narrow the search area," she suggested trying to sound helpful although she had no intention of turning the little ones over to her.

"We have a specialist on the team that has a background that is useful," Samantha continued. "We have asked for his assistance on other issues in the past. If you two work together, then maybe you can come up with something."

"That will help," agreed Christina. "When can I meet him?"

"Tomorrow night, I'll arrange a meeting with you and…"

"Commander John Reese," a man's voice called from the shadows.

Christina and Samantha turned in the direction of the voice. A dark figure was emerging from the shadows but had not fully stepped into a lighted area where they could see.

"She already knows him," the voice said, "yes, she knows him very well."

The figure stepped into the light.

"Mr. Smith, this is a surprise," Samantha said. "How did you know I was here?"

"I didn't," he said. "This is, how should we say, a happy coincidence perhaps. We installed a tracking device on Commander Reese's car. Tonight, someone took out my associate who was watching his house. When we activated the tracer, we saw that the location he came to tonight was the same area of the incident we had last night. We knew there had to be some connection."

"Last night?" Samantha said. "What are you talking about?"

"You killed Jake," Christina said, as she pushed Samantha aside.

"Yes," the man with Mr. Smith said as he smiled. "He bled like a stuck pig but he didn't give you away. The dumb shit, I might have killed him quicker if he had given you up. But he was too stubborn to make it easy on himself."

"Then you will die," Christina said her voice becoming deep with a raspy undertone. She took slow steps toward the man. "And I will not be quick as I pull your limbs from your body."

"Christina," Samantha said. "Don't do anything foolish."

"This man is mine. He must pay for the death of Jake," Christina said as she shot across the room at the man with such speed that no one else had a chance to react. She grabbed a handful of his hair and jerked his head back with such force, an audible crack was heard. Her other hand sliced at his clothing at such speed that neither Smith nor Samantha could distinguish the blurred movement. Next she slowly ran her long fingernail under his chin drawing a line of blood.

"Stop it!" Samantha shouted.

"Shut up!" Christina shouted.

"I'll use this if I have to," Samantha said as she raised her hand which contained the remote in her hand.

Christina released the man and he fell to the floor. She gave him a final kick, pushing him several feet from where they stood.

"Temper my dear," Mr. Smith taunted. "You haven't exactly been honest yourself. You contributed to the man's death you wish to avenge. Why don't you explain to us why you have been hanging around Commander Reese?"

"What?" Samantha said. "Reese? You know of him? Why didn't you say anything?"

"Oh, I think she knows more of him then we thought," Smith insinuated. "Christina has been a very naughty little assassin. I checked the tracking records and discovered she has been hanging with our good friend Commander Reese on numerous occasions. Until now, I didn't know what she looked like. I do know she even signed up for his class. I saw you there," he said pointing at her with his finger.

"What do you know?" Samantha demanded. "What did Reese tell you? Answer me!"

"I know enough," she said. "When you had me kill General Stone and Commander Scott, I learned of Commander Reese. I was curious so I went to see him to find out why the General had said certain things about him."

"You didn't report that," Samantha said angrily. She marched toward Christina with the remote detonation switch in her hand in a threatening manner. "How much does Reese know?" she demanded. "You tell me or I'll blow you to fucking pieces!"

"He knows enough," a voice said. Out of the shadows Reese strode into plain view of the rest of them. His face was contorted into a look that reflected anger as his eyes darted around but when they settled upon Christina his faced appeared a clear look of betrayal.

"Well isn't this interesting," Smith said. "Here we all are."

"Yes," Reese agreed, "here we all are."

"I have to know, Reese," said Smith, "how long did it take for you to realize your girlfriend was a murdering assassin as well as a vampire?"

"I didn't know," Reese said coolly as he looked directly at Christina. "She maintained her cover perfectly the entire time I was with her as she used me to get information. Apparently she is very good at what she does."

"You're shitting me!" Smith cried. "Damn cold blood and all. What did you think you were kissing there buddy? Flesh and blood? Well there is some flesh, although it is dead, and blood, yeah well there is some of that too but who knows whose it is."

"That's enough!" Samantha shouted. "We are wasting time." She turned her attention to Reese. "You will work together to find the girls."

"No," Reese said.

"No? What do you mean no?"

"I'm done with this," he said. "This and a lot of things," he said as he glared at Christina.

"I don't think so," Smith said as he drew his gun out from its shoulder holster. "We insist upon your cooperation in our continued working relationship."

"You know what, Smith?" Reese said.

"What?"

"Bite me."

"You've been hanging around your girlfriend too long," Smith said and then laughed. "I'm not into that kind of kinky stuff."

"But I am," a voice sounded behind him.

Smith turned to face the direction from where the voice had come from. A tall figure stepped into the light. "Who the hell are you?" Smith asked as he leveled the gun at his approach.

"My name is Dimitri Bicannoff and I am one that does bite."

"Screw you!" Smith said and fired.

The bullets passed harmlessly through his body and a smile appeared on Dimitri's face as he watched Smith's expression of murderous rage turn to fear.

"My turn?" asked Dimitri.

CHAPTER FIFTY-EIGHT

Reese watched as the gunshots passed harmlessly through Dimitri. His head ached from the gunfire which was deafening in the underground cavern. But the pain from the sound did nothing to dispel the feelings of shock and betrayal that Reese was feeling. Feelings that struck deep into his heart.

Christina was a vampire.

He became detached from what was happening around him as he wallowed in his own doubt and anger. He didn't want to believe what he had just heard but deep inside he knew it was the truth. All of it. She killed for the agency. Her latest assignment had been the murders of General Stone and Commander Scott and that was where she learned about him and the possible existence to other creatures like herself. She wanted to learn about them through him. She used him to find others of her own kind.

Her own kind.

He remembered the words that had haunted him when he had used that phrase to try and understand Dimitri and his own visions of what life as a vampire would consist of. Now it all seemed meaningless to him as he watched the expression of Smith's face change to reflect the natural fear of these creatures. Yes, you should fear them, all of them you perverted son of a bitch!

"Reese," a voice screamed at him.

"What?" he moaned as if awakening from a dream. "What?" he asked again as he returned to the present.

"Reese!"

Reese turned toward Samantha just as she stepped up next to him. She grabbed him by his shirt with tightly clenched fists.

"So you didn't kill them," Samantha said.

Reese faced the woman who now had a look of anger upon her face, the tightened lines around her eyes and the terseness of her voice was matched by her words. "You son of a bitch, you turned them loose. All of them?"

"All of them," Reese simply answered. He saw no point in hiding what was apparent. He knew that Samantha was extremely intelligent and would naturally conclude the truth after seeing Dimitri.

"What gave you the right?" she asked. "They could have been used to help your country, yet you chose to set them loose to prey upon innocent humanity."

"With one big exception," he added, "with you, they would have killed whom you chose, like her," he said indicating Christina. "But this way, it's random and not always human life. There's no innocence left to protect, it's all gone to shit."

The thunderous sound of the gunfire was replaced by the sound of the clicks from the now empty gun. Reese watched as Dimitri stepped into reach and backhanded Smith. The force of the blow sent the man across the hard cement floor for several feet before coming to a stop. He didn't get up.

"That's enough," Samantha shouted. She showed everyone the device in her hand. "This party is over unless you want to see Christina here blown to pieces. I offer you all a chance to be part of history."

Reese stared at the device and was surprised at how much it mirrored his own design that he had used with his team; however, he did not see a collar on Christina and he wondered what it controlled. Samantha continued, "Together we can change the world."

"No thank you," Dimitri said interrupting her, "we do not wish to change the world to fit the order that you want."

Christina laughed at Dimitri's statement. For a brief instant, they exchanged a smile. Reese saw it and felt anger and jealousy. He turned his attention back to Samantha trying to diffuse the situation.

"Samantha," Reese began, "it's over. All of this madness."

"No it's not," she said adamantly. "And you can be a part of it as well. Think what we can do John. We can make the world a better place."

"No, he said, "I have to agree with Dimitri on this one. You want to make the world into what you think is right even if it means killing to do so. I'm not into playing God."

Samantha's face turned angry as she looked at Christina and Dimitri who now stood side by side. With her free hand she removed a small handgun from her holster under her jacket and pointed it squarely at Reese. In her other hand she held the remote device out with her thumb poised over the switch. "John, I can't risk them falling into anyone else's hands. This is an 'all or nothing' offer."

Reese glanced over at Christina. For a brief moment their eyes locked but he refused to allow himself to linger upon them. The time to act was now. He returned his gaze back toward Samantha and he smiled and shook his head. "No. If we end it here and now, then at least the nightmare will be over."

There was a brief silence and then all hell broke loose. Samantha fired the gun and depressed the button on the device at the same moment. Reese saw the puff of smoke from the handgun as he heard an explosion which he knew was not from the gun, but from some explosive device off to his side.

A bomb was inside of Christina? Was that what the remote controlled? He had killed them both.

Whether it was from the explosion or the bullet, Reese found himself being lifted off the ground and hurtling through the air. Darkness settled upon him and, strangely enough, he welcomed it because death would finally bring an end to this madness.

Chapter Fifty-Nine

"Sir, we can't get hold of Reese," Commander Pattoon said to General Morris. "He's not answering calls at home or on his cell."

They were in the command center of the SEAL compound. "What about Smith?" asked Morris.

"Same."

"How sure are you about this information?" Morris asked.

"Reese asked me to check out any homes under the name he gave me and one came up. It fits all the possible search criteria."

"So you think that Reese was working on a hunch of some kind that led him to this house?"

"Yes sir. He seemed very interested in it. In fact when he gave me the name, his voice said it was like a challenge of some sort."

"What do you mean?" the General asked.

"He said it as if he knew the person and that they wouldn't possibly do anything so brazen."

"Interesting," the General said, "very interesting."

"We can have everyone in place in less than an hour," said Pattoon.

"What's your recommendation, Commander?"

"Time is critical. I suggest we move on it at first light."

"Where is the house? Bring it up on screen."

Pattoon pressed a few keys on the keyboard and an aerial map appeared on the screen. An arrow pointed to a house.

"This is it here. It's in the Ocean View area of Norfolk, and that's not at all far from here. It would have been very convenient the night of the operation as well. And, the house has a bomb shelter."

"Yes, I get it," the General said sounding annoyed. "And what was the other evidence you had?"

"Surveillance has two girls and three men on video but it's nothing more than a glimpse."

"Still it could be another trap," the General mused.

"That is a possibility," agreed Pattoon.

"Why the hell did Reese pick this moment to be out of contact?"

"Sir, with all due respect, Reese is an asshole," Pattoon spat out.

The General looked at Pattoon but said nothing. After what felt to the younger man like hours, Morris replied, "Commander Pattoon, Reese may be an asshole but at least he's an intelligent one. You on the other hand are just an asshole."

Pattoon appeared speechless as he struggled to say something. He finally settled on, "Yes sir."

"Now, have Commander Ritter go ahead with the operation."

CHAPTER SIXTY

Reese opened his eyes. When his vision finally came into focus, he saw that he was staring up at a ceiling made of smooth cement. One side of his head throbbed immensely and he raised his hand to touch it. A bolt of pain exploded through his head causing him to shut his eyes. As painful as it was, the pain did confirm that he was still very much alive. He was not sure if he should be happy or sad about this discovery and finally decided that ambivalence was perhaps the best he could do for the moment.

When the pain subsided and he was able to open his eyes, he examined his surroundings. He was in a large bed within a cavernous room. Although it had been extensively decorated, he took note of the cement walls and ceilings concluding that he was still in the underground compound. He remembered those last moments of Samantha firing her gun and pressing the button on the remote device. There was an explosion and...

"How's the head," a woman's voice asked him.

He turned his head slowly to see Christina standing next to the bed. She was still alive...

"How? What happened?" he asked. "The explosion, there was...it was inside of you?"

Christina took a step closer to the bed. "Samantha didn't know that I removed the explosive device from my own body. I kept it with me because it had a tracker built into it and she would have noticed the lack of movement eventually. When she showed up here tonight, I knew I had to get rid of it because before the night was over after I told her I was done with her and her organization, she was going to press that button. When the man admitted to killing Jake, I knew she wouldn't let me kill him so I used the opportunity to put the explosive device inside of his jacket."

"Who was Jake?" asked Reese as he winced from the pain.

"It's rather a long story. Get some rest. We can talk later."

Then he remembered, "The gun? Did I get shot?"

"No. When the explosion went off, she fired the gun at the same moment. Dimitri was able to push you out of the way of the bullet, but he had to use such force that you were thrown against the wall where you received the head injury. I think you might have a concussion."

"Oh," he said. Now that the immediate answers had been gotten, his feelings of anger and frustration returned. "Why didn't you tell me?" asked Reese. "Why didn't you tell me that you're a vampire?"

"We'll have a long talk later," she said. "You need to rest. Now sleep."

Reese tried to fight the fatigue and the pain, but he couldn't. In addition, Christina's suggestion of sleep offered a reprieve and he was glad to take it. He closed his eyes and drifted.

★★★

The darkness of the night passed into the light of the day. Christina could feel this as she exited her bedroom. There would be no rest this day with all that had happened and all that waited to be learned. She returned to the living room area of her home at the same moment Dimitri entered from another corridor. She stared at the man as he moved easily and effortlessly toward where she now was. She still had a difficult time believing that he, as well as the other man that had joined them, the one called Andre, were creatures just like her. They had been somewhat cautious in their brief discussions and had not delved much beyond her connection to the agency and Dimitri's and his men's previous affiliation with the military and Commander John Reese.

"I locked Samantha and Smith in the holding cells," Dimitri said.

"Good," she replied. She couldn't help feeling awkward in some way for she had never been in the company of her own kind.

"It is our way," said Dimitri, "the uncomfortable feeling of being in the company of others. If you are not used to it, it takes a while to become accustomed to it."

"You can sense me?" she asked.

"Your feeling is quite strong," he replied. "Come and sit," he said indicated the table and chairs. They both sat at the table, their hands folded in front of them and their eyes lowered avoiding making contact with one another.

"Where do we begin?" Dimitri finally suggested. "We have some sort of connection which I suspect is through our creator although he never told me that he had created another."

"I was created by Alexander," she began. "He probably did not tell you because he didn't want to share his failure with you."

"I don't understand," said Dimitri.

"It was so long ago," she said. "I am not proud of what I did. I tricked him with my anger into turning me into what you see. He did not know that my hatred was so intense that even as I neared death I was still able to attack him."

"But later, didn't he help?"

"There was no later," she said cutting Dimitri off. "He left me that night probably hoping that his mistake would die without the knowledge of what I was. I was totally on my own. I struggled to survive and to learn what I had become. When I realized my strengths and the power it afforded me, I walked the path of revenge for many years killing indiscriminately under the guise of revenge."

"He never mentioned it," said Dimitri. "We spent many years together until his death."

"You are lucky to have had the benefit of his wisdom. I wish I had. But I don't blame him for what he did - his leaving me. He seemed to be a good man and I think he tried to convince me that my anger would destroy me."

"This anger, do you still feel it?" asked Dimitri.

"No. I have finally rid myself of it and the chains with which it imprisoned me. I stayed with these people, doing their killing, because it offered me the opportunity to keep those feelings alive."

"What happened to cause you to rid yourself of it?"

"I had some kind of vision. Alexander came to me. He showed me how I could be somewhat human again; showed me that I could love and give meaning to my existence."

"Why now?" pressed Dimitri.

"This man, John Reese, he caused something inside of me to, I don't know, awaken perhaps," her voice rose slightly with the reflective question. "He made me think that it was possible to love again. He made me feel that I could leave my anger behind me and move ahead with these feelings."

"But you sought him out initially because of what you learned from General Stone about the existence of others like yourself."

"Yes that is true. I had no other goal in mind other than that in the beginning. I had planned to use him to get the information I wanted."

"You simply could have taken it from his thoughts," stated Dimitri.

"Yes I know," she agreed. "But I didn't want to do that. There was just something about him."

"And now? What shall you do?" asked Dimitri.

"I don't know," she said. "I am still sorting some things out. But tell me, you've known John Reese longer then I have, what do you think of him?"

"He is, interesting," replied Dimitri, "however he is a troubled man. He fears what life has to offer."

"I don't understand," replied Christina. "What does he fear?"

"It is not my place to tell you," Dimitri said bluntly. His change in demeanor did not go unnoticed by Christina.

"Why not, she asked, "why does this upset you?"

"What you seek is impossible," Dimitri said his voice harsh and direct.

"How do you know what I seek?" she answered in a tone that responded to his.

"As I said earlier," Dimitri said, "your feelings are known to me. I know that you believe that you love this man."

Chapter Sixty-One

Christina felt the sting of the way Dimitri had said the word, believe. "You don't know everything," she countered. "You may sense my feelings but you can't understand the motivation behind those feelings."

"I know enough," he said. "You have been consumed by your anger far too long to know the impossibility of what you seek. Would you turn him into a slave like the others you have used?"

"It's not like that," she said. "Those that I used were a matter of survival, there was no feeling beyond that."

"Yet you used them freely and willingly. Perhaps you even thought you loved them as well. Like your latest, this man called Jake. All these years you used him and now he is dead because of your 'matter of survival.' What did you promise Jake? What was the lingering thought that kept him from any chance of a normal life?"

The way Dimitri used Jake's name stung her like a sharp knife to the heart. "Yes I used him and I promised him life immortal - with me. It was wrong. Nothing I can do can change that fact. But that is all in the past. I have changed now."

"Have you?" asked Dimitri. "Our kind does not give up the past easily. Our friend Josip followed the same path as you and it ended in his death because he could not give up his anger."

"I have changed," Christina said, her voice firm.

"Perhaps you have," Dimitri said unconvinced, "but you have led this man to believe that you are something you are not. I saw the look on his face when he learned that you are a vampire. If you were so sure then why did you not tell him?"

"It was, I don't know, maybe because I wanted to learn what he knew at first, but then it... it changed. I knew that if I told him, I would have to use my persuasion on him and I didn't want that. For once in my life, I wanted this man to be of his own free will and to want me for what I am."

"This is madness," Dimitri scoffed. "Think of what you are saying. Even if he did love you, what would happen? Do you think there would be any form of a normal life for you? Can you watch him grow old and die? Or did you think he will become one of us?"

"The thought had crossed my mind," she said.

Dimitri immediately shook his head. "No."

"What do you mean, no?"

"This cannot happen," said Dimitri firmly. "Not now, not ever."

"Why not?" she demanded.

Dimitri rose from his chair with such force that it flew out from under him and skidded across the floor for several feet. "Will you play God? Will you be foolish enough to think that you can make this man into the one thing he fears most?"

"What do you mean? What does he fear?" asked Christina as she braced her hands against the table as if preparing to fend off an attack.

"You've seen his nightmare," Dimitri continued. "The man has become tormented by what he has learned of us. He loathes and cherishes our way of life! He wants to be like us but he cannot bear the loss of humanity his short life offers. To force him into this would be asking him to go against what he believes the most. He would live his life as a vampire with endless regret for what he gave up."

"You talk nonsense!" Christina countered.

"No, you talk foolishness," he shot back. "You refuse to face what you are. You believe that loving this man will return to you what you have lost through your anger."

"And that is what?"

"Your humanity."

"I think not!" she cried.

"You are a vampire, Christina! You are no longer human nor can you re-attain that through him. You belong to our kind now and for the rest of the time that you choose to continue this life. There are no other options, no halfway points that you can rejoin humanity."

"You can't talk for me!" she screamed at him. "I can choose my own way of life."

"Perhaps, but I will not allow you to make him into one of us!"

Christina rose from her chair and faced Dimitri. "You do not control me or what I choose to do." Her fingers dug into the sides of the table sending the sound of wood cracking and splintering echoing through the room.

Dimitri lowered his voice and tried to speak calmly, "Alexander made us with the intent to save our lives because he sensed that it was not our time to die at the vicious hands of others. He did not make us to create more pain and anguish in a world that already has as much as it can handle. There are things we need to do to help our own kind as well as humanity."

"And how would you help humanity?" she asked.

"By leaving it alone. Our kind was not made to interfere with the choices of the humans."

"Yet we kill them," she said pointedly.

"At times, but I believe this in an odd way is part of the process. We are not drawn to those that are full of life and participate in their society. It is the outcasts that we take. In addition, my men and I have not taken any humans in quite some time. We are content with the blood of animals."

"You speak as if you know precisely what we are and what we are meant to do. Who deemed you to be an authority?"

"While your life has been here in this country for many years doing the bidding of a few humans, my life has been one of discovery through the ancient texts. The one thing that I have learned and confirmed time and time again is that out kind has realized the importance of ignoring the humans and their existence. We have left it behind to pursue a quiet existence. This quiet existence ensures our survival through the centuries."

"You call what you have done, quiet? You were a pawn for the humans as much as I."

"All against our will, we were taken from our homes when Josip ignored what I have been telling you about. He got involved where he should not have. What happened to us should not have happened. I thought we could exist here but lately I have come to realize that we do not belong here. The West is too complicated. This place is all wrong. It is impossible to not get involved within the sphere of human existence."

"Maybe that was meant to happen. It is a part of our evolution."

"If we had arrived here of our own free will, then perhaps I might agree. But we were forced out of our natural environment."

"And what shall you do now?" she asked.

"We shall go home. I have decided to return to the Balkans with the girls. They have just begun their adjustment to their new way of life. I think it best to have them in an environment they are familiar with."

"I would agree with you on that," she said remembering her own time when she had to deal with her change. "They should be near home."

"And you should come as well," Dimitri said.

Christina looked at him sharply. "And do what?"

"You belong with your own kind. You can join us and be part of our group. The girls will need a mother figure to help them."

"And what of Reese?" she asked.

"He stays here. Where he belongs. He will have his books and research to occupy what remains of his mortal life."

"I will stay here!" shouted Christina.

"Will you not see the truth in what you suggest!" demanded Dimitri.

"I love him."

"You love what he represents: A mortal life. If you stay, you will watch him die. You have your own kind that needs you. The girls must have the guiding hand of a woman to help them transition."

"Dimitri," Andre said as he entered into the room holding a cell phone. "They have captured Iliga and the girls."

"What?" asked Dimitri. "We had other houses that they should have gone to first."

"Somehow they figured out where we were," said Andre.

"I sent them there," Reese said as he staggered out from the bedroom. "I had them do a search in the real estate records under your real name just for the hell of it. Apparently something came up and that's where they went."

"That was a foolish mistake on my part," said Dimitri. "I underestimated you again Commander."

"It doesn't matter now. We have to figure out some way to get them back," Reese said.

"You should not be up," Christina said to Reese as she rose from her chair.

"I'm all right," he said avoiding looking at her directly. "We have bigger problems to worry about. If they have Iliga, then they will figure out that the whole team survived. They will go all out to find you now."

"We can go to the compound and get them out as we did before," Dimitri said.

"I wouldn't count on that," said Reese. "They have strengthened security a lot since your break in."

"But we are still more powerful."

"Be that as it may, the chances of getting out of there alive would be slim. We have to take a different type of approach." Reese turned to Christina, "Who knows about this place?"

"Only Samantha and the people she works for," she said.

"That sounds about right, considering it's the agency. How are our friends?"

"Unconscious," Andre said. "I just checked on them a few minutes ago."

"Good," Reese said. "I need to make a call, and then I will go down to the cell and let Samantha out while you are all sleeping."

Dimitri, Christina and Andre stared at Reese.

Chapter Sixty-Two

Samantha awoke in her cell on a cot that smelled of mildew and decay of many years. Turning her head to one side she could see an array of cells that lined the corridor of the area she was in. It looked like some kind of holding area. She sat up and winced. She felt bruised on just about every inch of her body. She remembered being thrown back from the explosion and then being knocked unconscious by Christina, who should have been killed by the explosion, however apparently she had removed the device from her body and planted it on the man she had wanted to kill. What a smart bitch!

"Samantha," a voice called to her pulling her from her thoughts. She turned and saw Reese coming toward her cell. She noticed that his head had been bandaged, a red splotch stood out from the blood that had saturated an area of it.

"We have to move fast," he said. "They're asleep."

"You bastard! What do you want? You're one of them," she said almost hissing. "If I had a gun, I'd try and shoot you again but this time I wouldn't fail."

"Look," Reese said pleadingly, "I know this is going to be hard to swallow, but they had me under their control. I had no choice but to do what they demanded until this happened," he said as he indicated the bandage on his head. "The injury somehow blanks out their hypnotic control. It must affect a portion of the brain that is susceptible to suggestion. I've read about it, but didn't think anything of it until now."

"Why should I believe you?" she asked.

"Do you want out of that cell?" he asked.

Samantha was speechless for the moment as she appeared to not think of a reason why she would say no.

"Look," Reese began, "I had no choice. I was their prisoner and there was no way to stop what they made me do. I've been their slave ever since the last operation I went on with them. They made me switch the remote control devices so it looked like they were killed. They kept me where I was to substantiate the story, that way there wouldn't be any doubt about their deaths."

"Then why did that vampire save you when I was going to kill you?" she asked pointedly.

"Because I'm still very valuable to them; I have access to everything they need to keep their existence a secret. They have done this through the centuries, enslaving humans to do their bidding. Why do you think we haven't found the girls yet? It's because they know everything we do—through me."

"You could be lying. You're making this all up," she said.

"What good would that do me now? You're going to have to believe me," he said as he held up the key to the cell. "Your call. Do you want to stay in the cell and die or do you want to get out with me and try and salvage your vision for the future?"

She looked at the key and then back at him. She knew she didn't have much choice and her current situation didn't look like it would afford her any opportunity on her own. Besides, maybe he was telling the truth. It certainly explained a lot of things that had happened.

"If we can get Lieutenant Colonel Barkley out here," Reese continued, "we can get collars on all of them while they're still asleep, but we have to move now."

"Open it up," she said, "but so help me God, if you're lying, I'll skin you alive myself."

Reese slid the key into the lock and turned it. The door opened and she walked out into the corridor.

"What about Mr. Smith?" she asked.

"He's still out. We can come back later for him," answered Reese as he indicated the direction down the corridor.

In silence, they walked back toward the main area of the underground cavern. Samantha kept an eye on Reese as they walked. She couldn't help wonder if what he had said had been true. Had he been a prisoner all this time? It certainly explained a lot of things about the way he had acted.

"We can call General Morris and have him come out with a containment team," she said testing to see what his response would be.

"We can, but is that really what you want?" he asked.

"What do you mean?"

Reese continued, "Lieutenant Colonel Barkley I know I can trust. General Morris, I think, has his own agenda in mind."

"What do you know of him?" she asked.

"He's just like General Stone. He sees this as a way to achieve his own goals whatever the cost. If he gets involved, this might turn into something other than what you want. Isn't that why you had Stone and Scott killed?"

"They were incompetent," she said plainly as if there were doubt about the issue. "What makes you think he has his own ideas?"

"The man has body guards for Christ sakes. Have you ever heard of that being done before? I haven't. He doesn't like you or the agency involvement. He has protection because he fears you and when a man of his stature fears someone, the best way to get rid of that fear is to remove it. You should realize that more than I do."

"What are you suggesting?" she asked.

"As long as the military is involved, the chance of discovery remains high. You have the opportunity to start over and get it right this time and with more vampires."

Samantha eyed him suspiciously, yet she liked the idea of where he was going. After all, hadn't her original plan considered having Reese involved because of his knowledge and expertise with the creatures?

"I heard the vampires talking earlier," Reese continued. "Morris has found the two girls and the other vampire of Dimitri's group. They are being held at the compound. If we could somehow get them here, then you have the authority to make everything else go away."

"Why here?" she asked.

"This place is perfect. How long has Christina lived here without being located?"

"Over sixty years," she answered.

"We can keep all of them here and no one else will know about it. We know that the collars that I designed work. As long as they wear them we have positive control."

"But the girls got away last time even with the collars," she said.

"Yes, but Barkley and I questioned the med guy who made the elixir neutralizer. It is only temporary and he only gave them a small amount and what they had, they used it all up. It'll work better than whoever came up with the idea of the explosive device because they overlooked the fact that these creatures have no living DNA. Christina could have gotten away at any time she wanted."

She thought for a few seconds about what he was proposing. "Are you sure Barkley can be trusted?"

"Yes. He is the only one I trust and he has been in on this from the beginning. By the way, speaking of trust, I'm not too sure about your friend, Mr. Smith."

"He is a tool," she said without thought. "His methods are questionable but he gets things done. However, he is not a necessity to this project."

"Well for the time being then, how about if we leave him where he is?" asked Reese.

"Get Barkley out here, get the collars on them first, and then we'll see."

Reese picked up the phone and made the call.

CHAPTER SIXTY-THREE

When Barkley arrived in a vehicle that included the containment equipment, both Reese and Samantha met him. Reese instructed Barkley and Samantha which boxes to take with them and then hurried back inside. They placed the equipment on the floor and then the three sat at the small table discussing how they would proceed.

"We have three of them here," Reese said, "the toughest will be Dimitri so we do him first. The way in which we will proceed is that you two will cover me as I place the collars on them."

"Are you sure they will stay asleep?" Samantha asked.

"They should. However, if they don't, that is where you two come in." He turned to Samantha, "I want you to take the backpack sprayer that is filled with the elixir and stand in a position where you could spray them if need be. It won't take much so don't overdo the spray. Too much and it will kill them. One full spray should be enough. Sam will back you up with the machete if he has to take their heads off."

"I hope that is a last option," she said.

"It is," Reese agreed, "it's more of an intimidation factor then anything else. I don't think we will need it, but just in case, we'll have it available."

"Where is the remote control device?" she asked.

Barkley removed two of the devices from a pouch. "I've already tested them to ensure they work. All you need to do now is place your thumb over the pad and press the green button. This will allow the device to set to your DNA. If it senses anyone else's DNA, it will inject the elixir."

"Does that include our friends?" asked Reese. "Who do not have any DNA?"

"No DNA is the same as a different DNA. If the device senses the change, it will go off."

"Good," Reese said as he took the two remotes, he kept one for himself and gave the other to Samantha. Both of them went through the process of establishing the DNA pattern for each remote.

"Remember," Barkley began, "now that you have activated the remotes, the green button will inject the full amount of elixir, killing the creatures; the orange button will inject a tiny amount that can be used as a reminder of the control over them."

"Well then," Reese began as he looked at his watch, "It's a little past noon, so the timing doesn't get any better then that. Are you two ready?"

"Yes," Samantha said as she looped her arms through the backpack sprayer and hoisted it on her back.

"Good to go," said Barkley as he hefted the machete in his hand.

"Let's do it then," he said and they proceeded to the sleeping chamber of Dimitri and Andre.

The male vampires had chosen one of the open areas that were arranged as sleeping quarters for twenty to thirty men. Reese surmised it was probably to hold troops who had been lucky enough to have been assigned to the underground shelter in the event of nuclear war or other catastrophic event. In the center of the room, Dimitri and Andre had chosen two cots and placed them parallel to each other about twenty feet apart.

The group approached silently and took up position on the outer edge of the cot which Dimitri slept upon. Reese held the collar in his hands at the ready as he studied how Dimitri's head was placed. He kneeled down and looked to see if there was space enough to slide the collar underneath his head without disturbing him. He smiled at Barkley and gave him the thumbs up sign.

Reese slowly slid one end of the collar through the space between Dimitri's head and mattress, and reached around with his other hand to grab it. With an end in each hand, Reese brought the two ends together. They locked together with a resounding metallic click that sounded thunderous in the cavernous room just as Dimitri's eyes opened.

The vampire appeared surprised seeing Reese standing over him. He grasped Reese with both hands and tossed him effortlessly several feet away. Next his hands went to the metallic collar on his throat and he let out a thunderous howl. "No!" Dimitri screamed. "I will not allow this again!" He sat up, his hands still on the collar around his neck. Samantha and Barkley instinctively backed up in horror of the enraged creature.

Reese screamed to Samantha, "Give him a jolt to remind him!"

Samantha removed the remote and pressed the orange button. Dimitri jerked spasmodically and screamed again. Andre now awoke. Samantha turned her attention toward him and pointed the sprayer. "You move and you'll burn in hell," she cried.

Reese was back on his feet and moved quickly to where Andre still lay. Removing the other collar from his pouch he approached Andre with the device in the open position ready to put it on. The vampire hissed at Reese, baring his fangs in a threatening manner.

Reese spoke, "You may not give a rat's ass about your own life, but if you make a move, Andre, she'll kill Dimitri."

Andre looked in the direction of Dimitri who was still writhing in pain. His aggressive demeanor changed as quickly as it had arrived. Reese slipped the collar on him and then stepped back.

"Well that was a little intense," said Reese.

"How long will he be distracted by the pain," Samantha asked.

"It should subside fairly quickly," Barkley said.

"I want you to remain here," Reese said to Andre.

"I'll kill y-o-u," Dimitri muttered between clenched teeth. "Te-ar you limb from limb."

"Not today, my vampire friend," Reese shot back. "No more hypnotic control for you, thanks to the head injury you gave me. You and Andre are to remain here," he repeated. "We'll be back after we pay a call on Christina."

Reese and his group left the room.

"Are you all right?" Barkley asked Reese, "You've been getting beat up a lot lately."

"That wasn't too bad. We caught them off guard so he wasn't as powerful as he could have been. Let's hope Christina goes off better."

Chapter Sixty-Four

The three approached Christina's bedroom. Peering in from the doorway, they saw that she lay upon her bed asleep, apparently unaware of the disturbance that had taken place minutes ago with Dimitri and Andre.

"Wait a minute," said Reese in a low whisper. We need to switch tasks for this one."

"Why?" asked Samantha.

"Barkley and I will be more susceptible to her power because she is a woman. She might use that to her advantage to gain some time. You put the collar on her," he said to Samantha, "and I'll take the sprayer." Reese handed her the collar and showed her how it was to be fastened. Then he took the backpack sprayer from her and shrugged it on.

"Ready?" he asked.

The two nodded their heads in agreement.

"Let's go then," he said and they entered the room.

Unlike the sparse and unadorned quarters where Dimitri and Andre had been, this room had been arranged with much more care. The three of them silently walked around furniture and other objects that impeded their path to the bed.

Samantha, with the collar in her hands and outstretched in front of her, approached one side of the bed. Reese followed behind her and Barkley took the other side. Samantha looked at Reese who nodded to proceed.

"What do you intend to do with that?" Christina said as her eyes opened and she stared at Samantha who stopped moving toward her.

"Lie still," Reese said as he pointed the sprayer toward her.

"Why, John," she said, "this is not very gentlemanly of you; taking advantage of a woman while she sleeps." There was a sharp and mocking edge to her voice.

"You have never felt the effects of the elixir," Reese said, "if you resist us, you shall."

"I could never resist you," she said, her voice changing into a seductive tone. "Tell me what you want and I will do it for you, John. Whatever you want, John. All you have to do is tell me. Just send her away," she said indicating Samantha. "Once she is gone I can give you anything you want. Anything…"

"I can't do that," he said. "You have no power over me."

"Perhaps, I don't," she mused, "but I do over him," she said indicating Barkley. "If you try and spray me he will use that machete on you."

Reese turned toward Barkley. His facial expression appeared confused and dazed. The machete in his hands trembled as if he was undergoing some internal struggle for control.

"Leave her alone, John," he said in a voice that trembled and sounded unsure.

"Sam, give me the machete," Reese said trying to keep his voice calm and even. Sam's eyes remained focused upon Christina.

"He will only do as I say," Christina said, her voice confident and sure. "We are, as you say, at a stalemate."

"I don't think so," Reese said. "Before he can kill me, I will spray the elixir on you and you will die."

"Are you really going to gamble upon your quickness over mine?" said Christina. "You should know better, John."

"I should know better about many things," said Reese as he looked upon Christina. "But this is one thing I am sure about. You may have used me before with your hypnotic abilities, but this time it's different. You will allow Samantha to place the collar upon you or you will die."

"Idle threat," Christina said. "You can never kill me."

"Now who is gambling?" asked Reese. "Are you so sure that you're right this time? You used me and misled me. I thought you loved me but I know that was all a ruse and nothing more."

The smile from Christina's face faded slightly as she appeared to comprehend what Reese has just said.

Reese glanced over at Sam. His body was trembling; perspiration was pasted upon his forehead as he struggled to maintain some form of control over his body. Whatever was going to happen was going to happen soon, one way or the other.

"Before Sam can kill me, I will get off some elixir," Reese said, "that will give Samantha enough time to get the collar on you. So either way you lose."

Reese saw the effect that his statement had on Christina. Her facial features became stern and the red glow in her eyes became more intense. It was so intense, that even Reese wasn't sure if she was getting ready to attack or if she was going to allow them to proceed. "Put the collar on her now," said Reese to Samantha as he struggled to keep his voice even.

Samantha didn't move. She appeared to be frozen, her eyes wide with fear. "Samantha! Move! Put the collar on her now!" Reese said firmly.

His voice apparently woke Samantha from her fear. She moved quickly placing the collar upon the vampire. During the process, Christina's eyes never left Reese.

Reese didn't breathe until he heard the metallic click of the collar as it closed tightly around Christina's neck. When the collar was on, Reese heard the sound of a heavy thump. He looked to where Sam had been standing only moments before and saw that he was now lying on the floor.

"Put her with the others," Reese said to Samantha. "I'll take care of Sam."

"Revenge will be sweet and painful for you," Christina said, "that I promise you."

"Shut up!" Samantha said to Christina. "You and the others will follow our orders or you will die!"

"I escaped your control once, I will do it again," said Christina her voice sounding like a snarl of an animal.

"Not this time," Samantha said as she pressed the orange button on the remote control device she held in her hand. Christina writhed violently upon her bed for several seconds. When her seizure subsided, Samantha spoke, "Now you see what the collar can do. That was only a small amount of the elixir." Christina didn't say anything. But the meaning in the look she gave Samantha was clearly evident.

"Now get up and let's go," Samantha said forcefully.

As Samantha led Christina out of the room, Reese kneeled down next to Sam. "Sam, can you hear me?"

"What the hell was that all about?" said Sam. "One minute I'm standing here next to the bed and then I'm somewhere else, with her," he said indicating the now empty bed. "What happened?"

"Oh, not too much," Reese said, "you were merely ready to cut my head off with the machete, but other than that everything is fine now."

Sam gave Reese a disbelieving look. "You've got to be shitting me?"

"I wish I was, Sam. It was very close for a few moments there, even I wasn't sure what Christina was going to do, but Samantha got the collar on her and now she is taking her to join the others."

"God damn it!" Sam said. "This plan of yours better work, John."

"I hope so too," said Reese. "It sure looked convincing. Christina even had me wondering what was going to happen, Samantha probably bought it."

"So now what?" Sam asked.

"We made it through the first part, but now we move onto the second which is the hardest part. If we screw up one thing, the whole plan will backfire. So we have to make sure we get it right."

"Amen to that," Sam said.

Chapter Sixty-Five

After Samantha placed Christina with Dimitri and André, she rejoined Reese in the main meeting area of the underground cavern. "How is Lieutenant Colonel Barkley doing?" she asked.

"He's okay, just a little shaken up. How are you doing?"

"I'm fine," she said, "I was a little nervous back there. For a moment, I didn't know if she was going to have Barkley use that machete on you or not."

"That makes two of us," he said. "But luckily it worked."

"Yes it did," she said, the exuberance of the outcome was evident in her voice. "Tell me, would you have sprayed her?"

"In a heartbeat," he said without hesitation. "Now that they no longer have control over me, I hate them for the way they used me."

"How can we prevent that from happening again?" she asked. "We need to be sure that they never get control again."

"Sam and I learned that people on certain drugs are not susceptible to their influence. So he thinks he can come up with something that will deaden that part of the brain. I've read that some people, such as yourself, have a natural block to their influence, otherwise Christina would have used it on you."

"How long will it take to develop?" she asked.

"Not long, he's already on it."

Her face took on a curious expression, "You seem to have changed your opinion of these creatures," she stated.

"If they had taken you and forced you to do their bidding, wouldn't you feel the same way?" Reese said the anger in his voice evident. "I was nothing more than a tool for them to get what they wanted. When they were done with me they would have simply killed me. So yeah, I hate them!"

"Yes. I suppose I would feel the same way." She paused for a few seconds before going on. "And now you have the opportunity to do the same with them."

"Are you offering me a job?" he asked.

"If you want the job, it's yours," she said. "I need someone with your talents, someone who knows and understands the motivations of these creatures. We have a job to do John because this world is a terrible place.

Now we have the opportunity to fix everything that's wrong and make it right."

"You're really serious about this aren't you?" he asked.

"Oh yes John. I'm quite serious about this. I've been planning it for a long, long time and now I can see it all coming to fruition. You and I can do this. That is, as long as you have the stomach for it."

"You say, you and I, does that mean people like General Morris will not be included in this little plan of yours?"

"Like you said earlier, John, Morris has his plans, and I have mine. After what I've seen here today, I think we can do just fine on our own."

"We will need some support staff types," said Reese. "Lieutenant Colonel Barkley would be perfect for this."

"We can discuss all of it later John. First things first, you said earlier that we should probably get all the vampires located in this compound. Do you still feel that this is the best plan?"

"The sooner we get them out of General Morris's hands, the better off we'll be. The longer he has them, the more ideas he will get on how to use them. That would endanger your own plans for them, wouldn't it?"

"Yes. Yes it would," she agreed.

"Do you think you can get them moved here tonight?" he asked.

She thought for a few seconds before answering. "He has possession," she said, "even with my authority in this matter, questions will be asked and that might not be a good thing. It might be difficult if he doesn't want to give them up unless I bring in more personnel to assist."

"I don't think we need any more people involved," Reese asserted. "We still have an advantage."

"What's that?" she asked.

"They don't know that we have captured these three and as far as they know, we are still on the same side. We could just tell them we are taking them to be interrogated or on a training mission or something. Whatever story that gets them out of the way."

"And if they don't buy it?" she asked.

"Then we go to the back-up plan," he said.

"And that is?"

"We take them by force."

CHAPTER SIXTY-SIX

He had some time to kill, so Reese went to the area the vampires were being held in their mock captivity. He entered the room and found Dimitri and Christina in conversation. The sight of the two sitting so close to one another, almost intimate in appearance, shot a bolt of jealousy through Reese. He tried to contain the feeling as he cleared his thoughts and pushed aside his mixed feelings about her. He tried, but many of those feelings refused to be pushed aside.

He thought how she had been with him, the intimacy that they had shared and how he could have missed all the signs that she was a vampire. He remembered her caressing touch and contrasted it with her appearance of a few hours ago when she threatened to have Barkley take his head off. The image of the inflamed eyes and the extended canine vampire teeth along with her threats of death resonated in his thoughts.

He cleared his throat. Both of them looked at him. Reese had never thought of it before, but their similar geographical physical characteristics made them appear almost as brother and sister. Neither one spoke, but rather just stared at him with questioning expressions. Reese found himself focusing on the collars they wore around their necks. The sight reminding him of the beginning of the original mission.

"Samantha is on her way to the compound," he said, breaking the silence.

Dimitri and Christina separated, taking seats at opposite ends of the table that sat in one corner of the room. Andre sat off to the side examining a computer screen ignoring everyone else.

"So we wait," Dimitri began, "to see if your plan will work. I have my doubts that she will be able to get them out so easily." He rubbed at the collar that he wore. "I forgot how uncomfortable these things are."

"It's all we have for the moment," Reese replied, ignoring the obvious dig about the collar. His eyes kept drifting toward Christina who sat at the table with her hands folded in front of her and her eyes focused upon them. He wanted to wait for an opportunity to talk to her; however, those opportunities were beginning to fade quicker with every passing hour. Reese continued, "But if she can't get them out, then we will have to go in. All of us."

"It will be…interesting," Dimitri said as he stood from the chair.

He looked at Reese for several seconds and then at Christina. "Andre," Dimitri called, "we need to…" he hesitated, looking a bit uncomfortable, "we need to check the compound to see if there is any equipment we may need."

Andre looked at Dimitri, his face briefly betraying his confusion at Dimitri's request. They exchanged a quick glance and then Andre rose from the table he was sitting at and moved toward the door.

"We will be back later," Dimitri said to Reese.

They left the room without another sound. Reese knew that what Dimitri had just done was to allow him time to talk with Christina alone. They knew each other too well, he thought.

He directed his gaze toward Christina. So much had happened over the last twelve hours that changed everything he'd been feeling and believing. He'd been waiting all this time to talk to her and now that the time was here, he found it hard to begin. There was so much he wanted to say, but so little he knew how to express. He was angry at her and yet still felt the attraction he had since the moment he realized he cared for her. He had questions, but he wasn't sure he wanted to hear the answers. There was so much he wanted to say and no clue where to begin.

"Christina," Reese finally said. "Why? Why didn't you tell me?"

She raised her gaze to meet his. "Tell you what, John?" she asked. "That I was a vampire? That I was an assassin for your government? Or that I wanted to learn what you knew about others of my kind?"

"All of it," he replied.

"And what would you have done?" she asked. "Would you have understood my motivations? Would you have still wanted to make love to a creature of the night that preys on others?"

Reese paused and then said, "If you had given me the chance I …"

"What? You would have changed your mind about my kind? Do you think you could have understood what it was that drove me to do what I have done?"

"I don't know what your kind is capable of emotionally."

"Do you wish to study me?" she said sharply. "Is this a continuation of your research? Is that what I am?"

"No! Damn it! Please listen to me!" shouted Reese. "Can you imagine how I felt when I learned you were a vampire? You know enough about me to understand that I don't give in to my emotions. It's not the way I am. But with you I opened my heart to feelings that I thought I could never have again. If you had told me perhaps it would have been easier than hearing it from the lips of Samantha the psychotic spook!"

"Would that have really changed anything, John? Would that have softened the facts about what I have done?"

"The past is the past," he said.

"Not with you. For you," she began, "the past is your life. You make it your reality. You give it the power to create your fears. It haunts you John."

"This is not about me," he said.

"You're right, John, it's not about you but it is about us." She rose from the table and walked toward him. "Let's lay it all out on the table shall we. I didn't expect any of this to happen. When I sought you out, I had only the intention of using you to figure out what General Stone had insinuated before I killed him and discover what I could about the existence of others like me. But all of that changed when you made me feel... human again John. I haven't felt that way for a long, long time. It enabled me to see clearly for the first time in over sixty years. I learned that my captivity was of my own choosing and that I could break it if I wanted. And I did. This unexpected surge of emotions made me think I could once again be like I was, a woman who wanted to love and be loved."

"Was that so bad?" he asked.

"Not in its entirety," she said, "fantasy is a wonderful thing, John. But that's fantasy. Reality takes on a completely different light. Dimitri and I talked about things and the more I think about it the more I think he's right."

"About what?" Reese asked.

"Come on, John, think sensibly about this. We lead two different kinds of life, just like you say in your book."

"In time, we could adjust to a way of life," he said. "We can try?"

"What life? Do you think we could live happily ever after with a dog and white picket fence? A normal boring life in a suburban neighborhood? You can have tea with the neighbors at night while I hunt for food?"

"Maybe we can adjust," he said.

"You mean change," she said sharply. "That is what this is all about isn't it? One of us must change and yet neither one of us can. I can't become human and you can't become a vampire."

The words become a vampire shot through him like a knife being jabbed repeatedly into his abdomen. Anger, fear, and anxiety flushed through him trying to drown him. He struggled to find the words to speak but none came.

"You know I'm right about this John. I can see it in your eyes as we speak."

"But you've lived with humans before," the tone of his voice reflecting a mixture of confusion and anger.

"Yes, John, I have. There have been many like Jake over the years. I used them for their blood and protection by promising them my love and immorality. Then when they were near death, I just let them die. Is that what you want? You want to live an illusion of love and then die unfulfilled? Or would you like to end up like Jake, murdered by some agency who seeks control of my kind."

"You can give up what we have so easily?" he asked, his voice sounding defeated.

"Easily? Oh no, John. I've searched so long and hard for what we have. I'm not letting go of it easily. You will agonize over what we can do until it kills you, but I've caused enough pain in my lifetime to not want to cause anymore."

"I can..." he began as he grasped her hand and squeezed it.

"No, John, you can't. Your fear of the loss of your humanity will never allow it." She placed her hand on the side of his face. "And you're right. Do not give up your mortal life to live in a way that defies what has been given you."

The pain in Christina's voice reflected the loss of their future together, "I won't do it—not to you—not to anyone."

She released his hand, turned, and walked away from him.

Reese stood silently in the same spot for several moments. His anger began to rise as he thought what might have happened if Dimitri had not spoken with her. Would she have come to the same decision on her own? Or was he just looking for someone else to blame for his pain?

Reese marched off to find Dimitri.

CHAPTER SIXTY-SEVEN

Samantha walked into the compound's control center. General Morris was standing next to Commander Pattoon and both of the men looked up when she entered the room. "We've been trying to contact you for hours," Morris said. "We have the girls plus a bonus package."

"I was detained on other business," she said giving an air that it was not as important as what he had said. "This is good news, General, you are to be commended. What is this other package?"

"One of the original vampires from the Team of Darkness op," he said beaming. "Apparently one of them escaped when Reese had thought he had killed them. By the way, have you seen Commander Reese? We have some questions for him."

"No, I haven't seen him. However, that is remarkable news, General. I am very grateful for your actions in restoring the two girls to captivity."

"We wouldn't have found them if not for Reese's suggestion to check out a piece of property. He was right. They were right where he thought they would be."

"Have you been able to determine how the girls escaped?" she asked.

"No, they refuse to talk. Later we'll juice them with some of the elixir to make them a little bit more cooperative. We will find out how they did it."

"I cannot allow that," Samantha said firmly. "There can be no risks taken with such a valuable commodity."

"There is no risk," he replied. "Controlled bursts of the elixir will make them uncomfortable but…"

"No, General," she insisted. "They are agency property and I cannot allow that. If something were to go wrong they could be irreparably harmed. Besides, I have plans to move them."

General Morris moved closer to her. "And I can't allow that," he said. "My orders were to capture them and hold them here."

"My orders supersede anything you might have been instructed to do," said Samantha.

"Not unless your orders come through the Joint Chiefs," he said in a voice that rumbled with authority. He turned his eyes toward the two bodyguards that were watching the exchange and they moved closer.

"My last instructions were to cooperate fully with you in matters dealing with the capture of the creatures. They said nothing of removing them from this compound."

"We waste time on technicalities," she said. "You know that I can get the authority required."

"Probably," he agreed, "but until that time, the creatures stay here. I had a long conversation with the Chairman of the Joint Chiefs, General Stuttgart, the other day. It appears as though there may be some changes in the making regarding these creatures as well as the agency oversight into this operation."

"I doubt that," Samantha said, although she wondered how Morris had achieved his new found courage. Perhaps her superiors had decided that Christina was enough and that the situation of the escape of the girls jeopardized their own sixty year secret.

They may possibly have come to a conclusion that what they had was enough. The short-sighted bureaucrats may have decided to cut their losses and run. This would not be acceptable to her plan but if she had Reese on her side as well as all the vampires, then she could move on her own.

"I'm sure that all of this will be cleared up in a short time," she said returning to the conversation.

"Yes, I'm sure of it," the General agreed smugly. "In the meantime, you're welcome to attend the interrogation."

CHAPTER SIXTY-EIGHT

Dimitri was rummaging through supplies stored in the compound in the event some long ago emergency had required their usage. He heard Reese call his name and lifted his head seeing the man's obvious agitation. He could hear his accelerated heartbeat even with the distance.

"I am here," Dimitri said turning to Andre and the small stack of scavenged supplies. "Please take these items and move them into the other room." Andre, as always, did as he was told and left.

"What the hell did you say to her?" asked Reese as soon as Andre left them.

"I told her what she already knew. The truth," Dimitri said simply.

"You told her what you wanted to tell her," Reese said with a sharp tone in his voice. "You want her to stay with you and your merry little band. That's it isn't it? Maybe you even think you can have a little vampire family. Why not? Now you have a wife and kids to boot! Perfect symmetry as you love to say!"

"You are not approaching this logically," Dimitri said. "You seek what you cannot have."

"Who are you to tell me what I can and cannot have?"

"I see what you do not. She does not belong with you. She is not your kind."

"Since when have you become a damn expert on who belongs with whom?" Reese demanded. "You claim that your kind is as justified to live as any of God's creatures but now you're going to put restrictions upon which other of God's creatures your kind can mingle with? For Christ's sake, talk about being a hypocrite!"

"You take what I said out of context to suit your needs, Commander."

"Just as you do when it suits yours," Reese countered. "I'm tired of this bullshit, Dimitri. Why can't I, just for once, have some damn happiness in my life? She's special! When I'm with her I finally feel some peace."

"You would use Christina as the source for your peace, but time will reveal that she is not what you need."

"Oh no?" Reese said, "Then what is she?"

"She is what you fear and desire the most. She is the conundrum you will not face."

Reese remained silent for a few seconds as if contemplating what

Dimitri had said. Then he spoke firmly and answered with one word, "No."

Dimitri eyed him curiously.

Reese continued, "I did not know she was a vampire before I fell in love with her. I thought she was human."

"Surely you saw the signs," Dimitri said, exaggerating the words. "You are the vampire expert. She did not eat or drink. You only saw her at night. Was she not cold to the touch? Or perhaps she was warm because she had just fed."

The last words stung Reese as he struggled for words. "I was preoccupied with the search for the girls," he answered haltingly. "I was looking beyond the physical and…"

"You saw only what you wanted to see, but it does not matter," Dimitri said with a wave of his hands. "That does not change anything. She is what she is and you are what you are. You are a world apart. The only chance would be if you were to give up your humanity and become a vampire," Dimitri said as he stared intently at Reese. "And we both know that is out of the question. You are already torn between the two worlds, human and vampire, but your fear will prevent you from giving up your humanity. As it should. You were not meant to change. I agree with your decision. It is the right one. We never had that choice. Now we must live in our respective worlds and deal with it."

"You bastard," Reese said, "this is all about you isn't it? You want her to stay with you. Why? You're a solitary group; you stay together because you were together before you became vampires. Vampires don't make families."

"We were made by the same master. It is the only likely solution. She wishes to leave and so do we. She can help the children adjust to their new life. We will leave together and return to the Balkans one way or another."

"That's it?" asked Reese. "I don't get a say in anything concerning her? Do you have some power over her that makes her go along with what you want? Is that how you were able to turn her against me?"

"No. I have no power over her. For the first time in a long time, she makes choices of her own free will. She knows that what you seek is unobtainable. We should never have been here to begin with. This interference, in our case as well as Christina's, was brought about by humans who sought to use us. You agree that this was wrong."

"Yes! Yes! Of course I agreed. That's why you are still alive, remember? I set your asses free!"

"Yes I remember," said Dimitri, "alive and being hunted like wild animals. They'll use you to get at us. It will never end as long as we remain here. You must see that the best thing is for us to go home where we can once again become invisible as we were for centuries."

"You can go, I'll find some way to help get you out," said Reese, "but Christina stays."

Dimitri exhaled strongly. "You are stubborn. Why do you pursue this?"

"I have to," said Reese, as he shrugged his shoulders and offered no further explanation.

"Would you have her stay against her own will?" asked Dimitri. "Perhaps make her a prisoner, place a collar around her neck in the name of love?"

"Of course not," Reese said. "I just want her to make her own choice. I can accept that," he said. "If she wants to go, then she goes. But if she wants to stay, she stays. Either way, I want her to tell me so that I can see that it's the truth. You told me once that there are always options and that the key to surviving was adapting."

"Stop!" Dimitri cried. He stepped to within inches of Reese. "I have learned one thing about our dealing with mortal humans. They say one thing and mean another. I am going to say this only once. I will not change you!" Dimitri's voice was firm and unwavering, "Do not ask me. I will not speak of this again."

"You wouldn't change me even if I begged you?" said Reese. "If I decided that this is what I really wanted, you wouldn't do it? After all the shit you and I have been through?"

"No." said Dimitri and offered no more explanation.

"Damn you!" Reese cried. "You and your perverted philosophy of what is right and what is wrong! You and your..."

Dimitri was upon him before he finished the sentence. He picked Reese up with one hand and carried him from the room as if he was carrying a bag of wheat tossed over his shoulder. They left the storage room and moved quickly toward the confinement area.

"Enough is enough." Dimitri said. "I tire of this! We shall put an end to it once and for all!"

Chapter Sixty-Nine

"What are you doing? Where are you taking me?" Reese shouted as he struggled against Dimitri's hold on him.

Dimitri exclaimed, "I will end this madness of yours once and for all. I will show you up close what it means to be one of my kind!"

They entered the stockade area. Dimitri strode down the corridor between the cells with Reese over his shoulder. Only hours ago, Reese had come here with his concocted story to get Samantha to believe that he was on her side. Now only one cell was occupied; he could see Mr. Smith sitting on one of the cots. He looked completely at ease in the environment as if he was where he should be.

"Well, Reese," Smith began in his usual sarcastic tone, "I see you have your hands full. See, I knew you were into guys," he added indicating Dimitri. His next remark was made directly to the vampire, "Carrying him over the threshold, Big Guy?"

Reese struggled against the vampire's hold, trying to loosen the iron grip upon him. Dimitri ignoring the futile attempts walked up to Smith's cell door and ripped it off with one hand. He tossed it aside effortlessly the clang echoing loudly against the cement walls. The iron door slid across the floor for several feet before coming to rest with one last deafening clang of steel upon cement.

"What the fuck!" cried Smith.

Dimitri tossed Reese onto the floor next to Smith who'd jumped to his feet and stood looking at the vampire's fury being unleashed in front of him. Dimitri's eyes burned a deep crimson red, his fangs were extended fully and his fingernails had grown to several inches in length.

"Watch!" he instructed Reese. "Watch and see what it is to be a vampire, a murderer of mortal humans who kills uncontrollably and without conscience of what they do. Watch what it is you wish to become!"

Using one hand, Dimitri picked Smith up from the floor where he stood, obviously paralyzed from what he was seeing transpire only a few feet away. With his free hand, Dimitri sliced a long gash through the man's throat using one razor sharp fingernail. There was an audible exhalation from the exposed windpipe as if all the breath had decided to vacate Smith's body.

Dimitri then looked toward Reese who cowered on the floor in horror. When their eyes met, Reese looked away not wanting to see what was happening. Dimitri lowered Smith so that he lay next to Reese. The spook's eyes were wide with horror and he tried to scream but only bloody air bubbles escaped his severed throat. Dimitri grabbed hold of Reese's head and yanked it upright so that he was forced to look toward the suffering man.

"What? You don't have the stomach for this? Watch and learn!" Dimitri shouted in a voice that no longer sounded human, but rather as an animal who snarled with the intense ferocity of the kill. Dimitri sank his teeth into Smith's flesh and savagely sucked the blood from the body. The sound of chewing and sucking coincided with feeble struggles as Smith tried to fight back.

A few seconds later, Dimitri withdrew from Smith's throat, his lips and teeth covered with the man's blood. His eyes were so red that they looked to be filled with blood as well. He looked toward Reese, "Now," he said in a voice somewhat calmer than before but with an edge of sharpness in his tone, "it's your turn!"

"No!" cried Reese, his voice sounding weak and without authority.

"Yes, you shall," Dimitri said as he forcefully pulled Reese closer so that his head was now over Smith's throat. "Just dive into a human being and drink what remains of his life. Finish him!"

Dimitri pushed Reese's face into what was once the perfectly smooth flesh of a man's throat, but what was now a mangled ruin of flesh.

"Nooooo!" screamed Reese, the sound of his voice was gurgled as his lips tried to move against the onslaught of blood that oozed from the open throat.

"Drink! Damn you! Drink!" screamed Dimitri. "See what it is to have to depend on another for your life's sustenance. This man is on death's doorstep because of you! Can you live with that? What about the next victim! Or the one after that? Maybe they will have a family? What about the children who shall now be fatherless because you needed to satisfy your hunger! What of their love? Is it worth all that!"

Reese was only able to murmur garbled responses to his questions, but Dimitri could hear and sense the man's revulsion. Dimitri released his grip and rose from the floor to stand. Smith's body made its last reflexive jerk as life slipped from him.

Reese gasped at the air as he slid on the floor crawling back away from the body as quickly as he could manage. He stayed on his hands and knees until he slammed into the corner of the cell. His face was smeared with blood. He looked at Smith's body and then at Dimitri with eyes wide in disbelief and terror. He turned away and began to wretch into the corner; his spittle red with Smith's blood.

Dimitri returned to normal, his anger and frustration of the attack fading away. His nails receded, his canines retreating into his jaw. He stared at Reese knowing what he had done had been drastic, but he had seen no other alternative. He looked away hiding a guilty expression as he felt the blood of Smith coursing through his body. It had been a long time since he had taken a human, and although he hated doing it, the human blood created an exhilarating effect as it regenerated his own body in the way that animal blood never would.

"Is this what you want, Commander Reese? Is this the life you choose?" asked Dimitri in a calm voice.

Reese said nothing. He remained sitting on the floor spitting as he tried to clear the taste from his mouth.

"Animals can only provide so much for your body. If you think you will never have to take a human life, you would be fooling yourself. You will have to kill in the end."

"You didn't have to kill him," Reese said, his voice sounding raw as he spoke in between the spitting.

"He was inherently evil in ways you will be grateful not to learn." Dimitri added. "I made one of my God-like decisions as you called it earlier. I thought he should die. It is so much easier to destroy than it is to create. If you create, you must hope that what you have achieved is worth the risk. To destroy brings about finality."

Reese said nothing.

"Then what..." Dimitri began but stopped as he heard the sound of footsteps approaching.

CHAPTER SEVENTY

Christina heard the commotion and headed toward the confinement area. As she entered, she was not prepared for what she saw. John was sitting in the corner of the cell; his lips and lower part of his face covered in blood. Smith lay on the floor with his throat torn out. Dimitri stood just outside of the cell watching Reese intently.

"John," she murmured feeling nearly overcome with fear for him. What had he done? She fought the instinct that demanded that she rush to help him. She hesitated with the thought, something else is going on here; he wouldn't have killed Smith. She turned to face Dimitri.

"What's going on?"

"Dimitri said nothing. He merely continued to clean his face of what she could smell was Smith's blood.

"Tell me now!"

"Commander Reese was experiencing what it is like to be one of us," he said simply. "To see if it is truly what he desires to become."

"This is madness," she said as she felt her fear turning to anger. She knew that Dimitri would not turn John, so this was about one thing: Fear. "I thought you would be reasonable about this," she said to Dimitri.

"I'm the only one who is being reasonable," replied Dimitri, "he must be shown that this is not what he desires as much as you must understand that he cannot be changed."

"Don't you think I know that!" she screamed at Dimitri. "This was not necessary!" She turned from Dimitri and went into the cell. She knelt down and began to help Reese stand. He tried to push her away but she strengthened her hold on him and raised him from the floor. She could see the fear and anger in his eyes.

"John," she struggled to find the words, "let's get you cleaned up," she said. "I'm so sorry he did this to you."

She felt his resistance soften and then his grip tighten on her for support. "Can you walk?" she asked.

"Yeah...think so," he said, "just get me the hell out of here please. I feel so...dirty."

She led him past Dimitri without a glance and out to one of the showers in the large sleeping area. She let him go and turned the handles. He didn't bother taking off his clothes before stepping into the steaming water. Over the sounds of the water, she could hear him retching.

"John," she called, "I'll get you some clothes. Be right back."

She left the room in search of clothing in one of the other storerooms. As she searched, she thought about what Dimitri had done and her own feelings at seeing John lying helpless on the floor. She wondered if she had knowingly blocked from her own mind what Dimitri had understood all along. He'd known how John would react once forced to see what his life would be if he chose to become a vampire. Everything that he found revolting now, would become a way of life for him.

Yet she had accepted the changes relatively easily as had Dimitri. In some ways she found it hard to comprehend his reactions in comparison to her own at the change so many years ago. Why were they so different?

As she thought, she continued to shift through piles of old clothing until she found some uniform jumpsuits and picked out a size she thought would fit him. She stood and shook it out seeing it was a standard military style flight suit that she had seen in books. Unlike the clothes she was wearing, she immediately recognized the fact that the style had not changed in at least the 60 or so years that had passed since the clothing had been stored. The concept struck her as amusing that this clothing had not changed because apparently it was still as functional as when it was originally designed.

That was an interesting idea. Were people the same way? Were Dimitri and she alike because they came from the same time period? Was this why John was different because he came from a different time? Had the social, philosophical, and moral changes over humanity's passage on Earth changed the concepts of the mortal soul? Had time changed the human outlook to a point of what was conceivable and what was not? As people gave up superstition, had humanity itself become more precious to the human race?

Enough! She told her mind as it spun with possibilities of philosophical debate. She took the flight suit and returned to Reese. He still stood in the shower but there were no more sounds of retching. "John," she called, "Are you alright?"

"Yes," he said.

"I found a flight suit," she said. "I'll leave it here. I'll be in the other room. Okay?"

"Sure," he said. "Give me a few minutes."

She placed the flight suit on a wooden bench outside of the shower and followed her senses to some sort of lounge area where she found Dimitri sitting at one of the tables.

"How is he?" he asked.

"What" You're concerned now after what you did?" she said not attempting to hide her anger.

"I did what had to be done," Dimitri said flatly. "You know that."

A few seconds passed before she spoke. "He's still getting cleaned up," she said and then threw out a question that surprised even her, "Why are we so different?"

"What do you mean?" he asked.

"Have you ever met a modern day vampire? I mean one that was recently changed?"

"Only the girls," he answered.

"Why is that?" she asked. Before he could answer she continued, "What I'm getting to is if there are other vampires, which obviously there are," she said indicating herself, "why do we not know of them?"

"We are solitary creatures," he answered.

"Do you believe that?" she asked. "What proof of that do you have?"

"It is what I was told by Alexander."

"That just doesn't make sense."

"What do you mean?" he asked.

"Any race or species that seeks to survive forms communities. They seek protection in numbers from outside forces that would jeopardize their survival."

"It is what I seek now," Dimitri asserted. "You will join our group along with the girls. We do this in order to protect one another and survive."

"That's my point," she said. "Why now?"

"I do not follow what you are trying to say?"

"Why now?" she repeated. "You have been around all these years, and not only have you never joined with others, you've never even met any others. Why now? Why all of a sudden is there this big change?"

"Evolution?" he offered.

"Possibly, she agreed, "but what if it's something else. What if there are no others?"

"What are you implying?" he asked.

"If there are no others, then perhaps we do not have the capacity to create. You and I have both agree that we feel strongly against creating others—perhaps that is because we are not able to do so. Something inside of us, some genetic trait of our kind, prevents us from doing it. Perhaps we are all what remains of our kind."

"But Josip created the two girls. This destroys your theory."

"Or does it suggest that he was one of the few that had the ability to procreate?" she suggested. "Perhaps limited reproduction is some failsafe mechanism of our kind."

"You suggest much," Dimitri said, "but what does any of it have to do with us at this moment?"

"Change." She said simply. "Everything changes. We change as well as the mortals."

"Be specific," said Dimitri.

"As we are not the same mortals as when we were created, the mortals are not the same either. Evolution has changed both species. In some ways we have drawn closer together and in others we have grown further apart. Evolution is placing us onto a new path."

Dimitri's eyes widened at her assumption. "Are you implying that…"

"Christina?"

Dimitri and Christina turned in the direction of the voice. Reese emerged from the other room wearing the flight suit. His hair was wet from his shower and his complexion so pale, the lines of his face appeared deepened and he looked years older. His eyes fixated upon Dimitri.

"I should go," said Dimitri as Andre stepped into the room.

"There is a coded message from Samantha," he said, his voice sounding anxious.

"What does it say?"

"No option but to take by force," Andre replied. "Move quickly, chain of command deteriorating."

Dimitri and Christina turned their gazes toward Reese. "Commander?" said Dimitri, "Your suggestion?"

Reese's gaze still focused upon Dimitri. "We end this once and for all."

"And your plan is to what?" asked Dimitri.

Reese's eyes became sharply focused. "I want you to get the bodies of Smith and the other dead agent and burn them."

Chapter Seventy-One

"Did you get the neutralizer?" Reese asked as he braced himself against the wall. His skin was pale and his eyes vacant.

"Yeah," Barkley answered as he stared intently at Reese. "You look like shit, John. "And this is your doctor asking, are you alright?"

"Thanks Doctor," Reese replied. "But your flattery won't change a thing. Did our mad scientist give you any trouble?"

"No." Barkley continued. "He saw the green and he made the elixir neutralizer in less than an hour." Sam removed a small vial of a gold liquid from his coat pocket and handed it to Reese.

"Thanks, I really appreciate you doing this, but I can't ask you to go in on this one. If something should go wrong, you'll be implicated in the entire affair."

Sam looked at Reese, his facial expression perplexed. "I'll worry about me. What about you?" he asked. "What are you going to do?"

"I'll just claim I was under their influence," said Reese making it sound like the only possible explanation. "It worked with Samantha, it should work again."

"And if that doesn't work?" asked Sam.

"Well then, I'm in a world of shit," Reese said and smiled halfheartedly. "We'll leave you here, locked up in one of the cells. It will clearly look as if you were taken against your will."

"What are you going to do?" Sam asked.

"Simple. I'm going to waltz in there with Dimitri and the others and just take Iliga and the two girls out."

"Come on, John, be serious. How are you going to get into a secured compound with three vampires and get out with six?."

"I am being serious. We have the equipment van here. I plan to drive it into the compound and park it in the loading bay."

"You're crazy!" exclaimed Sam. "Do you need me to certify that fact before you go through with this? That way at your trial they won't be able to convict you due to your obvious insanity."

"Might not be a bad idea," Reese said in a somewhat somber mood, "perhaps I am."

"I was joking," Sam said, his face turning serious. "What the hell happened, John? What did they do to you?"

Reese looked at Sam and shook his head, a wry smile on his lips. "I wonder if they did it to me or if I did it to myself."

"Huh?"

"It's a long story," Reese said and then changed subject. "We're leaving soon, you want to pick out your cell and get some stuff in there? It might be a while before they get to you."

"I'm going with you," Sam said.

"Sam."

"Forget it, John. I've been in this since the beginning. Either way, I'll fall under suspicion no matter what happens. So the way I look at it, I have nothing to lose by going along with you. Hell. I might even add some credibility to this crazy plan you have in mind. They know I left with the van so if I bring it back, they won't think anything is wrong. Besides you'll need someone to administer the elixir neutralizer."

"I thought they drank it?" asked Reese.

"They do," Sam said and smiled, "but it must be under a Doctor's supervision of course. I'd hate to get sued for malpractice."

Reese's perplexed face softened. "Thanks," he said. "You're a good friend even after all I've done to you."

"Do you think we'll get a cell together at Fort Leavenworth?" Sam asked.

"Only if we're lucky," Reese replied. "Let's get the others. It's almost dusk."

Chapter Seventy-Two

As Samantha observed the two girls in person for the first time, one word resonated through her thoughts—perfection. They appeared so innocent that she imagined them not even having to fight to get through rigorous security measures; they would simply walk through them. Who would suspect such ferocity from two little girls? Now all she had to do was get them out of here and back to Driver.

During the time she waited for the interrogation to begin, she had been in communication with her superior at the agency. It was as she had thought; her orders were to cut their losses to avoid any implication into their current status. Apparently there had been a shake up in the current administration and any risky measures were not to be attempted. She was instructed to keep Christina and the two other vampires where they were at the abandoned base for the interim. She had accepted the orders at the same instant that she had decided she would disobey them entirely.

The fools! They don't see what we can do.

She would implement her plan without the approval of her superior. If the plan that Reese had in mind worked, it would come out perfectly and she would continue to increase her personal power and eventually change the course of history. She would control the agency while wielding the ultimate force at her command, her vampires. If the plan failed, she would be able to still salvage the three vampires and turn Reese in as the traitor. It was a win-win scenario.

"We're getting ready to begin," General Morris said interrupting her thoughts as he entered the observation room. She glanced at the two men that entered with him, the General's bodyguards. She watched, amused, as they assessed her as if she was some sort of threat. Well I am, boys. I am. she thought.

"They're bringing the one called Iliga into the interrogation room. This should be interesting," the General continued. "Finally we'll learn how they snuck in here and took the girls."

"I assume you have additional assets ready in case something should go wrong?" she asked. "These creatures are so unpredictable one never knows what to expect."

"Good point," Morris said. He turned toward one of his bodyguards.

"Have control shift all internal guards to this area of the compound."

"Yes, sir," the man answered and hurried off to comply with the General's orders.

Samantha casually placed her hand inside of her pocket. Her fingers closed upon the tiny cell phone and when she found it, she pressed the send message button. Her earlier pre-recorded message would be on the way to Reese, informing him that it was time to start the operation.

"He hasn't said a word since their capture," Morris said. "He's a tight lipped one."

"Maybe he can't speak," she offered.

"Or maybe he is in telepathic communication with the other two," the General said, his voice asserting authority and apparently newfound confidence in his information.

"Really?" she asked, interested in the General's new attitude.

"I've had Commander Pattoon go through Reese's files with a fine toothed comb. He's my new advisor on this project and he's suggested some things about these creatures that Reese was perhaps, how would I say, not as forthcoming as he might have been."

"I see," she answered. "Are you saying that you don't trust him?"

"No. He just doesn't see the big picture. He's not an operator like we are. He doesn't see the potential as we do."

"Potential?" she asked.

"The things we can do with these creatures," he said, his face almost glowing with anticipation. "We can change the face of modern day warfare."

Things have really changed, she thought. The way the General was talking and the way her superior had urged her to use caution, it sounded as if the administration had turned control completely over to the military since their recapture. At least for the time being.

"Yes I suppose we could," she said agreeing with the General. "We could do a lot of good with them."

"General Morris," a voice from a speaker called out. "Line one please."

Morris picked up the phone. "Morris here."

Samantha appeared to turn her attention back toward the girls while she listened to the General on the phone.

"Commander Reese and Lieutenant Colonel Barkley, the General said. "Go ahead and send them directly through."

The General replaced the phone. "Perfect timing," he said.

"Yes," Samantha agreed, "perfect."

CHAPTER SEVENTY-THREE

The van passed through the primary checkpoint and a deep sigh of relief came from Barkley as he shot Reese a puzzling look. "How the hell did you know that they'd wave us through and not search the van?"

"I didn't," Reese replied. "I was kind of winging that part."

Dimitri, Andre, and Christina emerged from where they had concealed themselves. Reese continued, "If they'd searched, we would have had to improvise, but knowing that the General might be anxious for us to get back to show off his prizes, I assumed he might instruct the guards to pass us through."

"Are you winging any more of this?" asked Barkley.

"Hopefully not," replied Reese. "The rest is up to you and them," he said gesturing with his chin towards the vampires in the back of the van.

Reese's cell phone rang. He removed it from his pocket and pressed the receive button. A recorded message in Samantha's voice played, "All personnel in main area of control center." Reese pressed the end button.

"She has them all in the main area," Reese said. "You're sure this gas is going to work?" he said indicating the canisters in the van.

"It will work, but we don't have enough to keep everyone out for very long. At the best shot, maybe fifteen minutes."

"That will have to be long enough," Reese said.

The van approached the entrance to the main loading bay. The large metal door rose as they approached and they drove inside. They parked the van and sat inside observing the area. They noted two guards on duty, both stationed by the door.

"Security is at a minimum in the bay," said Reese. "Their focus will be on the interrogation. I'll go and make my presence known while you," he said to Barkley, "deploy the gas into the ventilation system." He grabbed two compact gas masks from the rack in the back of the truck and placed them into a small carry bag. Next he turned his attention to the vampires.

"Remember, no killing," he said. "Most of them will be incapacitated by the gas. You get in, get the girls and Iliga and then drive this vehicle out of the bay. We have to blow this van as soon as it clears the bay to pull this off so don't waste any time getting out. I repeat, once you have cleared the bay, get out of the van as quickly as you can. If you're in it when the time comes, I will have to still blow it up. Make your way by foot to the vehicle we parked outside the security area. Drive back to the underground base and we will meet up later. Barkley and I will cover back here. Okay? Any questions?"

"And you believe these," Dimitri began indicating the bags of ashes from the bodies of Smith and the other agent, "will convince them of our deaths?"

"You'd better hope so," Reese said. "Let's go."

CHAPTER SEVENTY-FOUR

Reese walked into the control room and joined General Morris and Samantha. As he looked through the window, his eyes focused upon Iliga who was strapped into a chair in the otherwise empty interrogation room. Reese knew he had to give the appearance of shock that the creature was still alive when he should have been dead. After all, he had supposedly killed the entire Team of Darkness.

"What the hell?" Reese exclaimed. "Where did he come from?"

"Commander," the General said, "glad you could make it. I thought you might want to be here when we find out why this creature is still alive when you reported that it was dead."

"I'd like to know the answer to that myself," Reese said trying to sound surprised and confused why Iliga was still alive. "I killed them all that night when I activated their collars."

"Yes we are all aware of that, Commander. But, apparently something did not work as it was supposed to and that is what I intend to find out. If this one survived, then it is a likely assumption that the others survived as well. I want to find out where they are. I want them back. All of them."

"So do I sir," Reese said firmly. "So do I."

"Then we should begin," the General said as he clicked on a switch that opened communications to the interrogation room. "This is General Morris," he began, "I know that you are the creature called Iliga and that you were part of a military team. I want to know what happened to that team and how you broke into this compound and removed the two girls. The procedure of our little talk is quite simple. I am going to ask you questions. I expect answers to the questions. If I do not get answers I will inject quantities of the elixir in small dosages from the collar. Continued lack of response will result in larger dosages being released. Do you understand?"

Iliga said nothing. He remained motionless in the chair staring directly in front of him.

General Morris moved his hand toward a button on the console and quickly depressed it for a few seconds. Iliga shuddered in the chair, jerking his head back from the sting of the elixir that the General had administered.

"I asked if you understand?" the General repeated.

"Yes, I understand," Iliga said his voice angry. He glared up at the control area with eyes that glowed with fearful deep red.

"General," Reese began, "I would advise caution on how much and how often you inject the elixir. There could be long term effects that damage the subject."

"I will find out what I want to know, Commander," the General said, his voice hard and cold. "Is there perhaps something you do not want me to learn?"

The two body guards now turned their attention to Reese as if waiting for a word from the General to remove him.

"No, sir," Reese replied. "I just suggest caution because we don't know if there is any residual effect from the elixir."

"Well I guess we will find out then, won't we...ah..."

As the General stuttered on his words, Reese smelled the change in the air. There was a sudden heavy feel to it which he knew was the effect of the gas being released into the ventilation system. He could feel his eyes starting to sting.

"What the...h-e-l-l," the General groaned as he became unsteady on his feet. The two body guards stepped toward him but they too moved as if their coordination was now effected. Samantha, the smallest of the group was the first to collapse, her smaller body succumbing to the effect of the gas. Reese went to her and slid her out of the way of the men who were now staggering uncontrollably as the realization of what was happening overcame them. With his back to them, he slid one of the masks out from his bag and placed it on her. He then placed her face down so that no one would see the mask protecting her.

Reese was also beginning to feel the first effects of the gas. His legs became unsteady and his vision was beginning to blur. He took a few steps away from the group and lunged into one of the corners. During his faked collapse, he removed the second gas mask from his bag and placed it over his head. He lay on the floor, his face away from rest of them waiting for all of them to pass out.

Reese heard the thumps of the three men hit the ground, but he still remained on the floor. He wanted to allow Barkley and the others time to reach the main control room and turn off the recording devices. In order for his plan to work, there must not be any record of what was about to happen at least in the interior of the compound. The exterior cameras would continue to record what was happening which was necessary to the success of the story but that would come later.

Reese's cell phone rang. If all was going as planned this would be Barkley confirming the surveillance cameras had been disabled. He pressed the receive button. "We're in and the cameras are off," the muffled voice said.

"On my way," Reese replied, his voice also sounding muffled through the mask. At the sound of his phone ringing, Samantha had also arisen from her position. "Let's go," Reese said. "The clock is ticking."

The two stood and left the room. Reese knew the way and led Samantha toward the bay where Dimitri and the others would go as planned after they released the girls and Iliga.

CHAPTER SEVENTY-FIVE

"Ladies," Dimitri said entering the holding area imprisoning Ishma and Crema. "It is time to go."

The two girls looked up in surprise in seeing Dimitri, but their faces quickly changed to recognition and they both ran up to him and hugged him.

"We thought we would not see you again," Crema said.

"I promised you I would protect you. You are part of our family now," he said.

The girls stepped back from him and looked at Christina who was with him. They stared at her warily, but with interest. "Who is this?" Ishma said. "She's very pretty."

"This is Christina," he said. "She is one of us as well. She will help to raise you."

Christina looked at Dimitri, her facial expression sharp as if she had just been shocked by electricity. However her facial expression quickly changed to one of calmness and understanding. "Christina," Dimitri continued, "this is Crema and Ishma Laupki."

"Hello," she said. "It's a pleasure to meet you," she said.

"Hello," the girls said, "Ishma reached out for her hand. Christina grasped the tiny hand in hers. "You're very pretty," Ishma said.

"Thank you," said Christina and then added, "but you're even prettier."

"We will leave this place for good this time, I promise. Now we must hurry." Dimitri turned to Christina, "the neutralizer," he said.

Christina removed two vials from her pocket and handed them to Dimitri. He spoke to the girls, "As before this is to prevent the elixir in the collars from harming you; drink this and then we will be on our way," he added as he passed them on to the girls.

The girls took the vials and drank the liquid within them.

"Let's go, we will meet Andre and Iliga in the bay where we entered," said Dimitri. He then turned toward Christina, "then we will do what needs to be done."

Christina stared intently at Dimitri, but she didn't speak. Instead she just lowered her eyes and then nodded in agreement.

CHAPTER SEVENTY-SIX

Reese and Samantha arrived at the loading bay and found Barkley was already there appearing nervous as he fidgeted about. Reese noticed that Sam's eyes were drawn to the girls, whom he had not seen in person until this moment. He imagined that the sight of the collars around their necks probably stabbed at the man's heart. Reese couldn't help but notice the way in which the girls held onto Christina's hands. With one on each side of her, she appeared to be the perfect image of a mother with her two daughters. A family that he might be part of...

Then Dimitri stood next to Christina and Reese's immediate thought was that they looked like the 'picture perfect' family. He felt a pang in his chest, but he wasn't sure if it was jealousy or envy. The arrival of Andre and Iliga snapped him out of his thoughts.

"So far so good," he said, his voice still sounding muffled through the gas mask. "Remember, everyone outside will be watching what happens closely. So we can't make any mistakes. We have to get it right the first time around. Timing is critical. Samantha, Barkley, and I have to get back to our positions before everyone wakes up."

"There is a slight change of plans, Commander," Dimitri said as he stepped forward. He reached up and removed the masks from Samantha and Barkley.

"What are you doing?" Reese asked. "This is not the plan!"

"As you mentioned earlier, we are ending this, once and for all," he said.

Christina walked up to Reese and removed his mask. "I'm sorry, John. But this is best, for everyone."

Within seconds the three unmasked humans slumped to the floor. Christina knelt beside Reese and gently ran her hand along the side of his face as if memorizing it with her fingers so that she would always know its outline.

"Place the men where they were," Dimitri said to Andre.

"I'll take Reese back," Christina said firmly.

Dimitri gave her a stern look, but she ignored it. He continued speaking, "Place Samantha inside the van."

"But she will be killed," Christina said.

"She will never let go of her dream which means she will never let go of us for as long as she lives," said Dimitri. "There is no other way."

★★★

Christina carried Reese back to the interrogation control room where he had been when the gas was released. She gently placed him down on the floor then she removed a folded piece of paper from her pocket. She stared at it as if she was unsure what she wanted to do with it and finally placed the paper inside of one of Reese's pockets. She knew that Dimitri would not approve of what she had written in the note, or what she planned to do, but in this particular matter she did not care. What she did care about was John and what would happen when he woke up and he realized that it was all over and that he would have to deal with what was going to happen on his own.

She stared at his face and remembered things that they had talked about in those few precious moments they had shared when it seemed there were no differences between them. She hated leaving him like this, it was such a cold thing to do, yet Dimitri had insisted it was best. She knew he was right, but that didn't ease her heart about leaving John without saying what she needed to say to him. So, she had settled upon the note as the only viable opportunity left to her. Save one.

She had thought about it for a very long time, but when she had seen John's reaction to what Dimitri had done to him, she had almost changed her mind. It hurt to see it and she reminded herself that Dimitri had forced the issue in terms that bordered on horrific. If there were to be any chance, she would have to hope that she could accomplish this. But the more she thought about it, the more she started to question her earlier thoughts and there was no time left to decide. She leaned her head in close to John's and kissed him.

CHAPTER SEVENTY-SEVEN

General Morris awoke and sat up from where he lay on the floor. His head throbbed and his mouth felt paper dry. He immediately recognized the effects of what had happened. They had been gassed inside of their own secure compound with some form of nerve agent. How the hell had that happened?

The sound of his bodyguards and Commander Reese stirring from where they lay upon the floor drove the General's mind to wakefulness and an immediate need for information so that he could evaluate the situation.

"Get up!" he said to them as he staggered to his feet. "They gassed us! Those sons a bitches!" he said although he had no idea at this moment who "they" were. He grasped the railing and looked over through the glass window and into the interrogation room. Where the creature called Iliga had been, there was now only an empty chair.

"No!" he screamed, his voice filled with rage. "Not again!" He moved to the control panel and picked up the phone. "Control, this is General Morris, give me a status check on all the creatures!"

"Sir, we're just getting back on line, we were…"

"Yes! Yes! I know. We all were. Give me a God damned status check on all the creatures. Are they accounted for or not?"

Seconds passed until the voice confirmed what the General already suspected. "No, sir, they're all gone."

"Sound the alert and close all the gates to traffic! Nobody goes anywhere without me saying so. And I mean nobody, do you understand that?"

"Yes, sir!"

Morris turned in the direction of Reese and the bodyguards who were struggling to their feet and tried to remember the last thing that had occurred before he went unconscious. As he tried to remember exactly what had happened, he realized something was not the way he had remembered it. Something was different - and then it came to him.

"Commander Reese, where is Samantha? She was standing next to you the last time I saw her."

Reese looked at the General and said, "I, I don't know, sir. She was here and…"

"These agency bastards!" Morris screamed. "They just can't let go, they have to have it all! Well not this time! I'll have her ass!"

"Sir," one of the bodyguards said, "control reports that a van has left the main compound."

"Where exactly is it?" Morris asked.

"It's stopped midway to the main gate. It's just sitting there."

"Who's in it?" he asked sharply.

"Unknown. They refuse to identify," the bodyguard said.

"Use the probe cameras," the General said, "I want to know who's in there."

The guard relayed the General's order over his headset. Seconds later, one of the television monitors in the room flickered into life and an unfocused image appeared. The camera lens adjusted into focus and the image of the van came into view. The picture blurred again as the camera zoomed in on the windshield and Samantha sitting in the driver's seat.

"I knew it!" the General yelled. "The bitch is trying to get away with them. Have a containment squad get in there. She has the creatures inside the van and she's trying to get them out. If that van makes any move fire to ONLY disable the vehicle. Is that understood?"

"Yes, sir," the bodyguard said, "fire to disable," he relayed the information.

"Reese," the General said turning toward him.

Reese did not meet the General's gaze; he just stared at the image of Samantha on the screen. "Commander Reese!" the General screamed.

"Sir," Reese answered with a confused look still on his face.

"I want you to get down there and…"

"Sir!" the bodyguard said as he indicated that the General should look at the monitor. The van was moving forward and gaining speed as it approached the gate.

"Have the guards fire!" Morris ordered. "Disable that vehicle!"

CHAPTER SEVENTY-EIGHT

The effects of the gas left Reese's mind numb as he sorted through those last moments before Christina had removed his mask. Then, seeing Samantha on the screen sitting in the driver's seat of the van, further disoriented him. Had she tricked them all? He didn't think so. He saw no way she could have done it. Besides, he had seen her mask removed as well. So why was she in the van? If the plan they had originally designed involved blowing it up then she would be...

"Commander Reese!" The General's bellowing voice calling his name drove him abruptly from his thoughts.

"Sir," Reese answered; a confused look still on his face.

"I want you to get down there and..."

"Sir!" the bodyguard said as he indicated that the General should look at the monitor. The van was moving forward and gaining speed as it approached the gate.

"Have the guards fire!" Morris ordered. "Disable that vehicle!"

Reese was still looking at the General, trying to figure out what he had just commanded him to do when there was a flash of bright light from the monitor as the van flared into a tremendous fireball.

As the fireball turned into itself, Reese realized what Dimitri had done. The words echoed in his thoughts as he had used them, and then later when Dimitri used the same words: finish this once and for all.

Dimitri knew that there was no way that Samantha could be fooled into believing the vampires had been killed. She would pursue them to the ends of the earth if she had to in order to fulfill her goals of putting together a force capable of directing the world's affairs. The only way she would let go, would be to die. Even Reese had known this but he had not accepted the fact that it had to be done. Yet, Dimitri had. His damnable logic had seen it and he had taken action to remove the obstacle to their freedom.

"What the fuck did they do?" Morris was screaming. "I said disable the vehicle not blow it to fucking hell and back!" General Morris grabbed a chair and lifted it and hurled it against the wall. "Son of a bitch!" he screamed. God damn son of a bitch!"

Chapter Seventy-Nine

No one in the control room spoke for several seconds. General Morris's face was red with rage. He looked as if he would kill the first person that said the wrong thing.

"There were explosives in the truck," Reese said, breaking the silence. "I remember seeing them when we used the van on an earlier mission. A stray bullet must have hit them."

"Who the hell do you think you are?" Morris asked turning on Reese. "You're a God damned logistics officer for Christ sakes! These are experts out there. They shot to disable. Those bullets were well placed and not random."

"I'm offering an explanation," Reese said, "I don't believe that Samantha would have blown the van up. She may have been crazy but she wasn't stupid."

Morris eyed Reese. "I wouldn't put that option passed her. If she realized her plan had failed, she might have explored that avenue as a way out."

Reese saw the General was thinking about what he had suggested about Samantha. The man was being forced into a position where he would be blamed for the loss of the assets. He could not explain what happened unless he could come up with a scapegoat and even better, a scapegoat outside of his direct chain of command. In this case Samantha would provide one for him. She wouldn't be able to defend herself. She was the perfect fall guy.

Morris turned to the first bodyguard, "Get your ass down there. Have them get the fire out and sift through the wreckage. I want proof that the creatures were in there." Morris turned to Reese, "There would be evidence of their deaths, correct?"

"Yes, sir. If they were in there when it exploded, the separation of their head from their bodies would have caused them to internally combust. There should be evidence of ash."

"That's it? Only ash?" asked the General.

"Yes, sir. When they combust, even their skeletal frames turn to ash," explained Reese.

Morris seemed to mull this over for several seconds. Then he turned to his remaining two bodyguards and said, "Wait outside." The men left the room. "This has the potential to be quite a mess," he said to Reese. "If we find this ash, there will be questions."

"Yes, sir," said Reese. He saw it coming now. The General wanted every ally he could get when the questions were asked and that included Reese. If nothing else, Morris was predictable. Now Reese had to play him like a well used violin, carefully stroking the strings to get the tune just right.

Morris continued: "You remember what I said about this agency. Like a dog with a bone, they don't let go."

"Yes sir," Reese began, but then asked, "permission to speak candidly?"

"Go ahead."

"If I may be so bold as to suggest; there is nothing left for them to hang onto."

"What do you mean?"

"It's pretty clear to me that if Samantha took the creatures, which she obviously did, we have evidence of her being in the van while the rest of us were incapacitated, she was either working on agency orders or on her own. In either case, it was her recklessness that caused their demise as well as her own. If the agency admits to trying to take the creatures from military control, they lose. If they deny any involvement and she acted alone, they are in the clear and so are you."

"I see," Morris said. "Yes, I see." The General walked about the room as he considered what Reese had suggested. A few moments passed and then he turned and said, "Why don't you get down to the site and take a look. Bring Commander Pattoon with you as well. If you find this ash, let me know immediately."

"Yes, sir," Reese said as he turned to leave.

"And Reese," Morris called.

"Sir?"

"How did Samantha escape the gas? I didn't see her with a mask?"

"I don't know, sir," Reese answered. "She must have had it hidden somewhere on her."

Morris stared at Reese. "Yes, I suppose so. What other logical explanation could there be? I just wonder how she got through security with it."

Reese held his breath and waited.

"Get going," Morris said.

CHAPTER EIGHTY

As Reese headed for the remains of the van, he was joined by Barkley whose face appeared flustered and confused.

"What the hell happened?" he asked in a low voice not wanting to be overheard. "Why did they remove our masks? And I saw...she was...she was inside the van when it exploded. That's murder, John! That was not supposed to happen. What the hell is going on here?"

"I don't know," Reese said quietly. "None of that was my plan. It wasn't my idea; it must have been Dimitri's. He knew we would have objected if we realized what he was going to do, so they removed our masks."

"But murder, John?" Barkley repeated.

Reese stopped and faced Barkley. "Sam, I need you right now. Don't flake out on me. I need you to go to the van and find the ash we planted inside and confirm the deaths of the vampires."

"Yeah, sure," he said, his face still showing his mental anguish. "When this is over, I'm done. I would never have agreed to help you if I'd known we'd be part of killing."

"Sam, we had no way of knowing he was going to do that. I won't try and justify what he did, but they saw it as survival because we all know that as long as she lived, they would have to look over their shoulders."

"But you tricked her once, maybe you could have done it again?" asked Barkley. "There might have been a chance."

"I guess they didn't want to take that risk," offered Reese. He knew it was a weak answer, but it was the only one he could offer.

Barkley fell silent.

"Come on, let's get this over with," Reese said.

"Then what?" asked Barkley.

"Then I go out to the old base and get some answers," said Reese.

"You go alone," snapped Barkley. "We're finished."

Reese cursed Dimitri in his thoughts. Sam had been a good friend and the man had trusted him. But now Reese knew that whatever threads of friendship they'd possessed, were gone for good. Sam would always remember that he, although unknowingly, had played a part in Samantha's death.

CHAPTER EIGHTY-ONE

The van exited the Naval Amphibious base as an explosion lit up the night sky and then quickly faded away.

"It's done," Dimitri said to no one in particular as he looked out the window into the night.

Andre and Iliga sat in the front seats. The two girls sat in the far rear seats And Dimitri and Christina sat in the middle seats of the van.

"And now what?" Christina asked. "We destroyed our only hope of getting out of here. The woman could have been controlled and there might have been a way to get us back to our home."

"It was necessary," said Dimitri. "If it could have been avoided, I would have sought another way."

"Perhaps," replied Christina. "So where will we go now, back to the abandoned base?"

"No. That place is done with. You know that will be the first place that he will go when he finishes what he must do at the explosion site. We agreed that we would live the lie that we created this night. It is best for everyone. You left him a note, didn't you?"

Christina looked at Dimitri with a look of disbelief, but it quickly faded. "You don't miss much do you?"

"It's a survival trait," he simply answered.

"Yes, I left him a note" she said. "Still, he will go back to the old site and he shall go with hope that he can still salvage what he seeks. He might not seek a physical resolution, but will need peace in his thoughts and dreams."

"The dreams that plagued Commander Reese earlier will no longer haunt him," said Dimitri. "That part is over."

"Perhaps," she said, "but I wonder if he will only replace one nightmare with another. His soul is deep and the feelings that run through it are fast and strong. This, I know as well as I know myself."

"And this person, this self that you know, is this a person who sees the truth of what must be?" asked Dimitri.

"I see the truth but I also see the hope that there is always a chance for things no matter how far apart they may seem. Some things can, and do, change over time, but others always remain the same. We are creatures of basic necessity; there is no denying that just as I will not deny that

I love him. However, I see these girls," she said indicating Ishma and Crema, "and I see they need a mother, at least for a while and I have committed myself to that role. I will help them to adjust to their lives as best I can."

"Your hope is encouraging," said Dimitri, "as well as your desire for what you must do. We are committed to our kind first and foremost; this is something that is an undeniable part of us. We cannot harm one another or allow harm to come to one another. It is our law."

Christina gave Dimitri a sharp look. "You philosophize and rationalize, yet you miss what is important."

"And that is?" he asked.

"You said it yourself, we are creatures of evolution. We must change and adapt our ways if we are to survive. Yet in your own rhetoric, you speak of a resistance to change."

"I do what I know must be done," he said flatly.

"Does that make it right?" she said her voice threatening.

"I do what Alexander taught me to do. He was our master and we carry out his wishes."

"He lived a long time ago, in a different place and time. What he knew is gone. His time is not like this one. It is time to change again. Why are you so stubborn?"

"What is wrong?" Ishma asked from the back of the van. Her voice sliced through the heated debate of Dimitri and Christina, allowing them a few seconds to calm themselves.

"Nothing," said Dimitri, "we were just talking."

A few seconds of silence passed between Dimitri and Christina until Dimitri spoke, "We shall find a way home to our country. We shall live and survive as we have all these years. This much we agree upon?"

"Yes," Christina agreed. "I shall do this for a period of time. I have my commitment I must live up to. But it is only for a while because there are other things I must do as well."

Dimitri nodded and smiled. "We are not so much different from the humans are we?"

"What do you mean?" she asked.

"They seek to use us and we seek to use them: It is only the methodology that is different. It is in the same way in that I have avoided contact with them while you have sought them out and embraced them. Perhaps there is a compromise somewhere that can be obtained and I refuse to see it."

"Isn't that what life, whether mortal or immortal, is all about: Seeking a compromise?"

"I suppose it is," he agreed. "I have always said that but in terms of only our kind. Perhaps I have erred."

"Then this is something we must explore," she said.

"Gently," he said, "caution is always a good thing. Change can be a dangerous thing if it is approached too quickly."

"Then we make a good pair," she said, "the voice of reason and the voice of change. One offsets the other."

There was a sense of finality to her words and the conversation ended.

Dimitri turned his gaze back to the passing buildings as they drove on into the night and a future that he wasn't sure what was to come with it. As if sensing his uncertainty, he felt Christina's hand upon his.

Chapter Eighty-Two

The investigation of the burnt wreck came to an end as the morning sun rose in the east. The group of investigators marched back inside the compound for the briefing that had been scheduled to review their findings. The group consisted of Reese, Barkley, Pattoon, an explosive expert, as well as a forensic specialist. They all entered the main conference room and took seats around the large wooden conference table.

Shortly after their arrival, General Morris and another man, who Reese did not recognize, joined them. Although he did not know the man, the logical guess was that he was somehow connected to the agency. He was tall and skinny with bone white colored hair. His non-descript black suit seemed to hang loose from his shoulders. The man's facial features were sunken, which made Reese think of someone subjected to sleep deprivation once too many times. But the single feature that stuck out was the intensity of the man's eyes. They were the kind that gave you the feeling that they were looking right through you. In the man's hands he held a small leather covered book.

"Let's begin," the General said not bothering to introduce the man that had entered with him. "Let's start with what happened. Warrant Officer Black?"

Eyes turned toward the explosives expert, Chief Warrant Officer Black.

"The explosion was very hot," he began, "which is in line with the contents of the van. There were extremely flammable products that ignited in addition to the explosive compounds. The combination of materials caused the explosion to virtually vaporize everything inside."

"And this was caused by the gunfire?" asked Morris.

"Yes, sir. That appears to be the logical explanation," Black said, "as I mentioned the intensity of the explosion vaporized just about everything. I cannot find any other source of ignition for the explosion so in my opinion, it was the gunfire."

The man sitting next to the General leaned close to him and whispered something.

"Thank you, Warrant Officer Black," General Morris said, "You may leave."

After the warrant officer had departed, Morris turned his attention to Barkley. "Lieutenant Colonel Barkley, your findings if you please."

"Yes, sir. As the warrant officer mentioned, the intensity of the fire vaporized the contents. In terms of human remains, I found a few bone fragments but mainly ash. I checked the bone fragments for DNA and they positively match the woman known as Samantha. As to the ash, there's no way to tell who it belongs to."

"Not even by volume?" the General asked.

"No, sir. Volume would not be reliable due to the firefighting that was performed. Both foam and hoses were used so much of it would have been washed away."

"If you were to make an educated guess," Morris pursued, "would you say that there was enough ash for more than one or two people?"

"If I were to guess," Barkley emphasized the word "I would say that the amount of ash I found would have been enough to account for two or maybe three bodies. That is a WAG at best," he reminded. "And again, that does not account what was washed or blown away in the wind."

"I see," said the General. "Thank you." Morris turned his attention to Commander Pattoon, "Commander, your report?"

"Yes, sir, I reviewed the tapes of the van's departure until the time it blew up. The tapes revealed no one leaving or entering the van. Whoever was in there when the van departed this building was killed. In addition, the internal monitoring system was disabled during the gas attack; there are no images of what transpired for approximately fifteen minutes."

"Your analysis?" asked Morris.

"Whoever planned this raid miscalculated the amount of time required to accomplish everything. They had obviously planned to escape before anyone recovered from the effects of the gas. Their getting stuck between the gate and this compound was not expected. As to whether a bullet struck the van, or if one of the occupants decided to end it right there and not face capture, we will never know for sure."

"Thank you, Commander," Morris said. He finally turned his attention to Commander Reese. "Commander, is there anything further you like to add?"

Reese couldn't think of anything he wanted to add. The comments from the other team members seemed to cover all the bases that needed to be covered. However, the still unidentified observer looked unconvinced. Reese could feel his eyes boring into him. Still if this affair was to end, he needed to put all his cards out on the table to give the indication that he knew more than they did.

Reese began, "I think we have covered what happened here during the past few hours quite sufficiently as to a determination of what happened, however, I don't think we have discovered the motive."

The mystery man's countenance seemed to change and he shifted in his chair. His hands still clamped the book between them.

"You have something on your mind, Commander? Go ahead," said Morris.

"Well, sir, I can't help wondering why Samantha felt the need to remove the creatures from military control. Either she was under orders to do so or she had her own plan that was contrary to the thinking of her superiors."

"Interesting thought, Commander, but those issues shall be determined by a committee above this one," Morris said. "We will table that subject."

"Let him go on," the man said in a voice that was flat and unemotional. "I like to hear the Commander's take on this. Commander?"

"It didn't take much to see that Samantha was a..." Reese hesitated, "I'm not sure of the exact word I want to use. She was obviously dedicated to a cause, but a cause that she thought only she could accomplish. I always had the feeling that she was leading us in one direction while going in another. It was as if there was something she didn't want us to know."

"Where are you going with this, Commander?" asked Morris.

"It was things she said and the way she acted when she talked. It's as if she was planning something that involved a dramatic shift in how we would use the creatures. I almost got the feeling that they would be used as some kind of personal assassins to achieve some goal."

"Interesting thoughts, Commander," the unidentified man said.

Reese felt his eyes become sharply focused on him as if he wanted to say something but could not. When he finally did speak, it was in a slow, articulate manner, "I will take your thoughts under advisement. Of course if you had some kind of proof of what you suggest, that would help immeasurably. Do you have any proof, Commander?"

"No sir," Reese said, "nothing concrete."

Morris spoke up, "Commander Reese, do you have any thoughts on why the creature or creatures you said were killed were apparently still alive?"

"It can only be one of two things," Reese began, "either the remote device did not activate the injection device on the collars or the elixir in the collars had lost its potency."

"Or there was a deliberate release of the creatures," the white-haired man added. "Is this not a possibility, Commander Reese?"

CHAPTER EIGHTY-THREE

Reese paused for a few seconds to give the appearance that he was shocked to hear the accusation; however, he wasn't really surprised. As he had intended, this conversation had turned into a quid pro quo exchange. Reese indicated that he knew more about Samantha's, or the agency activities with Christina, and now the white haired man traded back that perhaps he suspected Reese was involved in the release of the vampires. Now they were on equal ground.

"I imagine that one might consider that a possibility," Reese said.

"However," the white haired man began, "given the nature of your impeccable service to this country, we would naturally not consider the possibility of such an action on your part. Just as Samantha's actions, although questionable, must have been taken because she believed it to be the best she could do for her country. Samantha is to be respected and remembered for her impeccable service and long career."

The man stared at Reese for several seconds and he saw that sharp-eyed appearance soften as they reached an understanding. The man turned toward General Morris and quietly said something to him, and then he stood up and left the room.

When the door closed, Morris turned to Reese, "What the fuck was that about? Do you have any idea who that man is and what power he has?"

"He was never introduced," Reese said, the sarcasm in his voice strong.

"You know damn well who he is, so cut the shit!"

"He asked me for my opinion and I gave it to him, sir" replied Reese and then said nothing more.

General Morris stared at Reese for several seconds before speaking. He appeared to be replaying the conversation in his thoughts. Slowly the angry expression faded and was replaced by a more cautious look. He turned his attention to all of them. "Gentlemen, we are done here. Over the next few days you will attend a final debriefing and then you will be returned to your previous assignments. As for you, Commander Reese, you will be returned to your retirement status. Thank you."

The men rose from the chairs and started to leave. "Reese," the General said. "Stay for a moment."

When everyone else had departed the room, the General said, "You're playing a dangerous game, Reese, a very dangerous game. However, I have to hand it to you; you played it well. Perhaps too well for your own good. You remember what I told you when the operation started, 'like a dog with a bone', remember?"

"I remember," Reese agreed.

"Good. I hope you live long enough to enjoy your retirement," the General said with a sarcastic grin on his face.

"You too, sir" Reese said as he pointed his index finger straight at the General's heart. The General's grin quickly dissipated. Reese smiled and then left the room.

CHAPTER EIGHTY-FOUR

Reese walked out of the compound and drove directly to the abandoned base. He found himself gripping the steering wheel so hard that his knuckles had turned white. He shook them and forced them to relax. During the drive he tried to push the thought from his mind that Christina would not be there. He suspected that Dimitri and the others were probably already gone because Dimitri had changed the operation to erase all indications of their existence. And he had, quite thoroughly, Reese had to admit. If nothing else, Dimitri was very thorough. Reese hoped that in terms of Christina, and Dimitri's insistence that they could not make their relationship work, his thoroughness had faltered.

As he entered the underground compound, he was greeted only with the sound of his own footsteps and their echo in the cavernous crypt. He checked every room and found no one. Finally he returned to the main area and he sat at a table in the room where he had last talked with Christina. He tried to imagine her voice – determined to remember every word of that conversation and search for clues as to what was planned.

"She's gone. Dead," a man's voice called interrupting Reese's thoughts. He turned in the direction of the voice and he saw the white haired man from the previous meeting at the compound.

"Such a pity," the man continued, "I wanted to kill her myself."

"What?" asked Reese. "Why would you want to kill her?"

"Let's say I have personal reasons," he said, as he raised the book Reese had seen him holding earlier.

"I don't understand," Reese said.

"I wouldn't expect you to. This book, she sent it to me. Its contents destroyed a part of me that I had put away for safekeeping. I'm not sure if that was her intent or if she was trying to make amends in her own way. I guess it doesn't matter anymore what she was trying to do."

"What was in the book?" asked Reese.

The man ignored Reese's question. "Still she was a very valuable asset to us. She will be missed."

"You mean assassin," Reese said. "She killed for you and your agency."

"Yes, well of course she did. That's what we do. Samantha will also be missed. She was a dedicated woman to the cause. A bit neurotic, but this kind of work will do that."

"Hazards of the job," said Reese.

The man laughed lightly. "Yes, well put. So tell me, what did Samantha offer you?"

"Excuse me?" said Reese.

"Come now, Commander, we both know what happened in that meeting. We reached a compromise which protects the reputations of both the Navy and my own Agency. Of course, there are... how would you say, unexplained elements of our stories that need not be gone into. Now, it's just you and me and I'm curious. What did she offer you for your services?"

The emptiness of the compound, as well as the one in his heart, left Reese uncaring about what this man knew so he told him the truth, "She wanted me to help her carry out her plan. I had the knowledge and background she needed and she thought I would be a valuable asset in her plans for using the vampires in a more aggressive manner."

"Ah, I see. And you agreed?"

"Let's just say that, at the time, I didn't have much choice in the matter."

"So she came up with this plan to get all the vampires out of the compound but ditched you in the end?"

"That's about it," agreed Reese.

"Such a waste," he said. "Samantha always followed orders explicitly. Until now. I was satisfied to keep the one vampire and let the military have the rest. But power corrupts completely and Samantha saw the power that she could wield if she had them all. She wanted to move more quickly than we were. But all of that is gone now."

"Some things were meant to be left alone I guess," said Reese.

"Perhaps, the man agreed, "but sometimes the future needs to be shaped. You could still be part of that."

"What? Are you offering me a job?" asked an incredulous Reese.

"I have an opening that needs to be filled."

"I'll pass on that one," Reese said with a wave of his hand. "I've had enough. Besides, my talents are currently not required."

"For now," the man said, "but at a later date they may again be needed."

"What do you mean?"

"You're an educated man, Commander. There are obviously other vampires out there. They just need to be found. Your services would be of great value in finding them."

"No. I'm going to have to pass."

"Are you sure? This offer may not come under such pleasant circumstances in the future."

"Is that a threat?" asked Reese.

"No. Of course not, merely a statement."

"Look," Reese interrupted, "I don't want anything to do with this. Not now, not ever. Do you think that I didn't take some measures when I was summoned back to active duty against my will?"

"Now it is my turn to ask, is that a threat?" the white haired man asked, his face turning severe in its expression.

Reese smiled, "No, of course not. Just practicing that art of compromise you mentioned earlier. A complete transcript of… how should I say? 'Questionable actions' is safely tucked away with legal instructions for its disbursement upon my death."

The white haired man stared at Reese. The severe look on his face slowly shaped itself into a grin. "We could have worked well together, but as you said some things are not meant to be. Have a nice retirement." Without another word, the man turned and left the underground compound.

Reese sat for a few minutes longer, feeling as if he could finally breathe again. The conversation with his white haired spook had been intense, but he thought he had handled it well considering he had bluffed his way through it. He hadn't left any kind of records anywhere, but now the thought seemed like it might be a good idea. Just in case.

Reese rose from his chair and walked into the room that had been Christina's bedroom. He took a last lingering look around and the clothes and adornments spoke to him of her. They reminded him of her personality and in his thoughts he could see her face as it had been those few nights they had spent together.

His eyes caught a glimpse of something familiar lying on a table. He moved toward it and saw that it was a copy of his book. She'd stolen the textbook on myths and religions he had used for the class he had only just started teaching before it was cancelled. He picked it up and flipped through it. Christina had dog-eared several of pages whereupon he had written about vampires. He felt a smile briefly touch his lips and then it vanished.

He kept the book in his hands as he turned and left the room knowing that he would never use it again.

CHAPTER EIGHTY-FIVE

When he got home, a wave of exhaustion plummeted upon Reese like a shower of bricks. He didn't want to think anymore. All he wanted was a hot shower and sleep. As he walked toward his bedroom to undress, he caught a glimmer of the red light of his answering machine flashing. He pressed the button and listened to the messages. First was a message from Commander Pattoon reminding him of the debriefing schedule the next day. Next, was a message from a telemarketer offering him a home equity loan. Finally, there came a message from a travel agency offering him a free trip to Disney World. He laughed at the Disney World offer, but then reconsidered. Maybe a trip to another type of fantasy world was just what he needed.

Exhausted, both emotionally and physically, he stood in the bedroom and began to undress. He caught his image in the full length mirror as he removed the flight suit that Christina had given him. Looking at himself, even he thought his features looked haggard and worn and that rest was probably the best thing that he could do at the moment. As he finished stripping down, he felt something in one of the pockets. He unzipped it and removed a piece of paper unfolding it and immediately recognizing the ornate script handwriting as Christina's. His legs turned to jelly, so he sat on the bed and read.

Dear John,

By the time you get this I will be gone with Dimitri and the others on our trip back to our home. I pray that all has gone well and you are safe. Everything happened so fast and there was no time for us to talk after Dimitri did what he thought was right—he knew that you were plagued with the nightmares of losing your humanity and he sought to make you see the truth that you tried to conceal from yourself. It was necessary, John, so that you could be yourself again. You need to be a mortal human and not some tortured soul that lies between the worlds of human and vampire.

As much as I wanted to stay and to be with you, I couldn't do it. Dimitri says we are from two different worlds and the gap that divides them is too far apart. Is he correct? I don't know. All I do know at this time is that I need to finish discovering what I am and what I can become. For too long I have allowed myself to wallow in the quagmires of anger and revenge. Being with you opened the floodgates of emotion and I can feel again. I can feel and now I can love. The feelings are both exhilarating and terrifying and the decision I need to make is one that I must do on my own. Will there be a later for us? I do hope so.

For now I am needed by Ishma and Crema to help them adjust to what they are now. We will be a family for a while John, working together for the sake of my race to ensure that we live on in the place that God or whoever has ordained for us to occupy. This time will allow me to think of a future as well as remember the past.

I am a selfish person, John. I could not leave without taking a part of you with me. I now have something that I will treasure for always. It will allow us to exist together in our dreams if not in our realities.

I do love you.

Forever yours,

Christina

After Reese read the letter several times, he let it fall from his hands and drift to the floor. He walked closer to the mirror and looked at his face. He could see the trace of the tears that had flowed down his face as he had read her words. He wiped at them with the back of his hand. Slowly he turned his head to the side and allowed his fingers to continue along the side of his neck. His hand passed over the rough stubble of beard and then came to the marks that he suspected would be there; two small punctures in the skin. She had taken a part of him. She had taken his blood.

He let his hand drop from his neck as he continued to look at his face in the mirror. He wasn't sure what he saw or what he was feeling at this very moment. Had he changed? Had all of this changed his feelings about mortality? The image of his reflection didn't offer any suggestions as to what these answers might be. He turned from the mirror and the questions that remained unanswered. As he headed toward the shower, he wondered what his dreams would be like tonight.

He turned the water on and listened to the sounds as it splashed off the tub floor. He felt a thin smile try to force its way upon his lips. The smile was associated with the message that had been on his answering machine - the one about the trip to Disney World and his chance to escape into a world of fantasy where the rules of reality no longer applied. Yes, he would take a trip, but not to Disney World.

Perhaps he could finally find that fantasy world of his dreams and live in it; now more than ever, he thought he was ready.

About the Author

Tony Ruggiero has been publishing fiction since 1998. His science fiction, fantasy, and horror stories and novels have appeared in both print and electronic mediums. His published novels include:

Operation Immortal Servitude: Book I of the Team of Darkness Declassified Files. The US military has developed a new weapon to be added to its arsenal—the creatures known as vampires. Tony uses his naval experience to write this dark fantasy thriller about vampires being used by the Navy SEALs. Ground breaking and fast paced, the novel is a characteristic mixture of the vampire lore of Anne Rice and the clandestine secrets of the military found in Tom Clancy novels.

Operation Save the Innocent: Book II of the Team of Darkness Declassified Files. Commander John Reese struggles with the decision he made to free the vampires, code name Team of Darkness. Unbeknownst to Reese, his efforts to stop the operation was undermined by the action of General Stone who secretly secured the bodies of two young girls who have now turned into full fledged vampires ready to be trained to become killers for the General's personal ambitions. However, General Stone is suddenly murdered in his home—his assassin is a female vampire, Christina, who has been controlled and used by a U.S. secret government organization, known as the Agency, to murder selected targets since her arrival in the United States over sixty years ago.

Alien Deception: Nothing is as it appears...nothing. Your whole life you think you understand who and what you are and then one day you learn that it is all a lie. So what do you do? You have lunch with the leading candidate for President of the United States...you and your alien friends.

Alien *Revelation*: Death has many meanings. For some it is an end, while for others it is a beginning. Yet, for one human/alien hybrid, it is a way to have one final chance to try and save his home, Earth, a son he has never seen, and find an enemy that just won't stay dead. The exciting conclusion to Alien Deception.

Aliens and Satanic Creatures Wanted: Humans Need Not Apply. Aliens, Satanic Creatures, and other alternate life forms have gathered together to make a stand for literary fairness. Move over pesky human...a change is coming. An anthology of short stories where the center character is not human; includes the award winning story, Lucky Lucifer's Car Emporium, as well as Electronic Bliss, Invasion or Subversion, and Going Up?

Tony is also a contributing author to *The Fantasy Writers' Companion* from Dragon Moon Press. The Companion picks up where The *Complete Guide to Writing Fantasy* leaves off. *The Fantasy Writers' Companion* takes on more advanced topics of writing, such as incorporating horror, incorporating mystery, developing a story in your favorite RPG universe, and exploring alternative cultures for world building. Tony's contribution is a chapter on the effective use of horror in fantasy. Other collaborative work includes *The Writers for Relief* Volumes I and II, *No Longer Dreams*, Breach the Hull and So It Begins.

Tony retired from the United States Navy in 2001 after twenty-three years of service. While continuing to write, Tony teaches at Old Dominion University in Norfolk, VA, Saint Leo University and the University of Phoenix.

For more information, please visit www.tonyruggiero.com.

OPERATION: ENDGAME

CHAPTER ONE

Reese slowly awoke in a gray haze to the sound of banging. It sounded like a hammer banging on a piece of wood. His surroundings began to slowly come into focus as the sound became clearer. It wasn't a hammer, but rather a gavel being banged on a desk. He looked around and saw that he was in a large room. The seats were full of military personnel in uniform. He was in some kind of a military courtroom.

"What the hell..." The room was full of conversational murmurs and combined along with the gavel banging, made Reese's head ache.

From what he could surmise, he was being court-martialed for something. He sat at a small table in the center of the room. He was wearing his dress blue uniform, the one he referred to often enough as the suit and tie outfit. The seat next to him, which he guessed would be for his attorney, was empty. He tried to move his hands and feet and found that he was shackled with chains. Reese wondered where his attorney was or if had he not been allowed to have one.

In the front of the room was a long table. Its occupants included three Navy officers, all of whom Reese recognized and all of whom he knew were dead.

The first on the left was General Stone, followed by Commander Scott and then Lieutenant Johnson. Stone and Scott's throats had been slashed, the gaping tear extending from ear to ear in the flesh clearly in view. There was no blood though, the wounds were clean. Johnson's wounds were less graphic; his body was full of bullet holes. Reese thought he could actually see light through some of the holes.

General Stone banged the gavel one more time and then laid it down. "I will have order in the courtroom," Stone said, his voice sounding coarse and scratchy - the way a man whose throat was slashed should sound - yet maintaining a tone of command. He turned his eyes toward Reese and that was when Reese saw the eyes, or rather the lack of eyes. The General's eye sockets were empty.

It's not real... Reese thought. It's a dream...that's all it is. I don't have any more bad dreams.

"Commander John Reese," Stone began, "you are charged with crimes against humanity; specifically in that you aided and abetted the creatures known as vampires, codename Team of Darkness; to wit you disobeyed orders and lied to superior officers on numerous occasions which led to the death of innocent victims all for your own benefit and amusement. Further, your actions have directly led to the deaths of Commander Scott, Lieutenant Johnson, Agency operatives Samantha and Mr. Smith and untold innocent civilian casualties. Oh, and also myself," he added with a wry smile. "That is the charge. How do you plead?"

"What's going on here?" Reese said, his voice sounding tiny and unsure in the courtroom venue. "This is absurd. It's nonsense. You're all dead. Dead by your own..."

"Commander Reese, I asked you how do you plead?" Stone demanded.

"I'm not going to plead anything. This isn't a real court!"

Stone slammed the gavel down abruptly. "Commander Reese! This is the last time that I will ask you. If you fail to respond accordingly, then I will enter a plea of guilty and have you sentenced immediately."

The audacity of Stone's comments struck a chord in Reese, even if it was a dream. "This is such bullshit. You can't do that! This is a military court of law," Reese said and then realized that he was arguing with someone in a dream. He knew it was useless and silly but still he went on with the first thing that popped into his head, "For starters, that's against the article of the code of military justice."

"Well, like you said, Commander Reese," said Stone. "To make matters somewhat easier and to streamline the entire affair, I decided to dispense with some of the specifics of the code. As you yourself said, this is a dream and we can pretty much do what we damn want in it—can't we?" Stone's empty eye sockets appeared to stare at Reese.

Reese felt his world turned upside down as he stared at General Stone. He didn't know what to say to that assertion. In fact he wasn't sure of very much at all right now. Dream or not—this was getting very weird and he did not like it.

He suddenly felt panicky and the urge to run to get away in his own dream. As absurd as the concept sounded, he felt he had to do it and now. He stood up abruptly, pulling the chains taut against his skin and having the strangest sensation. Pain.

It had hurt and hurt a lot. The shock that he had actually felt pain resonated not only where he had been shackled at his wrists and ankles, but in his head while trying to figure out how this could be possible. You can't feel pain in a dream. He looked at his wrist where the steel had been pressed against the skin, it was red and he could see the broken blood vessels just under the surface of the skin.

This can't be happening…

"Are you satisfied to the authenticity of these proceedings now, Commander Reese?" Stone said.

"I don't understand," Reese said. "How can this be?"

"The answer is simple. You have brought this upon yourself," Stone said his voice sounding cynical. "There's no one to blame. There's no one to try and protect you from what you have done. You will finally be held accountable for your actions. Your selfish and self-centered ways have caught up to you. There is nowhere to hide. No chance to manufacture another story to tell. This is your last chance to tell your story to this court. So how do you plead, Commander Reese?"

"I don't even have a lawyer," said Reese absently as his mind struggled to understand what was happening. He looked at the empty chair to his right and then turned back to General Stone.

"For the last time, Commander Reese, how do you plead?"

"Not guilty," the voice next to Reese said.

There was a sudden murmur of voices in the courtroom. Reese turned to his right and saw Dimitri standing next to him. "My client pleads not guilty," Dimitri reiterated.

"Not guilty," Stone confirmed in a voice that sounded with disgust, "And a reminder councilor that you need to be on time in my court."

"Of course, General. My apologies," said Dimitri".

"Dimitri, what the hell is this?" asked Reese.

"Not now," said Dimitri to Reese and then turned his attention to General Stone. "General, may I have a few moments with my client?"

"Granted, let's take a ten minute recess."

"Thank you, General," Dimitri said.

"You do realize it won't make much of a difference," said Stone and then he banged the gavel.

OPERATION: ENDGAME

CHAPTER TWO

Christina felt flushed with guilt as she stared at Reese's body lying sprawled on the ground at the naval compound. The look of shock was still on his face from when she had removed his mask so that he would succumb to the gas and join the rest of the humans. It had not been part of his plan but everything was happening so quickly and there were no other choices at the moment. As much as she did not want to think, much less agree with what Dimitri had said about the futility of a relationship with John, she needed time to think and decide what to do. Still she could not just leave him here without anything. She removed the folded paper from her pocket and slipped the note into his pocket. She leaned her head in close to his and kissed him on the lips and then moved toward his neck.

Gently she broke the skin with her teeth. She tasted his blood and at the moment she cleared her mind of everything with the exception of her thoughts and feelings toward him. She loved him and that was what she conveyed in those few seconds. No controversy, no questions, no feelings of right or wrong, simply sharing her innermost feelings of what she felt for him which would establish a connection.

She had done this procedure many times before, but in those cases she had gone much deeper in establishing a link based more upon control, such as in her relationship with Jake and the other humans that had served her. However, this time would be quite different. This connection would allow him to have the most vivid memories of her as well as a limited connection to her own thoughts if she allowed it. In time he would be able to immerse himself into those memories and feel as if he were actually there again. In addition, it would also allow her to feel his thoughts as well. In both cases the limitation was mainly based

296

upon the physical distance that separated them.

Seconds later she moved her face away from his neck while quickly wiping at her mouth. She did not want anyone to see what she had done. She placed her hand alongside Reese's face. "Goodbye, John."

Suddenly Reese opened his eyes. "Christina, don't go!" he said.

"I have to…" she said shocked. "I have to, John—please understand."

She was confused as to why the memory had changed. This was not the way it had happened.

The image of John Reese faded and slowly disappeared.

Christina forced herself out of the memory and returned to the present. As her eyes came to focus, she saw Dimitri standing in front of her.

"You were talking to yourself," he said.

Over his left shoulder she saw the brightly lit Econo Lodge sign and remembered that they had rented connecting rooms at this hotel. Over his right shoulder, she could see the sky; she remembered when she had first come outside it was black. But now it was gray and getting lighter as the sunrise approached.

Outside of their rooms she could see Andre and Iliga. Although they stood quietly, their eyes remained focused on the parking lot and the surrounding area looking for any indication that they had been followed or were being observed. They were like sentinels in the darkness she thought; always looking for something yet never finding it.

She returned her gaze to Dimitri's face. From the first time she had met him, she had thought that he was physically attractive, an obvious effect of being changed at a youthful age. His dark hair blended into his sharply defined face in a way that exuded confidence and trust—a natural leader. His eyes were normally dark and shiny which drew you into his persona. Yet now, his stoic and pensive look was becoming more prevalent since their escape. Even through his hard Slavic features, she could see his frustration and concern for their position in his eyes. He was obviously troubled as to what lay ahead for them.

"What you did was foolish," his voice not harsh or admonishing, but simply stating.

"What?" she asked.

"We are joined by the same maker, Alexander," he began, "and thereby linked together. That bond has gotten stronger since you joined us. And because of the strong emotions in that memory, I felt some of it as well. You took blood from Reese."

"I couldn't just leave him," she said. "I tried to explain that to you."

"You should have erased his memories for his own good," he said. "You should know better than to lead him on with false hopes. Have we not discussed it sufficiently enough for you to comprehend the error of what it is you seek?"

Christina felt anger surge through her. "How dare you judge me."

"I only state what is right and…"

"In your mind or opinion," she countered. "So stop judging my actions and look at your own."

Dimitri appeared confused.

Christina looked at him and felt a moment of guilt at what she had said. "Look," she began, "this ordeal has been quite frustrating for all of us. I understand your reasoning for what you have done to get the girls freed. And I agreed to return to Kosovo for the girls sake and so that I could think about all of this as well. But after that I am going to do what I feel is right for me."

"Including Reese?" He asked.

Christina sighed deeply and then spoke, "I believe I have already answered that."

"And what of your own kind," he asked.

"I will not have this discussion now," she said. "It's time to sleep." She turned to go back into the hotel room.

Dimitri placed his hand upon her shoulder. "We could be a family."

Christina looked at Dimitri. His hand was not forcibly grabbing her but rather holding onto her gently. She studied his eyes and saw that they had momentarily changed from the stoic and pensive look to one of hope and chance. She felt a flush of feelings of warmth emanating from him. She was both shocked and surprised by his expression of feeling and yet she found herself also scared.

She looked away from him and then reached for his hand and gently removed it from her shoulder. "I thank you for your concern—really," she said sincerely. But this is confusing enough without complicating it further."

She headed off to her hotel room that she shared with the two young girls. She opened the door, and finally let out the breath she had been holding, and went inside.

Coming in 2010